Thomas

By Sarah Shears

The Fairfield Chronicles
THE VILLAGE
FAMILY FORTUNES
THE YOUNG GENERATION
RETURN TO RUSSETS

THE SISTERS

and published by Bantam Books

Thomas

Sarah Shears

BANTAM BOOKS
TORONTO • NEW YORK • LONDON • SYDNEY • AUCKLAND

THOMAS
A BANTAM BOOK 0 553 40583 7

Originally published in Great Britain by
Judy Piatkus (Publishers) Ltd

PRINTING HISTORY
Judy Piatkus (Publishers) edition published 1989
Bantam Books edition published 1993

Set in 11/13pt Linotype Plantin by
County Typesetters, Margate, Kent

Corgi Books are published by Transworld Publishers Ltd,
61–63 Uxbridge Road, Ealing, London W5 5SA,
in Australia by Transworld Publishers (Australia) Pty Ltd,
15–25 Helles Avenue, Moorebank, NSW 2170,
and in New Zealand by Transworld Publishers (NZ) Ltd,
3 William Pickering Drive, Albany, Auckland.

Reproduced, printed and bound in Great Britain by
Cox & Wyman Ltd, Reading, Berks.

Chapter One

Memory went back no farther than his Third Birthday. Life began for him that day. It was the day he was breeched. It was the day he received the rocking horse. It was the day he fell in love with his Auntie Kate. All of equal importance in his young mind, yet each event marked the day for ever with special significance.

To be breeched was to be transported from babyhood to boyhood. The rocking horse was a present from Grandmama, who knew his passion for horses. It arrived just after breakfast, and he refused to have it carried upstairs to the nursery floor. All that day it stayed in the hall, and he galloped and galloped on Auntie Bertha's highly polished floor till his head was swimming and his stomach had fallen into his little kid boots.

Grandmama was the most important person in his small world. Mama was too gentle to be important. Only those who demanded attention were important – Grandmama, Auntie Kate and Thomas. He was Thomas the Third, it had been explained. The first Thomas was the founder of the big department store in the High Street – Thomas Brent & Son. The second Thomas, who was Grandmama's husband, had been killed by a runaway carriage horse, and Grandmama had worn black for so many years that everyone was surprised and delighted to see her in a new afternoon gown the colour of violets on his Third Birthday.

'In honour of my grandson,' she told her six daughters.

All had been summoned to attend the special tea party, but none was allowed to give a bigger or better present than the rocking horse.

His two sisters, Prudence and Arabella, had wanted to ride the horse, but he would not give it up that first day.

'It's mine!' he shouted, as he galloped across the hall.

'Yes, my darling, the horse is yours,' said Grandmama.

'It's my birthday,' he told all the aunties and uncles who came to tea that day. It was all very exciting.

'You kiss the ladies, and shake hands with the gentlemen,' Grandmama explained.

They arrived by cab from the station. Auntie Jane and Uncle Edward were the first to arrive, and Uncle Edward was wearing a black eye-shade, like the pirate in one of his picture books.

'Such a funny uncle!' he shouted.

'Not funny at all. The poor man cannot see with that eye,' said Auntie Bertha crossly (he called her the Cross Auntie).

'Uncle Edward had an accident and lost the sight of one eye,' Grandmama explained.

Auntie Grace and Uncle Henry were the next to arrive. They had come all the way from Switzerland. Prue and Bella found it in the atlas, because they were having morning lessons with Mama. Uncle Henry had a fat stomach and a jolly laugh, and he presented each of the three children with a golden sovereign.

Auntie Lucy and Uncle Basil were the next to arrive. Uncle Basil had been Mr Gregson till he married Auntie Lucy.

'And very nearly married the wrong girl,' said Norah, who carried up the mugs of early morning tea, and spent most of her day in the basement kitchen.

'Norah is not an auntie,' said Grandmama, decidedly.

'Norah is not a servant,' said Auntie Bertha, even more decidedly.

'What is she then?' Thomas asked Rose.

'Norah is a friend,' said Rose. Now Rose was not family. She was the nursemaid who took them for walks in the park, cleaned their boots, and polished the bassinet. Rose was nice, but you paid little attention to her because she was a kind of servant.

Last of all to arrive for that special tea-party had been Auntie Kate and Uncle Charles, and Thomas had known their importance by the way they were dressed and the way they behaved. It was clever of them to arrive when all the rest were seated at the tea table in the dining-room. His beautiful Auntie Kate curtsied most prettily, and Uncle Charles swept off his grey topper and bowed. Climbing on the seat of his high chair, he had called out to them, 'It's my birthday!'

Then came the moment that stayed in his memory.

'Many happy returns of the day, my darling!' cried the beautiful auntie, and he was enveloped in the feather boa she wore about her shoulders. Her perfume had a special fragrance, not like Grandmama's eau-de-cologne, or Mama's lavender water.

'You smell nice,' he said – and wondered why everyone laughed.

Grandmama had been quite taken with Uncle Charles, who kissed her hand.

'Showing off, the pair of them,' muttered Auntie Bertha.

'A perfect gentleman,' said Rose, in the quiet voice that was never raised in anger.

But Thomas heard both remarks, for his ears were sharp, and he missed nothing that was said at the tea table that day.

'A lovely child,' they said.

'So like his dear Papa,' they said.

'So bright and intelligent,' they said.

'Horrid little boy!' Prue whispered to her little sister.

Bella shook her head. She adored Thomas. Bella was his slave.

He loved the deep, masculine laughter of the gentlemen, and the tinkling laughter of the ladies, and he wondered why the gentlemen removed their hats and the ladies wore their hats for tea. He was wearing a paper crown on his golden curls, and a starched serviette tied about his neck. Since his second birthday, he had refused to wear a bib, said Rose, although he could not remember it.

Looking down the long table, he tried to count the number of people sitting there, but he could only count up to ten, then he had to start again. A place had been set for Auntie Kate and Uncle Charles at the far end of the table, and she waved and smiled frequently. He could not take his eyes from her. She was so beautiful. She laughed a lot, and her voice commanded attention. Her enormous hat was adorned with flowers and ribbons, and her gown with lace. A necklace sparkled at her throat and rings on her fingers. Dark lashes matched the fringe of dark hair on her brow. Her eyes still danced with mischief, and her laughing mouth was made for kissing – Uncle Henry declared.

'Go ahead, old chap,' offered her obliging husband. Grandmama was a little shocked.

'Behave yourself, child!' she scolded her naughty daughter.

It was fun! Everything was fun that day. 'Three kinds of jam – a veritable feast, my love!' Uncle Charles exclaimed.

Thomas was allowed to start with cake because it was his party, but he had to blow out the candles on the birthday cake. 'Watch me!' he cried, climbing on the seat of the high chair. One tremendous puff, and all three candles were out. Everyone clapped and cheered. Norah carried it away to the sideboard to cut in slices, and two of the aunties handed it round. Thomas ate only the sugar icing and a few of the silver balls. The cake was too rich.

'Greedy little pig!' muttered Prue, leaning across Mama.

'Hush, darling. It's his birthday,' Mama coaxed.

'Prudence is jealous of her little brother,' they said.

'What is jealous?' he had asked Grandmama.

'Wanting to possess something that belongs to another person,' she answered.

'Does she want my little sword?' he persisted.

'No, darling. I think Prudence would like your blue eyes and your golden curls because they are so like your dear Papa, and Prudence loved her Papa.' Both sisters had straight black hair, dark eyes and pallid cheeks. They were not pretty.

'But they have lovely eyes,' said Rose, who always defended them.

After tea, the uncles pushed back the table and they all played 'musical chairs' and 'hunt the thimble'. Auntie Kate kept hold of his hand, and when he tired of the games he sat on her lap and sucked his thumb.

'You smell nice,' he said, and fell asleep. That was four years ago.

Not any of the other birthdays had been as special as that Third Birthday, through no fault of Grandmama's, who had 'spent a lot of money she could ill afford,' said the cross auntie. Auntie Grace and Uncle Henry were not there for his fourth and fifth birthdays. They were living in very straitened circumstances, according to Grandmama, and could not afford the journey.

'But why doesn't Auntie Kate come? Are her circumstances straight?' he demanded, tearfully, when his fifth birthday had passed without a glimpse of her. Parcels had been delivered containing whole regiments of foot-soldiers, cavalry and cannon, and the battles were long and fierce on the dining-room floor.

'Thomas will want to play with soldiers because he is a soldier's son,' Uncle Charles had decided, when they went shopping in the toy department at Harrods.

But no amount of toy soldiers could compensate for his Auntie Kate. Grandmama was vexed. Two years had passed. 'They are so busy with their own affairs they have no time for the family,' she complained. 'If she doesn't come home for your next birthday, my darling, I shall go to London and fetch her!' Grandmama threatened, for she couldn't bear to see him so disappointed.

But she came! 'Where is my golden boy?' she cried from the doorway. He climbed off his chair and rushed into her arms. She was more beautiful than ever. She had changed her gown, her hat, and her jewels, but her perfume was the same. He was six years old, and he adored her. With his arms about her tiny waist, and his head on her breast, he could feel her heart beating and her soft breast sighing. It was the nicest sensation he had ever known.

When he was three, he had fallen asleep on her lap, sucking his thumb. Now he was six, he would sit on her lap and stroke her face, and all his senses would want to keep her for ever. Now he hated Uncle

Charles, who would take her away, back to London, and his sister Prue, who knew the meaning of jealousy, smiled at his foolishness.

Now he was seven, and the pattern of his life would change.

'Seven is a milestone for a boy, my darling,' said Grandmama unexpectedly one morning in mid-Summer, as they walked to the stables together for his weekly riding lesson.

'Why?' he demanded, carelessly, anticipating that exciting canter that followed the slow trot along the bridle path. He was not actually listening to the familiar voice that had ruled his small world as far back as he could remember. The voice that could be so stern, but for him was always indulgent.

'Why? Because it is time to leave the nest and spread your wings. A boy of seven no longer takes lessons with his mother and sisters. The next step towards manhood is preparatory school.'

'What is that, Grandmama?' he was paying attention now.

'It is a boarding school for boys up to the age of thirteen, when they are ready for public school.'

'Shall I like it?'

'You may and you may not, but there is no alternative. You follow in the footsteps of your Papa, as he followed in the footsteps of *his* Papa. It has been the recognized pattern for the sons of the upper class for hundreds of years. Your name has been entered for his old school at Brighton, and for Winchester.'

'But I want to go to Sandhurst.'

'Of course, after Winchester.'

'Will there be ponies at the preparatory school?'

'Yes.'

'Then I shall like it.'

Amelia smiled wistfully. Her adored grandson must discover for himself the harsh discipline that awaited him. Had it been a mistake, this indulgence? It had satisfied her own vanity, and her own intense longings for a boy-child. These tender years of his early childhood had brought her more happiness than all the years during which her own six daughters were growing up. What did the future hold for Thomas? Thomas the Third they called him. It was his Great-grandpapa who would pay for his education, as he had paid for his two youngest granddaughters at the Seminary for Young Ladies when the governess was dismissed. He had found a place for Kate and Lucy in his big drapery store, but that had been a sad mistake, for neither had completed the second year of her apprenticeship. Now the old gentleman had turned his attention to the young generation, and the boy Thomas would inherit that imposing emporium in the High Street when he came of age.

Thomas pushed his cap to the back of his head and swung the riding crop. He was not too dismayed at the prospect of boarding school, because he had no reason to be. Surrounded by love, and protected from every adversity, he knew no fear. Punishment of any kind had been forbidden by Grandmama. In her company he was well-mannered because he copied her example. He no longer pestered poor Maggie or kicked over her bucket of soda water.

'Good morning, Maggie,' said he.

'Good morning, Master Thomas,' she answered.

Grandmama was strict about table manners, but he sat beside her at the head of the table and copied her behaviour. When his high chair had been removed on his fourth birthday, a fat cushion was placed on one of the Windsor chairs.

Amelia had not quite finished what she had intended to say that morning, and she hesitated over the telling because it would remove the one adorable feature that she cherished.

'Those curls must be cut, my darling,' she said, her voice trembling with emotion.

'Why?'

'No boy of seven years of age keeps his baby curls. You would be a laughing stock. Rose will take you to the barber.'

'Will Rose want to keep my curls?'

'Rose will not be consulted. *I* shall keep them in a special box.'

He chuckled. It would be funny to see his curls in a box instead of growing on his head. He didn't seem to mind, yet for Amelia it was a major disaster. She watched him join the children already mounted on their ponies. Such a handsome little boy in his yellow jersey and jodhpurs.

She sat down to watch and wait on the bench provided in the yard, saddened by the thought of the inevitable parting. Prudence and Arabella would be pupils at the Convent, and Rose would escort them. It was only a short distance. September would see the start of this new chapter at The Haven. Her grand-daughters would be taught such ladylike pursuits as painting, embroidery, singing and playing the pianoforte. They would read aloud from Mr Dickens in the drawing-room after tea, and practise their deportment. It would seem she was putting back the clock, she sighed. The years were slipping away too quickly.

Kate and Jane had both sent invitations to Amelia. The children should be allowed to visit them before they started school.

'But who will take them, Mother?' Ellen asked anxiously. She had accepted the change in their young lives as something to be dreaded. Her children were growing up, nursery days were over.

'You will take them, of course,' her mother answered, tersely. Sometimes she felt impatient with her eldest daughter, who had been widowed on the Northwest Frontier of India when a stray bullet from a sniper's gun had killed her young husband. She had brought the two little girls home to The Haven, and Thomas had been born some months later. Ellen's dark eyes were haunted by the memory of the young husband, and the secret she must keep for ever locked in her heart.

'The children will love it. It will be their first train journey, and their first visit to Kate and Jane,' Amelia was saying. 'I am a little dubious of Jane's environment, I must confess. A Church Army hostel in the East End of London is not a very suitable place for our children, but they cannot visit one without the other. Jane would be hurt, and rightly so. She is a remarkable woman, and so devoted to good works. It will be an interesting experience for the children. I wonder what Thomas will make of it?'

Ellen sighed. It was always Thomas. She loved her son but had had little to do with his upbringing. Her will and her wishes had been over-ruled by a stronger personality. The years had slipped away, and now it was too late. Thomas would soon be a stranger, coming home for the holidays, shorn of his curls – a boy in an Eton suit who spoke a new language, the language of boarding school. But she would still have Prudence and Bella. Her eldest daughter was delighted at the prospect of boarding school for Thomas. She had hugged her dear, gentle mother in a passionate embrace.

'It will be lovely, Mama. Just the three of us and Rose.'

But Bella was in tears. Who would fetch and carry for him? Who would throw the ball for Thomas to bat? Who would read a bedtime story? Her small world would not be complete without Thomas.

Kate had sent money for their fares. It was not often that she remembered the genteel poverty her mother contrived to make an asset, not a liability. Amelia was too proud to ask for a bigger allowance from Thomas Brent. She had never been a favourite with her father-in-law. The four elder girls had been obliged to take over the household tasks, all but the washing and scrubbing, when they could no longer afford a cook and a housemaid.

A cab was ordered to convey the little family to the station that bright Summer morning.

'Ladies first,' Grandmama reminded Thomas, when he would have scrambled in.

They all were dressed in their Sunday best, Thomas in a white sailor suit and a sailor hat, and the girls in tussore silk frocks, straw hats wreathed in daisies, white gloves, white stockings and white kid boots.

Ellen was tense with nervous apprehension, and wished she might have brought Rose, but Rose had been unwell for some time, and only Ellen had noticed that she had lost weight.

So they boarded the train, and Thomas claimed one of the corner seats, and Prue the other. Two elderly gentlemen, immersed in *The Times*, peered at the children over their spectacles in a disapproving manner, so Ellen hushed her son's shrill, excited voice as the train gathered speed. The countryside slipped past the window. Bella and Thomas counted the cows and the horses, but the sheep were too numerous. Prue was wondering what would happen if the engine ran off the tracks. It sometimes happened to Thomas's toy engine. She was a nervous child, and her enjoyment of any special event was always marred by such alarming possibilities. She envied her younger sister and brother their starry-eyed pleasure in the journey.

'Mama, what shall we do if Auntie Kate is not there to meet us?' she asked, anxiously, as they neared the terminus.

'But she *will* be there. She promised.' Ellen smiled reassuringly, but her own anxiety was making her head ache.

'Mama! Why are we stopping?' Thomas demanded, shrilly.

'Because we have arrived at Victoria, young man.' One of the elderly gentlemen had folded his newspaper and was regarding the handsome little boy more favourably. Reaching for his hat, he bowed to Ellen, and observed, 'I must congratulate you, Madam, on such well-behaved children.'

'Thank you, sir.' Ellen's dark eyes were warm with such unexpected praise.

'There she is!' Thomas was the first to see her, and he dropped his mother's hand and ran to meet her.

'A gentleman removes his hat to kiss a lady.' Grandmama's voice prompted inside his head, and he skidded to a halt and snatched off his sailor hat. They hugged each other and laughed merrily. Other departing passengers stared indulgently for they made a pretty picture, the fashionably dressed young woman and the little boy who had snatched off his hat so gallantly.

'Darling boy!' Auntie Kate exclaimed. She loved the feel of his warm little body in her arms. If only he belonged to her! But Charles was not fond of children, and perhaps it was only the novelty of their rare meetings that appealed to her. They led such busy lives, there was no time for children. And she had to confess a total lack of that sense of devoted motherhood that Ellen possessed.

'You still smell nice,' Thomas was saying.

'Of course, because I always wear the same perfume,' she whispered.

'Good morning, Kate.' Ellen's gentle voice held a

disapproving note. Such emotional scenes were rather embarrassing on a public platform, but they were two of a kind, she had realized with a sinking heart – this flamboyant sister and her small son. Prue and Bella stood quietly beside her, waiting to be noticed.

'So there you are, my darlings! How charming you look in those adorable hats!' Kate swooped on her nieces and kissed their cheeks. 'That is the French way of kissing, a kiss for each cheek,' she told them, gaily.

Ellen could feel Prue shrinking from such affectation. Bella did not shrink from anyone, no matter how they affected her. She was too kind. 'Where is Uncle Charles?' she asked, for she had decided at their first meeting that he would be her favourite uncle.

'Unavoidably detained, darling. He sends his love. Some stupid Bill has to be passed at the House, and all members are honour-bound to be present. Isn't it tedious? Take my advice, darlings. Never marry a Member of Parliament or you will find yourself taking second place to a Bill!' she laughed.

Was she being serious? Prue wondered, clinging tightly to her mother's gloved hand. I should die if I got lost, I know I should die, she told herself. Such a crush of people. Such noisy confusion! She shivered in an agony of dreadful possibilities.

Thomas had deserted them. Rapturously happy, he skipped along beside his beautiful Auntie Kate. 'Where are we going?' he demanded.

'To Hyde Park. I have a carriage waiting. There is so much to see in Hyde Park.'

'Will there be horses?'

'Of course. All the best people ride in the Row.'

'Can I ride in the Row?'

'Not today, my darling, but it's a promise for the future. Will that do?'

'Yes.'

'We shall see the Household Cavalry. Such splendid fellows in their dazzling uniforms.'

'Shall we see the Queen?' asked Bella, when they had climbed into the carriage.

'Not today, darling. The Queen lives at Windsor. But I know of a dear little pavilion, serving the most delicious strawberry ice-cream. Would you like that?'

'Yes, please, Auntie Kate.'

'Why, the quaint little soul is really quite pretty when she smiles,' Kate decided. But her eldest niece had forgotten how to smile, or perhaps she had not yet discovered that a smile could transform the plainest features.

'What would you like to do, darling?' Her voice was coaxing. She was determined her part in the day's excursion would be a big success. After lunch, they were going to visit Jane in the East End. It was too ridiculous!

'I would like a drink of water,' said Prue, demurely.

'Water?' Kate had forgotten the taste of water – if it had a taste. 'Of course, whatever you wish, darling,' said she, graciously.

And when they had seen the riders in the Row, and the Household Cavalry, the carriage pulled up on the drive overlooking the pavilion, and Kate led her family across the grass to a white table, surrounded by chairs, and saw them seated. She ordered the ice-cream and the glass of water with the air of one who is accustomed to being served promptly.

'Isn't this fun, darlings?' she enthused, gaily. For all her extravagant gestures, she is still young at heart, Ellen was thinking. This was her right element – not the small, secluded world of The Haven, or the careful spending of a very limited allowance. Dear Kate.

The house at Onslow Square was most imposing. The door was opened by an elderly parlourmaid with streamers on her starched cap. She bobbed a curtsey. They were shown upstairs by an equally elderly housemaid. Kate was taking no chances with her husband's roving eye! Cook was fat and jolly, and well past her prime. The parlourmaid carved a plump chicken on the sideboard. Auntie Kate called her 'Harris'.

'Hasn't she got a first name?' Thomas whispered.

'Have you got a first name, Harris?' asked her mistress.

'Yes, Madam. It's Gertrude.' She went on carving the chicken.

What did these old-established servants really think of their bright young mistress? Ellen wondered. It must have been a shock after the quiet, orderly routine with Miss Lefeaux, Charles's sister, who ran the house before Kate arrived on the scene.

Very sensibly Kate had left it to Cook to provide

what she thought was suitable for the children who were accustomed to plain, wholesome fare, and the chicken was a good choice, with garden peas and creamed potatoes, followed by apple pie and custard. Kate was enjoying playing hostess to her young nephew and nieces, who had never seen her in such elegant surroundings. Charles had left a sovereign for each child. They were shown over the house, but Ellen was too polite to pass any comments on her sister's rather vulgar taste.

Thomas was impatient to be on his way, not because he wanted to leave Auntie Kate, but because he had been promised a glimpse of the Salvation Army Band, and children who wore no socks and shoes, so they were driven to the station, and boarded another train for the East End.

Jane and Edward were waiting to welcome them. Not even a cab was available, and they walked along the hot, dusty pavements and passed the public house where Edward had been slashed with a razor. The rough voices of the customers frightened Prue, and she wrinkled her nose disdainfully at the strong smell of ale. Such a well-dressed little family did not pass unnoticed, however, and the familiar faces of the Warden and his wife were greeted with 'Watcher Guv!' 'Watcher Missus!'.

Ellen was appalled when Jane scooped up a dirty infant from the gutter, wearing nothing but a filthy vest, and carried him back to his mother. A woman came to the door with her hair in curlers and her feet in a pair of men's boots. She could have been any age between twenty and forty.

''E's a right little bugger, this 'un, Missus. Can't abide being tied up, can yer, duckie?'

The baby chuckled and pulled on the curlers.

'What you got there then, Missus? That your fambly?' asked the woman.

'Yes, my family. Say how-do-you-do to Mrs Harrison,' Jane prompted. The children obeyed.

'Luverly manners,' said Mrs Harrison, approvingly, as they went on their way.

The hostel was a poor place, smelling of yellow soap and fried onions. There were no maids in starched caps with streamers, only Aggie, in a sacking apron, peeling potatoes at the kitchen sink. She welcomed them with a toothless grin, and dried her wrinkled hands.

'Shake hands with Aggie,' Uncle Edward prompted, so they all shook hands. (Grandmama had told them you do not shake hands with servants.)

'I got the kettle on, Missus, an' there's dripping for the toast,' said Aggie.

And Jane thanked her with a politeness that was as natural as breathing. They washed their hands in a bedroom with creaking floorboards and white-washed walls. The china basin was cracked, but the towel was clean. The pictures on the walls depicted scenes from the life of Christ – 'Suffer little children', 'The sermon on the Mount', 'The Raising of Jairus's daughter', 'The disciples on the Sea of Galilee'. A text hung over the bed. It read 'GOD IS LOVE'.

'I like it here, Auntie Jane,' said Bella. 'Can I come and live with you when I am grown up?'

The sisters exchanged a meaningful glance, but

they were not too surprised, for Bella was already deeply religious, and Sunday was her favourite day of the week. Attending church with the whole family was a pleasure, not a penance, and the climax of the day, singing hymns round the piano in the drawing-room, sent her to bed in a lovely glow of piety. She loved singing. Her voice was sweet and pure, but not strong. Now she waited for an answer to her question.

'We shall see, dear. You may change your mind. When I was your age, I wanted to be a cook! Come and help me with the tea. We shall need a lot of toast for the dripping, and I bought a dozen buns with pink icing.' (It would not do to mention they were halfpenny buns from a market stall.)

Thomas was taking his turn to wash his hands. His white sailor suit was crumpled and grubby with so much travelling.

'The band!' he shrieked. 'I hear the band!' and he raced downstairs.

They all gathered on the pavement, including Aggie, in her sacking apron. The Salvation Army Band was an important part of their lives. The men crowded on to the pavement with their mugs of ale, the women in their doorways, holding up bare-bottomed babies sucking dummies. And barefoot children pranced and sang, in shrill voices.

Onward Christian soldiers, marching as to war,
With the Cross of Jesus, going on before.

One ragged urchin made a lunge at Thomas with his dirty fist, and the child stepped back, surprised at

24

such a gesture. A fist was something he had yet to encounter at the preparatory school.

'It was only in fun. He would not have touched you, dear, because you were here with me, and we are their friends,' said Auntie Jane, and went on singing 'Onward Christian Soldiers' with Bella, who knew every word of every verse. So did Aggie.

'We was brought up with the Army,' she told Ellen. 'It ain't all dirt and drudgery, Madam, but you 'as ter be born to it to 'preciate it.'

'My sister and her husband were not born to it.'

'Nah,' Aggie scratched her head thoughtfully. 'Got ter 'and it to 'em, Madam. The wye they puts up with us.'

Aggie had her tea in the kitchen. She knew her place when the Missus had company. A picture of 'The Last Supper' over the mantelpiece in the parlour seemed to dominate the room, and the gentle gaze of the central figure followed Bella as she handed round the dripping toast.

'I don't like dripping toast,' said Prue, who had never had it. And Ellen, who would succumb to a sick headache as soon as she got the children safely home, asked Jane's permission to toast more bread, for Prue and herself, and spread it with butter.

When it was time to leave, they found Aggie at the kitchen sink, drying her hands on her sacking apron. Edward prompted once again. 'Shake hands with Aggie.'

'Luverly manners, the upper class,' she told the lodgers, as she served the supper.

'Wave to Mrs Harrison and the baby.'

'Wave to Mrs Thompson on her doorstep.'

'Wave to Peg-leg,' Jane prompted, as they walked back to the station.

Ellen, Prue and Thomas had seen enough of the East End to last a lifetime. Only Bella would go back, when she was seventeen.

They changed trains at Victoria and then settled down for the rest of the journey. Prue rested her aching head on her mother's shoulder and closed her eyes. Thomas chatted excitedly, and Bella listened.

'What did you enjoy most, my darling?' Grandmama would ask when they arrived back at The Haven.

'Dripping toast! I had three slices!' said he.

'Dripping on your toast? I wonder you were not sick.' Amelia was surprised at Jane.

But Thomas was not sick. Rose watched him with an aching heart. Tomorrow she would wash and iron the white sailor suit and put it away. It was the end of a chapter. The children would not need a nursemaid any more. Amelia had graciously offered her the post of sewing maid, and Rose was grateful. But the pains would get worse, and some days it was agony even to turn the handle of the sewing machine, but she did not complain.

It was Norah who found her in a state of collapse and carried her to her bed a few days after Thomas had left for his first term at the preparatory school. The doctor was called, but she was already in a coma, and she slipped away as quietly as she had lived.

When Thomas came home for Christmas, he would hardly miss her. With parties and panto-mimes, and so many presents waiting to be opened, he could not be expected to grieve for a nursemaid, and his fond Grandmama would not have him reminded of a chapter that had closed. Besides, he had brought home a friend. It was strange to hear the two small boys addressing each other as Cartwright and Henderson. Grandmama had not been consulted, and was rather vexed. She did not want to share her grandson, and would soon discover the truth of her own statement regarding the gentle Rose. The chapter was closed.

'Who is this boy? Hasn't he got a home?' she demanded, after he had been hurriedly bundled into the cloakroom.

'His parents are in India. He would have to spend all the holidays at school. You don't mind, Grandmama?'

'I do like to be consulted, Thomas.'

He smiled, disarmingly. To be called Thomas was a sure sign that she was displeased, but he knew how to coax her into a good humour. The hugs and kisses that were no longer allowed in public were as warm as ever, and he was quite irresistible. Without his curls, his handsome head was crowned with a cap of hair that shone like gold in the lamplight on that Winter afternoon.

When the other boy joined them – a frail-looking child, so obviously nervous – she forgot her displeasure and bade him welcome. They shook hands solemnly.

'It is kind of you, Ma'am, to invite me,' he said.

So that little rascal had deceived his headmaster into assuming the invitation was genuine! Now he

27

was regarding her with innocent blue eyes. But it was Christmas, and she must not be uncharitable.

'What do I call you, my dear? You do have a Christian name?' she asked, playfully.

'It's Roderic, Ma'am.'

'Well, Roderic, come and meet the rest of the family.' And she led the way into the dining-room. The Christmas tree nearly reached the ceiling. It sparkled with tinsel and coloured baubles in the light of the candles. Parcels were piled around the base. Tomorrow was Christmas Eve. Everyone had been busy. Paper chains were draped across the high ceiling. That would be Norah, for only Norah was allowed on the stepladder. A bright fire burned in the shining grate.

The two boys stared, wide-eyed. In their Eton suits with smooth hair and clean faces, their appearance was deceptively angelic.

That first term had been a revelation to Thomas. 'Bend over that chair, Cartwright.' The swish of the cane on his bare buttocks was an indignity he could not tolerate. He fought and struggled. But the hand on his shoulders was strong and relentless, and the Master was enjoying his role. It was a spur to his sadistic tendencies to cane a small rebel who refused to cry. Thomas was remembering his sore bottom as he gazed at the star on the top of the tree.

Amelia had sadly missed her grandson, but she had comforted herself with the promise of his company in the holidays. She had visualized the small figure, in his long nightshirt, climbing into her bed, to await Norah with the early morning tea. She had his favourite biscuits in the tin.

Shrieks of merriment and loud thumps across the landing had awakened her. Were they having a pillow fight at six o'clock on a Winter morning? What energy! She smiled indulgently and settled more comfortably in her warm bed. His sisters did not have pillow fights. They lay quietly waiting for the mugs of tea that Norah would bring at seven o'clock.

But the whole house was aroused by the squeals of laughter and the thumpings, and Amelia found her indulgence had been stretched to its limit by the time Norah arrived with the tea.

Norah had been brought up in a working-class family, and she welcomed the arrival of two small boys in a big house that had echoed to the clatter of Thomas up and down the stairs and his shouts of glee as he slid down the banisters.

The noise had suddenly ceased. Norah had taken in two mugs of tea and a plate of broken biscuits. Thomas had been promoted to his own bedroom on his third birthday, and had since enjoyed the privilege of sharing Grandmama's tea and biscuits. This privilege had lasted till the morning he left for school, and Amelia waited in vain for that practice to be resumed.

'Why must Thomas bring another child to upset all my cherished plans for the holiday?' she asked herself. Norah's homely face and cheerful manner only added to her vexation.

'I must speak to the boys. We cannot allow them to

29

disturb the whole household,' she told the woman who was neither family nor servant, but absolutely indispensable. 'Boys will be boys' was a statement she had made on more than one occasion, and she did not need Norah to remind her.

'I suppose so,' was all she said. And Norah climbed the stairs to the top floor with mugs of tea for Ellen and the girls. She would make a second journey from the basement with cans of hot water for washing. The boys would wash in cold water.

When they returned to school after Christmas, the water would be frozen in the jugs in their bleak dormitories, and they would wake to find snow had drifted on to their beds from the open windows. Fresh air was a fetish. They would have chilblains on their fingers and toes. It was a harsh initiation for small boys accustomed to the warmth and comfort of upper class homes, but it was traditional and there was no escape.

Prue and Bella were still missing Rose. Mama escorted them to the convent at eight o'clock and back home at four o'clock, but Mama did not bowl hoops or push the dolls' bassinet, or play ball in the park. They waited obediently in the main hall with the other day girls, supervised by one of the younger Sisters who was herself a 'new girl', subject to the strict rules and regulations. There were no playing fields for the girls, and their daily exercise consisted of a sedate walk on the promenade in a tidy 'crocodile'. Senior girls who were boarders enjoyed the privilege of walking in pairs, and were much envied by the juniors.

Prue was bored with the regimentation, and found the curriculum lacking in her favourite subjects, music and poetry. Ellen had encouraged her daughters in their individual tastes, but now they were obliged to conform to the standards and discipline of each class in turn, and the teaching Sisters were as varied and versatile as their pupils.

Bella accepted the discipline with her normal good humour, and soon made friends in her own age group, leaving Prue to feel neglected and resentful. Jealous of her younger sister's popularity, she despised the very qualities that would have spared her so many tears of self-pity.

Ellen was patient and gentle with her first-born, still excusing her behaviour as the result of an early childhood in India, and the distressing chapter of events that had brought them back to England. Prue remembered her handsome Papa in his scarlet uniform. She remembered Ayah, and the native servants who called her 'Missy Baba'. She remembered the smell of India, and the sun. It was the sun she still missed, for she was seldom comfortably warm, even in Summer, and miserably cold in Winter.

'When I am grown up, I shall go back to India,' she told Ellen. 'And you must come with me, Mama, for we don't belong here.'

'My darling, I could never go back. I had no sense of belonging to the Army way of life. A dutiful wife must accompany her husband to the far corners of the earth, if the need arises, but I have no husband now, and when you are married, you will not need your Mama.'

'I am not going to be married, because I shall never find a husband to compare with my dearest Papa. He was so very special, wasn't he, Mama?'

'Yes, darling,' she lied.

'Not one of the uncles would suit me for a husband, and supposing I found myself married to someone as hateful as Thomas? No, I have decided to be an old maid.'

'But my darling, you are only a little girl. You will change your mind a dozen times.'

'I don't change my mind. I always know what I want,' said Prue.

It was true. This first-born child could not be dissuaded. 'Love me best, Mama. Love me best,' she had sobbed when her baby brother was born. And she was still that same child.

Amelia lay tense and expectant, waiting for a tap on the door. Surely Thomas would say good morning before he went down to breakfast? But no, his door slammed, feet scampered across the landing, then shrieks of laughter as they slid down the banisters. Tears pricked her eyes. Seven years of devoted love, and every wish granted since he left the nursery wing on the top floor and moved down to his own room on his third birthday. Should one expect gratitude from children? Five of her six daughters had been amenable to her wishes. Only Kate was a rebel. Thomas was not sparing with his hugs and kisses, but had he ever actually said that he loved her?

She was deeply hurt by his selfish behaviour on the first day of the holiday. It was Christmas Eve, and once again she had spent more than she could afford, this time on a handsome sledge, to be delivered today. It was not going to be a white Christmas, but Thomas could take the sledge back to the school that was situated on the edge of the Downs, some distance from the town. The younger boys were allowed to take anything of a sporting nature to develop their physique. Next year it could be skates.

She heard Ellen and the girls follow the boys downstairs. She would see them later. This boy, Roderic, must have presents to open on Christmas Day. Ellen could take the girls shopping. She had planned to hire the station cab to take Thomas to Kong's for hot chocolate and sugar buns. Now she must take both boys. She sighed, and dabbed her wet eyes with a dainty handkerchief. Norah must see no trace of tears when she brought in the breakfast tray. Tears should be private.

It would not be the first time she had had to hide her disappointment; but there had been other much bigger issues. Six daughters, and she had longed for a son. Two granddaughters, coming home from India. Then, at last, a boy was born, and her family was complete. 'Thomas the Third', heir to Thomas Brent & Son and heir to 'The Haven' in Richmond Road.

Down in the basement breakfast room, Amelia's darling was stuffing himself with dripping toast.

'What shall we do first?' The question was addressed to Roderic.

'I don't mind, Cartwright. You choose,' was exactly what Thomas expected to hear.

'The rocking horse, then. It's on the top floor, and we shall get a second slide down the banisters.'

'I should like that.' His rare smile was not so dazzling as his young companion's, but rather sweet and wistful. His grey eyes reflected his thoughts, and the sadness of his first Christmas without his parents could not be completely dispelled by the friendliness of his present surroundings. To be with Cartwright for Christmas was something he had not dared to anticipate, and was too proud to suggest. 'A fellow must stand on his own feet at the age of seven' had been Papa's sensible advice on parting from his son. But he missed his mother. She was so gentle, and he missed Ayah and the native servants who had called him 'Baba Sahib'. In that household he had been regarded as a little prince. Now he was a mere scrap of humanity in the common herd – a small fish in a big pond. But he was lucky to have Cartwright's friendship, and he was grateful for the invitation.

Bella was watching him across the table. She was a little afraid that Thomas was going to bully him, and she felt protective towards the little stranger with the sad grey eyes and the sudden enchanting smile. Should she warn him about the broken stirrup? But Thomas would ride first, and he had broken it, as he broke everything sooner or later. Nothing was safe with Thomas, but perhaps Roderic had already discovered this.

'May I be excused, Ma'am?' he asked Mama respectfully.

'You may,' she answered.

'May I be excused, Ma'am?' Thomas echoed, his eyes dancing with mischief.

'You may.' To have an extra child for Christmas

was an unexpected joy for Ellen, and Prue would not be jealous of this little boy. Her heart ached for the child, and also for the mother, so cruelly separated by circumstances beyond her control.

But she had her children, and even Prue was not too old for a stocking. On such a limited income, she could only afford small gifts, but she had been collecting them since the children started school.

Tomorrow morning all four children would be sitting on her bed, wrapped in warm dressing-gowns, opening their little packets. All the big presents from Grandmama and the aunties would be opened in the afternoon. Norah would join them with mugs of tea and biscuits. She would put a match to the fire, already laid, and it would seem they were putting back the clock, in the old nursery. This, for Ellen, would be the happiest hour of the day.

Sipping the second cup of tea that Bertha had poured, she was remembering the faces of her five younger sisters in the firelight in those far off days, and the young nursemaid, still a child at heart, playing with Lucy's doll.

'Well, come along! We can't sit here all day!' Bertha's sharp voice reminded them.

Ellen sighed. Her offers of help were always rejected. After all these years, Bertha was still telling her elder sister, 'We can manage.' Norah, bless her, was the go-between.

Overhead, the thump, thump of the rocking horse brought memories of a different kind to Amelia, Kate learning to skip, and reluctant to wait to be taken to the park. Here, in the marriage bed, she had lain in the arms of her adored husband, Thomas the Second, and was reminded of her children only when a sudden noise or commotion on the nursery floor disturbed her blissful sensuality. Invariably it was the naughty Kate.

Thomas had been an indulgent father. The gentle Grace had been his favourite, but Kate had demanded more than her share of his attention from her earliest years, and would hang like a limpet on his trousered legs even before she could walk. Giving birth to six children, and all of them girls, had been a source of wonder and delight to Thomas, despite his disappointment that they had not been blessed with a son. Her own disappointment was so intense when their youngest daughter was born that she refused to look at her until the innocent little mite was put to her breast by an exasperated midwife. For such a small woman her breasts were full and her babies well-nourished, but she could not love them as she loved her husband. She lacked maternal feelings and it was left to Ellen, her firstborn, to mother her younger sisters which she did with a devotion that almost replaced that of the real mother – almost, but not entirely, for each girl in turn would try with pathetic eagerness to claim her share of love and attention from the dignified little person with the proud carriage who disliked being crumpled by clinging, childish hands.

The years had passed, her children had grown and developed their own individual personalities, but when she lost Thomas in that cruel accident, something vital had died that could only be recovered in the birth of her grandson. She saw in him her salvation, her pride and joy. She endowed him with qualities he would never possess, for it was Jonathan, his own father, he so closely resembled, not his namesake, his grandfather. In her passionate delight in the child's perfection, there was a kind of sensuality, but her foolish adoration could not hold him back from the natural growth of a normal, healthy little boy. In her lonely bed, on Christmas Eve, she listened to the thumping overhead and knew such acute pangs of desertion for which she was totally unprepared.

Both boys were lying flat on their stomachs assembling regiments of toy soldiers for battle on the dining-room floor when Amelia came downstairs, calm and controlled, but she felt quite drained emotionally. The trace of sadness in her blue eyes would pass unnoticed by all but her youngest granddaughter who was a particularly observant child.

Roderic glanced up from the field of battle, saw his hostess in the doorway, and sprang to his feet. 'Good morning, Ma'am,' he said, with a polite bow.

'Good morning, Roderic. I trust you slept well?'

'Yes, thank you, Ma'am.'

She knew her grandson would be furious with his playmate because he had been made to feel ashamed by his own lack of courtesy. The younger boy had not yet realized how important it was for Thomas to be first in everything, not lagging behind.

His mouth was sulky as he scrambled to his feet. 'Good morning, Grandmama,' he muttered.

'Good morning, Thomas. Have I interrupted at a vital moment?'

'Yes.'

'I do apologize. Shall you be ready for hot chocolate at Kong's? I have ordered the cab for eleven o'clock.'

He smiled, and kissed her cheek. His mouth was sticky, but she waited till she had left the room to wipe her cheek. Both boys would be chewing all day, and tomorrow they would eat the pink sugar mice in the bottoms of their stockings before breakfast.

She left them to fight their mock battles and went in search of the girls. They were on the way out with their mother, and were carrying their hoops.

'Don't stay too long in the park today. I shall want you to do some shopping,' she called after them.

'Just twice round the park, Grandmama,' said Prue, who didn't like to be hurried.

'Grandmama looks sad today,' said Bella, as they closed the green gate.

'I expect she was wishing she could put back the clock,' Ellen observed quietly.

'Why?' Prue demanded.

'A schoolboy grandson who brings a friend home for Christmas without consulting her must have been quite a shock, don't you think?'

'I suppose so.' Prue was looking pale today, her mother thought, but it was probably only excitement. There would be tears tomorrow before bedtime. It always ended that way on Christmas Day. Too much excitement and too much to eat – and Thomas with a toy pistol in his stocking! Perhaps it had been a foolish purchase, but he *was* a soldier's son, and an airgun would be dangerous. She, too, had been surprised and shocked by her son's behaviour, but Grandmama had only herself to blame.

'We are coming to help you make the mincepies, Norah,' Thomas announced importantly, when they had finished lunch.

Norah exchanged a meaningful glance with Bertha, who was not fond of children and was already feeling tired and irritable with all the extra work. Preparations for Christmas started in September when the puddings were made, and the children had to stir the mixture and make a wish before they started school. Bertha sighed, but Norah had no objection to small boys in her kitchen. Their noisy presence had already been announced at six o'clock this morning!

So they followed her down the basement stairs, and she rolled up their sleeves and tied tea-towels over their clean jerseys. When she had rolled out a strip of pastry, they stood ready with pastry cutters to cut the shapes to line the tins. The kitchen was hot, and their faces burned from the heat of the range. Strip after strip of pastry appeared on the floured boards, for Norah's big hands were quick and deft, but the boys' small hands were clumsy. Auntie Bertha was icing the Christmas cake on the sideboard and paid scant attention to the noisy group at the kitchen table. The boys had tasted a spoonful of mincemeat, but the suet clung to their mouths, and now each was waiting to sample a pie from the first batch out of the oven. The delicious smell floated up the basement stairs into the open door of the drawing-room, where Amelia was resting and Ellen was reading aloud to the girls in a subdued voice.

'It's not fair, Mama!' Prue whispered fiercely. 'How can we learn to cook if we are never allowed in the kitchen?'

'Perhaps we shall have cookery lessons at the Convent in the senior school,' Bella suggested, peaceably.

'Who wants to learn to cook Irish stew and suet pudding, and boiled fish on Friday? Ugh!' Prue pulled a face.

'Hush, darling. You will disturb Grandmama,' Ellen warned.

But Amelia could hear every word, and she opened her eyes to say, authoritatively, 'Prudence is right. You girls shall make the jellies and trifles for tomorrow's supper, and Norah will put them away in the cold pantry. That will be a nice little job for you after tea.'

'Thank you, Grandmama,' they murmured. And Ellen went on with the reading of the exciting adventures of the *Swiss Family Robinson*.

'Haven't we done enough?' Thomas was finding the job rather tedious, and the novelty was wearing thin.

'Not yet. We shall need at least four dozen, with three extra to dinner on Christmas Day and a dozen for Maggie, and about the same number for the carol singers this evening.' Norah went on rolling out strips of pastry, her homely face shining with beads of perspiration.

'Why can't Maggie make her own mincepies?' Thomas demanded.

'Because she can't afford to buy all the ingredients for the mincemeat. Your Grandmama always fills a basket on Christmas Eve for Maggie to take home, with enough meat for her big family, a pudding, a cake, a dozen mincepies, and sweets for the children. She does it every year,' Norah explained.

They could hear Maggie scrubbing the back steps, and Jackie barking furiously from force of habit.

'Will Jackie have a special Christmas dinner?' Thomas wanted to know.

'Of course. Bella will see to it.'

'Girls are stupid. They can't even catch a ball before it bounces,' said he, scornfully.

'Bella can skip up to a hundred, and Prue can run twice round the park with her hoop without stopping,' Auntie Bertha reminded them, for she liked to see fair play among the children, even if they were nuisances.

'You won't give everything to Maggie, will you Norah? Don't forget my tuck box to take back to school,' Thomas reminded her anxiously.

'Not much fear of that!' she laughed, as she dusted off a smudge of flour from his flushed cheeks, and gave each boy a mincepie, piping hot from the oven.

'Thank you, Ma'am,' said Roderic, politely.

As they ran back upstairs to continue with the interrupted siege of the fort, Bertha called after them, 'And don't drop any crumbs on my dining-room carpet!'

'Is it her carpet, Cartwright?' asked Roderic, innocently.

''Course not, Henderson. She only cleans it,' said Thomas.

Church bells were ringing when Roderic woke on Christmas morning. He lay very still beside Thomas, who was still asleep. The darkness was not at all frightening when he could hear another child breathing, and if he kept his eyes closed, he could see the nursery in the house in Calcutta, and Ayah dressing his two little sisters. He could actually smell the peculiar odour of Ayah's dark skin, for smells were such an important part of his early life in India. He was so terribly homesick, but it was not something you could talk about, even to your best friend, for Thomas would not understand; and when he wrote his weekly letter to his parents on Sunday afternoon, homesickness was a subject that was never mentioned. The letters began 'My dear Papa and Mama' and finished 'Your obedient son, Roderic'. In between, he would fill the half dozen lines with such items of interest that would please both parents.

At the beginning of his first term, he had written, 'I have been chosen for the junior cricket eleven, and I made five runs at the match yesterday afternoon.' That had pleased Papa, who had taught him to bat and bowl when he was six. It was never too young to start cricket, Papa had insisted. Last week he had written, 'My music master says I shall soon be ready

42

for the first examination.' That would please Mama who played the pianoforte most beautifully. 'We go to chapel twice on Sunday, and we sing the National Anthem every morning at Assembly.' That would please both parents who were so extremely patriotic the Union Jack was flown over the front porch on the Queen's Birthday. In next week's letter, he would have no difficulty in filling the whole page, for there would be so much to say about spending Christmas with Cartwright. He dried his eyes on the sleeve of his flannel nightshirt.

Church bells were sad on Christmas morning when your home was thousands of miles away. But everyone had been kind, and he would not cry any more. A girl called Bella had known he was sad because he had no presents to give anyone, and he had been taught to give as well as to receive.

'I do declare, I am like a magpie for I hoard all kinds of things!' she laughed. 'Come and see. You shall choose which you would like, and we won't tell the others,' she had whispered, after supper, and they crept upstairs. 'You see, I receive such *un*suitable presents as well as the suitable ones. You would never believe it,' she explained, as she turned out an extraordinary collection from the top drawer of the tallboy. 'Now, what should I do with scent or smelling salts, for I have no intention of fainting,' she giggled. 'Here we have hair-tidies, but my hair sticks tight to my head, and lace doylies are such fussy things. As for handkerchiefs, I get them every year, and I seldom have a cold. Now we will open these boxes and divide them up, two for each person.

43

Mama won't mind if we help ourselves to this crepe paper. There is red and green, and we use thread for tying the packages on the tree. The smelling salts would do for Auntie Lucy, who is coming for the day. She is not very strong, and liable to faint at the slightest provocation. The scent will do for Mama, even if she doesn't use it, for I do declare she is the easiest person in the world to please. Two of these Swiss embroidered handkerchiefs for Grandmama, and the plain linen ones for Auntie Bertha and Norah. And here is a hair ribbon for Prue. That leaves Thomas. There is nothing here for boys. Have you any money? A shilling would do. Thomas loves money. He never has enough of it.'

'I know, he borrows from me,' said Roderic.

'Does he pay you back?'

'Not always, but I don't mind.'

'No, he is so droll, one doesn't mind.'

But Roderic had only sixpence left from his last week's pocket money. They had spent it on marbles and marshmallows.

'It will have to do. We will wrap it in a lot of paper, so that he has to hunt for it, and only you and I will know what's inside,' she giggled. 'There, do you feel better now you have gifts for everyone?'

'Thank you, Miss Bella. I am extremely obliged to you,' said Roderic, with a gallant bow.

'You are quite the nicest boy I have had the good fortune to meet,' she said, with a pretty curtsey.

Yes, he liked Bella.

Thomas was yawning and stretching. The church bells were joyful now, not sad.

'Happy Christmas, Henderson!' Thomas shouted.

'Happy Christmas, Cartwright,' said Roderic, with a playful punch.

The church bells were still ringing when they crept upstairs, but Ellen was expecting them. Red candles were flickering on the mantelpiece, and a lamp was burning on the round table in the old nursery. The table was covered with a red chenille cloth with bobbles, but several of the bobbles were missing. The naughty Kate had taken the nursemaid's scissors and cut them off when she had been shut in the nursery one morning as a punishment, in the days of long ago. Prue and Bella had made paper chains, and Ellen had draped them across the low ceiling, and Bella had made stars from the silver paper they had saved from their penny chocolate bars. They looked very pretty stuck on the ceiling, and almost like real stars. Four fat stockings dangled from the mantelpiece, but they were no longer filled by Father Christmas.

'I do declare it was a sad day when Thomas discovered Mama filling the stockings,' Bella told Roderic, as he shyly received one of the stockings and climbed on the end of the bed beside Thomas.

When Norah arrived, a few minutes later, with mugs of tea and a plate of broken biscuits on a tin tray, she paused in the doorway to admire the scene. A very young-looking mother, with two long plaits and her dark eyes shining, who could have been an elder sister to the two little girls on either side of her, also with long plaits and dark shining eyes. At the bottom of the bed, two little boys, looking much too angelic at this early hour.

'Happy Christmas, everyone!' Norah bustled in, her starched apron crackling, and set the tray on the table.

'Happy Christmas, Norah!' they chorused.

Before she handed round the tea and biscuits, she lit the fire, and soon the sparks were flying up the chimney, and Roderic stopped shivering.

Norah pulled up a chair and sat down to watch. 'I wouldn't miss this for all the tea in China,' she told them, her cheeks glowing like polished apples in the firelight. Bella called her a silly, sentimental fool, but she didn't mind, for she understood Bertha, and her sharp tongue. For Norah, it would be one of the busiest days of the year, but when she had finished climbing the back stairs with laden trays, she would take off that white starched apron, and sit down with the family for Christmas dinner on this one day of the year when all were equal, and she would bow her head while Amelia said grace at the head of the table. Then the four sisters would be standing ready to serve the slices of roast beef that Mr Gregson would be carving at the sideboard. Two of the sisters and their husbands were missing again. Kate and Charles preferred to spend Christmas in Paris, while Grace and Henry could not afford the big expense of travelling from Zurich in Switzerland. Mr Gregson, who became Uncle Basil when he married Auntie Lucy, would have a little frilled apron tied over his striped trousers, and would try very hard to be jolly because it was expected on Christmas Day, but it was difficult for him to shed his self-importance as General Manager of Thomas Brent & Son.

Thomas had found his toy pistol and a black mask. He was prancing on the bed, playing the highwayman. 'Your money or your life!' he shouted, aiming the pistol at Norah, who flung up her hands and begged for mercy. You could always depend on Norah to join in a game of make-believe at any hour of the day. Bella and Roderic were giggling, but Prue was frightened.

'It's only fun, darling,' said Ellen, soothingly.

In her lonely bed, Amelia was also finding the church bells sad until a clatter of feet on the stairs, and a tap on the door, brought the four children into her room, to stand in a row and chant, 'Happy Christmas, Grandmama!'

'You may call me Grandmama, Roderic,' she had decided, last evening. 'Ma'am is much too formal.'

'Thank you, Ma'am – I mean, Grandmama.' He had smiled shyly, a little embarrassed.

Now she looked at the four children with their flushed cheeks and bright eyes, hugging the stockings they had refilled, and found them very endearing.

'Happy Christmas, and God bless you all,' she answered.

But they did not stop to kiss her. There was no time. Not a moment of this precious day must be wasted, for it happened only once a year. So they trooped out, and Roderic closed the door quietly. In the soft glow of the lamp on the bedside table, he thought Thomas's grandmama looked rather sad, and he would have liked to stay with her, to talk to

47

her about Christmas Day in the house in Calcutta, but Thomas was hissing, 'Come *on*, Henderson.'

Still in their dressing gowns and slippers, they raced downstairs. Fires were blazing in the dining-room and the drawing-room, but they chose the dining-room, because they could see the presents piled up around the Christmas tree, to be opened after dinner. The boys were eating the pink sugar mice they had found at the bottoms of their stockings. Squatting on the hearth rug, all four children emptied their stockings for the second time, and found something they had overlooked the first time. Prue found a miniature game of snakes and ladders, with a dice and counters, and Bella found a pack of cards for Happy Families. Four was just the right number for these games, and another hour slipped away before they were called to breakfast. Savoury smells of fried bacon and sausages greeted them as they clattered down the basement stairs, where another fire blazed in the breakfast room, and the glowing fire in the kitchen range was reflected in the steel fender and copper pans.

'Not dressed?' Auntie Bertha asked sharply, from behind the big tea-pot.

'We never dress till after breakfast on Christmas morning,' Prue reminded her. These two were always at loggerheads.

Ellen had followed the children downstairs, but she was fully dressed, and she kissed her sister affectionately. 'Did we disturb you, dear?' she asked, anxiously, for it was important to have Bertha in a good mood.

'Disturb me? You were making enough noise to awaken the dead!' she snapped, irritably, for her nerves were ragged, and she was dreading the hours when the children were let loose all over the house, for there were no restrictions on Christmas Day. They would be an even bigger nuisance today than at other times, she was thinking. And Thomas, with a toy pistol beside his plate, would be an absolute menace! In the flickering gas-light, his mischievous blue eyes defied her authority, and her grim mouth relaxed.

'Pass the sugar, Thomas,' was all she said, but Ellen sighed with relief. Even Bertha found her small nephew could be quite charming. The likeness to his father was most remarkable, the hair, the eyes, the gestures, all were Jonathan's. They said of his father that he could charm a bird off a bough, and his son, at the age of seven, had the same enchanting smile, so deceptively innocent, for getting his own way.

The children went back to their games of Snakes and Ladders and Happy Families after breakfast, but Thomas soon got bored because he was losing and dragged Roderic away to fight another battle with the toy soldiers, leaving the girls squatting happily on the hearthrug. Then it was time to get dressed for church, all in their Sunday best – the girls in grey coats and hats, kid gloves and button boots, and the boys in their Eton suits and school caps. They wore woollen vests and combinations under their suits, but Roderic was shivering as they trooped out of the green gate, led by Amelia in the black astrakhan coat and hat she had worn every Winter since she was widowed. Only Norah was left behind. Two plump chickens would be roasting slowly in the oven, and the plum pudding boiling in the big iron pot on the kitchen range. The table was laid ready for dinner, with a clean, starched cloth and sparkling silver.

Auntie Lucy, Uncle Basil and his mother would be waiting in the church porch, and after the service, they would all walk back together. Amelia had expected to see all her family gathered round the big table in the dining-room on Christmas Day, but three of her married daughters had their husbands to consider, and were no longer obedient to her wishes. They had all excused themselves.

'Like the people in the Bible, who were invited to a feast by the rich man,' Bella had reflected. But there was still quite a big family to eat all the good food provided.

They met the postman at the green gate, laden with packages, on his last delivery round. 'Compliments of the season, Ma'am,' said he, touching his cap to Amelia. The children chorused 'Happy Christmas, postman!' and Thomas demanded eagerly, 'Anything for us?'

'Only cards, Master Thomas.'

'Cards! What can you do with cards?' he scoffed.

'Put them on the mantelpiece with the rest,' said Amelia, smiling indulgently.

'Then I'll pop them in the letterbox and be on my way, for my family are expecting me back for dinner.'

'Have you got a big family, postman?' Bella always asked personal questions that vexed Amelia.

'Seven and a half, Miss Bella,' he answered. They all looked puzzled till he explained, 'Seven to sit down to dinner, and another expected in a couple of months or so.'

The children still looked puzzled. 'Come along, we shall be late for church,' said Amelia, authoritatively, for there was no telling where such an embarrassing subject might lead. She had done her duty for another year, as the head of the house, and the annual distribution of Christmas boxes had been made yesterday. The postman had received half-a-crown, the tradesmen a florin, and the delivery boys sixpence each. All had been invited into the kitchen for mincepies and cups of tea, or mugs of ale, according to taste. The carol singers had sung in the hall while the children sat on the stairs, and Amelia sat in the drawing-room. They sang the same two carols every year – 'While shepherds watched their flocks by night' (Thomas thought they were *wild* shepherds!) and 'Jingle Bells'. Then Norah came up from the basement to hand round a plate of hot mincepies.

'Dropping crumbs all over my polished floor!' Bertha grumbled.

'But it's only once a year, love,' Norah would remind her.

Amelia always thanked them graciously, and they went away, wishing there might have been a second mincepie and a hot toddy. They always fared better with a master than with a mistress!

Church bells were ringing again, and families were on their ways to all the churches and chapels in the town. A few of the upper class went past in their carriages, but the majority were walking. The children composed their faces as they followed Amelia into church. Thomas sighed, remembering the regiment of French artillery to be wiped out before dinner. Uncle Basil, Auntie Lucy and Mrs Gregson senior followed them in. Greetings would be exchanged *after* church. 'There is a time and a place for everything,' Amelia would say.

They were shown into the family pew by the churchwarden, in a frock coat and striped trousers. The pew was in the centre aisle, number six, counting from the back. Thomas always had the aisle seat, so that he could see what was going on, but today, since he was a schoolboy in an Eton suit, he would not stand on the hassock. Neither would Roderic. All along the row heads were bowed and eyes closed. It was a good moment to delve into a pocket for two sticky aniseed balls, to be sucked, not chewed. They had to last!

At the far end of the pew, Uncle Basil sat between his mother and his wife, equally attentive to both. Grandmama sat between her grand-daughters, and Bella sat next to Roderic. She smelled faintly of lavender soap, for she had found a tablet in her stocking, and when she turned her head to smile at him, her eyes were tender with the compassion she was feeling for this little boy who was thousands of miles from home on Christmas Day. Without speaking a word, she knew they were friends, would always be friends. When the choir passed by in their clean, starched surplices, singing the processional carol 'Once in Royal David's City' Bella sent him her prayer book, for she knew every word of the long carol, and she sang as sweetly as the robin that perched on the handle of the gardener's spade.

Thomas and Roderic could not sing, because of the sweets in their bulging cheeks, but it was not noticed, for everyone was singing all about them, as though inspired by the Bethlehem story.

'My Grandpapa!' Thomas whispered, as the grey-haired Vicar passed, stooping over his hymn book. Was he teasing? You never could tell with Thomas. Could a vicar be a grandfather? He must remember to ask Bella.

'Dearly beloved brethren' intoned the solemn voice when the choir had settled in their stalls and the carol was finally concluded. And those three words travelled across the miles to the English church in Calcutta, where the family attended every Sunday morning. Roderic closed his eyes; he could see his father, a tall, autocratic figure, in immaculate tropical suit, his mother in a gown of some flimsy material, and a pretty hat, and his two little sisters in white frocks and straw hats. It was a duty to attend church, Papa had explained. 'To set a good example to lesser mortals.' What did he mean by lesser mortals? Roderic had wondered, but you did not question Papa. You simply answered, 'Yes, Papa' or 'No, Papa', whichever was appropriate. Since Papa claimed the aisle seat, after he had ushered in his family, Roderic could see nothing more interesting than the ostrich feathers on Mrs Wetherby-Smyth's enormous hat. The Wetherby-Smyths were friends of his parents, and it was extremely important to spell the second part of their name with a 'y'. Their four little daughters were horrid children who smacked the face of their patient Ayah and called the native servants rude names. But the children of the two families all had to play together and share a governess, because Mr Wetherby-Smyth was a grade higher than Papa in the Civil Service, and because of something called protocol. Even so, Papa had a son, and the Wetherby-Smyths were still waiting – like the postman, who had seven and a half children.

When his eyes flew open, he found they were wet with tears, so he closed them again and sucked on the sweet in his cheek. 'Only girls and ladies cry.' 'Only those people with white skins are chosen by God to govern those people with dark skins.' 'When a boy reaches the age of seven, he puts away his teddy-bear and crosses the sea to England,' said Papa, authoritatively. But Mama was not so sure, and they both cried bitterly when they parted.

Bella was turning the pages of her prayer book and pointing to the place. He nodded. Then her warm little hand clasped his cold hand, and he was comforted. She knew he was sad. She would always know what he was feeling.

Back at The Haven, Bertha dragged off her coat and hat, draped them over a peg in the cloakroom, and hurried down the basement stairs to help Norah. Her pallid face was disagreeable, her grey eyes stormy. 'That's over for another year!' she told her bosom friend. 'Who wants to listen to a twenty-minute sermon on the origins of the Three Wise Men on Christmas Day? It's time that boring old man retired!'

Norah smiled indulgently, and poured a cup of tea from the pot on the hob. 'Dearest, he can't be more than sixty and Christmas Day is always a sad day when you have lost someone you love.'

Bertha sighed, and sipped the hot tea. 'I told Basil he could carry up the hot plates and start carving.'

'Good. The chickens are done to a turn. A pity to let them dry. Will you serve up the vegetables, love, while I finish the bread sauce and gravy? The pudding has been boiling for another three hours, and the mincepies can be warmed up in the slow oven.' Norah's face was flushed. Her strong, healthy body and calm mind revelled in the challenge of feeding the family well on Christmas Day. Maggie had filled the scuttles with coal, and baskets with logs before she left for home, last evening, and Norah had carried them up to the dining-room and drawing-room. She could hear the excited children playing tag overhead, but Bertha would soon put a stop to that, and have them seated at the table in no time at all.

Ellen and Lucy would be on duty at the sideboard, waiting to hand round the plates, and Amelia would seat herself at the head of the table, with a boy on either side. Then she would say grace. 'For what we are about to receive, may the Lord make us truly thankful.' And Bertha would lift the lids from the vegetable dishes. Everything was piping hot when it left the basement kitchen, but it quickly cooled.

The children showed scant interest in the first course. They were waiting for the plum pudding and the silver three-penny bits they found in the small slices. The girls had saved all theirs 'for luck', but Thomas, who was always short of money, soon found a reason to spend it. It was Thomas who would discover, the following year, that Norah kept the three-penny bits in her apron pocket, and slipped one into each slice of pudding intended for a child, and thereafter the coins would be mixed in the proper way and the children obliged to take a chance with the grown-ups.

'Why must you spoil everything?' Prue would complain.

Most of the afternoon was spent in distributing the presents from the tree, for Grandmama, who handed them round, made it last. Even Roderic found the ceremony rather tedious, for some of the presents were so small it was difficult to get enthusiastic over a tablet of soap, a lace collar, a pen-wiper, or a needle-case – these for the grown-ups, all carefully wrapped and tied to the branches of the tree. Uncle Basil stood by to cut them down.

'One at a time,' Grandmama insisted.

The ceremony over, the boys played with the regiment of Swiss Guards, from the Auntie and Uncle in Zurich, an expensive mechanical fire engine from the Auntie and Uncle in the West End, and a hand-made fort from the Auntie and Uncle in the East End. (Uncle Edward was clever with his hands.) Prue dressed and undressed her new dolls, and Bella turned over the pages of her new Bible.

Tea was a festive meal, with crackers to be pulled and everyone wearing a paper hat. It was a matter of principle that you wear the hat that fell out of the cracker you pulled with your neighbour, but Uncle Basil looked quite ridiculous in a paper bonnet, and Roderic had a crown about his ears! Such a feast – hot buttered scones, dainty bread and butter, three kinds of jam, gentleman's relish, Madeira cake, gingerbread men, and the rich Christmas cake that Auntie Bertha had iced and decorated.

'I couldn't eat another crumb,' Uncle Basil declared, patting his stomach. Auntie Lucy laughed indulgently, and thought her husband the life and soul of the party, but the rest of the family found him rather a bore.

'Now for the games!' Thomas shouted, gleefully, when the table had been cleared and pushed back against the wall.

'Musical Chairs, first, then Hide and Seek,' he told Roderic, and they ran around collecting chairs. Grandmama took Mrs Gregson senior into the drawing-room.

'Keep close to me and you might win. There is always a prize for musical chairs,' Thomas explained.

'And Thomas who wins it!' scoffed Prue, who had eaten too many chocolates between dinner and tea, and was feeling rather sick.

'I don't mind if Thomas wins,' Roderic told her. He didn't care much for Prue, so when the two boys were left circling the one chair, he kept running when Auntie Bertha took her hands off the keyboard and Thomas sat down triumphant – and received sixpence.

The rules for Hide and Seek had to be explained to Roderic. There were hares and hounds. Two hounds stayed at the home base and counted ten slowly, while the rest, who were hares, hid themselves anywhere in the house, and had to get home without being caught.

'It's fun!' Thomas insisted, but Roderic was not so sure.

'Me and you will be hounds,' he was told.

Prue went to hide behind the hallstand in the lobby. It was a frightening game, but she was too proud to admit she was frightened.

'TEN!' Thomas shouted from the dining-room, and she crouched lower and closed her eyes.

Roderic was instructed to search the basement. In the dim gaslight, he could see one of Bella's red slippers under the table and she squealed happily when he pulled her out, and claimed his first hare. People were running about upstairs, trying to escape, but Thomas was too quick for them. Why did everyone spoil Thomas? It's not fair, Prue was thinking. Footsteps on the stairs and protesting voices as the hares were driven back to the dining-room. Then silence, and the silence was more frightening than the commotion, because Prue could imagine Thomas creeping up on her, yet she was never actually prepared for his sudden attack. Crouching lower, her eyes tightly closed, she pressed her trembling hands on her stomach and wondered whether to bolt for the cloakroom and lock herself in. Then a hard, cold object was pressed to her temple, and a voice threatened, 'Your money or your life!'

She screamed, and the scream seemed to echo all over the house. They ran from all directions, and

Mama was the first to reach her, but not soon enough.

'My poor darling,' said Mama, helping her to the cloakroom.

'She's been sick on the floor. How disgusting!' Auntie Bertha complained.

'I'll clear it up,' said the practical Norah.

'But it was only FUN. It's only a toy pistol,' Thomas insisted.

'Of course, my darling, and it's Christmas,' said Grandmama, and went back to the drawing-room.

Bella was holding Roderic's hand. The scream had frightened him. 'My sister is very nervous. She can't help it. When she was little, she screamed an awful lot. Mama understands her. It's something to do with India, but I was too young to remember.' Bella had lowered her voice.

'Silly girl. You would think she was being murdered!' Uncle Basil told his wife as they waited for the game to be resumed.

'What happened in India?' Roderic asked quietly, as they sat on the basement stairs in the semi-darkness. They could hear Prue sobbing hysterically in the cloakroom, and Mama talking soothingly while Norah cleaned up the mess in the lobby.

'Our Papa was killed by a sniper in a skirmish at the garrison where the regiment was stationed on the Northwest Frontier.' Bella had repeated it so often, yet it still seemed strange, not real, as though it had happened to someone in a story. 'Prue remembers Papa very well,' Bella continued. 'She says he was very handsome in his scarlet uniform. She remembers climbing on his knee, and being fed with icecream. She remembers a person called Ayah who called her Missy Baba. Then, quite suddenly, Papa was no longer there, and Mama was packing trunks. They were going home to England, she said. She liked riding on the camel, but she didn't like the big ship because all the people were strangers, and she was still looking for Papa. She thought she would find him in England, but he was not here, only more strange faces, so she screamed. Then, one day, Mama explained that Papa had gone to live with Jesus in Heaven, and she stopped screaming, because that was something she understood. We said our prayers to gentle Jesus, you see. But I was too young, and I only remember this house.'

'Yes, I see,' said Roderic. But he wondered why two sisters who looked alike and dressed alike, apart from the colour of their sashes, should be so completely different.

'Come on, you two!' Thomas interrupted. 'You can be hounds if you like!' He was still brandishing the toy pistol.

'But it's pretend,' said Bella.

But not even Thomas could raise any enthusiasm for the game with Prue drooping in an armchair, pale as a ghost, and Mama sitting beside her, holding her hand.

Roderic and Bella were too slow to catch the hares, or perhaps they didn't try?

'Blind Man's Bluff is fun,' Roderic suggested, tentatively. It was one of the games they played at the birthday parties in Calcutta.

'So it is,' Thomas agreed, looking round the small group for a victim.

'I'll be blind man,' Norah offered, obligingly, and Uncle Basil lent his handkerchief. Norah was quick, and her arms were long, but the children dodged out of her way. Auntie Bertha was vexed, for she loved Norah dearly, and couldn't bear to see her being made to look foolish. Stepping in front of her, she was captured.

'You cheated!' Thomas shouted, accusingly. He had eaten too many nuts, dates, figs, preserved fruits and marshmallows between dinner and tea, and too many gingerbread men, and was feeling sulky, not sick. Thomas was never sick.

'Thomas!' the grown-ups exclaimed in chorus at such shocking disrespect, and he had to apologize before the game could continue.

Everyone had a turn at being blind man, then it was time for supper, and the three children, with plenty of energy to spare for some fresh diversion, hurried up and down the basement stairs carrying plates and dishes. There was a whole gammon ham, lambs' tongues, salad, home-made chutney and pickles, more mincepies, sausage rolls and the trifles and jellies the girls had helped to make. Nobody really wanted to sit down to another meal, but could not disappoint Norah, who had worked so hard on the preparation.

Prue was allowed to sit beside the fire and was persuaded to eat a little jelly. Uncle Basil surprised everyone by accepting a second helping of ham and tongue to oblige Norah – or so he insisted.

'Isn't he droll?' asked Auntie Lucy, with adoring glances at her spouse.

'I liked him best when he was Mr Gregson,' Thomas told Roderic after supper, as they all trooped into the drawing-room.

'The children have had enough excitement. We will finish the day quietly,' said Grandmama decidedly.

The grown-ups sank thankfully on to chairs and sofa, the children gathered round the piano. (Prue had recovered, and couldn't bear to be left out.) Grandmama smiled benignly on the four children, and touched the keys gently with her slender white hands.

'Away in a manger, No crib for a bed, The little Lord Jesus, Laid down his sweet head' the children sang. With his cap of golden hair, flushed cheeks, and innocent blue eyes, you could almost imagine that Thomas was the most angelic child who ever lived, Mrs Gregson senior was thinking, but she had seen enough, on her first Christmas Day at The Haven, to recognize the devil in disguise!

Everyone sang or hummed 'While Shepherds watched their flocks by night' and 'Oh, come all ye faithful'. Only Prue, Bella, and Auntie Lucy knew all the words.

Then Bella sang the first verse of 'Once in Royal David's City' and the spirit of Christmas was there, at the end of the day, in the pure, sweet voice of a child.

Chapter Two

'Shouldn't we do something about the children, my sweet, before they go back to school?' Charles asked, languidly, from a comfortable fireside chair in their drawing-room.

Kate was curled on the sofa, turning the pages of the *Strand Magazine*, studying the photographs of recent society weddings and pretty debutantes who had captured a beau of elegance and breeding during the Season. Kate sighed enviously, for she knew she had the looks and the personality, but would never be included on these pages unless her charming, but indolent husband bestirred himself at the House, where he was a backbencher, and attracted the notice of the Prime Minister. Since he was not in the least ambitious, it was most unlikely. As the wife of a cabinet minister in Her Majesty's Government, they could afford their own carriage, and a bigger establishment, with a butler to announce the visitors and pour the drinks. It would be fun, but it was wishful thinking.

'Will you get your head out of that confounded magazine, Kate, and answer my question!' Charles admonished, flicking the ash from his cigar on to the carpet.

Kate's dark eyes twinkled mischievously. 'My darling, I do apologize. What were you saying?'

'The children – shouldn't we do something about a treat before they go back to school?'

'Of course, darling. How clever of you to remember.'

'They *are* your relations.'

'But you do love them?'

'Love is a word that hardly applies to that recalcitrant little devil, and the girls are so plain.'

'I adore Thomas.'

'I know, and he adores you, but may I remind you, my sweet, you must be prepared for a change. Your adorable nephew is a schoolboy now, and a boy of seven will not want to sit on your lap, to be kissed and cuddled.'

'You're jealous, Charles! You have always been jealous of that child,' she teased.

Could one be jealous of a little boy, he asked himself, and decided one could when that particular little boy was Thomas. There was something between his young wife and the child that embarrassed him, but Kate would laugh at such a ridiculous notion. Twenty years her senior, he was beginning to wonder why he had married such a flighty little butterfly. He must have been a little mad to rush into marriage with a pretty little apprentice in the millinery department of Thomas Brent & Son, but the fact remained he could not have borne to lose her to young Gregson. She was a beautiful woman now, a charming hostess, and a delightful bed-mate. Could any man ask more of marriage? All his friends envied him, but they did not see the real Kate under that veneer of charming sophistication. Only the servants saw the ugly scenes between husband and wife after the guests had left.

As Cook would say, 'There was a time when the Master could please 'imself, but now 'e 'as ter please 'er Ladyship or there's trouble.'

'She wants 'er own way and she gets it.' The house-parlourmaid was not born yesterday, and she sadly missed the old regime, when Miss Eleanor was mistress of this house, and the Master still a happy bachelor, enjoying the best of both worlds with no strings attached – and wasn't that a gentleman's privilege? But it was an easy post if you turned a blind eye to those ugly scenes, and overlooked the insulting remarks. It was unlikely she would find another post where the mistress seldom interfered in a maid's duties, and was generous with discarded clothes. 'Beggars can't be choosers,' as Cook would say.

Just back from Paris, with several new gowns and dainty lingerie that Harris had unpacked, their young mistress was in a most pleasant mood, when favours could be asked.

When she had served the coffee and put more coal on the fire, Harris went away, closing the door quietly.

'They are taking those dear little children to the circus on New Year's Eve,' she told Cook, over a nice cup of tea.

'The circus!' Thomas shouted, excitedly, when

Grandmama had read aloud the letter from Auntie Kate the following day. 'And what fun to travel to London in charge of the guard.'

'Without Mama?' Prue asked, nervously.

Ellen shook her head. 'They are too young to be entrusted on such a journey. I do wish Kate would not propose such a hazardous arrangement. Anything could happen while the guard was busy on his normal duties, and Thomas is so venturesome,' she protested.

'I won't be venturesome, Mama, I promise. Cross my heart.' He was not sure what venturesome meant, but he would promise anything. Now he appealed to his Grandmama, for she would most likely over-rule any opposition by his anxious Mama, if only to prove she was still the one to decide such an important issue.

'We have never been to a circus, Grandmama, and it will be something special to swank about when we get back to school. Some of the boys were going to Switzerland with their parents for the Winter sports, and those who live in London will be going to a pantomime as well as the circus. You do see how important it is to do something really special, don't you, Grandmama?'

Such an appeal from her adored grandson could not be denied. 'I understand perfectly, my darling. Of course you must go.'

Thomas gave Roderic a playful punch and shouted gleefully, 'Isn't that absolutely top-hole, Henderson? Aren't you pleased?'

'I have not been invited, Cartwright.'

'Of course you must come. Don't be silly. Auntie Kate wouldn't mind. Isn't that so, Grandmama?'

'Your Auntie Kate is seldom surprised at anything, Thomas. One extra child is unlikely to cause her more than a moment's anxiety. Your Uncle Charles will be there. No lady would dare to take a party of children to the circus without an escort. It would not be safe.'

'The lions will be shut in their cages, won't they? Nobody will let them out?' Prue shivered with fear at such an awful possibility.

'If they do, the lion tamer will drive them back with his big whip,' said Thomas, who had seen pictures in the *Boy's Magazine*.

'I shall sit next to Uncle Charles, then I shall feel safe,' Prue decided.

'So shall I. He is a very safe-guarding person,' said Bella.

'A *responsible* person,' Grandmama corrected, automatically.

Neither of the girls was keen on a visit to the circus. They would have enjoyed the ballet at Covent Garden, but Thomas would be exceedingly bored, and Auntie Kate had chosen the circus to please Thomas. Everyone wished to please Thomas. It was natural.

Roderic would have been quite content to spend the rest of the holiday playing with the new toys, and endless games of Snakes and Ladders. He, too, had seen pictures in the *Boy's Magazine*, and his heart ached for the wild animals in captivity – for the king of beasts, in cages, and magnificent elephants

67

lumbering round the ring, tail to tail, sea-lions climbing ladders, and baby chimpanzees dressed in frocks and bonnets, pushed in bassinets. It was cruel. But Thomas was his best friend, and he would have to pretend. He had already discovered there were two boys. There was Roderic and there was Henderson, and there was a time for each.

When the guard had handed over the children and received a handsome tip from Uncle Charles, they stood waiting a little uncertainly till Thomas stepped forward and proffered his hand.

'How do you do, Auntie Kate? How do you do, Uncle Charles,' said he, with a polite bow. 'May I introduce my friend Henderson. You may call him Roderic.'

Kate suppressed a strong desire to giggle. Charles was right in his assumption that her young nephew would have outgrown her hugs and kisses. But he was still adorable, and her eyes danced with mischief as they shook hands. This was going to be fun. Both boys were neatly dressed in Eton suits, and had removed their caps for the introduction. The girls had bobbed a small curtsey, and Charles was kissing them affectionately.

'Well, my darlings. How charming you look in those pretty little capes with the matching caps, and those are the muffs we gave you, are they not?' Kate asked, gushingly.

'Yes, Auntie Kate,' they smiled shyly.

'We have brought our thank-you letters,' said Bella.

'We have written all our thank-you letters, but

Thomas has not written a single one,' Prue informed them, importantly.

'There was no time. We were too busy. Only silly girls write letters in the hols,' Thomas declared, and Kate was in full agreement with her darling boy.

Charles gave a hand to each of the girls, and they walked beside him feeling very proud to be escorted by such an important gentleman who was a Member of Parliament, and had a seat in the House of Commons.

'But you could hardly expect the poor man to remain standing,' Prue had volunteered, very sensibly.

The boys walked sedately on either side of Auntie Kate, and stood back politely while she climbed into the waiting cab, followed by the girls and Uncle Charles.

'Grandmama would be very pleased to see such good manners,' Bella was thinking as the cab moved away from the station forecourt.

The four children reacted differently to the blare of the trumpets and the beat of the drums as they entered the big tent with the glaring lights and the smell of animals and saw-dust. It was another world, far removed from anything they had yet experienced in their short lives.

For Prue, it was frightening, and she clung tightly to Uncle Charles's hand.

For Bella, there was magic in the scene and in the atmosphere.

For Roderic there was pity for all the wild animals in captivity, and a tightness in the throat.

For Thomas, there was excitement, glamour and fascination and he settled on the bench beside Auntie Kate and looked about him with eager curiosity.

They hadn't long to wait for the colourful parade, led by the ringmaster in his resplendent uniform and beautiful girls in scanty dresses and sparkling sequins. Then came the animals with their trainers, the trapeze artists, the horses and the clowns. They circled the arena, and the large audience applauded – rows and rows of parents and children for whom this was the annual Christmas treat.

Thomas enjoyed every moment and clapped every act enthusiastically, but when the horses appeared in their gaudy trappings, tossing their proud heads disdainfully, he stood up, tense with anxiety, lest those leaping figures, springing on their backs, should harm his special favourites.

Kate watched her small nephew with mixed feelings, a little jealous of those creatures who could claim his undivided attention. The quiet little boy on her other side smiled shyly and whispered, 'Cartwright is the best rider in the whole school. He can already jump the hurdles.'

'Clever boy – and you?'

'I can only trot.'

'Never mind. I expect you are clever at your lessons?'

'Not clever, Ma'am. Only average,' said he, modestly.

The girls could not bear to watch the trapeze artists, and closed their eyes. Charles and Kate exchanged meaningful glances. Prue hid her face during the lions' act, and Roderic sat with clenched hands and shuddered when the trainer cracked his whip, while Thomas missed nothing of the whole performance, and would have liked to see it all over again. Uncle Charles purchased strawberry ices in the interval, as the band played military marches.

And Kate's 'darling boy' decided to become a ringmaster, not a soldier!

With the boys back to boarding school and the girls as day pupils at the Convent, the small household at The Haven settled down to a quiet period, till Easter – too quiet for Amelia, who missed the lively company of her grandson, and found the short Winter days rather dreary.

When Norah and Bertha had removed all the Christmas decorations and replanted the tree in the corner of the front garden, among the laurels, the rooms looked bare.

With only a rare visit from Kate, a monthly visit from Jane, and a promised visit from Grace for the Summer, Amelia found herself sauntering round the shops, where the January sales were in full swing. She was not tempted to buy, however, for she had overspent at Christmas, and her quarterly allowance from Grandpapa Brent was not due till March. Hot chocolate at Kong's in mid-morning used up another hour or so, for there was no hurry. Norah, Bertha and Ellen would be coping with all the chores, with Maggie for the hard work. They did not expect Amelia to soil her hands.

She had made no friends in Worthing, and hardly

knew the meaning of loneliness, but for seven years she had enjoyed her role as Grandmama, and her special place in the affections of her young grandson. She wished she could put back the clock and have those seven years all over again, for she had not yet become reconciled to this small independent schoolboy, who answered to the name of Cartwright, and avoided her hugs and kisses. It was too late to transfer her affections to her grand-daughters. Children are wary of such obvious disloyalty. They were shy with her, and saw her as a person to be respected and obeyed.

She did not share their confidences. She would hear them chattering to Bertha and Norah about the teachers and the girls at the Convent. For that brief hour after tea they would take turns to play their little pieces on the piano, and to read aloud from Mr Dickens. Now that they could have music lessons at school, for a small extra fee, Amelia had stopped teaching them. It had been a laborious task, for neither of the girls showed any talent or an inclination to persevere. They could practise their scales and simple pieces on the dining-room piano, before tea, and she would shut the door on their poor performances! As for reading aloud, they were no better and no worse than her own daughters, but it did not occur to her to ask if they would prefer another author.

Prue enjoyed *Grimm's Fairy Tales* and *Tales of King Arthur and his Knights*. Bella found the Bible stories quite fascinating, but the children were not consulted, and Ellen never interfered. Grandmama's wishes and Grandmama's authority were never questioned.

Ellen was a devoted mother, and her children revolved about her, with their constant demands on her time and her affections. It was Mama they loved, and their small world at the top of the house was a safe haven now that Thomas had been removed. When he came home for the holidays, he would bring Roderic, and they had nothing to fear from that well-behaved boy.

Even Prue liked Roderic. 'He listens when I tell him about *my* India, and I listen when he tells me about *his* India,' she told Bella. 'I think he likes me best,' she added, importantly.

Bella knew he was just being polite, and her own feelings for Roderic had nothing to do with politeness.

Lucy was expecting a baby, and Basil had acquired a new status as a prospective father.

'One would suppose such a state to be unique. I have no patience with such ridiculous self-importance,' Amelia scoffed. If the truth be known, she was more than a little vexed because she was not allowed to interfere with this happy event. Lucy had firmly established herself in a household where her delicate constitution was regarded as a sacred trust, and she had never been so cherished. Her every wish was gratified, and Mrs Gregson senior, a devoted mother-in-law, was ready to do battle on Lucy's behalf whenever Amelia set foot in the door.

They had not taken to each other, and Mrs

Gregson senior had decided to refuse all future invitations to The Haven. *Her* grandchild would be every bit as beautiful as that detestable child who had had his own way over everything that day, and was not even scolded for frightening his sister into hysterics with that toy pistol.

Acting on the doctor's advice, Lucy spent most of the day on the couch in the drawing-room, pampered and protected from every disturbing influence, while her fond mother-in-law busied herself with making the infant's layette. Lucy was not to tire herself, but whenever she felt inclined, she could manage a small bonnet or bootees. Basil spared no expense on the purchase of a cradle, a bassinet, and the largest teddy bear in the best toyshop in town. Lucy's adoring spouse had never been more attentive, or more aware of his responsibilities. His dear little Lucy had proved a most obliging bed-mate once the initial shock of the wedding night had passed. Her sweet acquiescence to his demands had pleased him enormously, and no man could have been more surprised or delighted to discover a child had been conceived. Not for a single moment had his thoughts been allowed to wander to the tantalizing picture of the bewitching Kate in the passionate embrace of that scoundrel Lefeaux. His dear little Lucy was so amenable and he was the happiest of men – or so he convinced himself.

'Why don't we see Greggy any more, Mama?' Prue demanded, one Sunday afternoon, as they waited for the gong to summon them to tea.

'Uncle Basil would not come without Auntie Lucy,

74

'darling, and she is indisposed,' Ellen told her eldest daughter as she smoothed her hair and rearranged the bow of ribbon she wore on Sundays.

'But it's weeks and weeks. What is the matter with her?'

Ellen sighed. Such a delicate subject could no longer be avoided, but she had been hopeful the birth would be announced, when no explanation would be necessary. 'Auntie Lucy will shortly be blessed with a darling little baby, and Uncle Basil will be a proud Papa,' she explained, carefully.

'Greggy a Papa? But how does it come about? I mean, our Papa had already gone to Heaven to live with Jesus when Thomas was born.'

'That is so.'

'I don't understand, Mama. Is there some mystery or something too shocking to be discussed?'

'There is no mystery, my darling, and nothing at all shocking, but you are too young to understand.'

'Understand what?'

They were getting into deep water, and Ellen was embarrassed by her daughter's questioning mind, not for the first time.

Bella seemed to be absorbed in the tale of *Uncle Tom's Cabin*, and her tender heart ached for poor little Topsy, but she lifted her head to say, 'Millicent Savage, who is my best friend, told me there must be a papa as well as a mama to make a baby.'

Ellen blushed with such acute embarrassment, she could only stare at her younger daughter.

'She doesn't actually know how babies are made,' Bella confessed, with all innocence.

'I should think not indeed!' Ellen was much disturbed. She had thought her little girls would be safe at the Convent.

'I told her she was mistaken, for Jesus had no papa, and she insisted that Joseph was his rightful papa, so I asked Sister Cecilia to settle the matter,' Bella continued. 'There was no papa. It was a virgin birth, she told us. And we had to copy out "Jesus was born of the Virgin Mary" twenty times. So you see, Mama, Greggy may have been quite surprised when he was told he would soon be a proud Papa.'

'There's the gong. Come along. We mustn't keep Grandmama waiting.' And Ellen followed her growing daughters down the stairs with mixed feelings of shock and apprehension.

With the first pangs of childbirth, Lucy was startled into an awareness of pain. She had always been afraid of pain, and Amelia was right in her assumption that her youngest daughter, overshadowed by the dominant Kate, had found refuge in sick headaches, fainting spells and tears. For nine months she had enjoyed being the focus of attention, with nothing more than a little discomfort and distress at the ugliness of her swelling belly. But Basil had assured her she was beautiful and that he adored her. Nobody had warned her, however, of the travail she had still to endure before the child in her womb could be safely delivered, and she was still ignorant of the actual process of birth. It was all a complete mystery, but one did not ask such intimate questions of one's husband or one's mother-in-law. For instance, how did the child get out of the womb and become a living person? And would the miraculous process of delivery be accomplished through her 'private parts'? To be ignorant of the facts of life had not disturbed her unduly. It was Kate who was so curious.

The marriage bed had been a mystery, but she had survived her wedding night with its unpleasant disclosures, and had submitted to Basil's demands with a sweet willingness that was typical of her docile nature.

When she cried out with the pain that was unlike anything she had yet experienced in her short life, her mother-in-law was there to calm her fears, and Basil was sent post-haste for the midwife. It was Sunday morning, and the church bells were ringing for Matins. The midwife, a bustling, competent little body, showed no surprise when she was still in attendance twelve hours later.

'The first child is always a bit awkward, but you won't have no trouble with the second,' she prophesied, cheerfully.

'Never again!' Basil had vowed, for he couldn't bear to listen to those agonizing screams.

The midwife had taken time off for several substantial meals, and a short cat-nap on the couch, but Basil and his mother had eaten nothing but toast with frequent cups of tea, and were quite exhausted.

'There's something not quite normal. Best get the doctor,' the midwife finally decided.

Basil was instructed to call at the doctor's house on his way to work on the Monday morning. He was glad to get away, and had never been more thankful to see the premises of Thomas Brent & Son. With Lucy's screams still ringing in his ears, he found the quiet sanctuary of his private office quickly dispelled such a shattering reminder of his own regrettable part in the agony of childbirth. Reminded that he had had no breakfast, he rang the bell, and ordered coffee and ham sandwiches. In his role as general manager, his confidence was restored. In his role as a prospective parent, he had been made to feel both inadequate and guilty, awaiting the birth of his first child. 'Never again,' he told himself, as he sipped the hot coffee.

The doctor was annoyed that he hadn't been called earlier. A complicated birth should never be left to the midwife, he asserted, as he administered a soothing draft of laudanum and set to work on the delivery. Now he could see the reason for the complications. The child was being delivered feet first, and when he held the tiny scrap of humanity in his hands, there was no life. A still-born child was always distressing, but the mother was more important. So he handed the child to the midwife, and leaned over the young mother. Her pulse was weak, and her glazed eyes unseeing. Her head drooped, and her gentle spirit departed with nothing more than a tired sigh.

Six months had passed, and Basil, still suffering from a sense of guilt he could not dispel, received a little note, in a neat, copy-book hand. It read 'Dear Greggy, Please come to tea on Sunday. We miss you. Your devoted nieces, Prudence and Arabella.'

'Are we nieces, Mama?' Prue had asked, because

she liked to be certain of her relationships.

'You are nieces by marriage,' Ellen answered.

Another Christmas had passed with the normal celebrations for the sake of the children, and Roderic had been included as naturally as though he actually belonged to the family. Lucy's name was not mentioned, but Amelia's thoughts were sad as she lay in her lonely bed, listening to the church bells on Christmas morning, and Ellen was remembering the gentle little sister she had mothered in those nursery days.

All four children had once again climbed on to her bed with their bulging stockings. How much longer could they continue with these childish practices, she wondered.

'Just one more year, please Mama,' Prue had begged, for she couldn't bear it to finish. Neither could Norah, so deeply involved was she in every big and small event in her adopted family.

For the same reasons that had prevented them the previous year, neither Grace, Kate nor Jane could join the rest of the family. They had all attended Lucy's funeral with their husbands, all attired in the deepest mourning, and Amelia was back in the black dresses, hats and gloves she had worn for such a long period after the death of her husband. They all were kind and warmly sympathetic to the young brother-in-law, so sadly bereaved, but he seemed to perform the necessary obligations in a state of dazed disbelief.

'Time will heal,' the practical Bertha predicted when they had left mother and son together.

Since that day, all communication between the two

houses had ceased, and it was doubtful whether Basil would ever have set foot in The Haven but for the tender reminder that he was missed.

'Shall you go, dear?' his mother asked, anxious to find some small diversion or new interest to take his mind off the tragedy.

'I'll think about it,' he answered, automatically, and the silence between them was pregnant with the sadness that would soon become morbid.

'They are nice children,' the mother prompted, patiently. In his own grief, her son had not given a thought to his mother, who had lost a very dear daughter-in-law, and the only hope of a grandchild, for Basil had sworn never to marry again, or to father another child. It was a drastic decision for such a young man, but she could understand his feelings. Lucy had been too frail for motherhood. In their grief, mother and son had drawn a little apart, and their long silences were not companionable but a barrier to mutual confidence. So she waited hopefully for a return of the old happy relationship they had shared since the day her son carried the unconscious girl into the house.

It was strange that he should lose both the Brent sisters – Kate by her elopement with Charles Lefeaux, Lucy in childbirth. Now his work was his salvation, for in the hours he spent at Thomas Brent & Son there was little opportunity for private thoughts. His grave young face held a severity that reminded the apprentices of his authority. For recreation he took long walks on the promenade, averting his eyes from the bathing machines and the poignant memory of happy Wednesday afternoons.

'Please come to tea. We miss you.' Every brisk step was punctuated by this childish invitation. Could he bear it without Lucy? The invitation bothered him. It could not be ignored. 'We miss you.' It was probably true, for he was fond of those two little girls, especially Prue, and they were fond of him. Now, at last, his mind was made up. He would go to tea on Sunday afternoon.

But first, a polite little note to Amelia: 'Dear Mrs Brent, May I take tea with you on Sunday next, if this is convenient? Yours respectfully, Basil Gregson.'

The reply came back by return post: 'Dear Basil, Thank you for your note. We shall be pleased to see you at about four o'clock on Sunday. Yours sincerely, Amelia Brent.'

The die was cast, but he approached the hour with something akin to panic and would have cancelled the appointment but for disappointing the children. When the cab drew up at The Haven, the green gate flew open, and two excited little girls were there to welcome him. He paid the cabby and stood there, smiling shyly. Then they were in his arms, their hugs and kisses falling like benison on his sad heart, and he wondered why he had waited so long.

'Oh, Greggy!' breathed Prue, ecstatically, her dark eyes glowing. 'It seems such an age since we saw you.'

'And there is so much to tell you,' said Bella, as they dragged him into the house.

They were all there to greet him. Amelia kissed his

cheek. Ellen, Bertha and Norah shook hands. Nothing had changed at The Haven. The faint smell of gas drifted up from the basement. The grandfather clock ticked away the hours in the polished hall, and the special Sunday tea was laid so invitingly on an embroidered cloth.

Seated between the two girls, Basil gazed at the empty space where his dear little Lucy had once sat, and he shivered involuntarily. They plied him with scones and strawberry jam, and the hot, sweet tea from the big silver teapot was just to his liking, but he listened to the chatter of the two little girls, and wondered how soon he could leave. It had been a mistake to come here after such a long interval. The warm feeling of being accepted back into the bosom of the family had not lasted, and his heart was desolate. To revive old memories could only bring heartache. The chapter was closed.

'We have a favour to ask,' Prue was saying, and the present moment claimed him. 'Will you teach us to swim? *Please*, Greggy,' she pleaded.

'We are free on Wednesday afternoons,' Bella added.

'Perhaps Uncle Basil has other plans for Wednesday afternoons?' Ellen suggested.

He shook his head. He had no plans.

'*Please*, Greggy,' they chorused.

'We day girls are so despised by the boarders. It would be so very satisfactory to be able to claim one small victory. Not one of the girls in my form can swim,' Prue explained, earnestly.

'Or in mine,' Bella echoed.

'I see.' He glanced at Ellen for confirmation.

'I would bring them down to the beach and stay with them, so you would not feel responsible,' she told him.

'And you did teach Auntie Kate to swim,' Prue reminded him.

Yes, he had taught Kate. Would he ever forget that lovely shape in the ugly costume, the clinging arms, the tantalizing wet mouth? Could he bear to be reminded? But these two children were innocent of such seductive thoughts. It would be a new chapter, a new interest, unconnected with the past when he had loved both Lucy and Kate.

'I could bring a picnic and a big flask of tea,' Ellen was saying. She wanted him to agree. It would be so enjoyable.

'That would be nice,' he said, still undecided. He hadn't been to Kong's for tea since that awful day when Lucy had tried to drown herself, but tea on the beach would disturb no bitter-sweet memories.

'It would be such fun, Greggy dear.' That was Kate speaking. In some ways Prue was very like Kate, but she would never be a beauty with that lank black hair and pallid skin. Only the dark, expressive eyes saved the piquant face from plainness. But Prue would never be a nonentity, for there was so much character, so much intensity in the child.

'The water is still cold,' he warned them.

'We don't care, do we, Bella?' said Prue.

'No, we don't care,' Bella echoed, obligingly. If Prue suggested jumping off the end of the pier, Bella would oblige!

'Very well. Then it's settled.' And Basil gasped as two pairs of throttling arms wound round his neck.

But memory played tricks on that sunny afternoon, and Prue's childish form in the clinging costume was a disturbing reminder of Kate. With her long hair tucked under a rubber cap, Prue's eyes were wide with a fear she could not hide; the intensity of her determination could be felt so acutely, and his own body was trembling. Kate had pretended to be afraid to attract his sensuality, but this child was too young for pretence.

They had left Bella sitting on the steps of the bathing machine with her mother, awaiting her turn for the first lesson, but there would be no need to coax the younger girl, for she seemed to be born without fear. He supposed all children were born without fear, and Bella's early years held no disturbing memories of India and an adored Papa who disappeared.

'Do you trust me, Prue?' he asked, as she clung like a limpet round his neck.

'Yes, Greggy,' she answered, with chattering teeth.

'You have a funny way of showing it,' he told her, his voice gruff with an emotion he could not define.

'I do! I do!' She was struggling to control her tears. It had seemed such a wonderful idea and she had practised the strokes on the hearthrug. But the hearthrug was warm and steady, the water was cold and lapped about her stomach, and the sea was so vast, it seemed to go on for ever.

'Well, I can't stand here all day, waiting for you to

make up your mind. I shall count ten, and if you are not ready I shall carry you ashore.'

The threat was a challenge. She couldn't bear to be deprived of her small victory over those hateful boarders. 'I'm ready, Greggy,' she faltered.

'Good girl.' He lowered her gently into the water, felt her shuddering breath, and ached with pity. Cupping her chin with one hand, he grasped a handful of sagging costume. Her small body seemed weightless between his two hands, and it took all her gasping breath to cover a few yards.

'Splendid,' he encouraged.

But she was already exhausted, and her body went limp and she floundered helplessly.

'That will do for today,' he told her, kindly, and lifted her up.

'I nearly did swim, didn't I, Greggy?' she asked, with chattering teeth.

'Nearly.' He smiled and kissed her wet cheek.

He felt no disturbing emotion with the younger girl, only amusement, as she flayed the water with such exuberance; his grasp was slipping and she was partly submerged.

'Where do you think you are going? If you are thinking of swimming the Channel, I must warn you the coast of France is twenty-two miles away!' he teased.

Spluttering and giggling, he lifted her up. She spat out a mouthful of sea water, and her dark eyes were glowing. 'That was absolutely spiffing, Greggy! Once more, *please*!' she pleaded.

They both glanced towards the bathing machine,

but Ellen had taken the shivering Prue inside, and would be rubbing her down and helping her to dress.

'I won't tell Prue I had two turns. It would be unkind, wouldn't it?' said the loyal little sister, as she flopped back on the water. They all knew that Prue's jealousy was something that could not be cured. It was part of Prue. She couldn't help it – as Bella would say. It would certainly have provoked a scene had she witnessed the prolonged swimming lesson.

'Like a duck to water,' Basil was thinking. And when at last he lifted her up and held her against his chest, her streaming face laughed up at him. There was a joyousness about this child that her sister would never know. The gift of laughter was a precious gift. To have a child like Bella would be a blessing to any parent, Basil thought, as he carried her ashore and sat her down on the steps of the bathing machine. Then he plunged back into the incoming tide.

The long Summer holiday that year would be remembered by all four children as one of the happiest Summers they had known. Day after day the sun shone from a cloudless blue sky, and the beach echoed to the happy shouts of children. Each day, from Monday to Saturday, followed the same pattern, and nobody had any wish to change it. Norah packed a hamper, and the two boys carried it to the beach. The girls carried towels and bathing costumes, and buckets and spades.

The two boys had been taught to swim in the sea at Brighton, where two young masters escorted a group of the younger boys every Saturday afternoon. They travelled from the rambling old house at the foot of the Downs by wagonette to the seashore, and were forcibly ducked into the ice-cold water at the start of the Easter term.

Thomas was soon swimming like a fish, shaming Roderic for his poor performance. Such spartan methods of teaching were not uncommon. Preparatory school for boys of the upper class was to pave the way to manhood. No two boys were alike, but all were treated alike. There was no escape. In the Winter months they were taken for long walks on the Downs, and spent endless hours in the 'gym', vaulting the wooden horse and hitting the punch ball with boxing gloves. Small hands and feet suffered with chilblains, and small boys, miserably homesick, endured all the harshness of this spartan discipline with admirable fortitude. Cricket was another hazard, and the hard ball a frightening object to youngsters hitherto accustomed to cricket on the lawn with a tennis ball.

But now they were free, and Ellen shepherded her small flock to the beach with a sense of joyous participation. The bathing machine could be hired for an hour, morning and afternoon, and all four children were warned to keep to the shallow water. Only on Wednesday afternoons, with Uncle Basil to supervise, were the boys allowed into deep water, while the girls were kept in the shallows. Bella longed to join her uncle and the boys on Wednesday afternoons, but Prue would not be left. When the tide went out beyond Ellen's anxious gaze, the boys built a castle on the firm sand, working like beavers with the tin spades, then standing back to admire their handiwork while the girls ran to and fro, filling the tin buckets with water for the moat. Then the boys played endless games of leap-frog, while the girls searched for shells to decorate the castle. The girls liked to paddle in the pool at the base of the high breakwater, but the boys ran along the top, and jumped into the pool with a mighty splash that annoyed Prue. It was always Thomas who led the way. It was fun. Everything was fun, and teasing was second nature to Thomas.

For Ellen, the holiday was a pleasant change from her rather lonely existence when the children were at school. To get away from the house, and Bertha's nagging tongue, was a relief, and to compare her own children favourably with other children delighted her maternal nature. With an old straw hat on her piled-up hair, and a faded print dress, she soon acquired a healthy tan. So did the girls and Roderic. Thomas was so fair, his skin scorched, and Ellen went prepared with camomile lotion. All four children wore hats. There were no bare heads to be seen on the beach in that day and age. And children could remove their shoes and socks for paddling, but to remove any other garment it was necessary to enter a bathing machine and close the door.

Ellen took off her gloves, but nothing more. She sat all day on the beach with legs and arms decorously covered, and a high collar up to her chin. Only common day-trippers removed their boots and stockings 'to give their corns a good soaking'. But such shocking exhibitions of ugly feet did not encroach on the select beaches to the west of the bandstand.

The boys drank lemonade, the girls drank tea. They ate every crumb of the food that Norah provided, and enjoyed the hot supper in the early evening. The family used the back entrance every weekday. The young dog, called Sam – Jackie had died of old age – barked excitedly as they crossed the yard, and whined dismally when he was left behind. But Norah would soon find a meaty bone to compensate for his disappointment.

'Why doesn't Norah come to the beach with us?' Thomas wanted to know.

'Because Auntie Bertha can't be left alone to do all the work now Mama is on holiday with us,' Prue explained.

'They are not working all day. They could join us in the afternoon if they wished, but Auntie Bertha dislikes the beach,' said Ellen.

'Norah would like it. Why does she always have to please Auntie Bertha?' Thomas argued.

'Because she is very fond of her, darling.'

'Is being very fond the same as loving?'

'Yes.'

'Then I am loving Henderson and he is loving me, and boys are not allowed to love. It's soppy, and only girls are soppy,' said he, shouting with laughter.

'They are not! You are still a horrid little boy, and have no manners!' Prue usually had the last word. Even on holiday they crossed swords. Bella was the go-between.

Amelia also disliked the beach, and could not be persuaded to set foot on the shingle. She was too dignified, too fastidious. Neither could she bring herself to walk as far as the promenade with a family of children in their shabbiest clothes, trailing buckets and spades, towels and bathing costumes. She made the excuse that they always left before she was ready, then she took a cab and arrived at the bandstand just in time to hear the first item on the programme. A sun-shade protected her complexion, and her youthful features belied the fact that she was a grandmother. The silver hair, piled so becomingly on her proud little head, was most distinctive. Her daughter remembered their mother with hair as fair as Grace and Lucy, for she had turned white overnight with the shock of her husband's tragic death in a carriage accident. Something of herself had died that day.

She had not loved her children as she had loved her husband. Amelia was too proud to admit her faults, and she knew she had been unfair to her six daughters and her two grand-daughters in her preference for the opposite sex.

It was only in the rare company of Charles Lefeaux, her charming, cultured son-in-law, that she felt a whole woman again, because he flattered her with compliments not paid to her since she lost Thomas. She actually envied Kate her husband, for he reminded her of her own long-lost husband, and brought back poignant memories of a time – all too short – when she had known that she was truly beloved.

Her thoughts wandered on these Summer mornings, and the military band was nothing more than an accompaniment to these memories. She could see herself in the hip-bath that the housemaid had filled with hot, scented water for her daily bath, and see Thomas, sitting on a chair, admiring her swollen belly. Being pregnant was no handicap, for there was no shyness between them. The marriage bed had been enjoyed, not endured, and it was only after his death that she realized it must have been a very unusual relationship in that day and age, where a woman was not expected to be a lover, or to share her husband's sensuality, only to submit herself to his demands. Childbirth had not ruined her figure or her health, and Thomas had always found her desirable at every stage of those six pregnancies.

She sighed nostalgically for her lost youth and her lost love. Then she remembered the golden boy on the beach, and her sad eyes brightened.

'Cartwright again. Who else would have the audacity to kick a ball through the window of the Head's study?' the irate housemaster demanded of his colleagues as they shared the mid-morning break for cocoa.

The start of the Autumn term had brought the usual difficulties with small boys who had been allowed too much freedom in the long Summer holiday.

'Has Cartwright confessed to kicking the ball that smashd the window?' a junior master asked. The usual procedure, for a serious offence, was to line up the entire form and threaten each one with the cane, when the culprit usually confessed.

'The Head is fuming. The ball landed on his desk and upset the inkpot.'

'Great Scott!' the junior master exclaimed in horror. This was his first term, and he was being very careful not to give offence.

'Have you seen Cartwright since he confessed to the crime?' drawled Peterson. Everyone knew his opinion of the Head; the masters were a close fraternity and they shared a common bond. They all liked teaching small boys and disliked a Head who practised sadism on innocent or at least exuberant heads.

'I saw him through the broken window. He was sweeping up the broken glass.'

'That was a dangerous job for an eight-year-old.'

'That's what I thought. His lordship was standing over him clutching the cane. I pity that poor little wretch. He won't be able to sit down comfortably for a week or more.'

'Cartwright is not afraid of him,' said Peterson. 'He is afraid of nothing, and nobody will break his spirit.'

'Why is that?' the new young master asked, as he sipped the lukewarm cocoa.

'A chip off the old block, so they say. Old Bates remembers the father. He came to a sticky end on the Northwest Frontier. A devil for punishment it seems.'

'Is Cartwright the Second destined for the Army?'

'So he says. He's a cheeky young scamp, but so darn enthusiastic, he would break his neck to win. Can't bear to lose. No sense of loyalty to the herd. A self-important little beggar, and why not? With those looks and such confidence, he will never have to struggle for recognition.'

'The right material for Winchester and Sand-hurst?'

Peterson nodded. 'Little Henderson gets my vote. It takes a nice nature to play second fiddle to Cartwright,' his housemaster asserted, as they filed out of the room.

It was not the first time that Matron had anointed a small boy's buttocks with soothing lotion, but the Head had been particularly severe with this young offender, and the weals were bleeding. She supposed he deserved it, and she dared not spare too much sympathy for the child. She owed her allegiance to the Head, but she had seen the result of too many vicious canings to have any respect for the man. Nearing the age of blessed retirement, Matron was ever more careful than usual to share her private thoughts only with one other member of the staff, Monsieur Dubois, who taught French and Music.

'There, that will do, Cartwright. Come back after supper for another application. It won't be the first time you've had to sleep on your stomach, young man.'

'No, Ma'am.' He pulled up his pants, thanked her politely, and walked away, stiff-legged. Henderson was waiting to greet him with a violin tucked under his arm. He had just finished his half-hour lesson, and his ears were tingling. Monsieur Dubois was a fiery little man, whose hands inflicted such stinging blows it was surprising that his young pupils had not lost their heads!

Thomas grinned painfully, and accepted a sticky aniseed ball.

'Does it hurt frightfully?' the younger boy asked, the tears threatening, for he could not bear to imagine the pain and indignity of such a severe punishment. He had suffered a couple of strokes on several occasions for being found in the company of the culprit. The Head would not hesitate to cane half-a-dozen boys for one offence.

Thomas sighed. 'It's not the caning I mind about. It's having to miss my riding lesson. I shall hate watching.'

'You could help with the new boys still on leading reins.'

'Yes, I could.'

'There goes the dinner gong. You coming, Cartwright?'

'No, I'm not hungry. I feel rather sick. Matron will excuse me.'

Roderic looked worried, but hurried away. It was a punishable offence to be late for a meal. The culprit was compelled to stand to attention till the meal was over, when he would be served with bread and water.

When Matron had rustled past in her starched apron, Thomas wandered into the recreation room to play a lonely game of darts – reserved exclusively for senior boys. Whack! Whack! the jerky movements hurt his sore bottom, but he was pleased when he scored a bull's-eye!

Any boy who excelled at games was popular, and Thomas fell easily into that category. New boys tended to hero worship, and Thomas accepted their homage as readily as he accepted Roderic's loyal friendship.

Had Grandmama known about that sadistic headmaster, she would have removed him from the school, but it was doubtful whether there existed a preparatory school with more lenient views on discipline in that day and age. It was all part of the process of character training. Strangely enough, Thomas had no intention of reporting such harsh treatment to Amelia's sympathetic ears. He liked the school. He liked showing off his skills on horseback, in the playing fields, and in the sea, for even a few of the superior senior boys were impressed. He had been getting bored at home, having lessons with his sisters, waging interminable battles with his toy soldiers, and having his every wish gratified. At the age of seven the time had been ripe for the company of boys and the rough and tumble of a battlefield in which he found himself outnumbered in his innocent initiation.

A year later, Thomas was no longer a raw recruit, but an established member of a system calculated to produce the Empire builders of the future. There was also the question of heredity, and following in the footsteps of a parent who may or may not have achieved a measure of success academically, but was remembered for his exploits in more daring and dangerous fields. Thomas had been reared as the heir to a man who had died heroically for Queen and Country, and his self-importance sprang from the roots of that deed. Thomas had recounted the tale with many embellishments to the dozen small boys in the dormitory during the first week of his first term and captured the imagination of his admiring audience. No other boy could boast a parent with such a stirring history of bravery and dedication to duty. He had literally stepped into Jonathan's shoes.

At the age of twelve, Thomas was elected Head Boy, and he enjoyed this worthy status for a whole year, when it was time for the next chapter of his young life – Winchester. This was a rude shock to his self-esteem, for he crashed from his pedestal as an idolized hero to the very lowest degree of a miserable existence as the 'fag' of a prefect. 'Slave' would have been a better word to describe the insults and humiliation to which he was subjected. There was no escape, for this kind of punishment was also considered necessary for future Empire builders. It was part of the system, the long-established tradition, that together with cold baths, cross-country running to a state of exhaustion, and the rugby scrums, were calculated to make men of shrinking thirteen-year-old boys.

But Thomas survived. His spirit was not broken, and no tears were shed. Young Cartwright, it seemed, was indestructible – a pretty boy, coveted by other prefects as a pet and plaything, but surprisingly immune from such sensuous pleasures. His appearance was deceptive. It was simply that he had already discovered the attraction of the opposite sex – in his adorable Auntie Kate! It was inevitable. He had fallen in love at the age of three. Twelve years later, his initiation was performed as naturally as breathing. Her 'darling boy' was an apt pupil. Tall and slender as a reed, the young virgin body was as beautiful and desirable as Kate had expected. She had tired of Charles, and had other lovers in the intervening years, but none to excite her more than her nephew, on the verge of manhood. It was fun! Everything was fun!

'Call me Kate, darling boy,' she insisted.

For Thomas it was the sweet in the bitter-sweet years at public school, for he joined Kate and Charles on their holidays abroad, and Kate was lavish in her presents and generous in her allowance. She encouraged his extravagant tastes and sense of self-importance. If Charles ever suspected their relationship, he made no mention of it, for he, too, had tired of the young woman with whom he had eloped in such impulsive, and rather foolish, haste.

The pattern remained almost unchanged for Prue and Bella, with Roderic spending his holidays at The Haven, for he was part of the family now, and had his own room. Indeed, he felt a deeper attachment to his adopted family than to his own in Calcutta. His sisters had not been sent home to England, but had kept their English governess, so he became more attached to Prue and Bella, especially to Bella, with whom he shared a spiritual affinity and a desire to work with Jane and Edward in the slums.

While Thomas was enjoying the luxury of a villa in the South of France, Roderic and Bella were spending part of their Summer holiday in the slums. Since

Roderic was expected back in Calcutta, to enter the junior ranks of the Civil Service at the age of eighteen, no mention was made of these activities in his weekly letters to his parents.

As for Prue, she had decided to teach. There would be a place for her, as a pupil-teacher, in the junior school of the Convent, under the supervision of Sister Hilary. Neither of the girls had been urged to adopt the Catholic faith during their years at the Convent, but Prue was impressed by the ritual and the solemnity of the many Holy Days in the church calendar, and inclined towards the doctrine while still attending St Matthew's every Sunday morning with the rest of the family. Such inclinations would have displeased Amelia, so were not mentioned.

The age of innocence was past for all four children.

Chapter Three

For Ellen, the years of her son's growth and development also held a bitter-sweet flavour and a mixture of pride and pain as she watched him grow into manhood in the image of Jonathan. The enchanting smile was false, the candid blue eyes could lie.

Only a filial sense of duty brought him home for a week or so during the long Summer vacation in those final years at Winchester. Christmas was spent in the Austrian Tyrol with Gerald Buckley and his family, a friend who had long ago replaced Roderic in his affections. Easter was spent at Farthing Hall, their country estate in Warwickshire.

Only Thomas had changed, but the serious young man to whom he had pledged eternal friendship at the age of seven was so firmly established in the affections of the family that jealousy and resentment divided them. Thomas was a stranger in the house where Amelia still held the reins and still adored her grandson. He found her adoration a little tedious now, but her pleasure in his company compensated for the estrangement with the rest of the family. It was no use to pretend. They had grown apart. Their small world was too small for him, and their old-fashioned ways ridiculously out-dated.

The house that had once seemed so big and important had shrunk. It was old and shabby, and the only servant was a half-witted girl who scrubbed the floors, did all the washing and dribbled on her sacking apron.

'Where on earth did you find such a repulsive creature, Grandmama?' Thomas demanded when he first set eyes on her.

'I didn't find her. I acquired her. You remember Maggie?'

He nodded.

'This is Rose, her youngest daughter.'

'Rose!' he exploded with laughter. 'Could anything be more inappropriate?'

'One gets used to her. Somebody has to do the hard chores, and she is a good worker.'

'What happened to Maggie?'

'She died. She had a hard life, but she was born to it, and never complained.'

'I remember thinking it was fun to kick over her bucket of water when she was scrubbing the front path.'

'Fun for you, but not for Maggie.'

'Were you cross with me?'

'I was never cross with you.'

'Never?'

'Never.'

'Darling Grandmama.' He kissed her cheek, and wondered if this was a good moment to mention he was stony-broke and heavily in debt. Twenty pounds was a lot of money, and Grandmama would want to know how he had incurred so much debt. He would tell her the truth, and hope for her understanding. She had always excused his faults with the assumption that 'boys will be boys'. Now that he had grown to manhood, would he be excused for 'sowing his wild oats'?

In the station cab, driving along the wide carriageway adjacent to the promenade, after they had called in at Kong's for hot chocolate and sugar buns, Thomas was silently turning over in his mind the best approach to the sordid little story. The warm pressure of her little gloved hand, and the faint scent of eau-de-cologne brought back a fleeting memory of his first visit to Kong's on his third birthday.

'Is anything wrong?' Grandmama enquired. 'You are very quiet this morning.'

He sighed, and squeezed her hand.

She smiled and prompted, 'Is it so very serious?'

'Promise you won't disown me? I couldn't bear it if I was banished from your sight for ever.'

'My darling boy, what a dreadful thought!' she chuckled.

'Tell me.'

He turned his face to look at her – a handsome, boyish face, with eyes of intense blue that matched her own. But it was a man's voice that answered her.

'I have put a girl in the family way, and the father is demanding twenty pounds to keep his mouth shut.'

Amelia gasped. 'A servant?'

'Yes, a housemaid at Farthing Hall.'

'That was extremely foolish, Thomas.'

'I know.'

'I mean, it was foolish of you to believe that girl's story. She could have slept with a groom, or a footman, or even a stable boy. It's happening all the time.'

'I thought you would be shocked.'

'Not shocked, only surprised at your foolishness. I thought you had more common-sense.'

'It seemed the honourable thing to do.'

'Honour is not expected in the servant class. Honour is expected between gentlemen. Remember that in future.'

'Yes, Grandmama.'

'Was she pretty?'

'Yes.'

'Of course. One would not expect otherwise. Does your friend Gerald know?'

'Yes.'

'Anyone else?'

'Only you.'

'There is no need to tell your mother. She would be deeply shocked. I have often wondered about my eldest daughter. She is so prim and proper, yet she bore three children. She probably married for the sake of motherhood, and the marriage bed had no further use for her. Poor Jonathan!'

'You are very advanced in your views, Grandmama.'

'Advanced? My dear boy, you are not only your father's son. Your grandmother can claim a small share in your person. Heredity is a fascinating subject. I am no prude. I acutally *enjoyed* the marriage bed with your grandfather. Where do you suppose your Auntie Kate inherited her naughtiness? I could only pretend to be shocked,' she confessed, with a candidness that was so like Kate.

But what would her reaction be, he wondered, if she knew they were lovers? A very different kettle of fish. No, it must remain a closely guarded secret.

'You may have your twenty pounds, Thomas, but I shall deduct it from your allowance each month,' Amelia was saying.

'Thank you, Grandmama.'

'One must expect a young man to sow his wild oats,' she added, as they turned towards home.

From his young niece by marriage, Basil had found a measure of comfort in her affection and a kindred spirit who was so completely different from his dear little Lucy in every way, so that he was not reminded of that gentle creature.

Prue had grown tall and had put up her hair. The dark eyes held a haunting beauty, and high cheekbones lent character to a countenance so often disturbed by uncontrolled emotions. Prue was an earnest young woman and her own worst enemy, as Amelia would say, caustically, for there was no love between them.

But Basil enjoyed her company because he had been shocked into contemplation of his own sensibilities by the death of his young wife. The Haven was once again the place where he was always sure of a welcome. There was no shyness in their relationship, and he regarded Prue with the easy comradeship of an elder brother for a younger sister. 'Greggy' was Prue's confidant, and she saw in him a likeness to the adored Papa who had disappeared so mysteriously in India. She felt safe with Greggy, but would not have felt safe with a younger man. Greggy escorted her to the weekly concert at the Assembly Rooms in the Winter months, and they took long walks over the Downs on Sunday afternoons, where they discussed such earnest topics as Art, Music and Literature. These walks were educational. They held hands and were so engrossed in their own self-esteem, they hardly noticed the beauty of the rolling Downs, or the soaring song of a lark in mid-Summer.

Bella had outgrown Greggy, and had her own friends. She was teaching at Sunday School on Sunday afternoons, and playing strenuous games of rounders and tennis at the Convent on Wednesday afternoons. In the holidays, she had Roderic for company, and for Roderic there would never be another girl to equal Bella. Her lively personality had endeared her to family and friends alike, and for Jane and Edward held the promise of a worthy recruit to the Hoxton Mission.

These were lonely years for Ellen, however, with her children growing into adulthood and no longer in need of her constant supervision. On her solitary walks with Sam in the park, her thoughts would wander to those happy years when her children were small and dependent, and she was the centre of their world.

Amelia was a law unto herself, and did not need the company of her daughter. Bertha and Norah were still inseparable. So under the same roof were four women, divided and isolated, with only the bonds of family and habit to hold them together.

Thomas was travelling to London one Friday evening in early Summer during his last year at Winchester, to spend the weekend with Kate while her husband was engaged on parliamentary duties in his constituency, when he found, to his extreme embarrassment, that he was facing a framed advertisement in bold type. It read: THOMAS BRENT & SON, HIGH CLASS DRAPERS, HIGH STREET, WORTHING.

Not one of the passengers in the crowded compartment would know of his relationship, so there was no need for his embarrassment, but it was all the fault of Grandmama, who was rather a snob. It was said of his great-grandfather that he was just 'a glorified tradesman' and it was true, for he had started his working life as an errand boy at the age of ten. A self-made man, he had one son who had enjoyed the advantage of a public school and university education. And for all the snobbishness of her upper-class origins, Amelia had fallen in love with Thomas the Second and married into trade.

Still staring fixedly at the advertisement, Thomas found his thoughts wandering to the elderly gentleman with the bristling whiskers and the stern countenance that had always softened in the company of the small boy he had made his heir. Once every month, he had been taken by the hand and escorted round the big store. Proud as a little prince, he had acknowledged the bows and curtsies – actually intended for great-grandfather – with a slight inclination of his curly head. They had lunched at Watson's Chop House, and he was driven home in the carriage, where Grandmama would be waiting at the green gate, in her best afternoon gown. It had not surprised him that the elderly gentleman had not been invited into the house, for, at that early age, nothing had surprised him. He had kissed the whiskered cheek and climbed down from the carriage, clutching the precious half-crown that he never failed to receive. Smiling and bowing, as he had been taught, he watched the carriage drive away. It was a long time ago, but the memory was fresh.

During his first term at preparatory school, great-grandfather had died, very suddenly, of a stroke, and there had been no time to fetch the boy to his bedside. Now, a decade or so later, Thomas was remembering his first reaction to the news had been the loss of a halfcrown!

'It does not signify, my darling,' Grandmama had reminded him sympathetically.

And he had no doubt what she meant. But he did not question her authority, and had still received the halfcrowns. Great-grandfather had kept his word, and Thomas was his sole heir, with a trustee appointed till he reached the age of twenty-five. In the meantime, the estate would pay school fees for the three children and a small allowance for Amelia, who found herself once again in the grip of genteel poverty. Thomas had been sheltered, was still sheltered, from such financial embarrassment, for he could always depend on Auntie Kate for a 'loan' with no obligation to repay.

Since that extraordinary affair, soon after his fifteenth birthday, when his beautiful Auntie Kate had invited him into her bed in the absence of her husband, he had received a regular allowance, in strict confidence of course, and a request 'Call me Kate, darling boy'.

He smiled at the memory, and all those early memories were forgotten as the train rushed towards Victoria. It was understood that whenever Charles was absent from home and Thomas could think of a feasible excuse to travel to London, he would do so. But it was no longer a novelty, and Kate was rather possessive. In three years he had outgrown the cloying adoration and found it rather tiresome. He would not need her at Sandhurst, and would discard her as easily as he had discarded Roderic when they left preparatory school, and intended to drop Gerald at the end of the year when he was no longer useful for holidays. On second thoughts, he would have to see Kate occasionally, for her allowance paid for the wine and cigarettes to which he had become addicted in the past two years or so.

A law unto himself, Thomas felt no loyalty to old and trusted friends. In his search for new faces and new pleasures, he was indebted to a father for whom he still retained a boyish hero worship. It was, perhaps, the only lasting sentiment in his fickleness.

Kate was instantly aware of her nephew's mood when he climbed into the carriage and kissed her cheek. His mouth was sulky, but she knew how to coax him into a good humour. 'Dinner at the Café Royal, followed by the current attraction at Drury

Lane — whatever that may be — and I thought we would have a day at the races tomorrow? How does that appeal to you, darling boy?' she asked, coyly, as she tucked her arm in his and smiled.

'My dear Kate, I am yours to command,' he answered, meaningly, glancing at the plunging neckline of the fashionable evening gown. The French perfume was rather heavy on this warm Summer evening. Kate was hardly aware of her surroundings as they drove through the park, and bemused with her own girlish prattle, she had not noticed that her nephew's eyes wandered repeatedly to the young lovers on the park benches. Now the woman at his side was revealed as a middle-aged matron, posing as a young girl.

He followed her into the Café Royal like a sulky boy. Not yet nineteen, he *was* a boy, and could not hide his feelings. Kate had put on weight with her idle life and too much indulgence in mid-morning snacks of hot chocolate and pastries at Slaters. She was plump as a spring chicken, Thomas was thinking, disrespectfully, and that gown was too tight.

'Order what you fancy, darling, and we will have a bottle of champagne,' said Kate, with lavish disregard of expense. She was perfectly at ease in these ornate surroundings of red plush and gilt and glittering chandeliers. The fashionable clientele in London's most popular restaurant could include the current star of the West End stage, dining with a peer of the realm, cabinet ministers, a Texan millionaire, and even Royalty, for a table was reserved for the Prince of Wales who found it amusing to dine with a party of theatrical friends that included his mistress.

It was clever of Kate to order champagne, and her handsome young nephew soon recovered his high spirits. There was nothing like champagne to loosen the tongue, put a sparkle in the eye and set the pulses racing. Thomas had amusing stories to tell of their escapades at Winchester, and she wondered how they ever found the time to concentrate on their studies. Once again they were mutually enchanted, and when they had toasted each other in the last glass of champagne, and he leaned across to whisper, confidentially, 'Shall we go straight back to Onslow Square?' her eloquent eyes answered him.

She giggled girlishly, and saw herself as the same age as Thomas. Sharing a bath of hot, scented water in the bathroom Charles had installed the previous year, they played with light-hearted abandon, their prelude to the rites of love. It was not in their nature to waste time or thought on the absent husband, and the shared bath had the same intoxicating effect as the champagne. Kate's plump little body, slippery with scented soap, held a seductive intimacy for her young lover.

When they were thoroughly excited, they climbed out of the bath, dried each other with warm towels, and ran, naked, into the bedroom. Kate was panting as she stretched on the bed, and opened her arms and gasped, 'Take me quickly, darling boy.'

It was Thomas, not Kate, who lay exhausted some time later. When the door opened quietly and Charles stepped inside, Thomas was drowsily suckling Kate's breast. Shocked into wakefulness, they sat up and stared, wide-eyed, at the tall, distinguished figure immaculately dressed, laughing at their discomfort.

'Caught in the act, my sweet! And cradle-snatching, forsooth!' he mocked.

Thomas was already out of bed, pulling on trousers, shirt, jacket and shoes. Pushing socks and tie into a pocket, he stood waiting for the punishment he expected and deserved. But Charles flung open the door and barked, authoritatively, 'GET OUT, BOY! GET OUT AND STAY OUT! UNDERSTAND?'

'Yes, Sir,' Thomas muttered – and fled!

Kate had pulled the bedclothes up to her chin, and when the door closed on Thomas, she was a little afraid of the husband who stood there. The cynical smile was more threatening than anger.

'What are you going to do?' she asked.

'I am going to spank you,' said he, taking off his jacket, and hanging it carefully over the back of a chair.

She smiled; she liked being spanked. It excited them both, and they made love. Emotionally immature, it suited Kate to be chastised like a naughty child.

Flinging the bedclothes aside, Charles looked down at her with a thinly disguised expression of contempt, and she saw he had picked up one of his leather slippers.

'Turn over!' he ordered.

'Please forgive me, Charles. I promise it will never happen again,' she pleaded, tearfully.

'I said turn over.'

'Wait! I can explain,' she covered her breasts with

her plump little hands, and her dark eyes were anguished.

He rolled her over and began to whip her fat little buttocks with the slipper. She screamed and struggled under the relentless pressure of his hand.

'You are hurting me, Charles.' She was sobbing now with pain and fear, for this was no ordinary spanking, and he was acting like a madman. He *was* mad – mad with jealousy, for her plump thighs were still damp.

When a trickle of blood dropped on the white sheet, he lifted his hand from her shuddering body and the slipper fell to the floor. There was no compassion in the eyes that had once adored her. To be cuckolded by a mere boy, and her own nephew, was more than his pride could forgive.

Ignoring her moans, he pulled on his jacket and went out. The front door slammed.

The servants had huddled in the kitchen. They had heard the screams.

'It's no more than she deserves,' said Cook – and put on the kettle for a fresh pot of tea.

The long night passed. Nobody came near her, and she was too ashamed to ring the bell for the maid. She knew the servants' loyalty to Charles, and now, when she most needed attention, there was nobody to wait on her, nobody to care how she suffered. Every nerve in her body seemed to be quivering, and her soft flesh was smarting with the punishment Charles had inflicted. Her eyes were swollen with crying, and the breast that had cradled the head of her young lover was still throbbing.

But her constant fear, during that long night, was losing Charles, and when he did not return home in the morning, or send a message, she spent the day in bed, and had the parlourmaid serve her meals on a tray. She was still the mistress, she reminded herself.

It was not the first time Charles had spent the night at his club, but it *was* the first time he had seriously considered divorcing Kate. His own infidelities were forgotten. It was a gentleman's privilege. But a wife must not be allowed to flaunt her lover with such embarrassing disregard of his sensibilities. It was humiliating and unforgiveable. He thought of asking for his sister's advice, but they had lost touch, and he knew exactly what she would say.

'I told you so!' for she had warned him he had made a grievious mistake in offering marriage to the pretty little apprentice when he could have had her as his mistress and still kept his freedom.

But Eleanor hadn't known Kate as he knew Kate. She was cunning as a little fox, and she had deliberately trapped him into an elopement by wearing that blasted betrothal ring and declaring she was pledged to Basil Gregson. His infatuation had not lasted, and he knew that he had been a fool, but divorce might ruin his career, and he could not take the risk. He would frighten Kate – had already frightened her.

Having arrived at this sensible conclusion, he took a cab and went home in the late evening, and found Kate lying on the couch in the drawing-room in a state of abject misery. She looked so forlorn and wretched, he was tempted to take her in his arms, but resisted the temptation when she demanded, petulantly, 'Where have you been?'

'At the House. There was an all-night sitting.'

'But that was twelve hours ago. I have been quite ill with anxiety. What have I done to deserve such inconsideration?'

'Do I have to remind you?'

'But it was only fun. It does not signify. You are my husband, and I love you.'

'And you don't love Thomas?'

'Of course I love him. He is my darling boy. I love him like a son.'

'A son who suckles your breast in our bed? What blatant effrontery!'

'I can't help it. I have said I am sorry, and it won't happen again. What else can I say?'

'There is no need to tax your brains, my sweet. I doubt whether you would find a solution to our misunderstanding, if such it can be called. But I must remind you, Kate, that adultery has to be paid for.'

'How?'

'Divorce.'

'*Divorce?* Charles, you wouldn't!'

'I would, and I shall, unless you swear, on your bended knees, never again to take a lover.'

'I do! I will!' She slid off the couch and fell on her knees at his feet, gazing up at him with frightened eyes. Her face was puffy, her hair uncombed, and she smelled of sweat and stale scent. Was this slovenly creature his fastidious Kate?

'Say it. Say it after me,' he dictated. 'I swear by

Almighty God I will never again take a lover, and will keep my marriage vows.'

She repeated the oath, and did not question the reference to Almighty God. They attended church because it was expected of them, and Charles was very conscious of his position in society. But she would promise anything to be reassured of her comfort and security as Charles's wife. She had no pride now, only a mind frantic with questions, and sore buttocks, and a sense of utter injustice. Was that all? Was he satisfied now that he had seen her grovelling at his feet? She still knelt there while he delivered his ultimatum, his hands clasped in typical masterly attitude under his coat-tails.

'There is no further obligation to pretend under our own roof. The servants are fully aware of the situation. Our relationship is our own concern. In public, however, I shall expect you to behave with decorum and with a pleasing manner, attributable to a devoted and affectionate wife. It should not be too difficult for you have quite a flair for playing a part, haven't you, my sweet?'

She shook her head, too choked to speak, and stumbled back to the couch.

'By the way, I shall be sleeping in the dressing-room,' he added – and poured himself a drink. He did not offer her one. Such discourtesy was so unlike Charles, it was not only proof of their estrangement, but of her fall from grace.

When he had swallowed the drink, he turned to her with a mocking little bow. 'Good night, my sweet. Pleasant dreams,' said he, and went out of the room. The study door opened and closed.

She felt betrayed by her emotions. How could he be so cruel? Sex was the very breath of life. He knew it. They were two of a kind. Why did he have to spoil it now with such arrogance? Angry tears wet her cheeks. Charles was being totally unreasonable, and she would not tolerate being so humiliated a second time. A typical gesture of a domineering Victorian husband. But she was not, and never would be, a typical Victorian wife.

She sat up, dried her eyes, and began to make plans – secret plans, that she would put into operation at the earliest opportunity. She loved secrets, but she was not very clever at keeping secrets. This time she would be more careful. In future, she would not use the marriage bed. That had been a mistake. One of the servants must have betrayed her, but she would have her revenge. She was still the mistress.

Her darling boy had looked positively devastated. Next time he came to Town they would meet at an hotel, but not in the West End. She would give him time to recover, poor lamb.

In the meantime, there was Colonel Fraser-Archibald. She giggled, and forgot her misery in the recollection of his old-world courtesy that day at Slaters, when her little white lie had not been wasted on unsympathetic ears. For a lady to be seen lunching in a public restaurant without a male escort was inconceivable, and Kate was fully aware of the raised eyebrows and whispered comments. Pretending to study the menu, she was actually blushing with embarrassment.

'Pardon me, Ma'am, if I intrude, but am I addressing Mrs Charles Lefeaux?'

Kate raised her eyes and met the admiring glance of a grey-haired gentleman with a ruddy complexion, bristling military moustaches and piercing blue eyes.

'That is correct, Sir,' Kate answered, demurely. 'But you have the advantage, for I have no recollection of your name?'

'Then may I introduce myself? Colonel Fraser. Your servant, Ma'am,' said he, bowing stiffly from the waist.

'How do you do, Colonel.' Kate inclined her head graciously. 'You know my husband, Colonel Fraser?'

'Very well. We are members of the same club, and we often share a game of chess. He beats me nine times out of ten,' he confessed modestly.

'So that is how he spends his time when I am awaiting his homecoming?' she chided.

What a dashed attractive woman, he was thinking. Lefeaux is a very lucky fellow.

'May I sit down, Ma'am?' he asked, and she answered, 'Please do.'

'You were expecting your husband to join you for lunch?'

'Yes.' The little white lie slipped out on a sigh. 'I sometimes wish he were just an ordinary clerk at a city bank with regular hours of duty. It is so very vexing to be kept waiting.'

'Now you are making me feel guilty, Ma'am.'

'Why should you feel guilty?'

'For the games of chess, when he should be at home with his charming wife.'

Kate smiled disarmingly. The waiter hovered, and she ordered soup and an omelette, for it was one of the days when she had decided to diet. It would not last. She was too fond of her food.

'Have you lunched, Colonel?' she asked.

'Yes. I was just about to leave when I saw you arrive, alone. You do not object to my company till your husband joins you?'

'Not at all. Indeed, I am much obliged, for I find it exceedingly embarrassing.'

'Just so.'

'You have a wife, Colonel?'

'Alas, I lost her, on the eve of my retirement. This past year I have felt like a ship without a rudder, just drifting through the days.'

'Are you not young for retirement?'

'I have served for the specified twenty-five years. We had planned to retire to Worthing, but when Jessica died, I decided to stay in London, sold the house, and moved into bachelor chambers at Albany. It's a lonely life for a man.'

'I am so sorry.'

'Are you really? I mean, sorry enough to keep me company for lunch one day in the near future?'

'Shouldn't you be asking my husband's permission, Sir?'

'I will do so, Ma'am.'

'Then we will await his decision.'

'Just so, Ma'am. I stand rebuked.'

'You are forgiven, Sir,' said she, with a saucy glance.

The Colonel was not entirely innocent of scheming.

He had watched and waited for just such an opportunity, since he lunched every day at Slaters. A virile man, bereft of his wife at middle-age, must find solace in the arms of another, and the Colonel had heard rumours that Lefeaux and his wife were estranged. Servants spread the rumours. Valets and lady's maids were particularly guilty of such indiscretions. Now he was almost certain that this elegant young woman was just getting her revenge. He would play her game. It would be an amusing diversion, and Lefeaux need not suspect, if they were discreet. Instantly aware of her sexual attraction as he faced her across the narrow table, there was no mistaking the invitation in those revealing dark eyes! By God! he was more than willing to co-operate!

When Thomas left the house in Onslow Square, smarting with indignation at such an humiliating dismissal, he hastened to the nearest hotel where he washed and tidied himself in the cloakroom. The unsuspecting attendant, believing him to be a guest, provided him with a clean towel, and received the small tip gratefully.

In the comfortable smoking room, Thomas lit a cigarette and ordered a brandy. There was really no need to feel so badly about this affair. It was quite amusing, he decided, philosophically. After all, he had escaped scot free, and it was Kate who would be paying the penalty for their naughtiness. He supposed Uncle Charles could be quite formidable as a cuckolded husband. But what to do with the remainder of the weekend? That was the question.

He was not due back at college until tomorrow night, and his only other relatives in London were Auntie Jane and Uncle Edward, and he had hardly given them a thought since that first visit to Hoxton with Mama and his sisters. He remembered the squalor and the ragged barefoot children capering to the band of the Salvation Army. It would be fun to visit them again. He would make the excuse that he had called at the house in Onslow Square and found Auntie Kate was staying with friends for the week-end. Since the two sisters had nothing in common, and seldom met, it was unlikely that his little white lie would be questioned.

So he set forth by train to the East End, and gave no further thought to the unfortunate partner in the escapade. On this warm Summer night, half the female population of Hoxton seemed to be sitting on their doorsteps, or gossiping at the market stalls, still doing a brisk trade at this late hour. The squalor was appalling, and the unpleasant stench quite disgusting as he stepped from the station forecourt on to the littered pavement. From the open door of the public house, the raucous voices of tipsy customers mingled with the strains of a mouth-organ. Babies crawled in the gutter, or were carried on the hips of puny little girls, staggering under the weight. Ragged small boys played leap-frog in the street, their bare feet hardened by the cobbles.

Thomas stood hesitating, knowing he had to run the gauntlet of this frightful place to reach the safety of the Mission.

'Blimey! A blinkin' toff!' yelled a red-haired

urchin, leap-frogging over his three companions. Surprised by the unexpected diversion, they all gathered round to inspect the visitor, obviously bound for the Mission. With their bright eyes and grubby faces, and their mocking attitudes, they made a formidable obstacle, and Thomas had never felt so outnumbered or so inadequate.

'Give us a penny, Mister,' cajoled the red-headed urchin, with a disarming grin.

'If you ain't got a penny, a 'n'appeny will do. If you ain't got a 'n'appeny, then God bless *you*!' they chanted. It was the age-old chant they chorused at Cannon Street and London Bridge stations on the eve of Guy Fawkes. The fifth of November was one of the highlights of their boyhood.

'I don't carry pennies and halfpennies,' Thomas reminded them loftily, and pushed them aside.

'I don't carry pennies or 'n'appenies' they mimicked, as red-head snatched off the straw boater and darted away down the street.

'Here! Come back! Come back I say!' Thomas gave chase, feeling extremely foolish, for the boys were too quick for him. Tossing the hat from one to the other, they darted round the market stalls and jumped over the babies in the gutter. The hat went sailing through the open door of the public house, was caught neatly by a hefty stevedore from the docks, who sent it spinning over the heads of the startled customers, straight into the hands of the youngest urchin, who was off like a shot with his prize. Yells of laughter followed the boy down the street.

'Them kids is a proper scream,' chuckled a blowsy-looking woman, suckling an infant, on her doorstep.

'Alfy! You give the genalman back 'is 'at!' yelled Alfy's mum from a bedroom window. 'Jew 'ear me! Thinks 'e's the cat's whiskers that little bugger since 'e learned 'is letters from the Missus at the Mission,' she complained to nobody in particular.

Thomas stopped running. Not even a rugby scrum at public school had prepared him for this. Some way ahead he could see the boys lined up on the pavement, urinating in the gutter, and when he finally reached the open door of the Mission, his Auntie Jane was standing there, convulsed with laughter at the sight of a small boy with a straw boater hanging around his ears and her nephew hatless.

'Thomas! What on earth are you doing here?' She greeted him with open arms and a warm hug. She smelled sweet and clean in this sordid background, and he was suddenly aware of her courage and fortitude.

'Do 'e belong to you, Missus?' red-head demanded.

'Of course. He is my nephew.'

'What's a nefew?'

'The son of my sister.'

'Cor blimey. We never meant no 'arm.'

'I am sure you didn't. It was all good fun, but enough is enough. Give Thomas his hat, Alfy.'

'It's goin' ter cost 'im a penny, Missus.'

'Very well.' She produced a penny from the pocket

of her faded print gown, and Alfy snatched it eagerly, and handed over the hat.

'Thanks, Missus!' they chorused, and gathered round.

'A farvin each? What jew fink, Alfy?' cajoled the leader, who still had the last word. And they belted for the market stall and the sherbet bags.

'I shall never be able to wear this hat again,' Thomas complained, holding it disdainfully by the brim.

'Yes you will. I will give it a good scrub with a nail brush, and it will be as good as new in the morning. You *are* staying overnight?'

'If you can accommodate me.'

'Of course. There is always room for one more. We keep one of the attic rooms for latecomers.' She did not question the reason for the unexpected visit, so there was no need for the white lie.

'Leave the door open. It's quite stifling with it closed.' She led the way to the kitchen. Was she so accustomed to the stench of the filthy street that she no longer noticed it? Thomas wondered, and sat down at the well-scrubbed table to await the inevitable cup of tea. Nothing stronger than tea or lemonade at the Hoxton Mission.

'What did that woman mean about the boy learning his letters?' he asked, curiously, as Aunt Jane carefully measured out a spoonful of sugar.

'I am teaching him to read and write. Not only Alfy, but a dozen small boys. They are so keen, and it takes them off the street for an hour or so in the morning. The girls have their turn in the afternoon, but they have to bring the little ones who play quite happily on the floor with empty match boxes and a few stones to rattle in empty cocoa tins. The mothers think I am wasting my time teaching girls to read and write. They see them as little drudges, dragging around younger brothers and sisters, like little old women. Why shouldn't girls have equal opportunity to learn? I feel so strongly about it, Thomas. It's one law for the male and another for the female in all classes of society, and I don't agree with it. I suppose the Queen sets the pattern, and it suits the majority of males to see themselves as superior beings! I'm sorry, dear. Take no notice. There is no stopping me when I get on to my favourite hobby horse,' Jane confessed as she sipped the weak, sugarless tea.

Her cheeks were flushed, and her grey eyes bright with indignation in the need to express herself to another human being other than her husband, who was not always in the mood to listen.

'I had no idea you felt so strongly about it, Aunt.' Thomas was genuinely interested. 'How was it possible that she and Kate could be sisters?'

Jane smiled reflectively. 'It goes back a long way, dear. Your Grandmama wanted a son so desperately, poor darling, she could not hide her disappointment. We all tried hard to please her because we wanted to be loved for our own sakes. She couldn't help it. It was not her fault, but her misfortune that she couldn't get close to her own children. Kate was the most determined, and she did succeed in getting a lot of attention with her tears and tantrums. She was so naughty, so determined to get her own way. Dear Kate. Is she happy now, I wonder? She changed her mind about having a child when Lucy died in childbirth. But Lucy was always delicate, so it did not signify.'

'Aunt Kate adored me when I was little, didn't she?'

'She still adores you, Thomas. You were the one topic of conversation the last time we met at The Haven. Your Grandmama was rather piqued because you had not been home for Christmas. Winter sports with Gerald and his family had taken priority, I understand.'

'Grandmama can be rather possessive.'

'I know, but she loves you dearly. You were like a little prince in that household. Even your Auntie Bertha succumbed to your charms!'

'Prue hated me. She still hates me.'

'Hate is too strong a word, dear, and she couldn't be blamed for feeling jealous when you had so much attention. It was natural.'

'Do you always make excuses for everyone, Aunt Jane?'

'I try to be a good Christian. It's what we are born for. It's my job, and every job needs to be worked at wholeheartedly. Body and spirit should be involved. Common-sense as well as common prayers. We share the same creed as the Salvation Army and serve the same God. It's not all preaching, and it's not all what you have seen today. Behind the scenes you will find loyalty and affection, kindness as well as cruelty, and so much courage. I would not change with my sister

Kate. This is my world, and, God willing, I shall spend the rest of my life here.'

'But it's so squalid, and you are so clean and fresh. How can you bear to have those dirty ragamuffins in your house?'

'They wash their hands and faces at that sink.'

'It seems such a waste of time.'

'Nothing is wasted. If only one child out of the dozen benefits from my teaching, it will have been worthwhile. It could be little Alfy, for he's bright as a new button. He wants to be an engine driver, and why shouldn't he be an engine driver? Ambition is a splendid thing. Then there is Mary O'Brien who sings like an angel, and has already sung solo with the Salvation Army band at the Citadel. One step leads to another. Do you realize how privileged you are to have your steps paved with tradition? To follow in your father's footsteps has been guaranteed since the day you were born. You see what I mean?'

'Yes, Aunt, and I am suitably humble.'

'That is something you will never be, my dear nephew, but I agree with Kate, you could charm a bird off a bough! Ah, here comes Edward with our youngest lodgers.' She lowered her voice. 'These boys were running wild and living on their wits. Edward rescued them. He spends every evening with them after supper, in a gallant attempt to keep them out of the public house. They usually go down to the docks when the evenings are light, and lend a hand with the loading and unloading, hoping to get taken on as apprentices. They are working in a jam factory, and it's very tedious.'

Thomas was standing to shake hands with his uncle, and he smiled in a superior way at the seven lads who followed him in and snatched off their caps. They could have been any age between twelve and sixteen, and they glowered at the young toff who was doing his best to be friendly.

'Good evening,' said he, and they muttered, ''ullo' and scuffed their bare feet on the cracked linoleum.

'Good evening, boys,' Aunt Jane greeted them warmly.

'Evening, Missus,' they chorused.

'You will find bread and cheese in the dining-room, and I will make a fresh pot of tea. Whose turn is it to fetch and carry this week?'

'Me an' Bert,' the smallest boy answered.

'Then you can fetch the tea in ten minutes, Dave, and help Bert with the washing up when you are finished.'

'Yes, Missus.' They disappeared into the dining-room that was also used as a classroom. Jane's blackboard was propped against the wall, and a pile of slates on the window sill.

'You look tired, dear.' Jane kissed her husband's cheek and he sat down in the old wicker chair with a sigh of utter exhaustion. A black shade covered the sightless eye. Badly damaged in the accident, it was not a pretty sight, and he was so sensitive about his appearance. He still suffered with bad headaches and, when he was shy or nervous, the impediment in his speech was more noticeable. He was shy of this elegant young man with the cultured accent, drinking tea in their homely kitchen, because Thomas had

126

grown in the likeness of his father, Jonathan, who had treated him with contempt when he was an overworked curate lodging at the Vicarage. He could see the Vicar's youngest son in that handsome head and brilliant blue eyes and condescending smile. Why should he look down his nose at these destitute lads in their ragged clothes, with their rough speech? And what had brought him to Hoxton when he had not troubled to visit them since that one visit as a little boy? He had no place in their lives, or in Edward's affections, but Jane was obviously pleased and proud to see her nephew, and would not question his shameful neglect. His dear Jane excused everyone. There was always a reason or an explanation. What should he do without her?

She had poured a cup of tea and carefully measured out two spoons of sugar. She went without sugar in her tea, but would not deprive Edward, who had such a sweet tooth. She hoped he was not too tired to show a spark of interest in her nephew, who would soon be embarking on an Army career, and she smiled with relief when he looked up to ask, 'W-what are your p-plans, Thomas?'

'My immediate plans, Uncle?'

Edward nodded.

'To spend the Summer vacation at a crammer establishment at Salisbury, prior to the final examination for entry into Sandhurst. I have passed the preliminary, but that is only the first step, you might say. It's going to be dashed uncomfortable, slogging away on all those subjects to acquire the specified number of marks. All work and no play this

Summer, but I mean to pass. Nothing in the world is going to stop me now.'

'It m-means so m-much to you?'

'It means the difference between life and death. I should die of boredom if I had to settle for anything but an Army career.'

'That s-sounds like your P-papa.'

'Tell me about him, Uncle Edward. You knew him personally, did you not, before he married Mama?'

'We w-were not cl-close. Jonathan w-was the Vicar's youngest s-son. I was the humble c-curate.'

'Your uncle is too modest, Thomas,' Jane interrupted, as she brewed another pot of tea for the boys. 'The Vicar depended on Edward for most of the parish visiting, and all the hospital visits, also the almshouses. He taught at Sunday School, was responsible for the boys' club and the weekly Bible class. What more could be expected of a curate? When we met and fell in love, there was no time for courting, and Edward was not invited to The Haven till we were actually engaged to be married. Mother could see no future for one of her daughters married to a poor curate!' She chuckled at the memory. 'Love will find a way. The Church Army came to the rescue; otherwise my poor darling could still be the curate at St Matthews. A warden for the Hoxton Mission must be married. It was a heaven-sent opportunity, wasn't it, my dear?'

'So you ins-sis-ted, my love,' Edward teased, affectionately. He had succeeded in getting away from the subject of the Vicar's youngest son. It was not his nature to discredit anyone, but Jonathan's reckless behaviour and selfishness had not endeared him to the unfortunate young lodger in that household. His Mama's spoilt darling and the despair of his pious Papa, it had been a relief when he finally departed for India with his regiment. A fond mother's nervous breakdown, and a small plaque in the church were the only vestiges of his existence – except for his children.

Here, in their humble kitchen, smelling of yellow soap and pickled onions, sat the very embodiment of that arresting personality. The likeness was not only remarkable, but rather frightening. Would Thomas survive such a perilous path, or would a second tragedy deprive poor Ellen of her only son? It was a morbid thought, but Edward's thoughts were seldom optimistic. Only Jane could dispel the bouts of deep depression since that ghastly accident, only she could banish the bogies that threatened his sanity.

He closed his eyes, weary of the long, exhausting day, serving his Master.

'Time for bed! We have to be up by five o'clock. Our lodgers start work at six.' The practical Jane was already on her way, locking doors and windows against night intruders. Every loaf of bread had to be safe-guarded against the hungry scavengers who prowled the streets at night. Their loyalty had to be a positive thing, and her own sympathies engaged with those actually living under their roof. Jane's warm heart was often saddened by the plight of so many homeless boys for whom there was no room at the Mission. As soon as sufficient funds could be raised, the Church Army would provide a Mission at

Stepney; there was a desperate need for more Missions in the East End.

When Jane had shown her nephew to the small, bare closet reserved for latecomers, she kissed his cheek affectionately. 'God bless you, dear. Sleep well,' she said.

He could hear Aggie snoring in the adjoining closet, for the walls were thin and every sound magnified. When the boys came to bed in their dormitory room, he could hear them skirmishing.

Far removed from the rest of the family, in the pleasant township of Zurich in the Bernese Oberland, Auntie Grace and Uncle Henry lived in quiet contentment and happiness, in modest comfort. The romantic love affair that had blossomed in the disturbing atmosphere of the Bayswater house, had lost none of its sensibility. A less determined man than Henry Halliday might have been defeated by so many obstacles in his path. His whole nature had changed, and he was no longer the self-important, rather pompous individual who had greeted his wife's new companion that fateful Sunday, and recognized in her gentle manner, frail beauty and calm temperament the very antithesis to his ailing, nagging wife, who held the purse strings. Ambition had driven him from the struggling ranks of the working class into upper-class society, and into the arms of the adored only child of a wealthy merchant banker. One glance at the dark-eyed clerk who attended her in her carriage had been sufficient. Beatrice Courtney had met her future husband and would not be dissuaded from the marriage. Nothing but the threats of suicide if she did not get her own way finally convinced the besotted parent that she was serious. Promotion was instantly arranged, and the lucky clerk removed from his high stool in the counting house to a position of authority. His dress, his speech, his behaviour enjoyed a rapid change, for Henry was too astute to neglect such an unexpected opportunity.

As Henry Courtney-Halliday he challenged anyone to guess the humble background he had discarded, together with his family and former colleagues in the counting-house. But such a loveless marriage had to be paid for, and Beatrice had succumbed to an imaginary weak heart after the birth of a stillborn child, and spent most of her days reclining on the drawing-room couch, nursing a lap dog, and attended by a succession of bored lady's maids.

Grace Brent had been the last, and the most successful. She was a lady. She had a pleasing manner and a gentle nature, and she played the pianoforte with a delicate touch that her mistress found most soothing to her nerves. But the atmosphere in such a divided household, where the servants took sides with either the master or the mistress, and the violent scenes between husband and wife became more and more unbearable, and Grace, already suffering the early stages of consumption, gradually became seriously afflicted with the disease, and finally collapsed.

Then it was time for Henry to declare his love for Grace. She was sent post-haste to a sanitorium in

Switzerland at his personal expense, and he moved out of the Bayswater house that was still his wife's property, and handed in his resignation at the bank. It was a tremendous challenge to his self-esteem, and his downfall was as sudden and dramatic as his promotion. In the meantime, Grace hovered between life and death. She was allowed no visitors for eighteen months, and her letters were censored for anything of a disturbing nature.

During this anxious period, Henry obtained a post as a clerk in the Zurich branch of the London bank, withdrew his stocks and shares, and purchased a small cottage. With an elderly housekeeper to attend to his simple requirements, he settled down to a daily routine of work and hopeful anticipation of Grace's ultimate recovery. When, at last, he was allowed to visit her in the sanatorium, she hardly recognized the same man, in his gentleness and humility, and he, in turn, was shocked into the evidence of how nearly he had lost her. His own robust health seemed a mockery to this frail creature, too weak to walk for more than a few yards, and his strong virility, long since subdued by his determination to wait for the recovery of his dearest love, was tortured by her frailty. There would be no sudden improvement in his patient's condition, the Herr Doctor reminded him. That she was alive was in itself a miracle.

Another six months had passed before he was allowed to remove her from the sanatorium to the cottage, still under the care and supervision of the Herr Doctor, cosseted by the motherly housekeeper, and adored by a man who was neither husband nor lover. Grace was no longer obliged to hide her feelings; secure in his devotion, her gentle nature was content. To share the marriage bed was not for Grace the ultimate conclusion to their relationship – but for Henry it was.

When, at last, he obtained a divorce from Beatrice, he married Grace, with only the housekeeper and a colleague from the bank as witnesses to the simple ceremony. They saw themselves as the happiest couple in their adopted country. Tenderly, almost reverently, they were finally united as man and wife. They spent their honeymoon drifting across the lake of Thun in a small pleasure steamer, with a party of tourists, eating and sleeping in spotlessly clean pensions on the lakeside, in idyllic surroundings suggestive of *Grimms' Fairy Tales*. Snow-capped mountains, pine forests, meadows sweet with Summer flowers, and his beloved, with a healthy tan and a new awareness of the man who had forfeited so much for her sake – what more could Henry ask of life? He had suffered and paid for his mistake in years of misery and frustration, tied to a woman who owned him, and who made no secret of the fact.

Never again would he grasp success and security in upper-class society. Their friends and neighbours were tradesmen, shop-keepers, teachers and watch-makers. Grace wrote a dutiful letter to her mother every week, and occasional letters to her favourite sister, Ellen. She remembered all the family birth-days with small, inexpensive gifts, carefully selected to suit each recipient, and sent money to her nephew and nieces that she had saved from her housekeeping allowance with careful budgeting.

The calm serenity and unselfishness that had endeared her to her father and elder sister in those early years at The Haven, and supported her through the troubled years, was amply rewarded at last. She loved to sit and watch the sturdy figure, striding homewards with the air of a man who knew exactly where true values were to be found. She was his sweetheart, his darling girl. She had never been so loved, or so grateful for this new lease of life, to share with her dear Henry.

The days passed peacefully and pleasantly, with Henry away all day, and her daily routine almost unchanged since they had settled down together after their short honeymoon. There was time for the painting she had neglected, time to play her favourite Chopin, time to sit and dream, time to stand and stare. The balcony faced a wonderful panorama of distant mountain peaks, dazzling in the bright sunlight of the long Summer days. With the forest of dark pines, it seemed to belong to a fantasy world, under a blanket of snow. She had captured both the Summer and the Winter scenes on her canvases, but was too shy to display them to visitors. Henry praised them extravagantly, however, and would not allow her to hide her light under a bushel. Now they were finished, and hanging on the whitewashed walls of the cottage.

She continued to add to the collection, so that she would have a more personal gift for the birthdays of her mother and sisters. Even her two nieces had begged for a picture each now they were grown-up young ladies, with their own rooms at The Haven.

Only Kate and Charles had visited them, more out of curiosity than affection, for they had nothing in common. Grace and Henry had entertained them with the simple pleasures they themselves enjoyed, and the housekeeper had provided appetizing meals, but it was alien to the Londoners' gregarious way of life, and they were obviously bored by the end of the first week, when Charles invented an urgent appointment at the House.

As Henry and Grace walked back, after seeing them off at the station – with hugs and kisses, and lavish praise for their hospitality – Henry observed, candidly, 'The simple life is not for those two, my darling girl.'

'I used to envy Kate in those early years, when we were growing up at The Haven,' Grace mused, as she took his arm.

'She was so lovely, so animated, she always knew what she wanted, and she usually managed to get it, often at the expense of poor little Lucy, but her moods were as variable as the weather, and we never knew what to expect from her. Now she has everything that money can buy, and she is still beautiful, but she is not happy. What is she still searching for, my dear? What has gone wrong with that marriage?'

'They are two of a kind, sweetheart, and that is not a good recipe for a happy marriage. Look at us, my love. No two people could have started out with such opposing views, or such differences in character and mentality: an extrovert and an introvert, a demanding egotist and an undemanding saint.'

'No!' Grace interrupted. 'You were too prejudiced in my favour. My thoughts and my feelings were not at all saintly, I do assure you, Mr Halliday! For a humble lady's maid to be secretly in love with her employer was deceitful. It was cheating because Beatrice liked me, and was kind to me, most of the time.'

'I know, and I was jealous, because you seemed to prefer her company to mine.'

'But I was engaged for that purpose, was I not?'

'True.'

'It was quite impossible to please you both, and you were so intolerant.'

'True.'

'Oh dear, it all seems to have happened in another life, to another person. Everything that happened before the breakdown has the quality of a dream, but I must have been very innocent and naive not to recognize the danger when we first met. Ellen recognized it.'

'Had you known what I felt for you that day, would you have stayed?'

'There was no choice. I was rather useless as an unpaid servant, and Bertha was constantly complaining that I had to be reminded to change the linen, or to use the right brush for the stairs, or to throw out dead flowers. It was true, Henry. I was hopeless, and Bertha was so efficient. She kept the house immaculate. Mother decided to send me away, and she had the last word on everything. But I *was* upset, and I cried myself to sleep every night for that first week.'

'My poor darling.' He kissed her glowing cheek, and remembered how pale those cheeks had been, and how enchanting her tall, willowy figure and small gloved hands that he had held for a moment longer than politeness dictated because he was already in love with her, and wanted to touch her.

'What were we talking about before we started reminiscing?' Henry asked, reluctant to leave the subject of falling in love at first sight.

'The advantages of being opposites,' she teased.

'And you were envious of Kate when you had no need to be. I would not have noticed Kate if I had known you all in those early years, and I certainly would not have eloped with that irrational young woman. I feel sorry for Charles. Kate behaves more like a spoilt child than a mature woman. He knows he has made a mistake, but he has to abide by it because a divorce would ruin his political career.'

'And because he lacks your courage and resolution, my dear,' Grace reminded him gently, as he pushed open the gate.

The years had dealt kindly with Amelia. She was still a young-looking woman with a trim figure. She carried herself with a proud dignity that was often mistaken for haughtiness.

She had missed the lively company of her adored grandson, but comforted herself with the knowledge that he was fond of her because he still spent a week of the Summer vacation at The Haven, and two days

137

at Easter, when she arranged all kinds of pleasures for his entertainment. His gentle, uncomplaining mother had long since accepted the close relationship between Amelia and Thomas. Their personalities were too strong to fight. Her two daughters still needed her, if not so often or so urgently now they were grown up. She never went away and she loved to hear a young voice calling 'Mama! Are you there?' as one or the other raced up the stairs.

'Yes, my darling. I am here,' she would answer, her dark eyes tender with love.

Prue was a pupil teacher at the Convent now, and boarded there. Bella worked at the Hoxton Mission all the week, and came home on Sundays. They both had stories to tell, and both were equally involved in the work they had chosen.

Roderic was training with the Church Army, and living in a hostel, but he spent his free Sundays once every month at The Haven. Bella still saw their friendship as one between a brother and sister, but Roderic would have liked to see an engagement ring on her finger.

'You need not be afraid that I shall run off with one of those tough young lodgers at Auntie Jane's. I haven't her capacity for loving every Tom, Dick and Harry. Besides, I love you, Roddy dear,' she had reminded him, and he had to be content with that. In the opinion of his parents, Roderic had disgraced himself by choosing such a degrading occupation in London's East End when the Indian Civil Service offered such bright prospects. They had washed their hands of their only son. His only regret was losing touch with his mother and sisters, but Ellen and her daughters had amply compensated for this unavoidable breach in his own family.

Roderic and Bella would need a further two years of practical experience before they would be offered a joint post at one of the Missions in Stepney. They could have argued that Edward and Jane had been appointed in their early twenties, but it did not signify. Edward was not a product of public school but Grammar School, and when he left school, he went straight to St Matthew's Vicarage under the exacting guidance of the Reverend Cartwright. Jane had the practical domestic experience, including cooking, that was necessary for a warden's wife. Bella had not been allowed in the kitchen at The Haven, and could hardly boil an egg when she joined Auntie Jane after leaving school. But Jane was in no hurry to lose her, for she had taken the place of the daughter she had always longed for. Training her niece for the hazardous life ahead had its funny moments, however, for Bella was a born clown. She had a rare and wonderful gift to see the funny side of a situation bordering on calamity. Her chuckling laugh was so infectious. Even Edward could not fail to respond to such a good humoured young woman.

The two sisters were close and affectionate, yet they had little in common, and often disagreed on both secular and religious matters. Prue had adopted the Catholic faith after much soul-searching. She was so intense, so devout, so passionately eager to prove herself worthy of the privilege accorded to her. Still emotionally unstable, she leaned on Basil for support and encouragement. Basil was the father-figure for whom she had searched in vain as a child, and 'Greggy' was kind and patient and lonely.

Their relationship was so strongly established, and so widely accepted, it was agreed they should take a holiday together one Summer, and when they saved enough for fares and spending money, Ellen wrote to her sister Grace, who was delighted, and Henry most agreeable, as always, to any suggestion that would give pleasure to his darling girl.

'Why not bring Bella?' Grace wrote. 'The two girls could share the spare room. In any case, Basil will be sleeping on the couch in the sitting-room, or a lounge chair on the balcony, whichever he prefers.'

But Bella was much too busy learning how to cook nourishing stews, cakes and pies for the lodgers, how to budget the meagre housekeeping allowance and how to 'make do' in a dozen different ways. She could not see herself lazing on Auntie Grace's balcony, gazing at the view, or drifting across the lake in a pleasure steamer.

'No, thank you. I like it here, and we do get plenty of entertainment one way and another,' she pointed out. It was true. Bare-bottomed babies and barefoot urchins provided a constant source of amusement to a young woman reared in the genteel environment of The Haven.

Roderic was disappointed when he heard that Bella had turned down the invitation.

'Be patient, dear. Your turn will come,' Ellen reminded him. 'A honeymoon, perhaps?' she added, for Roderic had becomer dearer to her than her own son over the years.

'Bless you, Ma'am. You are very kind,' he answered, gratefully, and went back to his duties with renewed hope.

To embark on such a journey was quite an adventure, and neither Basil nor Prue could be called adventurous by nature. They preferred the conventional, the conservative, and were consequently shy of exposing their ignorance to fellow travellers. All the family, including Basil's mother, had gathered on the station platform, and they had departed with many last-minute instructions to take care, and to be sure to send the telegram on arrival, a copy of which had already been decided: 'Arrived safely, Love Prue and Basil.'

'One would suppose we were starting on a journey to the Far East with all this fuss and bother,' Basil remarked, irritably, when at last they were on their way. 'It's only Switzerland, and some people take a holiday there every year and think nothing of it,' he added.

'That is true, but not us, Greggy, dear. It's most exciting, I do declare. I could not sleep a wink last night, and could eat no breakfast. After all, we can always pretend to be seasoned travellers. We are not stupid.' Prue took his hand, and settled down with a sigh of relief and complete confidence in his ability to get them safely to Zurich.

Basil had removed his straw boater to wave to the little group on the platform, and now he tossed it on to the rack, where the porter had placed their luggage. They were travelling second class at Uncle Henry's suggestion. First class was a luxury that only Charles and Kate could afford, and third class was for those in poor circumstances; that included Jane and Edward. In actual fact, Basil was feeling a little apprehensive, and not at all sure that this holiday was a sensible arrangement. Was he the only person to realize their relationship had changed in the past twelve months, and had to be conducted with the utmost discretion? His feelings for this girl, young enough to be his daughter, were no longer paternal, or even the feelings of an elder brother. He was in love with Prue. He knew all the symptoms.

There had been a time when he was in love with her two youngest aunts, Kate and Lucy. Lucy had been so trusting, so naive, and when she died in child-birth, he was so shocked and stunned, he felt he was guilty of murder. Conscious-stricken, and firmly re-solved to refrain from any further sexual relationship, he had accepted the sympathy and companionship of a little girl. But little girls grow into big girls, and big girls into young women. Once again he was involved, and he was afraid.

When Prue took his hand and cuddled close to him, he had the strongest desire to draw off her glove and kiss that cool hand – Prue was never hot or sweaty, not even on the hottest day. What would be her reaction? Disgust? Fright? Hysteria? Her trust-ing innocence knew nothing of sex or its dangers. A man could lust after a woman as Charles Lefeaux had lusted after Kate, only to discover that sex was her only attraction. But he had married Lucy, and exchanged tenderness for passion, and a new sensitivity he had not known he possessed when she was carrying his child.

Now this was something else, something different, something precious that must not be hurt or destroyed. But when the natural fondness of a man for a child had suddenly revealed itself as love for a young woman, he was shamed by feelings he could scarcely control. Now his loins were trembling. She was still a child at heart, he reminded himself, and those thrusting breasts, so tantalizing under the tight bodice of the dark travelling dress, were the only evidence of her maturity. Her total dependence on him to solve her problems, to dry her tears, these were the actions of a child, not a grown woman.

Bella had matured. She had stepped from childhood into the world of adults and responsibility without fear, without tears, and without too much of the soul-searching that had so disquieted her elder sister.

When Prue took off her hat, and settled her dark head on his shoulder with a deep sigh of contentment, Basil asked, gruffly, 'Happy, dear?'

'Deliciously happy, Greggy darling.' She closed her eyes, and snuggled closer.

He sighed, but not with contentment. Would he ever escape from the bonds of being a father-figure? he asked himself, as they embarked on a holiday fraught with danger emotionally. And she was not even aware of it.

She must have dozed on the first part of the journey. She was so quiet, and her breathing so regular, he could feel the rise and fall of her breasts. She wore no scent or jewellery, and her breath was sweet. In every sense she was different from the others – from Kate, who loved scent and jewellery and fashionable clothes – from Lucy, whose flaxen hair always smelled of lemons, and who wore nothing but the cameo brooch for sentimental reasons, and the wedding ring. All the sisters had received similar brooches from their father that last Christmas before his tragic death. Only Kate had discarded hers for something new, as she discarded everything. He still kept Lucy's brooch in his stud box because he liked to be reminded of her when he dressed. To forget her would be too easy, now that he had Prue's unfailing devotion and companionship. He had almost forgotten the bitter-sweet relationship with Kate, but not quite.

Comparison was a mistake. But he knew for certain that if he had been sharing this empty compartment with Kate, she would not be sleeping! A wry smile twisted his lips. He had not seen her for a very long time, but she would not change. She was like a flame that lit the passion in a man. She seemed to know by instinct what others of her sex had to learn. She had taught him how to make love in the most unlikely places. They had even made love in the sea! Yes, he had been jealous of Charles Lefeaux, who had not waited for the marriage bed to discover whether his bride was still a virgin. They were two of a kind and well matched. Self-important and self-indulgent. A week or so after their holiday in Zurich with Grace and Henry, there had been cards from

Italy. Perhaps it was the only way to keep Kate happy, to be constantly searching for some fresh diversion, new acquaintances.

He could never have satisfied Kate if they had married. To be the wife of the general manager of Thomas Brent & Son had pleased Lucy enormously, but Kate would soon have been bored. And sharing his mother's house would have meant being torn apart between the two, for his mother had taken an instant dislike to the fashionable young woman her son had introduced as his betrothed, and so glad to welcome Lucy in her stead.

His thoughts had wandered, and he had hardly noticed the passing countryside. Now they were approaching Victoria, and he roused Prue with a gentle kiss on her cheek.

'Wake up, dear. We are nearly there,' he coaxed.

She opened her eyes, those dark, expressive eyes, so like her mother's, that rarely smiled. 'Have I slept for a whole hour, Greggy? It seemed no more than ten minutes.'

'You were tired. You were too excited to sleep last night, so you said.'

'Did you sleep?'

'Yes,' he lied.

Yawning and stretching her long, slender body, she picked up her hat – a straw boater, similar to the ones her two aunts had worn that last Summer they had all been together. 'Will I do?' she asked.

'Very nicely,' he answered, and tucked a wayward strand of hair in place. He was feeling more composed, back in his familiar role as the father-figure. 'I will go first and help you down,' said he.

He hailed a porter to take their luggage to the cab rank, then paid the porter, and directed the cabby to drive them to Liverpool Street to catch the mid-day boat train to Harwich. In the cab Prue was full of praise for his assurance.

'They will think we are seasoned travellers, won't they, Greggy. You are so very capable.'

'Thank you, Madam!' he teased.

'Oh, but it's true! All this would be quite frightening if you were not here. Indeed, it would be utterly impossible even to contemplate such a journey.' She clutched his arm and stared wide-eyed at the confusion of cabs and carriages moving away from the station into the stream of heavy traffic. With the clatter of wheels on the cobbles, her voice was scarcely audible. 'I do wish we had brought Mama. She has not yet visited Auntie Grace, and she is her favourite sister.'

'Your Mama is a poor traveller. She was very ill on the journey home from India.'

'But that was years ago, and she was very unhappy. She did feel better when the ship stopped rocking. She sat in a deck chair and I sat on her lap. Bella sat on a rug, playing with her doll. It was a rag doll. We both had rag dolls that Ayah had made.'

'You remember all that, but you were only three?'

'I remember more than that. I remember Papa.' For a brief moment, a shadow clouded her face, then it was gone. 'You were there, waiting to receive me, at the end of that long journey, so kind, so comforting. It was all so RIGHT – to find Papa at the journey's end. Only you were not Papa, as you explained so very gently that I understood. Yes, you may smile at my foolishness, Greggy, dear, but some memories are so precious, I want to relive them, over and over again. What should I do without you? I couldn't, and that is the truth.'

'Nonsense! Silly girl,' he chided, and patted her hand.

The next stage of the journey was quite uneventful, then came the bustle and excitement of boarding the steamer to the Hook of Holland. Once again Basil took charge, and Prue found herself seated on deck with a cup of very strong, sweet tea, while fellow passengers crowded about the rails, waving farewell to relatives and friends.

The sun was shining, the sea sparkling, and their holiday had really begun to feel like a big adventure, especially when an elderly couple joined them on the bench and began to speak in a foreign tongue.

'German?' Prue mimed.

'Dutch,' Basil answered her in mime.

She wished they were speaking French, for then she could have aired her slight knowledge of that language, and probably discovered they could not understand a word! It was such a beautiful language, as Sister Valentine had demonstrated in her twice weekly lessons at the Convent.

The boat rocked gently as they left the harbour, and the vibration under her feet unsettled her stomach. Out in the open sea the swell increased and suddenly the strong sweet tea rose in her throat. She had no time to reach the rail. Sour vomit spilled on her dress and into her gloved hands. She was shamed into tears. All in the space of a few seconds, the lovely adventure had turned into this ugly, embarrassing situation.

Basil was too surprised and shocked to do more than fumble for a clean handkerchief and to murmur soothingly, 'It will pass, dear. Try not to worry.'

'Excuse please. Your vife is best to lie down below. Stewardess a kind voman,' the motherly Dutch woman suggested, also offering a clean handkerchief.

'Thank you, Ma'am.' Basil took her advice and they went below, where the smells of the dining-saloon brought on another attack in the alley-way.

'This is awful. I wish we had never started on this journey,' Basil was thinking, dismayed by such a violent reaction to such a gentle swell.

'Leave her to me, Sir. She needs to lie down.' The stewardess had arrived, and Basil handed over the distraught girl with a sense of relief. They disappeared into a small cabin, and the door was closed. A steward brought a mop and a bucket of disinfected water to clean up the mess. Basil apologized profusely, and slipped a shilling into his hand.

'Don't you worry, Sir. Me and the stewardess 'as been doing this job for 'arf a lifetime. We got strong stomachs, see. Your wife is a bad sailor, but she'll be all right once she sets foot on dry land again. There ain't no accounting for sea sickness. Some folks is sick even before we leave 'arbour. Just looking at the sea is enough, you might say.'

'Is that so?' Basil murmured politely. The combined smells of vomit and fried onions were quite nauseating, and he hurried back on deck where a second steward had to be thanked and given a shilling for cleaning up the mess.

Leaning on the rail, he enjoyed the clean, sweet air, the warm sun, and the gentle swell. Then he found a quiet corner and a vacant deck chair, and sat down to contemplate this unexpected interruption to their pleasure. Prue could not help being such a poor sailor, but with her nervous temperament, he should have realized the excitement would be too much. 'Prue is highly strung.' How often he had listened to that explanation for the tears and tantrums of childhood. Ellen was such a patient, indulgent mother. It was only bad temper that should have been corrected in early childhood.

He sighed. Would his mother remind him he was making a rod for his own back to marry into the family for a second time? She could be right. He had drifted into a situation that was not premeditated. The change in their relationship was inevitable. It satisfied his ego to be so indispensable, to be thought so capable, so manly. At Thomas Brent & Son, he was respected and admired by the young apprentices, and more than one of the departmental manageresses would have been happy and proud to wear his betrothal ring. He was good-looking, and he was no fool; but what did the future hold for such a relationship? Would Prue accept or reject his proposal? Where would they live if he married Prue? He could not take her to his mother's house, or the bed he had shared with Lucy. There was plenty of room at The Haven, but would Amelia welcome her ex-son-in-law as the husband of her grand-daughter? So many unanswered questions. If only he could make up his mind.

'Excuse me, Sir,' the steward interrupted. 'Your wife is asking for you.'

'Is anything wrong?' he asked, anxiously, as he followed him down the companionway.

'Not that I know of, Sir. The stewardess asked me to fetch you.'

'Your wife.' 'Your wife.' Was it so apparent to complete strangers? Yet Prue wore no ring on her ungloved hand. Could they be mistaken for lovers.

The stewardess was standing in the open doorway of the small cabin. 'Your wife has had a good sleep, Sir, and she is feeling so much better, I think you could try her on deck again. It's such a lovely day.'

'Greggy.' Prue was sitting on the edge of the bunk. With a faint colour and bright eyes, she certainly looked better.

'Thank you for taking such good care of her,' he told the woman, gratefully. This time it was half-a-crown he handed over. She bobbed a curtsey. It was not often her services were rewarded so generously.

'Take one of these clean rugs, luv, in case it blows up chilly later,' said she.

'You are very kind.' Prue was always polite. The Convent teaching had left its mark on both girls.

Basil took her hand, and they climbed the companionway.

'They ain't married, Nell, but what do it matter? You an' me don't fret about such formalities, do we, old girl?' The steward winked at the buxom little figure in the starched white cap and apron.

'Not so much sauce from you, Charlie Brown, or there won't be no more cuddles!' she retorted, and slammed the door.

The steward brought another deck chair, and they settled down comfortably with the rug over their knees.

'Such a kind woman. She took off my dress and sponged it while I slept, and she washed my gloves. Were you very ashamed of me, Greggy dear?' Prue asked.

'I was surprised and shocked, but not ashamed.'

'The stewardess thought we were married, and I was too ill to contradict her.'

'I wish it were true. Would you marry me, Prue?' There it was said, and could not be unsaid.

She turned her head to look at him, and all his doubts vanished. Her eyes were soft as velvet, and a smile trembled on her lips. 'Oh *Greggy*! I wondered if you would ever ask me, and I do love you so much.'

'Then why, in heaven's name, did you not tell me, you silly little goose!'

'Because it is not proper for a young woman to declare her love. That is what we have been taught at the Convent.'

'You mean, the Sisters spoke of such matters?'

'But of course. They are most concerned with our sensibilities. Did you suppose such matters were never mentioned?'

He nodded, mutely, too astonished to believe in such an extraordinary revelation.

'It was not Mama who taught Bella and myself the

151

facts of life. She is much too shy, too modest, and she would be so terribly embarrassed, poor darling. It was Sister Valentine who approached the subject of intimate relationships between a man and a woman with such delicacy it was not at all improper. When we started menstruation, it was so obvious, we were sent immediately to Sister Valentine for private instruction. I remember I was so terrified, I really thought I would bleed to death. She was so calm, she had seen it all before so many times, and when I had stopped crying, she explained that menstruation was a natural function, and that I was no longer a child, but a young woman. "You must be taught how to protect your womanhood. Man is made in the image of God, but he fell from grace in the Garden of Eden, so his thoughts are not always worthy. You must guard against deception and flattery. You must learn to discriminate between what is true and what is false. The Blessed Virgin Mother sets the pattern for all women. Safeguard your virginity. Keep your body clean and healthy, and your thoughts pure. Do not speak of menstruation as a curse. It is a blessing, a sign that all is well, and that the womb is ready to receive the seed that will grow into a child when Holy Matrimony has been sanctified." Are you shocked, Greggy dear?'

'My dearest girl, I am absolutely astounded. Here am I, hardly daring to mention the word betrothed for fear of scaring you away, and you have been waiting for me to declare myself. Forgive me, my darling.' He kissed her mouth for the first time. It was wet and warm, and her breath still a little sour.

But it did not matter. Nothing mattered, only this wonderful realization of perfect harmony and understanding. It had grown and developed through the years. The father-figure had paved the way to ultimate happiness. Soon, very soon, his role would be changed.

'I love you,' he said.

'I love you,' she answered.

There was so much to talk about. So much time had been lost, and he was no longer young. Yet neither Kate nor Lucy had given him this kind of assurance that all was well. There had always been reservations because of his reluctance to lose his role as self-appointed escort of the two girls. All this had happened before Ellen brought her fatherless children home from India.

Now he looked at the girl beside him with the eyes of a lover, and saw in her all the beauty and all the qualities he most admired. Prue was his last and dearest love. He knew her as he knew himself, knew this glowing young woman who was even now insisting, 'I want to belong to you, Greggy darling. I am not afraid of the marriage bed because its mysteries have been explained. It is ignorance of the facts of life that breeds fear. One day, perhaps, for our grand-daughters, there will be no more mystery, no more fear.'

'Could it not be a bad thing, too much freedom, too much knowledge of the opposite sex? It could be dangerous.'

'You are probably right.' She stroked his cheek, and he caught her hand and touched it with his lips.

'How soon can we be married?' she whispered.

'What would you say to being married in Zurich? There would be an English church, and your Uncle Henry would know how to arrange a special licence. This holiday could be our honeymoon. What do you say?'

She flung her arms about his neck. 'I should like it beyond anything in the world. To go home as man and wife. What a shock for everyone! Grandmama will disapprove, of course, but then she has always disapproved of me, and I have tried so hard to please her. Mama will say I am too young for marriage, but it does not signify, for she herself was married young.'

'She will probably think I am too old for you, and she will be right.'

'For me, my darling, you are exactly the right age. I could not contemplate marriage to a mere boy, a stranger, even if I had met such a person.'

'Where shall we live, my love? We must be practical.'

'Must we?' She giggled happily. 'There is your position to be considered, Mr Gregson. The General Manager of Thomas Brent & Son could not be accommodated in lodgings!'

'And for obvious reasons we cannot live at your house, or mine.'

She made no answer, and sat back in her chair, frowning thoughtfully. 'Are there any empty rooms on the top floor of the store?' she asked.

'Several.'

'Then you and I will go together to see the lawyer.

We can make a cosy little nest for ourselves. It will be so very convenient for you to live on the premises, and I shall learn to be a good housewife. So, that is settled.'

'There speaks the great-grand-daughter of Thomas the First!' he chuckled, as his arms closed about her.

The remainder of the journey held the quality of a dream. They ate, and slept, and talked, and were so engrossed in one another, their fellow travellers did not exist. They missed the novelty and excitement of their first journey abroad in the enraptured self-absorption of lovers the world over. Their eyes, their lips, spoke of love.

But Prue did not have the courage to go through with such a sudden proposal. Despite her knowledge of the facts of life, she was puzzled that there were things she didn't know. And the disapproval of her grandmother seemed to reach as far as the centre of Europe. As for Greg, he decided he had to endure the frustration of being so near his beloved Prue for the whole time of their holiday, and just make do with holding hands and stolen kisses.

Grace and Henry reacted with tact and consideration, and put up with the love-struck couple with great indulgence. They exchanged glances which spoke of their understanding of what had been an even more unusual courtship than their own.

Chapter Four

The guard had blown his whistle and waved his green flag when the tall young man, with a bulging portmanteau, burst through the barrier and ran, with long, loping strides, along the platform. A door flew open, and hands reached out to drag him in.

'Stand back! Stand back there, you young fool!' the guard shouted importantly, as the powerful locomotive, puffing clouds of smoke, moved away. Then he slammed the door on the sprawled figure and, still muttering, hopped easily on to the step of the guard's van.

Thomas picked himself up and grinned at his rescuers. One had retrieved his hat, the other his portmanteau. 'Thank you, gentlemen. That was uncommonly decent of you!' he gasped.

Two pairs of eyes, grey and brown, studied him with interest, for he was worth a second glance. With his vivid blue eyes, fair complexion, and his handsome head, crowned with a cap of hair the colour of ripe corn, he seemed to take command of the situation with the natural confidence of a born leader. Since the others had been feeling apprehensive, they welcomed the stranger with a good grace.

'Sandhurst, Gentlemen, I assume?' said he, glancing from one to the other.

'That is so,' said the elder, a sturdy figure with a ruddy complexion, brown eyes and hair.

The younger man nodded. His lean, gangling appearance gave the impression of a youth who had outgrown his strength. His eyelids fluttered nervously, and he blushed like a girl.

The newcomer thrust out his hand. 'Thomas Cartwright, at your service, Gentlemen,' said he, and grasped the elder's firm hand.

'Albert Henry George Vickers. My friends call me George,' he recited, with bored familiarity.

'Holy Smoke! How did you come by such a collection?' Thomas demanded.

'Two grandfathers and an uncle,' Albert Henry George explained, with a shrug.

'And you, my good fellow?' Thomas enquired of the younger man.

'Lancelot Andrew Beverly Curtis-Browne – hyphenated, with an 'e',' he added, apologetically. 'My friends call me Lance.'

Thomas shouted with laughter and clapped him on the shoulder. 'It's downright inhuman to saddle a fellow with such a burden.'

'The only boy in a family of girls,' Lancelot Andrew Beverly explained, with a shy smile.

'Then I seem to have been uncommonly fortunate to be blessed with only one name. The family refer to me as Thomas the Third. I will tell you the story of the others some time, but now, let us be seated and get properly acquainted before we arrive at this worthy institution, for I have a strong feeling that protocol will demand we bow our heads in subjection. Heaven knows, they tried hard enough at public school, but they didn't quite succeed with me,' he chuckled. 'I suppose Winchester is typical of the rest?'

'Grammar school could have been worse,' said George, amiably.

'Eton was hell.' Lance shuddered at the memory.

'It has a savage reputation. They say that battles are won on the playing fields of Eton, and that every new boy has to defend his honour, stripped naked, in the initiation ceremony?'

'Something of the kind,' Lance admitted, in his quiet, cultured voice.

'Well, when we have been enrolled as gentlemen cadets at the Royal Military College they cannot treat us with such total disregard of our age and dignity – or can they?'

'I think they can,' George mused, 'though I am speaking from hearsay. My father was commissioned from the ranks. He was not trained as an officer, but so many officers died in the Crimea, he was given command of his company at the battle of Balaclava, where he was mortally wounded. The citation described him as a brave and gallant soldier. It was this recommendation that got me a place at Sandhurst. We have no army tradition in my family. My forbears were peasants, and to this day own nothing more than a tumble-down farmhouse and a few acres of grazing land for sheep and cattle. I am not ashamed of my humble heritage.'

'Very commendable, my dear fellow,' Thomas agreed. 'And you, Lance? How do you come to be here?'

'For me, there was no choice. With three generations of army tradition, it was expected.'

'What would you have chosen, had you been allowed to choose?'

'To live in Paris. To be an artist.'

'An artist? My dear fellow, you could have starved in a garret.'

'At least I should have proved something. I am my mother's son. She understands, but her wishes are over-ruled. My father has the last word on everything. Look at me! Be honest, Gentlemen. Do I *look* like a leader of men?'

'In 18 months you will not recognize yourself.'

'No, because to all outward appearances I shall look like all the rest, moulded into the same pattern, but I shall still be the same person fundamentally. You cannot make a silk purse from a sow's ear. I hate the sight and the feel of a rifle. I hate the thought of killing in cold blood. My uncle was Master of Hounds, and I was expected to enjoy the hunt. I followed the field on my mare. Her name was Bess. I was blooded at the age of seven, and disgraced myself by being sick. I always shut my eyes when the hounds tore the poor fox to pieces. He was so beautiful.'

'Cheer up, my good fellow. You have found friends. All for one and one for all. We will call ourselves The Three Musketeers – George, Lance and Tom. I salute you, Gentlemen!' Thomas announced dramatically. His confidence and gaiety were so infectious. Good looks and personality established his right to leadership. Even Lance could face the future with less anxiety. All three leapt to their feet, grasped hands, and shouted, 'The Three Musketeers!' with boyish enthusiasm.

'You haven't told us, Tom, how you come to be here?' George reminded him, when they were seated once more and the train was gathering speed towards their destination.

Thomas launched into the tale he so enjoyed telling. At preparatory school, small boys had listened spellbound in the dormitory after lights out, and Roderic had not been the only one to hero-worship the handsome youngster who could not only ride, but jump all the hurdles, who could swim like a fish, and run like a hare; who cared that his energy and enthusiasm were not apparent in the classroom? He was always the first to take the blame for any misconduct and the thrashing that followed, and that alone entitled him to hero-worship.

At Winchester the tale had been told with more embellishments, as befitted the age and intelligence of his listeners. It was Gerald who had seen in him the very qualities that he himself lacked, and Thomas had accepted his admiration and loyalty, and all the privileges the friendship entailed, for Gerald's family, in their ancestral home, had shown him another aspect of life so very different from the small world of The Haven. Holidays abroad, first-class travel, parties and picnics, and debutante balls. All these delights were enjoyed during those years at

Winchester. Now Gerald had gone up to Cambridge, and they had lost touch. Thomas had no sense of guilt in neglecting the young man who had given him a taste for the privileged class of society. This was a new chapter, and each chapter brought new friendships, new adventure, new opportunities to prove himself the worthy son of that heroic parent whose face had smiled down on him from the silver frame on the mantelpiece as far back as he could remember. 'Say good morning to Papa,' his fond Mama would say, lifting him out of his cot.

Now he could sense that George and Lance were most impressed by the tale of the gallant young subaltern. For a man to die in the service of his Queen and country was an honourable death, and his son had every reason to be proud. The commanding officer had indeed written to his Mama, but he had never seen the letter, for it had happened before he was born. It had taken only a little imagination, however, to conjure up the contents of that letter. It was full of praise for Sub-Lieutenant Jonathan Cartwright's bravery and devotion to duty. Etc. Etc.

Thomas got quite carried away by his own eloquence. In young Lance he could see the beginnings of that hero-worship his ego demanded. So he smiled, and his blue eyes were moist with emotion, when he had finished the tale.

'I shall ask to be commissioned in my father's regiment. It could be posted to the Northwest Frontier for a period of five years. I shall marry, of course. It is more or less expected, I understand. Young officers are less prone to temptation with beautiful native girls!' he laughed. 'So, my dear fellows, I intend to absorb every aspect of this eighteen months' course of training. A little fun, perhaps, will not come amiss. All work and no play makes Jack a dull boy, they say. But the girls can wait. We can pick and choose when we are ready. Shall you fellows marry for love or money?'

'For love, among my own people. I have known Jenny since she was a little girl. She will wait for me,' said George.

'Very commendable,' Thomas agreed.

Lance shook his head. 'I see myself as a bachelor uncle, distributing half-crowns to nephews and nieces.' He smiled his diffident smile.

'And I shall look for a beautiful bride with a handsome dowry, since I cannot abide to be poor!' Thomas declared.

He will get what he wants, George was thinking. Who could resist such devastating charm?

More than 200 young men poured off the train when it reached its destination. The platform was crowded with all types, in a great variety of dress, with individual taste. Dark and fair, with a sprinkling of red heads, they laughed and joked and jostled each other in the greatest good humour. Railway porters were swept aside. They were grown men, and could carry their own bags. Some sort of conveyance would be provided no doubt; if not, they would walk.

So they swarmed out of the station, followed by the scornful glance of the guard who had seen it all before. 'Bloody young fools! They don't know what they've signed on for. Get them into that bloody uniform, and you won't tell t'other from which,' he muttered.

An elderly porter, leaning on his empty trolley, was more tolerant. 'They be only lads. Good luck to 'em,' said he.

'Holy Smoke!' The imposing edifice was even more impressive in reality than in the prospectus they had all received, and Thomas whistled. Silence fell on the chattering groups, and they snatched off their hats as they filed into the entrance hall.

Thomas lifted his head and glanced about him with a confident air, feeling entitled to be standing where his heroic father had once stood under the gilt-framed portraits of former governors and a likeness of the Queen looking down on their serious young faces. George squared his shoulders. Lance blinked nervously and moved closer to Thomas. For some, it was all too formal and impressive, and they would have run away but for the jeers of their companions and the anger and disappointment at home. There was no escape. The majority, however, awaited the Governor with mixed feelings of doubt and hope. They were no longer boys to be herded into classrooms and dormitories and thrashed if they misbehaved. Soon they would be called 'Gentlemen Cadets'. It was a proud title.

Silently, reverently, they stared at the man whose entrance was greeted by a clicking of heels and smart salutes from a bodyguard of instructors. A tall, distinguished figure in his immaculate uniform, with a row of medals and ribbons on his chest, his stern features relaxed for a moment as he studied the rows of eager young faces. A veteran of several campaigns, his appointment as Governor to the Royal Military College had been the climax of a brilliant career. His sense of dedication and feelings of responsibility were renewed with each new batch of recruits. There would be professors to teach the theory, and instructors to teach the practical – all worthy chaps. But it was the Governor to whom they all turned for advice, and his authority was absolute. It was a lonely and often a hazardous authority, for in time of war it was his painful duty to send young subalterns to their respective regiments, only partially trained, and not yet ready for combat. Loyalty to the Queen and a stern sense of duty must be so embedded in the mentality of every cadet leaving the Military College that they would not hesitate to obey any order. A man must first learn to *take* orders before he could *give* orders, the Governor was saying, and his strong, resonant voice echoed to the rafters. This was one of the fundamental issues on which the Royal Military College had been founded, and nothing had changed, he insisted. Individual achievement would be recognized. Insubordination and slackness would be punished. Confined to barracks on bread and water was not pleasant, but discipline must be maintained. The professors and instructors had heard it all before many times.

The raw material was there, waiting to be moulded into shape, but leaders were born, not made, some were thinking. Their patience – and impatience – would be rewarded at the end of eighteen months by the sight of a long column of cadets, in strict formation, marching to the tune of *Colonel Bogey* at the passing-out parade. So they listened politely to the Governor's speech and searched the rows of boyish faces for any distinguishing feature that would help to provide a clue as to the personality.

Standing a little apart from the rest, three young men, of widely different appearance, were grouped together in what appeared to be close harmony, but there was something about the central figure that was worth a second glance. Bold blue eyes and a handsome head. A young Viking? Flanked by a sturdy figure with a determined chin, and a lanky fellow, blinking nervously and looking positively terrified, the young 'Viking' was strikingly different. That air of such supreme confidence, with a hint of arrogance, was not a quality that instructors and professors cared to observe *at the start*. It would be interesting to see whether that confidence was justified, ex-Sergeant Major McFarlane was thinking.

'That will be all, Gentlemen.' It was only a short speech, but its effect was indelibly stamped on young minds. Doubts were removed and hope substituted for fear. A sigh that conveyed both relief and determination broke from the throat of every one of those new recruits. They were here, at last. Even Lance was smiling shyly at his companions, and he braced his hunched shoulders.

'Nothing very original in that speech, my dear fellows. I could almost have written it myself,' Thomas muttered as they moved away.

'I thought it was quite apt. Makes one feel better for listening,' Lance ventured.

George kept his thoughts to himself. Sensible fellow!

There was no time for Thomas to air his views any further. That would have to wait till they found themselves together again during Mess. The public school system had prepared the majority for the strict observance of rules, and for the discipline, but it hadn't prepared them for long hours of concentrated effort of mind and body. Even those, like Thomas, who had attended a crammer establishment, were surprised by a regime so totally lacking in sympathy and tolerance. Public school had moulded and shaped them, but it had taken all of five years. Here, at Sandhurst, everything had to be learned in eighteen months. Mind and body must be welded into a coherent whole, and for all their willingness, it would take all their strength and endurance, for they had only recently attained manhood.

The Three Musketeers were allocated a bedroom containing three hard truckle beds, three cane chairs, and a large wardrobe, its whitewashed austerity suggestive of a monk's cell. They were singularly pleased, however, for this concession to their new-found friendship.

The rest of the day was confined to formal introductions to professors and instructors, and becoming acquainted with their environment. For George, who had attended a local grammar school daily, it was quite a revelation, this initiation into communal living, but he was sensible enough to hide his ignorance.

For Thomas and Lance, who had both suffered the

rigours of the traditional public school system, it was just a matter of adjustment. They would still play an occasional game of rugby, but the gymnasium, with its formidable vaulting horse, would tax their aching muscles to the limit.

They had all studied the prospectus, and it had seemed a reasonable document, but the morrow would prove they were mistaken. It read:

TIME TABLE

Reveille	– 6.30 a.m.
First study	– 7 – 8 a.m.
Breakfast	– 8 a.m.
Surgeon	– 8.30 a.m.
Parade	– 9 – 10 a.m.
Second study	– 10.20 – 11.20 a.m.
Third study	– 11.20 – 12.30 p.m.
Fourth study	– 12.30 – 1.30 p.m.
Luncheon	– 1.30 p.m.
Riding	– 2.00– 3.00 p.m.
(2 classes)	– 3.00 – 4.00 p.m.
Drill	– 3.00 – 3.45 p.m.
Gymnastics	– 4.00 – 5 p.m.
Sword exercises	– 6 – 7 p.m.
Mess	– 8 p.m.
Lights-out	– 11 p.m.

It was truly a formidable programme. At the end of the day, The Three Musketeers collapsed on their hard truckle beds with groans of protest. Every muscle in their bodies ached intolerably, their minds were confused by a thousand facts, and their brave hearts faltered and questioned their ability to endure such a rigorous system for eighteen months. Lance was too exhausted to speak.

Their day had started at 6.30 a.m. and they had been put through their paces by a team of instructors who seemed bent on breaking their spirits.

As for the professors, their knowledge of military history, regimental protocol, etc. etc., was infallible.

'It don't signify. Half that stuff don't apply to this day and age,' Thomas complained, stretching his painful legs. Then his tired eyes brightened. 'The riding class commends itself, does it not? And the horses are superb.'

'You and your horses!' George mocked – and fell asleep.

It was soon apparent that individual effort and achievement were regarded favourably. The public school team spirit was not so constantly enforced. Cadets were sifted carefully, and their potentials studied and reported. Even in those early weeks, when they obeyed orders instantly and automatically, there were signs of potential officer material. It was apparent in Thomas Cartwright and in Albert Henry George Vickers, but not, unfortunately, in Lancelot Andrew Beverly Curtis-Browne. It would take more than a few hours of drill to straighten those hunched shoulders and put purpose in his marching feet and confidence in his hesitant manner. But he tried hard, and with much encouragement from his two companions, he would eventually make the grade.

The roars of the ex-sergeant-major were executed

to make every raw recruit tremble in his new army boots, and there were a few in that original crowd of young men who would slip away, defeated by the system, and leave no trace in the annals of the Royal Military College.

But once they were issued with their uniforms, there was a noticeable difference in the swinging arms and the marching feet on the parade ground. They marched proudly, and saw themselves as splendid fellows. Dress uniforms were worn for church parade and for formal occasions when they were inspected by visiting VIPs, and on rare occasions by Her Majesty the Queen. Battle dress was their normal wear. It was plain and useful. In their uniforms the cadets appeared singularly alike. Bareheaded, they were easily distinguishable, however, for no two heads and no two pairs of eyes were exactly alike.

While Thomas and George were soon displaying their skills in riding and shooting and gymnastics, Lance was quietly gaining marks with the learned professors. He was interested and attentive while his companions were only at lectures out of compulsion. Their energy and enthusiasm for outdoor activities was boundless, but their minds still baulked at the theory. They were well matched, these two, and riding was the only class where Thomas was the undisputed leader. With horses there was a gentleness and sympathy that was lacking in his human relationships. The observant George was heard to remark, amiably, that in his opinion Thomas would love no woman as well as he loved his horse. It could be true. He had yet to find a woman who would take priority over his army career.

Sandhurst was proving every bit as absorbing as he had anticipated. He had hardly a thought for the family at The Haven; and as for his discarded friends and the adoring Kate, all of whom wrote regularly, assuming he must be homesick, Thomas had no time for them.

Grandmama and Kate still sent his allowance that he spent on beer and cigarettes in the hostelry with George and Lance, whenever they could slip away after lights-out without being discovered. With his gregarious nature, Thomas seemed to need the stimulating companionship of fellows who drank too much beer, laughed too loudly, and recounted shady tales of their performances with the opposite sex. George and Lance went along because Thomas expected it, and he usually managed to over-rule their objections. George would have preferred a quiet pipe in the smoking room, and Lance an interesting book in the library. 'One for all and all for one,' he would remind them, with that irresistible smile. He was popular at the hostelry; for one thing he always had money to spend, and for another, he could always cap a naughty story with one of his own. True or false, what did it matter if it raised a laugh? He was not so popular in the Mess, however, where other gentlemen cadets could equal his charm and his self-confidence. One in particular – Lord Cecil James Fothergill – whose ancestral home in Northumberland could boast a bed in which Queen Elizabeth had slept, was decidedly hostile. He picked his companions with fastidious care, and ignored the rest, including The Three Musketeers.

Such haughty condescension, as may be expected, affected Thomas as a red rag to a bull. He couldn't bear to be ignored. One evening, after a particularly gruelling day, the enmity between them flared into open conflict too sudden to be prevented. Thomas overheard the sneering remark, 'That conceited young pup!' It was too insulting to be tolerated, and his Lordship found himself sprawled on the floor, cradling his aching jaw. Pushing away the helpful hands, he staggered to his feet.

'Nobody strikes a Fothergill and gets away with it!' he growled, and lifted his foot.

Thomas collapsed with a groan, clutching his testicles. It was all over in a few seconds, and he was given a chair-lift by his two companions and carried back to their quarters in agony. Writhing on the bed, he vowed to get even with the bastard, but after a thorough dressing down by the Governor the following morning, he was persuaded to change his mind. Such incidents, prompted by high spirited young gentlemen, could be expected, but not repeated, and Thomas was no fool. The note of warning in the Governor's voice could not be ignored, but neither could the incident be forgotten. It was some consolation, however, that his Lordship was severely reprimanded by the Governor: 'Only a cad lifts his foot to his opponent.'

By the month of May, the cadets were expected to be ready to display their skills at the annual Sports Day, when relatives were invited. After five months of laborious and concentrated effort, the instructors had to admit among themselves that the fresh batch of recruits had earned their favourable commendation, but not so much as a whisper of praise escaped their closed ranks, and the gentlemen cadets did not expect it. Keen rivalry was the spur goading them on to further effort, and Sports Day the opportunity to prove themselves worthy of their calling.

At the opening ceremony, resplendent in dress uniform, more than 300 cadets marched in strict formation, like toy soldiers on parade. In brilliant sunshine, it was a sight to warm the heart and bring proud tears to the eyes of doting mamas, sisters and sweethearts. The band played a stirring tune, and the parade ground echoed to the stamp of marching feet. Everyone was impressed. It was a proud moment for Grandmama Brent, a dainty little figure in an afternoon gown of tussore silk in a delicate shade of mauve, with a matching sunshade and a beribboned hat. Surrounded by her family, she looked much too young to be the mother of Ellen, Grace, Bertha, Jane and Kate, for all had been anxious not to miss such an important occasion. They made a pretty picture in their Summer finery, flanked by Charles, Henry and Edward in grey toppers and morning dress. Prue was on the arm of Basil, to whom she was officially betrothed, and Bella on the arm of Roderic. Norah was there, of course, to complete the family group. Thomas was fully aware of all of them.

At a distance of fifty yards or so, the cadets looked so alike that there was some disagreement on his exact position in the column. Kate insisted the central figure in the third row was Thomas. Jane thought he was on the outside of the seventh row, and Grandmama, who had the last word, as usual, spotted Thomas in the *back* row!

Ellen was too choked to speak. She had put back the clock a quarter of a century, and that tall, handsome figure in the last row was Jonathan Cartwright, her betrothed. It was Jonathan who would walk towards them with his long, loping stride when they were dismissed, and he would kiss her cheek, for he did not care who saw this token of affection.

'You are looking very beautiful today, my sweet,' he would say, with mocking blue eyes, and she would blush like a school-girl.

But the splendid figure who saluted smartly, bowed to Grandmama and smiled disarmingly on his family was her son, Thomas, and there *was* a difference, for Thomas *did* care that he was being watched, and had no intention of bestowing his kisses on any expectant cheek. Ellen had found Jonathan's self-importance a little tiresome on official occasions, but it was nothing compared to that of her handsome son, who stood before them in all the splendour of his young manhood, smiling and bowing, but unapproachable. He was a stranger now, this splendid young man, a worthy product of the Royal Military College, and the family had no place in his new world. In a few short months he was stamped for a lifetime with the pride and principles of an army career.

'Did you see me?' he asked.

And in that question the family recognized the ghost of the small boy, on his third birthday, astride his new rocking horse. 'Watch me! Watch me!' he had cried, imperiously.

'My darling boy!' gushed Kate, stepping out of the family group to kiss his cheek. He stiffened and shrank from her embrace. The French perfume he had once thought so alluring he now found cloying. She felt his withdrawal. It was hurtful, but she was a good actress, and her ravishing smile had not faltered. Only her dark eyes betrayed the hurt to her pride. She knew she could never reclaim the young lover she had lost, but she chatted brightly to cover her embarrassment.

'You look marvellous, darling. I am so proud of my handsome nephew. We wouldn't have missed your Big Day for anything. We can't stop for the sports, unfortunately. We are meeting our friends at Victoria *en route* to Monaco, don't you know, for the Whitsun vacation. Isn't it exciting? Come along, Charles, darling, we mustn't keep them waiting.' She took his arm and her ravishing smile swept the family group. 'You will excuse us, won't you, Mother?' she asked, but did not wait for an answer.

Charles bowed, reluctant to leave, but anxious to avoid a scene. It was not true. There was plenty of time. He had booked seats on the night express, and he would have enjoyed watching the sporting events. He shook hands with Thomas, and recalled their last meeting. That virile young body had been lying in the arms of his wife, stripped naked. 'Au revoir, my 'dear fellow,' said he, with a nonchalant air. What did it matter? What did anything matter? He had long since tired of Kate, but it suited him, this parody of a happy marriage. They walked away, arm in arm, and Grandmama stared after them with pursed lips.

'That poor man. He looks positively haggard. I am ashamed of my daughter. One of these days she will find herself without a husband, and who could blame him?'

Thomas made no comment. He suspected that Kate had already taken another lover.

She was soon forgotten. This was Thomas's day. Chairs were provided for the ladies to watch the main events. They would be served with ices while the gentlemen went away to watch the rifle drill, the archery contest and the sword displays. The cadets had changed into battle dress.

In the riding classes, Thomas distinguished himself, as expected, closely followed by his sworn enemy, Lord Cecil James Fothergill. Such superb horsemanship brought cheers from the proud fathers who had seen it all before, and from younger brothers who could hardly wait to participate, as well as the uncles, like Edward, whose youth had been spent in very different circumstances.

There had been no money to spare for Jane to have a new dress for the occasion, but Ellen had re-trimmed last Summer's Sunday best and the straw boater, a relic of many summers, suited her young-looking, unadorned face. They had left two of the Salvation Army lasses in charge of the Mission, and Jane's child-like pleasure in every event was sufficient reward to Edward, who would have preferred to spend their free day watching the traffic on the river with a picnic meal. This gathering of sophisticated society was not Edward's idea of enjoyment, and Thomas was not a favourite with this uncle-by-marriage.

As for Prue, she had not changed her opinion of her good-looking brother who still managed to steal all the limelight on the few occasions they met. She was not impressed by his skilful handling of the spirited horse he had been allocated.

'Showing off, as usual,' she scoffed, but was careful to lower her voice so that only Basil heard. And Basil was so much in love with his dear girl he agreed with everything she said and did. They were wondering how soon they could slip away without annoying Grandmama, who had insisted on their attendance. Both had been granted a free day, and could think of better ways of spending it. They planned their wedding for August, when the rooms on the top floor of the drapery store would be ready. It would cost Basil all his carefully hoarded savings to furnish their future home, for Prue would have nothing but the best materials for curtains, best quality carpets, blankets and linen, and solid mahogany furniture. Wedding presents would provide silver, china and cutlery. Prue had always had her own way, and Basil would find his second wife had few of the wifely virtues of the sweet compliant Lucy. His dear girl would be exacting and possessive, and this second marriage in the family would need all his patience and tolerance. They held hands and whispered endearments to one another on Thomas's Big Day, and when Henry, Edward and Roderic went off to watch the other events, Basil excused himself.

'Don't go, Greggy, darling,' Prue whispered. 'Stay here with me.'

So he stayed.

'Silly man!' muttered Grandmama. 'He is making a rod for his own back!' Prue had never been a favourite with Grandmama.

'Do you wish you had settled for Sandhurst?' Henry asked Roderic, as they walked away together.

'No, Sir. I should have made a poor cadet. There is no army tradition in my family, and no incentive to be shaped into officer material.'

'Thomas seems to have all the necessary qualities for leadership.'

'Thomas is a born leader. Even at prep school those qualities were easily recognized.'

'Are you still good friends?'

'Not close friends, Sir. We have lost touch. I admire from a distance.'

'It's quite a considerable distance, is it not, my dear fellow, between London's East End and this?' He spread his arms to embrace the splendid panorama of the Royal Military College. The band was playing a Strauss waltz to entertain the ladies in the absence of the gentlemen. A few privileged children were playing tag, and groups of pretty girls linked arms and chatted excitedly about their favourite cadets. All had brothers at Sandhurst.

'Charming, aren't they?' mused Henry, who still

had an eye for a pretty girl. His adored Grace only smiled when his eye wandered. His darling girl was his dearest love.

'When are you going to marry that nice little Bella?' he asked his young companion.

'As soon as we both have completed our training.'

'For the Church Army?'

'Yes.'

'A different sort of army, eh?'

'Very different, Sir.' Roderic smiled shyly.

'It wouldn't suit young Thomas.'

'No. He thinks we are quite mad, Bella and I.'

'I am inclined to agree with him, my dear fellow. Was it necessary to choose a profession – an unrewarding profession – in such a squalid environment?'

'Service to the poor and under-privileged has its own reward, Sir.'

'I daresay you find it highly commendable in these two young people?' He had turned to Edward to include him in the conversation, but Edward was feeling the heat, and his head ached. Henry's robust health and hearty manner seemed to emphasize his own disability.

'We d-did not p-persuade them. They m-made up their own m-minds,' he answered, haltingly.

'Quite so, my dear fellow. Quite so.' Then he changed the subject, for he was not really interested in these pious opinions. His gregarious nature found the company of friends in the local tavern more to his liking.

Thomas had been chosen to compete in the

musketry, but failed to gain a place in the finals. His attention had wandered for a few seconds because of the close proximity of his hated rival. All his senses were aware of him, and he could not hold his concentration.

'Bad luck, Sir,' called Henry from the touchline, when the shot misfired. It was George, with his steady nerve, who won the contest.

But Thomas was at his best in the sword display.

'By Jove! Our man is truly magnificent!' Henry declared.

'It's the challenge, Sir. Thomas cannot resist a challenge,' said Roderic, the faithful disciple.

'I wouldn't care to be on the wrong end of that sword in combat,' Henry shivered.

When the sporting events were over, Thomas introduced his friends, and they escorted their respective families over the college precincts. Lance had taken no part in the sporting events. Only the best were chosen. The honour of the College was at stake. His bevy of sisters could not hide their disappointment, and his stern parent was only partially appeased by the assurance of his professors who vouched for distinction in his studies.

'As for the rest, give him time, Sir. Remember the fable of the hare and the tortoise,' reminded the jovial Professor Haddersly.

'Can't say I do,' muttered the disgruntled parent, and walked away. He wished he could claim young Cartwright for his son that day. Lance was his mother's son. The father judged that he would never make an officer. But he was wrong. Qualities of leadership have many guises, and cannot be determined by brilliant tactics alone, but by courage and resourcefulness, and Lance would have both at the right moment.

Tea was served in the Mess for the visitors who came from a distance by train, but the majority had their own carriages and coachmen. A quick change back into their dress uniforms after the sporting events, the cadets barely had time to snatch glasses of cold beer. They were hot and sweating, and ready to call it a day, but were still on duty, and there must be no slacking till the last of the station cabs had rolled away.

Prue and Basil had asked to be excused from the tea-party, and slipped away to catch an earlier train to London. They would spend the late evening deciding on a pretty colour-scheme for the nursery. Prue was pregnant. It had been all too easy to make love in their future home on Wednesday afternoons with the store closed, and the caretaker in the basement. After her initial shock and repugnance, Prue had found herself very happy to consummate her feelings towards Basil. But she had reacted hysterically to the doctor's confirmation that she was carrying a child. 'I don't want a child! I want only you!' she cried.

And Basil, who had sworn never to inflict the sufferings of childbirth on any other woman, was in a state of nervous apprehension. They were hoping to keep the secret to themselves till after the wedding, but Ellen had already guessed, and wished her daughter would confide in her.

When Thomas had assisted the ladies into the station cab, he leaned over and kissed Amelia's flushed cheek. 'Thank you for your company, Grandmama,' said he, gallantly.

'It was a proud pleasure, my darling,' she answered, her eyes tender with love.

He saluted smartly and bowed as the cab rolled away.

Ellen's dark eyes were sad. I am his mother, but he does not kiss me, she thought. She was not important in his young life. She never had been. Now it was too late. He was too involved in his military training to give a thought to the woman who had carried him in her womb on that long journey from India, and seen him grow in the likeness of the father he had never known. A little over a year and he would be going back to that far off country where he was conceived. He would take a wife, because it was expected. She would be young and beautiful, a fitting complement to his own young beauty. It saddened her to think of this innocent girl, unaware of the dangers she had to face, the homesickness, and the heartbreak. Thomas would not hesitate to lust after other women when she became pregnant. His mother was not blind to his faults or his weakness for a pretty face. She had seen it all before, and suffered the anguish of rejection. Thomas might be loyal to the regiment, but not to his wife. Jonathan's blood ran in his veins.

'Why are you looking so sad, Mama?' Bella whispered, as they drew up in the station forecourt.

'I was thinking of your Papa. In that uniform the likeness is so very remarkable.'

'And that makes you sad?'

'Yes,' she sighed.

Bella pressed her hand affectionately. She supposed Mama was lonely now her children were grown up, and she was torn between love for her and love for Roderic. It was so difficult to separate one from the other, yet she had done so, and the future must lie with Roderic and the Church Army.

For a month in the Summer the cadets were living under canvas, with all the discomforts of camping. In Summer storms they were drenched to the skin, and in sweltering heat they were sweating profusely. It was a rehearsal for the conditions they would encounter in wartime.

Living rough was not a state that appealed to Thomas or Lance, but George enjoyed it thoroughly. From early childhood he had been accustomed to living conditions his two companions could not even visualize in their comfortable, upper-class environment. It had hardened him, and he was less inclined to chills and fevers. Early morning ablutions in the open air were no hardship for George, who had washed under the pump in the yard at home. Meals cooked and eaten outdoors, with stew and dumplings invariably for the main course, reminded him of the plain but wholesome fare in the farm kitchen.

In place of their normal studies, they were instructed in map reading and long route marches, carrying heavy packs on their backs, with all their equipment. They rode for miles over rough country, where rabbit holes and hidden ditches could unseat the unwary. It was not a holiday, they were re-minded, and the hostelry was out of bounds. Sentries were posted at strategic points.

Deprived of their room. The Three Musketeers had no privacy, and Thomas, in particular, found the crowded sleeping accommodation most restrictive.

'You may be glad of this experience one of these days, Tom,' George reminded him one morning, as they breakfasted from a tin bowl on lumpy porridge and a thin slice of fat bacon, sandwiched between two thick chunks of bread.

'They do say that a soldier marches on his stomach. In which case, this particular soldier won't get far,' Thomas grumbled.

Lance ate uncomplainingly of the food that was shovelled out into tin bowls or on to tin plates. Since the Sports Day, and the obvious displeasure of his stern parent, he had lost heart, and was once again beset by doubts and fears. He envied Thomas the nice family of aunts and uncles, the fond mother and sisters, and the adoring grandmother, all so obviously proud of him.

It was in a depressed state of mind, with his thoughts wandering, that he failed to see the deep ditch the other riders had negotiated. His horse stumbled, and he was thrown heavily to the ground. Some hours later, he awakened in the sick bay with his right arm in splints, his head bandaged, and his body stiff with bruises. It was cool and quiet, and a gentle breeze stirred the muslin curtains. He lay there, disinclined to move, and strangely comforted by his surroundings. His mind was clear, and his thoughts no longer troubled by his father's displeasure. It had never been any different, so why had he been so disappointed and discouraged?

Since he was removed from the nursery at an early age, and sent away to a boarding school, his mother had been the only person who cared, and her love and understanding the only lifeline to which he could cling in a boyhood singularly devoid of close relationships. He had not expected to see her at Sports Day, for she seldom attended any formal occasions with his father. Her delicate health was due in part to child bearing; too many children too quickly. He would see her again for a brief period before he joined his father's regiment as a junior subaltern. In the meantime, he had Thomas and George, two splendid fellows, who had included him in everything since that day they met on the train. He was grateful for their friendship. They had taught him the confidence he had been sadly lacking, liked him, and teased him, as though he were a younger brother.

In a few short months, he had almost forgotten his wretched boyhood. He was a man. In future, neither the rifle nor the vaulting horse would defeat him! With this satisfactory resolution he fell asleep, and dreamed he was leading his men into battle on a white charger, clothed in the suit of armour worn by one of his forebears, at the Battle of Agincourt!

The weeks and the months slipped away. The cadets had a week's leave at Christmas to spend with their families, but the majority, including The Three

Musketeers, were glad to get back to Sandhurst and the world of men. Disciplined, hardened and keen, they had already established a liaison with the army that only ex-soldiers could teach. The Governor, at the head of the establishment, was not just a figurehead, but a personality, known, admired and respected for his own record of military service.

Lance was out of action for several weeks and had the option to go on leave, but preferred to spend his convalescence on further studies. He would need special coaching in shooting, drill and fencing as soon as he could use his right arm. With so much time to spend on his studies, it was not surprising that he finished the course well ahead of Thomas and George in theory, although some way behind in the practical.

To the utter disgust of Thomas, his hated rival achieved the coveted title of Best Cadet of the Year and led the column of marching cadets at the passing-out parade. George was included in the top ten, but Thomas had only himself to blame for being placed at number thirteen, since he had lost a number of marks after Christmas for insubordination, and had been confined to barracks, on bread and water, for a whole week. But Thomas would always be in trouble with superior officers, because of his quick temper, unless he learned to control it. It was humiliating to discover George had beaten him, for George was a plodder and had none of the advantages of a public school education. But George was a very determined plodder, and Lance had helped him with his studies.

There was an element of sadness as well as eager anticipation during those final weeks at Sandhurst. It was doubtful whether the three good friends would meet again once they were posted to their respective regiments. For Thomas, however, the exciting demands of Aldershot quickly dispelled any lingering regret at parting with George and Lance. It was a world that included women and children, and the strictest protocol was observed.

In a very short time Thomas was enjoying the social life of the regiment as well as the disciplined routine of drills and parades. As a junior subaltern, he was invited to his first ball and, being Thomas, fell in love with the beautiful daughter of his commanding officer! It was a most romantic affair, and inevitable from the moment they faced each other in a quadrille. Rosalind Maitland was seventeen, a wilful, high-spirited young lady, accustomed to getting her own way, with an indulgent father. Her mother had died in childbirth, and she had been taught the usual accomplishments of a Victorian miss by a string of anxious and agitated governesses, none of whom had succeeded in controlling such a difficult pupil. They matched each other perfectly, in every way – a golden girl and a golden youth, in a setting that suited them both to perfection. A tiny, dainty figure in her first ball gown of ivory satin, trimmed with rosebuds, she was shoulder high, and her blue eyes danced with mischief.

They had been formally introduced. Protocol had to be observed, and she had already danced with the senior officers and was entitled to enjoy the rest of the evening with the young subalterns. Thomas would be yet another to add to her many admirers. It was fun to flirt and tease when you were just out of the schoolroom, and knew yourself to be very pretty indeed. Yet she found, to her discomfort, the blue eyes that met her own were not deferential, shy or embarrassed. They were mocking, and she disliked being mocked. He was, after all, a very junior subaltern from Sandhurst, and she the only adored daughter of his commanding officer!

He had taken her little gloved hand in his own gloved hand, and she could feel its strength, and his tall, erect figure, in the immaculate dress uniform, held a strong fascination. For all her pretence, Rosalind was as innocent and ignorant of the opposite sex as the majority of young ladies in her class of society. This particular young subaltern was the handsomest in the room but it was instinct only that told her he was different. Her heart fluttered like a bird in her breast as she lifted her proud little head and returned his bold glance.

'You are holding my hand too tightly, Sir!' said she, haughtily.

'I am fully aware of it, Madam!' he retorted, quite unabashed – and squeezed it harder.

Chaperoned by the Colonel's sister, there was no opportunity to do anything more than play at a mild flirtation, and the subalterns who had already claimed the remaining dances were unlikely to forget. As the spoilt darling of the regiment, she could pick and choose, and more than one ambitious young officer had hopes of a betrothal in the near future.

The regiment would be sailing for five years' service in India, and only six months remained of their term in Aldershot. Six months for the un-married men to find themselves wives; six months for the married men to find themselves expectant fathers.

Colonel Maitland watched his lovely daughter with fatherly pride, and more than a little anxiety. If only her mother had lived, he would not feel so respon-sible. The years had passed so quickly, and the regiment had already seen service in the Far East under his command. Rosalind was still a child, too young for marriage, he told himself, then remem-bered he had married her mother at the same age – a man old enough to be her father, in love for the first time in his life. Rosalind was the living image of his lovely Celia, and there was pain as well as pride in the grey eyes that could be cold as steel when occasion demanded. He wanted her happiness. He wanted her to choose wisely from the officers on his staff, but he knew full well that when she fell in love, wisdom would have no part in it. Impulse, instinct, these feminine qualities would decide, and he, the fond parent, could only wait and watch, and smile indulgently at her naughtiness.

'Just look at that little minx! She is quite incorri-gible! She flirts with every one of them, irrespective of age or rank,' his sister complained, fluttering her fan in some agitation.

'Let her alone, Millie. It's her first ball, and she is wearing her first ball gown. And she knows she is the prettiest girl in the room.'

'I daresay, but too precocious for my liking. If I had had my way, she would have been left in one of those respectable establishments for young ladies, not dragged halfway round the world with a stupid governess, too insipid to assert her authority.'

'You know I could never leave her behind. She belongs to the regiment.'

'And she will probably marry some besotted young fool with nothing but his Army pay to support them both.'

'If she is happy with her choice, I shall not complain. One thing is certain, Millie. It will not be a civilian. Now that really would upset me. But all her young companions are here, within her own familiar environment. All her short life she has been surrounded by the regiment, was born and bred to the sound of marching feet and the beating of drums. It's in the blood, Millie.'

His sister sighed. She was no longer young, to be dragged halfway round the world again, for the second time. It would be so very pleasant to spend a little time with her married sister in Broadstairs, and get to know her nieces and nephews. But she would never leave Teddy and that troublesome child to the care of native servants. A firm hand was needed and a watchful eye, for they were not to be trusted. Native servants on the Northwest Frontier of India would be no different from the native servants in Singapore, and she would do her duty as a Christian. Both her health and her temper suffered in the tropics. It was unfortunate that the regiment was once again posted to a climate that disagreed with her digestion. One could not be too careful. Native servants must never be left to their own resources. Water must be boiled, and hands washed, before handling food. Their ignorance was appalling, and their habits quite disgusting. Wasn't it due to her untiring efforts in Singapore that they all had escaped that wretched epidemic of dysentery? But Teddy had assured her that in India all the wives and children of the officers, with their English nurses and governesses, would be sent to one of the hill stations for three months of the year, and she would naturally be included in that welcome exodus from the plains.

She had seen photographs of the spacious bungalows, set in pretty gardens, with lawns and flower beds, gay with English flowers. There would be afternoon tea on the lawn, and no need for those bothersome mosquito nets on their beds. The men would join them for a month's leave, and then there would be all kinds of entertainment: tennis parties, picnics, riding in the hills, gymkhanas and sports days. She had read all about it in one of Mrs Henry Wood's novels – or was it Mr Dickens? Although an avid reader, she seldom remembered the name of the author.

She was a born worrier and could always foresee trouble. Leaving Teddy to the careless attention of native servants while she enjoyed a long holiday in the hill station had already presented a problem. She had reminded him of that awful epidemic of dysentery in Singapore, and he had promised to eat all his meals in the Mess, and kissed her affectionately. They were very close, in spite of their differences over Rosalind.

Thomas was sulking. He had wanted to claim the

supper dance, but it was already promised to a dashing, dark-eyed subaltern, very much favoured at the moment, and with the advantage of three months in which to get acquainted. A stab of jealousy made Thomas realize that he had again met his match. The rivalry between the two would be as bitterly contested as that at Sandhurst; the price was the Colonel's daughter.

He watched her walk away on the arm of the young subaltern, and cursed himself for a fool. He should have realized that the men would outnumber the girls by two to one, and that all the dances had been claimed in advance for this particular girl. He had lingered too long in the Mess, enjoying the company of his fellows, a group of young officers already betrothed to girls in their own parts of the country, to whom they would be married before the regiment sailed for India. One of them had mentioned the pretty daughter of their commanding officer as a mere child, only just out of the schoolroom.

His eighteen months at Sandhurst in a world of men had not prepared him for the atmosphere of Aldershot, where women and children, and young, unattached maidens were so much in evidence. The ranks had their own families housed in crowded barracks some distance from the officers' quarters. Thomas had cast a cursory glance at the drab-looking women and the swarms of children as he cantered past on his well-groomed horse on his arrival last evening. The husbands and fathers would present a formidable force when assembled on the parade ground. It was his duty to get to know the men of the battalion to which he had been allocated. He would do his duty, and they would not find him lacking in qualities of leadership. But he would not win their loyalty and affection as George and Lance would do so naturally in their respective regiments. Indeed, his sergeant had already sized him up with the unflattering comment, 'Conceited young bastard!'

Dancing dutifully for the rest of the evening with the bevy of unattached maidens, so obviously hoping for an attachment, Thomas smiled and bowed so gallantly that each in turn felt she had made a conquest. All the time, he had eyes for only one in that crowded ballroom, and when she swept past in the arms of her partner in the last waltz, he had the strongest urge to claim her and waltz her away. She met his look boldly, provocatively, in passing. There was no shyness in her eyes and none of the coyness he had found so irritating in his other partners. Indeed, her glance had been so challenging, he could feel his pulses racing, and his step faltering.

'I beg your pardon, Ma'am,' he said contritely to the plain little mouse of a girl in his arms.

'Don't mention it, Sir,' she whispered, with a sigh of resignation. Poor Mama! Her three plain daughters had no dowry to attract a future husband and all were doomed to the state of spinsterhood. Her future as a governess had already been decided. The handsome young subaltern behaved impeccably when the dance was over. He escorted her back to her Mama, smiled and bowed, and she curtsied and thanked him prettily, but it was expected, and it was just a formality. She smiled at his retreating back.

Thomas would have been surprised; she was really quite pretty when she smiled.

His duties kept him occupied during the day, but at the haunting notes of the bugle at sunset, and the lowering of the flag, he was free to join his fellow officers in the Mess.

The handsome, dark-eyed Welshman made no pretence of his dislike for the newcomer, however, and his surly manner was deliberately objectionable. Having already established himself as a favourite with Rosalind, he had no intention of losing his claim to a blue-eyed charmer who fancied himself a lady-killer. Rosalind had teased him about young Cartwright, pretending to be enamoured by his good looks and dashing air, so he was on his guard. His dark eyes held a challenging directness, and his singing Welsh voice a thrilling resonance.

The first time she heard him sing at the carol concert, she found herself falling in love with a voice. Emotionally immature and easily swayed by poetically romantic thoughts, she had endowed the young Welshman with qualities he did not possess. He sang as naturally as he breathed, and his stubborn pride and nasty temper were held in check in her company. Always on his best behaviour with Rosalind, he was seen in his true colours in the Mess. 'A surly young blighter' was the general opinion. To have won the favour of the Colonel's daughter massaged his vanity, and he saw himself betrothed to the fair Rosalind before the regiment sailed to India.

It soon became apparent in the close community of

the garrison, where nothing could be hidden for long, that only two of the young subalterns were competing for the hand of the Colonel's daughter, and their rivalry became a topic of interest and amusement in the Mess. Bets were placed, and the odds were constantly changing as first one, then the other seemed to be favoured on those early morning rides. An accomplished horsewoman and fearless in the saddle, she would challenge her escort to a gallop as soon as they were out of range. A groom always accompanied them at the Colonel's insistence, but Thomas soon discovered he could be bribed to lag behind. Providing they all returned to the stables together, nobody was any the wiser.

'Where is the groom?' Rosalind demanded, as he reined in his spirited horse one morning after the gallop.

'We seem to have lost him, Ma'am,' Thomas replied, innocently. Both were flushed and breathless, and their horses were sweating. 'We must walk them till they have cooled down,' he decided, and slid from the saddle.

'You think very highly of your horse, do you not?' she asked.

'Very highly, Ma'am,' he agreed, as he lifted her down.

'Stop calling me Ma'am!' she ordered.

His hands were clasped about her tiny waist, and his eyes were mocking. 'What do I call you then?' he asked.

'I have a name,' she retorted.

'Miss Maitland?'

'Correct.'

'I will try to remember,' said he. Dropping his hands, he turned away to speak soothingly to the horse, and she was piqued by his indifference. It had been a disturbing moment when he lifted her down, and her heart was still fluttering.

It was the first time she had been alone with him, and she had not expected to receive less attention than the horse. Now he was walking away, leading the horse, and she followed slowly, choked with angry resentment.

When he had walked the horse for a distance of fifty yards or so, he stopped to look back, and his heart missed a beat. She had tried to spring up on to her horse's back. Startled by sudden movement, the animal had reared and plunged nervously. She was hanging round its neck when Thomas reached her. Her hat had fallen to the ground, and she was convulsed with laughter as he lifted her down for the second time.

'It was so funny,' she gasped. 'I do declare I have never tried to get on to his back this way before, and he doesn't care for it, do you, my darling?'

'It was foolish. You could have been badly injured,' he scolded.

'And your fault, Sir!' It was her turn to scold. Her moods were as variable as the weather.

'I do apologize, Miss Maitland.'

'And so you should. Put me down.'

'Not till you say I am forgiven.'

She couldn't bear it. She thought she would die. Surely he must hear her heart beating? 'You are forgiven.' Her voice was a whisper, and when he set her down, she swayed, and he caught her in his arms.

'Rosalind,' he murmured huskily.

They both were caught up in a moment of such ecstasy, all pretence was abandoned. She lifted her head and breathed 'Thomas' and he kissed her trembling mouth with a tenderness he did not know he possessed. She closed her eyes and shivered. David had stolen kisses, tentatively, always a little afraid that his daring might end their relationship. There was a difference. Thomas had no doubts and no hesitation. There was a masterliness about him that she found deliciously exciting. For the first time in her young life she was totally enslaved, and she lifted her arms and clasped them about his neck. Starry-eyed, she gazed up at him. She was like a child who had just been given an unexpected gift.

'I love you, I love you,' she said, with trusting innocence, for he was almost a stranger.

'My sweet Rosalind.' He kissed her again, and they clung together. She was so tiny, she swung from his neck, and he held her close, pressed to his strong, virile body. Their two hearts beat as one.

It was unlike anything Rosalind had imagined in her girlish dreams, and Thomas was more handsome and more wonderful than the knight she had imagined.

As for Thomas, he felt it was so infinitely sweet and precious that no impure thoughts should be allowed to desecrate such tenderness. Yet the thoughts were there, and his racing pulses proclaimed the urgent need to possess her. But this was no wanton housemaid to be bedded for a shilling, or the impetuous Kate, with her blatant appeal. This was the girl he would wed if he played his cards discreetly – an innocent child, fresh from the schoolroom, adorable in her young and trusting admiration.

He took her face between his hands and gazed into her starry eyes, blue as the sky on a Summer day, and he wondered afresh at her beauty. Every feature was perfect, framed in the mane of golden hair, for today she wore it loose. She was the loveliest creature he had ever known, and the most desirable, but desire must wait, and he must not lose control. It would not be easy, for they were two of a kind, indulged from infancy, demanding in their arrogant self-esteem. She was so intense, so wilful, this adorable Rosalind.

'My sweet, we must be careful. The groom could be watching us, and your father might prevent us from meeting if he knew we were in love.'

'But I shall tell Papa I wish to marry you.'

'Not yet, my sweet. It is too soon. I am a new-comer to the regiment, and I have to prove my worth as an officer before I can ask for the hand of the daughter of my commanding officer.'

She pouted when he unclasped her clinging hands. 'You don't love me!' she said, accusingly, and turned away.

'I adore you,' he said, his voice broken with emotion.

And she turned back and took his hand, and pressed it to her cheek. 'There are tears in your eyes, my darling. What is troubling you?' she asked.

'Your father – he may have other plans for his lovely daughter – a captain, a major perhaps.'

She shook her head and smiled at his distress. 'Papa would never stand in the way of my happiness.'

'You are sure of that?'

'Positive.'

He bent his head and touched her lips with his hungry mouth. But the hunger must be controlled, and his aching loins must wait. Three months, or more? It would be intolerable, this waiting period, and he still had to fight his rivals – with fists, not swords.

'We are pledged, my sweet. Now we must go back. I am on duty in less than an hour, and I have to change.' He lifted her into the saddle, and ran back to his own horse. Swinging himself into the saddle with easy grace, he lifted his head and laughed aloud. The gods had favoured him yet again. Grandmama would be so pleased and proud. He would write and tell her he was betrothed to the lovely daughter of his commanding officer.

'It is only what he deserves. Only the best is good enough for my adored grandson,' she would tell the rest of the family.

But Thomas had reckoned without the natural impulse of a young girl in love to declare her love. 'Be careful!' Thomas had warned; carefulness was not a quality she recognized.

Breakfast was the worst time in the day to confront a man with anything of a personal or domestic nature, and Colonel Maitland was no exception. He liked to glance through the copy of *The Times* that he found folded neatly beside his plate every morning. Punctuality was a fetish. Rosalind was only a few minutes late, but he had already finished his porridge and started on bacon and eggs. He had breakfasted alone after his wife died, his young daughter ate with her nurse or her governess, and his habits had become a matter of disciplined convention. Having adjusted to the new regime of allowing his daughter to be there to pour his coffee, he expected her presence on time. So he stood up to greet her, without the customary smile of welcome, and reminded her gruffly that she was late.

'Good morning, Papa.' Ignoring the gruffness, she kissed his cheek affectionately. Even the most indulgent of parents have moments when requests for favours are not welcome, but his young daughter had not yet been expected to practise patience.

When the servant had brought in the boiled egg to which she was accustomed, he withdrew quietly, and they were alone. Still in her riding habit, for she would be riding again later with a party of young friends and the attendant grooms, she looked much younger than her seventeen years, her hair tied back with a ribbon, her cheeks glowing and eyes bright.

'Papa, something wonderful has happened!' said she, leaning towards him.

His mouth twisted in a wry smile. She had a way of looking at the most ordinary events through rose-coloured spectacles, an admirable trait that emphasized her extreme youth. At any time other than breakfast, he would listen to her excited prattle with a mixture of tolerance and amusement.

She did not wait for his response, but announced with breathless importance, 'I have fallen in love.'

'Again? Who is it this time?' he teased. She had been falling in and out of love since puberty, when her delight in her little pointed breasts had embarrassed her governess and amused her indulgent Papa. The music master, the dancing instructor, the groom and every good-looking subaltern had endured her girlish infatuation for brief periods. She was like a butterfly in her pretty flutterings.

'This is the man I intend to marry,' she told him.

'Rubbish!' he contradicted, testily.

'It's true. We are pledged.'

He frowned. 'Who is this man?'

'Second-lieutenant Cartwright. His name is Thomas.'

'The newest and youngest subaltern from Sandhurst?'

'Yes, Papa.'

'How dare he!' Now his grey eyes flashed with an angry gleam, and his voice was curt. 'Since when has this young scoundrel seen fit to take such a liberty?'

'This morning. It was so very romantic, Papa. He is so handsome, so masterful, so altogether divine.' She sighed ecstatically.

'What was the groom doing while all this ridiculous nonsense was taking place?'

'He was – he was lagging behind.'

'These early morning rides must stop. I will not have you exposed to such blatant effrontery. I shall speak to this young man very severely. The groom has obviously been bribed, and I will not have my daughter made a laughing stock in the stables. The time has come to practise a little dignity and restraint, for my sake, if not for your own. As for being pledged to a man who joined the regiment but three short months ago, I have never heard of such a ridiculous notion. Let me hear no more of this, Rosalind!' He pushed away his discarded breakfast, dabbed his mouth with the starched napkin, flung it on the table with an impatient gesture, and stood up.

Rosalind had never been more surprised and shocked, but she quickly recovered. 'I shall marry him! You can't stop me!' she declared, passionately.

'We shall see about that, Miss!' he retorted, and left her sitting there, too choked to eat, and too furious to realize what such a threat could entail.

So Thomas faced his commanding officer some hours later, made more than a little apprehensive by the summons. There could be only one reason, for he had been particularly careful in obeying the orders of his superior officers and had not neglected his duties to his men. The grey eyes that had welcomed him so cordially but a few short weeks ago were cold as steel, and the atmosphere in the office could be cut with a knife.

The Colonel surveyed his young subaltern, and noticed, not for the first time, the military bearing, the alertness, and the fearless glance in the compelling blue eyes. He knew the history of every young officer who joined the regiment, and heredity counted for a great deal in the character and mentality. Leaders were born, not made, but even so they had to learn to control their own actions, their thoughts and emotions before they could be trusted with authority. He had no favourites, but recognized the qualities of leadership instantly.

'So, Subaltern Cartwright, my daughter tells me you are pledged?' A cynical note had crept into his clipped voice, and he tapped impatiently on the desk with a pencil. 'Well, are you or are you not pledged to my daughter?' he barked.

'We have an understanding, Sir,' Thomas admitted.

'What exactly is an *understanding*?'

'We have declared our love, Sir.'

'Indeed? A simple matter, no doubt, with the groom bribed to lag behind?'

Thomas was feeling rather foolish, standing there, stiffly to attention, explaining the impulse that had prompted such a promise. Silly little fool! Why hadn't she kept her mouth shut? Love could wait. The regiment came first, would always come first, in his priorities.

'My daughter has only recently left the school-room. She is still a child, with a child's sensibilities. It was not the behaviour of a gentleman, Subaltern Cartwright.'

'No, Sir.'

'Do you intend to pursue your advantage?'

'No, Sir. I am persuaded it was a grave mistake.'

'You swear?'

'I swear, Sir.'

A sigh escaped those tight lips, and the grey eyes softened. The subject was dropped. A more urgent matter had presented itself since early morning.

'You may stand at ease,' he told his young subordinate.

'Thank you, Sir.'

'I wish you to report forthwith to Captain Vincent. He is an authority on manoeuvres, and each company in turn receives instruction. Two subalterns and a sergeant accompany each group. Choose your men carefully. Subaltern Jones and Sergeant Murphy have already been delegated. All equipment must be carried, including provisions for fourteen days. It is a test of endurance. No tents. Sleeping rough and getting the feel of the territory chosen. A kind of rehearsal you might say for a reconnoitre on the Frontier; not in numbers, of course. We patrol the Northwest Frontier with small groups of carefully selected men, under one officer. The smaller the group, the more likely they are to succeed. The tribesmen are born to it, and know every inch of the terrain. We cannot emulate their tactics, but we can follow the example of our predecessors. It is a sacred trust, handed down to us. We have the men. We have the horses. We have the new rifles, but we still have a lot to learn. You follow my meaning?'

'Perfectly, Sir.'

'That is all. You are dismissed.'

Thomas sprang to attention, saluted smartly, and marched out of the room. He was sweating profusely, but he was also tremendously relieved, for he had not known what to expect in that formidable presence. To get away from the garrison on these manoeuvres was as good as a reprieve, for he had been getting bored with all the drills and parades.

Captain Vincent was a taciturn individual and a strict disciplinarian. As for Sergeant Murphy, his voice alone was enough to make the newest recruit sweat! He chuckled, gave his horse an affectionate pat and vaulted into the saddle.

'Jason, my beauty, we have won another round,' he confided.

Jason snorted and tossed his proud head. A stallion with Arab blood in his veins, and a man on his back who knew no fear, would challenge those frontier tribesmen on their scruffy mounts – or die in the attempt.

Aunt Millie, the Colonel's sister, who breakfasted in bed, had heard the raised voices in the dining-room with some surprise. Her brother was normally a most agreeable man and seldom raised his voice under his own roof.

Settling her stiffened limbs more comfortably, she poured a second cup of tea from the dainty tea-pot, and wondered what had provoked his anger with the child he adored. The arthritis was gradually crippling her movements, but she did her best to hide the infirmity from her brother, and the doctor had prescribed small doses of laudanum for the pain.

She was spreading marmalade on a slice of toast when she heard the running footsteps on the stairs. Then her niece's bedroom door opened and closed with a slam. A moment later, the unmistakable sound of sobbing reached her ears, but caused no dismay and very little sympathy. It was an emotional age, and her temperamental niece often gave vent to her feelings in a flood of tears. So she finished her breakfast and took up her copy of the *Morning Post*. The sobbing gradually subsided, then all was quiet. To offer comfort at such times was a mistake. 'Go away! Leave me alone!' was the petulant response to her last attempt. It would pass, she told herself, without her interference.

Whatever had gone wrong would be put right at the end of the day, and there would be smiles and hugs and all would be forgiven. Teddy was to blame for spoiling the child. She had warned him repeatedly that he was making a rod for his own back, but he would not listen. He had seen her naughtiness and high spirits in the schoolroom as proof of her intelligence, but the governesses would have preferred a more amenable pupil. Now that she was finished with the schoolroom, her wilfulness had become a disturbing factor between brother and sister, and they were constantly in disagreement. Millie was not looking forward to a five-year sojourn in India. Indeed, she was dreading it. But her duty was plain. Teddy saw no danger in his daughter flirting with every good-looking officer in the regiment. They flattered her, and she teased them with her favours, first one, then another.

'Let her alone; 'tis a harmless pastime,' he insisted.

Millie put the paper aside. She could not concentrate on national or international affairs with her mind on a domestic problem in her own small world.

Rosalind was a favourite in her own circle of friends. All daughters of the regiment, they had known each other since childhood, but the other girls had been left at boarding school when the regiment was serving in the Far East. Now these same girls had grown into young ladies of marriageable age, and their fond mamas were on the alert for suitable husbands committed to sailing to India. The garrison was their natural environment, and they had no need to look elsewhere. Their daughters, whether plain or pretty, had been taught all the virtues of Victorian womanhood, together with the usual accomplishments. They could play a little Chopin and Brahms on the pianoforte, accompany any gentleman desirous of singing a drawing-room ballad. They could paint a pretty landscape and sew a fine seam. They were charming partners in the waltz and the quadrille, and they listened attentively to any subject, no matter how boring, that was introduced. But they were all of a pattern, moulded by the conventions and principles of upper-class society. Rosalind was strikingly different.

When Millie had bathed and dressed, she tapped on the door of her niece's room and went in. Rosalind was lying fully clothed on the bed, sleeping soundly, exhausted by her weeping, no doubt, poor child, her aunt decided, and went out, closing the door quietly. It would not be the first time of recent months that she had cried herself to sleep, and when she awoke, the reason for the tears would be forgotten. In some ways she was still a child with her tears and tantrums, yet she could be such an amusing companion on a shopping expedition in town, a Summer picnic, or a performance of a Shakespeare play on a Winter evening by their own group of talented players.

She was at the difficult age of seventeen – part child, part woman, ignorant of the facts of life, yet obviously attracted to the opposite sex. If only her indulgent brother could see the danger.

It was mid-morning when Rosalind awoke, with a heavy head and no desire to move. The crumpled riding habit was proof that her troubled dreams had not exaggerated the situation. Papa had been so stern. She had never known him to speak so angrily. But he was *old*. He must be nearly fifty years of age, so what could he know of love? She recalled every precious moment of that brief encounter.

'Thomas.' She whispered his name, heard his voice, husky with emotion, felt his strength as he lifted her down. She had been kissed before. It was fun to tease, and to boast of stolen kisses to her friends. But this was different. They had declared their love. They were pledged. Such rapture could not be contained. Why had Papa been so angry? Couldn't he see that she wanted to marry Thomas more than anything in the world? She would die if he was forbidden to see her again. Never in her whole life had she loved anyone as she loved Thomas. It had happened so suddenly, she was near to swooning. What was happening to Thomas now?

If Papa had ordered him to stay away, that order must be obeyed. Such a junior officer had very little authority, and very little status. Protocol had to be observed. But she loved him, and he loved her.

When the door opened to admit Aunt Millie, with the mid-morning hot chocolate and biscuits, she complained sulkily, 'I don't want it. Please take it away.'

'But you had no breakfast, dear.'

'I was not hungry.'

'What has happened to upset you?'

'You must ask Papa. I have no wish to discuss it.'

'Very well, dear. I do not wish to pry.' Aunt Millie sat down on the edge of the bed. 'Drink a little of the hot chocolate and you will feel better.'

Rosalind sighed, and sat up, pouting with annoyance, and Aunt Millie placed the tray on her knees.

'Wouldn't you feel more comfortable if you took off your riding habit?' she suggested, tentatively. 'Unless you intend to ride with the Browning girls?' she added, for the twins were particular favourites.

Rosalind shook her head. 'I don't know what I want to do. My head aches.'

'A short walk in the fresh air would be best. We have to exercise the puppy.'

'I had forgotten the puppy.'

'It has not forgotten you. It has been whining outside your door.'

'Why did you not let it in?'

'A bedroom is no place for a dog.'

'What does it matter? I shall ask Papa.'

'Drink up your chocolate and I will let it in.'

The puppy was a recent gift from Subaltern Jones, and quite a novelty, since her other admirers sent flowers or chocolates. But it was a thoughtless gift, and the Colonel had not appreciated such a gesture from one of his junior officers. It was presumptuous.

His sister was inclined to agree with him. In any case, it would be left behind when the regiment sailed for India. Quarantine restrictions had to be observed, and there were no facilities for dogs on a troopship.

The puppy was scratching at the door, and it slipped in quickly when the door opened, barking joyously.

'Not on the bed, please, dear!' Aunt Millie pleaded.

It was too late. With a single bound it was there, cradled in the girl's arms.

'Now I shall never get it house-trained. Really, Rosalind. You would try the patience of a saint,' declared the poor woman. And she picked up the tray, went out of the room, and limped downstairs.

She had to admit, however, as the day wore on, that her niece was looking pale, and her normal high spirits had completely deserted her. Only the puppy enjoyed the walk. A light lunch was served at midday. Rosalind picked at the grilled sole and creamed potatoes, and refused her favourite chocolate pudding. She was not hungry, she insisted, and would lie down till tea-time. Her friends would be informed that she did not feel like entertaining them. They would be disappointed, and obliged to take tea in the drawing-room with Miss Maitland and their fond Mamas, who would gossip about the latest scandal and the trouble with the servants.

It was all very boring. It was such fun to spend a Winter afternoon with Rosalind in her cosy sitting-room, chattering about their favourite subalterns, re-trimming their bonnets and arranging their hair in becoming styles that would most likely meet with disapproval. The twins would play duets on the piano, and Davies would carry up a heavy tray of tea at four o'clock.

It was futile for her aunt to argue that lively company was exactly what Rosalind needed, with her spirits so low. She could be as stubborn as a mule when she made up her mind, Aunt Millie reflected, as she watched the girl climbing the stairs with the dragging steps of an old woman.

Unfortunately, it was the one day in the week when the Colonel dined in the Mess with his senior officers, and would not be home till late. He had probably forgotten the incident at the breakfast table, but his anger had left his daughter in a state of dejection that even the puppy had not dispelled. It was back in its basket in the kitchen.

When she had given instructions for a tea-tray to be served to Rosalind at four o'clock, Aunt Millie settled down to enjoy her visitors. The privileged few invited to take tea with the Colonel's sister would not fail to inform their rivals. She had her favourites, and they basked in her good opinion.

They were all away by six o'clock, when she went upstairs to change for dinner and found her niece once again lying fully clothed on the bed. There were traces of tears on her pale cheeks, and the poor child was so exhausted with weeping that she could not be wakened.

'Rosalind! Wake up, dear. Rosalind!'

There was no response. Aunt Millie sighed. Whatever had gone wrong between father and daughter would have to be put right or there would be no peace for any of them. It was inconsistent, and so unlike her brother to be so angry with the child. Of course she was upset.

The tea tray was untouched on the bedside table. She left the door open, changed her dress and shoes, and went down to a lonely dinner. Her own company was a poor substitute for the lively conversation she normally enjoyed with father and daughter. Davies had explained that she had left the tea tray, and had not disturbed Miss Rosalind who was fast asleep. Another tray was sent up at seven o'clock, and this time it was brought down.

'She's that sound asleep, Ma'am, you would think she were dead,' the servant reported, testily. She was not a young woman to be traipsing up and down stairs with trays.

The words echoed in her mistress's mind with sinister persistence. Once again she climbed the stairs to take a closer look. Once again she raised her voice. 'Rosalind! Wake up, dear. Rosalind!' Grasping her shoulders, she lifted her up and gave her a good shake. The head lolled drunkenly. Drunk? Why should she touch the Colonel's whisky when she had never had anything more than a small glass of sherry before dinner? No, it was not whisky. There was no smell to her breath.

'Rosalind,' she whispered, and clasped the girl to her chest in a frantic embrace. She was very frightened, and in her fright her normal sensible reaction completely deserted her.

'Davies! Davies!' she shouted.

'Is something wrong, Ma'am?' the servant enquired, blandly from the doorway.

'Find the groom. Tell him to fetch the Colonel. He is dining in the Officers' Mess. Tell him to come immediately. Miss Rosalind is ill. Hurry, woman, hurry!'

'Yes, Ma'am.' Davies sighed resignedly. Such a fuss and pother.

It seemed an eternity to Millie that she sat on the bed, cradling the girl in her arms. All her complaints and disagreements were forgotten. She would never forgive herself if the child died. As for her brother, she dare not anticipate such a tragedy. His wife's death had left its mark on him. He would not marry again. Rosalind had grown into a replica of the mother who had died in giving her birth. The likeness was so extraordinary, it was quite uncanny.

In less than half an hour, Davies had the door open but was thrust aside. A moment later he was standing there, breathing heavily. 'What is it, Millie? What has happened?' he demanded.

Millie shook her head, too choked to speak.

'Give her to me,' he said, gently, and he took the limp little form and laid her back on the bed. Chafing her cold hands, he coaxed, 'Wake up, pet. It's Papa.' There was no response. Davies was hovering in the doorway. 'Tell the groom to fetch the doctor,' he barked.

'Yes, Sir.'

The whole house was astir now. Servants always responded more quickly to the Colonel's orders, it was noticed.

'How long has she been this way?' he asked his sister.

'Several hours. I thought she was sleeping. Poor child, she has been so upset all day, and hardly touched her food. You should not have scolded her so severely, dear. You know how sensitive she is. Did you have to be quite so angry? I have never seen her so distressed.'

'How would you have reacted if the child announced she was pledged to marry a young subaltern she had known for a few weeks?'

'*Marry*?'

'Yes, marry. And very determined, I can assure you. You can't stop me, she informed me.'

'And what did you answer?'

'I can't remember. I was so angry.'

'You could have reasoned with her. It was unlike you to walk out and leave her in tears.'

'She was not in tears when I left. She was defiant.'

'But she has since been weeping till she was utterly exhausted.'

'I'm sorry.' He was still clasping her hands, and his voice was husky with emotion. 'This is something more than exhaustion. It seems more like a coma.'

'I'm frightened, Teddy.'

'So am I,' he confessed, with anguished eyes.

The Army surgeon had been called out by an anxious midwife earlier in the day, and had only just started on his evening meal after delivering the child. The young officer had been profuse in his thanks. It was their first child, and they had been married for only seven months. It was not the first time the doctor had reluctantly agreed to call it a premature baby. To save face in such a patronizing huddle of gossiping matrons, it was sometimes necessary for the doctor to bend his own principles. The silly young fools had learned their lesson. His wife was clucking impatiently.

'Who would be a doctor's wife?'

'Who indeed, my love?' he agreed, and kissed her cheek. The groom was waiting with the horses, and they rode away.

Davies had the door open. She took his hat, and he hurried upstairs. He was no stranger to this house, and he remembered that night of sadness when he had delivered the child and lost the mother. Such tragedies in his profession were unavoidable, but always upsetting. It seemed such a cruel fate for a man to lose his wife and be left with an infant.

He greeted the Colonel and his sister with his accustomed gruffness and bent over his patient. The pulse was weak. He lifted an eyelid. Miss Maitland was explaining the situation in great agitation, but he cut her short.

'The child is drugged,' he told them.

'*Drugged?*' the Colonel exclaimed, in horrified disbelief. His sister was weeping. 'But how? When? There is nothing in the house,' the Colonel protested, spreading his hands in a helpless gesture.

'The laudanum, Ma'am. Where do you keep the laudanum I prescibed for the pain?' the doctor was asking.

'In the bathroom cupboard.'

'Will you fetch it, please?'

She hurried away, and came back with the bottle. 'It's half empty, Doctor.' Her voice was choked.

'Not enough for a fatal dose, but she must be awakened,' said he. Turning back to his patient, he slapped her cheeks, then dragged her off the bed.

'Take the other arm, Sir. She must be walked,' he told the Colonel.

Limp as a rag doll, her head lolling, they dragged her between them, back and forth, along the corridor, Aunt Millie weeping and protesting at such rough treatment.

'It's the only effective treatment I know for a coma, Ma'am, and it could take an hour or more.'

'I can't bear to watch it.'

'Then don't watch, Ma'am. You could ask Cook to have some strong coffee ready.'

'Yes, Doctor.' She went away, dabbing her eyes, and left them with the unconscious girl.

'I had no idea you had prescribed laudanum for my sister. She had never complained to me that she was in pain. What's wrong with her?' asked the Colonel, testily. As if he hadn't enough on his mind without an ailing sister.

'Miss Maitland is not a complaining lady, but she suffers acutely from arthritis for which there is no cure. Small doses of laudanum relieve the pain, temporarily.'

'And put my daughter's life at risk?'

'A million-to-one chance that she would need such a drastic remedy for her depression, and she is unlikely to repeat such an impulse. She is going to feel very sick and wretched for several days. What happened, Sir? She is normally such a happy child.'

'I blame myself. I lost my temper.' He sighed. 'How could I be expected to know she would react so foolishly?'

'She is very young, Sir, and highly strung.'

'Yes.'

'Was it a strictly private matter?'

'No, that is, I thought I had dealt with it and the young man in question, but now I must confess I was too hasty. My daughter tells me she is in love with Subaltern Cartwright. He joined the regiment but a few weeks ago, straight from Sandhurst. She tells me they are already pledged. It's sheer nonsense, and I told her so. What can I do? She has always had her way with me. She must marry the fellow.'

'It would seem to be the answer to the problem, Sir. Your daughter is a very determined young lady. Would you say this Subaltern Cartwright was an ambitious fellow, with an eye for promotion?'

'That would apply to the majority. I liked the fellow. He took all the blame for such a hasty decision, but, knowing my daughter, he would need to be completely indifferent to her blandishments to resist the temptation. If she has her way, and I couldn't risk a repetition of this, he will find himself married to a very strong-willed young woman, with a complete lack of obedience. She knows she can pick and choose, and I must admit her choice is understandable. They are well matched in looks, and Cartwright has the making of a fine officer. What more could I expect, Doctor? There is nothing in this world more important to me than my daughter's happiness.'

'Then the sooner she knows, Sir, the quicker the recovery.'

And they continued to walk her for another hour or so, till she lifted her head, opened her eyes, gave a shuddering breath, and began to retch. The doctor carried her into the bathroom, where she was violently sick. 'Better up than down, my dear,' said he, with gruff kindness.

But she was still too weak to stand, and clung to her father with the pathetic helplessness of a child. In all her short life she had never been so close to death, and both were aware of the tragedy that had been averted, and too choked to speak.

'We will have that coffee now, if you please,' the doctor called downstairs.

The Colonel sat on the edge of the bed with his arm about the girl's shoulders, holding the cup to her lips while she sipped the hot, strong coffee. Gradually the colour crept back into her pale cheeks, and she stopped shuddering. Aunt Millie sat beside her, smoothing the lank hair from the damp forehead, talking soothingly. And Davies hovered in the doorway, waiting for further orders, her mouth agape. She, too, had been badly frightened. 'Shall I serve the whisky in the drawing-room now, Sir?' she asked.

'An excellent suggestion, eh, Doctor?' the Colonel agreed.

'Don't leave me, Papa,' Rosalind pleaded, tearfully.

'I shall be back in ten minutes, pet. Drink another cup of that strong coffee. We don't want you falling

217

asleep again. We have the doctor to thank for waking you up.'

'I didn't want to wake up. I wanted to die.'

'Why should you want to do that when you have the whole of life before you?'

'Because Papa would not let me marry the man I love.'

'Supposing I told you he had changed his mind?'

The Colonel smiled and kissed her cheek. 'Only if you promise never again to give us such a nasty fright.'

'Dearest Papa. I promise.'

Peace was restored, and once again Rosalind had her way.

'What she really deserves is a good spanking, and I hope she gets it from her future husband,' the doctor told his wife, as he finished his interrupted meal. 'I don't envy that young fellow. She will make life hell for him if she does not get her own way. They will fight like cat and dog, I shouldn't wonder.'

'My dear, how dreadful!'

'Not for some. I have known married couples who actually enjoyed fighting for the pleasure of making up. It's just a question of hormones and heredity, of course. Two strong personalities are much more likely to disagree, especially when the woman is the stronger of the two. A man likes to be the master in his own house. I was fortunate, my love, that you never disputed that right.'

'Why should I? Surely a wife should know her place?'

'It's a debatable point, Sophie, and the young

generation of women are not so inclined to adhere to the principles and moral standards of our gracious Queen. Times are changing, and the Colonel's daughter, as a newly married wife, could have quite a sway among the other young wives in a garrison town in the Punjab. It won't be like Aldershot, you know. With the many servants and too much time on their hands, and their husbands often away for weeks on end, that's when the trouble starts. Boredom can be responsible for a whole lot of misunderstanding and mischief.'

'They could have babies.'

'So they could, my love. What a simple solution!' he teased. Then he saw the pain in her eyes, and was sorry for the teasing. Their only child had been stillborn. It was a long time ago, but a woman never forgets the child she has carried in her womb.

When Thomas reported to his Commanding Officer some three weeks later, the Colonel hid a sly smile behind his hand, for his future son-in-law had suffered a black eye since they had last met.

'One of the mock battles quite realistic, eh, Cartwright?' he asked.

'No, Sir. I acquired this last evening, after our return to base. I was expecting it, Sir.'

'Indeed?'

'Yes, Sir.'

'May I enquire the reason?'

'A private matter, Sir.'

'Ah, just so. Defending your honour, no doubt?'

'Yes, Sir.'

'And your opponent?'

'Subaltern Jones, Sir.'

'Also defending his honour?'

'Not exactly, Sir.'

'What other reason would provoke an officer and a gentleman into combat?'

'The right to compete for the hand of your daughter, Sir.'

'I see, and Subaltern Jones had heard a rumour that he might be too late?'

'Yes, Sir.'

'All is fair in love and war, Cartwright.'

'I told him he was mistaken, Sir, and we were not pledged.'

'Yet you still had to fight?'

'He said I was a liar, Sir.'

'So you are.'

'I beg your pardon, Sir?'

'Subaltern Jones is speaking the truth. The entire garrison has been buzzing with rumours since you left, and servants gossip. Nothing is sacred in a garrison town. Surely the Mess was humming with this particular rumour last evening?'

'Yes, Sir.'

'But you did not believe it?'

'I – I was appalled, Sir.'

'Quite frankly, I was never more frightened in my life. I thought she would never awaken.'

'It was laudanum, wasn't it, Sir?'

'Yes. The Doctor prescribed it for my sister Miss Maitland, and Rosalind helped herself from the bottle.'

'She could have died, Sir?'

'Yes, with a larger dose.'

'I would never have forgiven myself, Sir.'

'I would not have blamed you. My daughter has been badly frightened. I have her promise it will not happen again, but she is so impulsive, so much a victim of her emotions, I could not risk a repetition. Subaltern Cartwright, I am asking you to marry my daughter.'

'Yes, Sir, with the greatest pleasure, Sir!' said he, with a smart salute. And they shook hands gravely.

It was a very subdued young woman who rode out with her future husband that same evening, when he had finished his duties for the day. They rode in silence at a steady trot, till they reached the familiar landmark of that previous occasion. There they halted, and Thomas lifted her down. Her blue eyes swam with tears as she reached up a hand to touch his disfigured face.

'Don't cry, my sweet,' he coaxed.

'Does it hurt terribly?'

'Not any more.'

'My brave knight. I do love you so terribly much. I would die if you did not wish to marry me.'

'My foolish love. Of course I wish it. Shall I go on my knees to you? There. Give me your hands. Will you marry me, Rosalind? I love you devotedly, with all my heart.'

'Yes, Thomas. I will marry you and we shall live happily ever after, for it's so terribly romantic, is it not?' She sighed, ecstatically, and flung her arms about his neck. 'Kiss me, my darling. I do so adore your kisses.'

His arms tightened round her tiny waist, and he kissed her trembling mouth. Had she no conception what such closeness did to a man? he wondered. It would take all his self-control to wait for the marriage bed. All his pulses were racing, and his loins demanding. He had never before denied himself the pleasure of sex. But this was his true love, and he would swear to be faithful. His intentions were honourable, and he saw himself as the perfect husband. She was adorable, so sweet and trusting, and she loved him so much she had nearly died. He was profoundly touched by such devotion.

So they clung together, and were lost to the world, as all lovers are lost, in a dream too fragile to withstand the realities of waking.

Chapter Five

If Ellen felt hurt that the wedding invitation was addressed to Amelia and not herself she hid the hurt as she had always managed to hide it since the day her son was born, and his grandmother claimed him. Ellen would never fight for her rights and privileges as a mother. Her love was kind, infinitely maternal, unselfish. In her dark, expressive eyes could be read the travail of all motherhood, and all the doubts and disappointments, the constant fears for her children's safety.

The days were long and lonely in the old nursery suite at the top of the house. She did all her own chores, so there was no extra work for her sister, Bertha, and she joined Amelia, Bertha and Norah for meals at the big table in the dining-room, where Amelia still presided over her depleted family. One Sunday in the month, Bella came home to The Haven with Roderic. After the East End of London, they both enjoyed the comfort and the good food that Norah provided. Ellen enjoyed their company, and listened avidly to their tales, both sad and amusing, among the people they had sworn to serve. Letters were exchanged each week, so they kept in touch.

Ellen wrote regularly to her two daughters every

Sunday afternoon, since she was seldom invited to visit her eldest daughter, less than a mile away, and heavy with child. Since her marriage to Basil, Prue had become rather strange and distraught in her pregnancy, and Basil found himself tied to a quarrelsome young wife, jealous of the two hours he spent with his own mother on Wednesday afternoons when the store was closed, and suspicious of his casual acquaintance with the female staff at the store. He often wondered whether it had been a mistake to marry the girl, young enough to be his daughter. They both had suffered from the transition period. To find herself pregnant had been a shock to Prue. She did not want a child. She had planned a cosy little nest for two, on the top floor of Thomas Brent & Son. There was a side entrance and a back staircase, so they would be completely private. As the wife of the General Manager, she would preserve her dignity, and not associate with the staff. The rooms had been nicely decorated, and tastefully furnished. They even had a bathroom, a luxury The Haven could not afford.

Then all her lovely plans had been shattered by the doctor's pronouncement that her frequent 'bilious attacks' were, in fact, the early morning sickness of pregnancy. The shock had been so devastating, she had not fully recovered, and was still blaming Basil for such indelicacy!

'How could the wife of the General Manager preserve her dignity with a belly so swollen one would suppose she was giving birth to twins? And how could the child's bassinet be conveyed from the top floor to the ground floor?' Prue demanded, irritably.

'My dearest girl, there is a service lift and a porter,' he reminded her, with quiet patience.

In the meantime, she was housebound by her own pride and obstinacy. Ellen was not surprised. Prue was highly strung, and Basil must make allowances for her nerves. When the child was born, all would be well, she wrote, under separate cover, to her son-in-law. He read the letter in his private office, where he would retire at mid-morning to drink coffee and mid-afternoon to drink tea. It was the one peaceful interlude in his busy day.

His mother-in-law was a sweet woman, but no match for her elder daughter, her son, or her own mother, with their strong personalities.

Constantly harassed in his private and public life, Basil looked back on his carefree youth, and wondered why any man should wish to change the happy state of bachelorhood for the bonds of marriage. For the second time he was conscious of a sense of guilt. Lucy had been too frail to bear his child and Prue too immature. Being a wife had not changed her mentality. Why had he expected it?

'We shall not be going to the wedding, so why should we spend money on a present?' Prue argued.

Basil was deeply shocked by such reasoning. 'I don't understand you, dear. Your own brother!'

'It does not signify. There is no love between us. Why should I pretend?'

'There is such a thing as family loyalty and affection.'

'Not for Thomas. I should not care if I never saw him again. Nothing was ever the same after he was born. I had a wretched childhood. The entire household revolved around him. It was too ridiculous. He knew his importance even before he could speak a single word. He had only to yell for someone to run to give him what he wanted. Everyone adored him. As for Grandmama, the sun rose and set on his golden head. It still does. It sickens me. So, he is to marry the Colonel's daughter! Grandmama must be absolutely delighted, for it would be exactly what she had in mind for her precious darling. Only the best is good enough for Thomas!' She yawned, expansively. 'Do what you like about a present. Ask Mama to select something suitable.'

'Very well, dear,' he agreed. It was useless to argue. For the sake of peace he had become a 'yes' man. Yet it brought no peace, so perhaps he should have been firm and masterful. It was too late now. It would be dangerous to assert his authority at this stage of her pregnancy.

'Patience and tolerance, my dear fellow,' the doctor had advised.

Never had nine months dragged on so interminably. The early-morning swim was a tonic that rejuvenated his slack muscles and refreshed his tired mind. Even that small measure of independence offended Prue. She resented his glowing cheeks and bright eyes. The cap of fair damp hair gave his face a boyishness that was sadly lacking for the rest of the day. To hear him running down the stairs after he had served her with early morning tea and biscuits was a further reminder of her own condition. Heavy with child, she lay back on her pillows while tears of self-pity wet her cheeks. In his early morning exuberance, he seemed to be gloating over her own heaviness of spirit, and the chaste kiss on her brow was a mockery and a betrayal of the love that had blossomed on that first holiday together. It could well be their last holiday, for how could they travel with a young child?

Basil had been her lover for only a few short weeks, when they had delighted in each other's bodies. It had been such a sudden revelation, and more than a little frightening, till she discovered how completely his desire for her could be used as a bribe to obtain anything on which she had set her heart. But it had not lasted, for when he knew she was carrying his child, he stopped being her lover and became a fussy and rather tedious husband. She distrusted such obvious devotion, and these tender kisses on her brow, and she reasoned that he must be going elsewhere for the pleasure and satisfaction of intercourse. In another woman's arms, he would be kissing a wet, yielding mouth, and fondling her breasts. How she hated that other woman who had stolen her lover and left her to weep, with her swollen belly! Visions of that hateful woman floated before her anguished eyes. She was very fair, with blue eyes and altogether desirable. Her thoughts had wings, and she saw them together in the sea, clad only in their clinging bathing costumes, and she knew for certain they were sharing the bathing machine. Her tears flowed afresh, and her heart ached with an awful desolation, so that when he returned after his swim, her lashing tongue accused him of all the deceptions her warped mind had visualized in his absence. The dark, expressive eyes that had once been as soft as velvet, were black as onyx in her pale, distorted face, and he stared at her with a heavy heart, all the pleasure of the early morning swim completely lost in such a tirade.

'My dearest girl, what *are* you talking about?' he remonstrated, mildly. 'There *is* no other woman. I love you, Prue. You are my wife, and soon to be the mother of my child. What have I done that you should accuse me of such treachery?'

'Your blushes give you away. How do you dare to stand there and tell me you are not guilty of adultery?'

'*Adultery?*' he laughed, mirthlessly. 'My dear, you can't be serious?' He sat on the edge of the bed. He smelled fresh and clean after the swim, and the blush on his cheeks was a healthy glow from the exercise and the cold nip in the air.

She wanted to believe him, but her stubborn pride refused to listen. 'You lie!' she screamed, and smacked his face.

He frowned and shook his head. 'Never do that again, Prue,' he said, with quiet dignity. Then he stood up and walked out of the room.

'Come back! I didn't mean it. Basil, darling, don't leave me. I feel so ill, so frightened. I must be mad to think such dreadful thoughts. Where are you? Why don't you answer?'

His footsteps echoed on the stairs and a door

closed. She covered her face with her hands and sobbed, distraught.

When the daily housekeeper arrived to start on her duties, she found her young mistress in a state of collapse, and the kitten the Master had bought for her companionship lapping a puddle of spilled milk on the kitchen table. There was no sign of the Master. A cheerful, bustling little body, she had long since decided that young Mrs Gregson had been foolishly spoilt, and needed a firm hand. But she knew her place, and she needed the money to cope with a drunken husband and a tribe of children.

'Lawks-a-daisy, Ma'am!' said she, snatching off a battered straw hat in the doorway. 'What be the trouble then?'

'My husband has deserted me,' moaned the poor girl, from the depths of an untidy bed.

'The Master would never do that, Ma'am.'

'Yes, he would, and it's all my fault. I said the most dreadful things.'

'Then all you 'as ter do, Ma'am, is ter say you be sorry.'

'But he has gone!'

'Now don't you fret, duckie. 'Tis bad for the baby. Men are touchy in the early morning, but they come round after they've eaten a good breakfast.'

'But Mr Gregson has had no breakfast, so he won't come round.'

'Did 'e leave any message 'bout lunch?'

'No, I don't think so. I can't remember. I was too upset.'

'Well, I daresay we shall get the porter coming up

later on. Now, let me tidy you up, Ma'am, afore I get your breakfast, and you'll feel a lot better.'

'I don't want any breakfast. I am not in the least hungry.'

'Jus' a nice cup of tea and a nice slice of buttered toast? What jew say?'

'All right.' Prue sighed, resignedly, too weak to argue. All her passion had been spent. She bathed her face and combed her hair, listening for Basil.

To go home to Mother, to the quiet atmosphere of the house but a short distance away, and the comforting arms of a woman who had known sorrow and survived tragedy, was very tempting, and he stood, hesitating, at the side entrance, watching a station van unloading goods. That would be a coward's way, and only a temporary release from this traumatic chapter of their early married life. He was still his mother's son, and she would welcome him with gladness, for he saw very little of her since his marriage to Prue. But his first loyalty now was the young wife he had left in that cosy little nest they had planned together, with such high hopes.

In this building that housed his public and his private world, Prue's insistence on absolute privacy had isolated them. They had no friends, no social life. She was jealous of his popularity with the female staff, for he treated them well, and was always ready to listen to their grievances. This was his life, and his future was here. He *had* to stay. Pride had no place in his thoughts today. Too much pride and passion had already been spent in that upstairs apartment. He shivered at the remembrance.

When he saw Mrs Atkins bustling along on the opposite side of the road, carrying their shopping in her shabby carpet bag, and her hair slipping untidily from a battered old hat, his grim mouth twisted in a wry smile. She was one of the old breed of servants. The salt of the earth. She could manage Prue with her cheerful good humour, so he fled to the sanctuary of his private office before she crossed the street, and left her to climb the stairs. She would cook his breakfast, but he would not be there to eat it. As soon as the office boy came on duty, he would ring for coffee and toast. Then a blessed half-hour before the store opened. But first he must change his clothes. He kept a suit of clothes, several clean shirts with stiff collars, a cravat, and a pair of patent shoes in the small wardrobe in the office for just such an emergency.

It was not the first time that Prue's nagging tongue had obliged him to escape to the office in the past few months, but it *was* the first time she had slapped his face, and his cheek still tingled. In the striped trousers and tailed coat, with his damp fair hair and his troubled blue eyes, he was reasonably satisfied with his appearance in the long mirror. The customers would have no cause to complain, or the staff suspect that his private life was so badly disorganized that their General Manager had actually contemplated going home to Mother!

'Patience and tolerance, my good fellow,' he reminded himself of the doctor's advice as he settled into the swivel chair behind the desk. Both had been tried to their limits today, and he would not attempt any reconciliation until tonight, when the store was closed. Mrs Atkins would cook a meal for Prue, and eat her own share in the kitchen. He would leave his assistant manager in charge in the lunch hour, and take a stroll to the Chop House. Prue would have plenty of time to repent of her naughtiness.

A sharp rap at the door, and Prue was banished from his thoughts. 'Come in,' he invited.

A cheeky face, well-scrubbed with yellow soap, peered round the door. 'Good morning, Sir. Did you ring, Sir?' asked young Albert, respectfully. The eldest of Mrs Atkins's brood, at twelve years of age a master of diplomacy, he was dressed for the part in one of Thomas's discarded Eton suits. His hair was plastered with water, and his boots polished. They were mutually attracted, the man and the boy, for Basil could see himself at the same age, scrubbed and clean, presenting a satisfactory appearance to the house-master at his prep school.

He greeted the boy with his customary smile. 'Good morning, Albert,' said he. 'I stayed too long over my swim this morning. The tide was exactly right. So I had no time for breakfast. Could you rustle up a cup of coffee and a couple of slices of toast in the staff kitchen, before Ivy takes over?'

'Leave it to me, Sir,' said Albert, with a broad grin. To get the better of Ivy was one of his many pleasures in his busy day. The boss was a real gent, and Ivy was a disagreeable old bitch. There were no shades of grey with Albert, only black and white.

The wedding was a splendid affair. Thomas and Rosalind the handsomest couple, and the bevy of six pretty bridesmaids, with their muslin gowns and mob caps had all the young, unmarried subalterns relishing their own courtships. The sun shone on the dazzling uniforms, and church bells were pealing as the long line of hired carriages, adorned with white ribbons, carrying relatives and friends of the bride and groom, rolled slowly along the route. A crowd had gathered at the lych gate, and children were perched on the wall. A military wedding was always popular in the garrison town.

In the packed church, the women chatted and the men sat quietly, nursing their hats, waiting for the bride. Thomas and his best man stood stiffly to attention. The fair head and the dark both proudly erect, their eyes staring fixedly at the chaplain in his clean, starched surplice.

But it was Rosalind's day, and she intended to steal the limelight every single moment. It was her right and her privilege. Hadn't she almost died of love when she thought she was denied?

The chattering stopped, and the congregation rose in a colourful tide under the old rafters as the organ swelled in volume, and the lovely young bride swept past on the arm of her proud Papa, regal as a princess, in her wedding gown of ivory satin, the long train held by two small pages. The veil that covered her face would be lifted when Thomas stepped forward to claim her. She felt all her senses responding to the admiration, the joy and the wonder that surrounded her. All her young romantic dreams had been realized. Her heart fluttered like a trapped bird under the tight bodice.

She knew they were going to live happily ever after. He was so very handsome, his blue eyes so teasing, his smile so devastating, his kisses so tender. Being in love with Thomas was the most exciting and wonderful experience of her whole life – and she was already seventeen years of age!

Only one small incident marred the ceremony. A small choir boy, overcome by the scent of lilies and carnations arranged so tastefully on the choir stalls, sank to the floor in a faint, and was carried out by two embarrassed seniors.

Thomas was proud of his family in the reserved front pews. Even Bertha had purchased a new hat for the occasion. As for Kate, she almost stole the show in an enormous hat, draped in ostrich plumes, and her plump bosom in a most revealing gown caused quite a sensation among the senior officers. For Amelia, it was the proudest day of her life. She had eyes only for her adored grandson, and her voice was choked with emotion as she joined in the singing of 'Love Divine'. Her pride and joy was mingled with sadness, however, when she reflected on the inevitable parting later in the year. The regiment would be sailing for India and would be away for five long years. A silent prayer was offered to Heaven that he would be kept safe on that treacherous Northwest Frontier where a sniper's bullet had killed his father.

Ellen was also praying for her son's safety, and for his happiness. She did not envy that lovely child, for Thomas was his father's son, and would not be a faithful husband when the poor girl was enduring nine months of pregnancy in the suffocating heat, the dust and the discomfort of that strange country. She had met her future daughter-in-law for only a few minutes at the reception in the Officers' Mess last evening, when Rosalind had been surrounded by a merry crowd of young officers, all a little intoxicated with the wine the Colonel had ordered. Thomas had been flushed and excited, showing off his bride-to-be with a proud possessiveness. After she had left, and the family were driven back to their hotel, Thomas would enjoy his last night of freedom with his fellow officers, and he would be undressed and put to bed by his batman in the early hours of his wedding day. Yet here he was, resplendent in his scarlet uniform, with no sign of a hangover, the envy of those who had flirted with Rosalind and hoped to win the hand of the Colonel's daughter.

Ellen was crying quietly, a dainty lace-edged handkerchief pressed to her trembling mouth. She was back in time to her own wedding day, with Jonathan claiming her, 'for better, for worse, till death do us part'. Her poor darling, so soon to renounce those solemn vows, so soon to die.

'Don't cry, Mama,' a soft voice whispered, and a small gloved hand rested on her arm. She had forgotten Bella, her dear younger daughter, who would be the next to marry.

Ellen smiled tremulously. 'They are both so beautiful, aren't they, my darling?' she whispered back.

Bella nodded, and turned to Roderic. She knew exactly what he was thinking. Only a few more months, and his long courtship would be rewarded, not in this elaborate setting, but in the Church Army Mission at Hoxton.

He squeezed Bella's hand. Seven years he had waited, then a further seven years – like Jacob, serving and waiting for his beloved Rachel. The trappings of a fashionable military wedding meant nothing to these two. They did not serve the Queen. They served her poorest subjects.

What would be that lovely child's reaction, Kate was wondering, if she knew her handsome young husband had lain with his Aunt Kate? She sighed nostalgically for that delightful chapter of self-indulgence and the exquisite pleasure of his beautiful body in her arms. Never again would she know such happiness, for happiness, for Kate, was physical and her delight her own demanding sensuality. The tears she shed in the church that day were tears of self-pity, for her elderly lover was so tedious, his breath stank of whisky, and he grunted like a pig when he made love.

It was not love. Why did she pretend? A middle-aged matron, near to swooning in her tight corsets, she was still a very attractive woman, but not to her own husband. Charles had long since discovered he had married a very stupid woman. He too was remembering. To be cuckolded by a boy of seventeen was a gross insult to his pride. He had never forgiven Kate, and had taken a mistress to soothe his vanity, a gentle, undemanding creature, tucked away in a small apartment in Bloomsbury. He was not surprised by Kate's tears, and had no inclination to comfort her. The French perfume he had once found so alluring, was too overpowering, her gown too revealing, her cloying sentimentality too forced. He would never know how she came to belong to that nice family of sisters, and that dignified little mother for whom he had the greatest respect and affection.

It must have been quite a relief to that family when he had married Kate. But his infatuation was quickly replaced by the certain knowledge that he had made the biggest mistake of his life. Nobody would suspect they had not shared the marriage bed for more than three years – only the servants, who would probably gossip with the tradesmen, but since all their bills were paid regularly, he did not expect any repercussions from that quarter.

His wandering thoughts were rudely interrupted by the thundering blast of the 'Wedding March', and the bridal procession down the aisle. A momentary hesitation, then recognition in a pair of mischievous blue eyes, and Charles smiled and bowed, as man to man. All was forgiven, if not forgotten. Young Thomas could not be blamed for such a foolish indiscretion. He really was a handsome fellow. Proud as Lucifer on his wedding day, because he had won the hand of the Colonel's daughter. What did the future hold for them? Love at first sight could be dangerously deceptive – a spark kindled into a flame, a mirage, a fantasy of self-indulgence. But who would want to listen to his gloomy observations today? So Charles gave his arm to Kate, and they followed the slow procession out of the church.

The swords of the Guard of Honour gleamed in the

bright sunlight, the bells were pealing, and a shower of confetti descended on the handsome couple as Thomas handed his bride into the waiting carriage. Someone had tied an old boot on the back for luck, and several pots and pans to make a good clatter. Six exuberant young subalterns had removed the horses and were prancing in the shafts, intending to draw the carriage! The Colonel watched with fatherly indulgence, flanked by his senior officers, with pursed lips and frowning brows. The carriage moved off to the cheers of the crowd, and Aunt Millie, dabbing her eyes with a damp handkerchief, confided to Amelia, 'It's a true love match, Ma'am. Your grandson is the handsomest man in the regiment.'

'Indubitably,' Amelia agreed, with a triumphant smile.

The huge marquee was suffocatingly hot, and the stewards were sweating profusely over the laden tables. A buffet wedding breakfast was the only answer to the crowd of guests, and the officers had been instructed to see that everyone was served with refreshments. Champagne corks were popping, and the buzz of excited chatter and the clatter of crockery almost drowned the band, playing so energetically on the parade ground.

Rosalind sipped the champagne and giggled happily as Thomas fed her with tasty morsels from his own plate. Papa had spared no expense. The heat and the champagne were making her feel quite light headed, and she clutched Thomas's arm and whispered, 'Take me out, darling. I feel a little faint.'

He picked her up and carried her out. In the lee of

the marquee, she lay in his arms and dropped her head on his shoulder.

'Feeling better, my sweet?' he asked, anxiously.

'Yes, thank you.'

'How soon can we get away?'

She stared at him, wide-eyed. 'Who wants to get away? It's fun. It's our wedding day, and I am enjoying every minute. We must stay for the dancing. You know how I love dancing. Put me down. We must circulate among our guests. Don't look so sulky, silly darling.'

'I want you to myself. Why do all these fellows feel entitled to kiss you?'

'I like being kissed. Are you jealous?' she giggled happily, and took his arm. 'Come along. I can see your men lined up with their sergeant, waiting to be presented, and you haven't spoken to your family. Smile, darling. That's better.' She patted his cheek, affectionately. If only he knew how much she was dreading the end of the day, when they would be alone together in a strange hotel in London. Papa had booked a suite at Brown's Hotel. Dear Papa. Being married to Thomas was so very delightful, for she loved him to distraction. Surrounded by a milling crowd of guests and admiring officers, she had smiled till her face was stiff, but she was haunted by the spectre of the marriage bed. Nobody had explained. The subject was much too indelicate for Aunt Millie. So it remained a complete mystery. The twins, who fancied themselves enlightened on matters pertaining to the opposite sex, had even suggested the marriage bed could be rather fun. The only problem in their particular case was finding *two* husbands and *two* marriage beds, since they had always shared everything, hadn't they? Having no brothers, their knowledge of the opposite sex was every bit as vague as Rosalind's, and confined to a few stolen kisses in the conservatory, and the close proximity of a partner in one of Mr Strauss' delightful waltzes.

'But how will you decide who is in love with whom? Supposing you both fall in love with the same man?' Rosalind had raised the question and caused quite a flutter of anticipation for it was a vital question, and their fond Mama most anxious to find husbands for her twin daughters.

So nothing was settled, and Rosalind was still as ignorant as ever, and most decidedly apprehensive now that the night was fast approaching.

When the veil and the orange blossom had been removed, and the train of her wedding gown draped over her arm, Thomas bowed to his bride, she curtsied prettily, and they circled the ballroom in the first waltz. Now all her fears vanished in the pleasure of the dance, for Thomas danced divinely. She knew he was the envy of his fellow officers, and she could see the admiration in their eyes as they drifted past. She danced with every one of them, and their gallantry and charming compliments pleased her enormously. Only Subaltern Jones had spoiled everything by claiming a kiss in a secluded corner behind a potted palm. His dark eyes were sulky, and his lips were hard. Clasped in a passionate embrace, she struggled free.

'*Mister* Jones, you are taking liberties!' she reminded him, haughtily.

His singing Welsh voice was husky with emotion. 'I love you, Rosalind, and you knew it. Why did you have to marry that conceited young pup?'

'You are speaking of my husband, Mr Jones.'

'It used to be David. I thought you liked me?'

'I *do* like you – David.' It was true. There was something strangely compelling in those dark eyes. He made no pretence to charm, and his attraction was not only in his singing voice, but in the intensity of his Gaelic moods. His rare smile had to be enticed. David Jones was not very popular among his fellow officers, but his men would have died for him, and might still be required to do so if all that was told and written about the Northwest Frontier were true. Thomas had not yet achieved such obvious devotion, but he was trying hard. David was more single-minded, more sincere.

Rosalind was touched by his declaration of love and laid her little gloved hand on his sleeve. 'I do like you enormously, David, but it's Thomas I love. I am sorry.'

'Don't be sorry. Be happy, my dearest.' His own gloved hand was gentle on her flushed cheek. Then he bowed and walked away. She did not see him again till after the honeymoon.

'My sweet, I blushed with embarrassment at your stupid mistake! Whatever possessed you to sign your maiden name?' Thomas demanded, in a hoarse whisper as they walked away from the reception desk.

241

'Because I was nervous, and because I am not yet accustomed to signing my married name, and do not speak to me in that tone of voice,' she answered, testily, her own voice quavering in a way that should have warned him she was very near to tears. 'And do not call me stupid. I am not a stupid person!' she added, her blue eyes flashing indignantly.

'But don't you see, beloved, they may think we are not married?'

'Then they would be very stupid, since we are spilling that horrid confetti on the floor. It does not signify. Papa is well known to the management in this hotel, and he booked our rooms. Why should we care what a mere clerk supposes? He is only a servant.'

'I *do* mind. Servants gossip. My reputation is at stake. I was desirous of leaving a good impression should we wish to visit this hotel again.'

'Poof! I find you *intolerably* conceited, Subaltern Cartwright,' said she, snatching her hand away.

Were they quarrelling? Thomas was aghast at such a possibility. He apologized profusely as they climbed the stairs, and was so contrite, he actually went on his knees to her as soon as they were alone together. Clasping her tiny waist, he gazed up at her with such imploring humility, she was almost ready to accept his apology.

'Forgive me, my sweet. I do understand. Of course you were nervous. I blame myself for not warning you. To tell you the truth, sweetheart, I do believe I could have signed for both. The clerk did attempt to speak to me, but I was not listening. What a silly

fellow you have married to be sure! Am I forgiven?'
Now that it was too late, he remembered the kindly
advice of Aunt Millie, only a few short hours ago.

'Rosalind reacts very strongly to criticism. You
must be careful, dear boy, not to upset her dignity.
She is very proud, very self-willed. It will not be easy
for you. The Colonel has spoiled her rather foolishly.
Unless you are prepared to let her have her own way,
you are asking for trouble. Persuasion and flattery,
Thomas. These are your weapons against such a
determined and self-willed young woman.'

He had thanked her. She meant well, but he had
not expected to be reminded of her sensible advice so
soon after their marriage. Did he really want a docile
little wife? It would be so boring. His beloved was so
adorable when she was angry, and he knew he would
be tempted to upset her in order to see the angry
tears in her eyes, and the quivering childish mouth.
It was a game they would play if it pleased her to see
him on his knees – a game of pretence, for he was too
proud to beg. It was so easy.

'Forgive me, my sweet.' Even to hold her thus was
agony. He could not wait to take off her clothes. The
day was too long, and they still must put in an
appearance in the dining-room. It was expected.
'There is a time and a place for everything,' as
Grandmama would say, and the marriage bed was
waiting in the adjoining room. He would take her,
and know the exquisite satisfaction of mastery. His
naughty little wife must be punished for all her
tantrums since their betrothal. He smiled, in anticipation, and took her face in his hands.

'Kiss me, sweetheart,' he breathed. He could be tender, and he could be cruel.

The head waiter bowed in the doorway, and they followed him to their reserved table. There were flowers on the table, and a bottle of champagne in a bucket. The other guests looked up and smiled knowingly, as they passed. Thomas wished he had ordered the meal to be served in their private suite, but he had been too taken up with appeasing Rosalind.

She seemed to be enjoying the attention, though she had no appetite for the roast chicken, normally her favourite dish, and she crumbled the bread roll on her plate. Thomas was hungry, and finished the chicken the waiter carved on a side table. They drank their health in the champagne, and had eyes only for each other. They were still being watched.

'Such a handsome couple, and so absurdly young,' sighed a plump, over-dressed matron, enviously, as she was served with a dish of strawberries and cream.

Rosalind was sipping the second glass of champagne when she remembered the marriage bed, and nearly choked. Thomas offered a clean handkerchief, and watched her scarlet face and streaming eyes most anxiously.

'Shall we go?' he whispered, and she nodded mutely.

'Will you be coming back, Sir?' asked the waiter.

'No.' Thomas was curt, and considerably embarrassed as he led his bride away.

'My head aches,' Rosalind complained, when the door had closed on their privacy.

'Take off your hat,' he suggested, kindly.

She was looking at him with wide, frightened eyes. The bed had been turned down, and a new night-gown and nightshirt folded neatly on the sheet. They sat on the edge of the bed, and she laid her aching head on his shoulder while he spoke soothingly.

'Why are you so frightened, my sweet? There is nothing to fear between husband and wife. Everything is natural. Have you been listening to those old wives' tales?'

'Nobody has told me anything. That is why I am so frightened.'

'Would I hurt you when I love you to distraction?' He smiled, encouragingly, and knelt to remove her new satin slippers that matched her new gown. 'Relax, sweetheart, and I will undress you,' he coaxed.

She pushed him away. 'Leave me alone. I can undress myself.'

'Very well, my sweet. I will get undressed in the dressing-room.' He kissed her affectionately, but she did not return the kiss.

He undressed quickly, his own hands fumbling, went to the bathroom, and wrapped his naked body in the bath-robe. He was proud of his body, and the women who had loved him had found it beautiful.

When he opened the bedroom door and stepped inside, he caught a glimpse of a childish face with frightened eyes, and a mane of golden hair spread on the pillow. He must be gentle. He turned down the lamp, dropped the robe on the floor, and climbed into bed. He had already erected.

'Don't be frightened, sweetheart. It's only your husband. Your adored Thomas,' he breathed, reaching out for her.

The voluminous nightgown covered her completely. It was buttoned at the neck, and fell in flounces over her feet. It was his first encounter with a nightgown since he left the nursery.

'Where are you, my sweet?' he teased, playfully.

But she clung to the garment in feverish desperation, resisting all his efforts to find a way in. What had he expected? He was not very imaginative. All his short life he had taken what he wanted. To be refused was alien to his nature. He sighed, fretfully.

'So you don't love me?'

'I *do*! I *do*!'

'Then let me feel you, *please*.'

'You won't hurt me?'

'Haven't I promised on my honour?'

'Yes, but I am still frightened.'

'My poor sweet.' He found her mouth in the darkness, but her lips were tightly closed, and without the sensuality of his probing tongue, her body was tense and unresponsive.

When his hand reached up to fondle her stomach, she shivered involuntarily, but he persisted, his hand gradually creeping up till it cupped her breast. Time stood still while he wrestled with the twin desires to be gentle, and to take her by force. To rape his innocent young bride on their wedding night would be a dastardly act, unworthy of a gentleman, but this was a kind of torture, and his patience was exhausted.

246

Flinging the nightgown over her head, his mouth fastened hungrily on her breast. His teeth were sharp, and she was gasping for breath in the folds of the gown. It was then that she became aware of his nakedness, and clenched her hands to push him away. One hand closed on a hard object between his legs. With a stifled scream of horror, she rolled over and buried her face in the pillow.

'My sainted aunt!' he exploded in an agony of frustration, and slid out of bed. Switching on the lamp, he looked down at the tumbled head on the pillow and heard the frightened sobbing, but felt no compassion. At that moment of rejection, he could have strangled her, and felt only that she deserved it. Hurt pride was a bitter pill for Thomas to swallow, and he was trembling with the anguish of unrequited love – or was it lust? No, he *did* love her. He thought he had found his true love, the perfect love, in this innocent young virgin. Had he been mistaken?

Pulling on his clothes, he cast a final glance at the huddled little figure in the bed, and went out. The night porter raised a hand in salute. Nothing surprised him, after watching the idiosyncrasies of the upper class for nearly forty years. The tales he could tell would fill a volume, but he had no talent for writing them down. The military, in particular, were renowned for their practical jokes and boyish escapades, and this handsome young subaltern still wet behind the ears would be no exception. Something was definitely wrong upstairs, sure to goodness, his canny Welsh instinct informed him. Why should a bridegroom be taking a walk on his wedding night when he could be enjoying himself with his bride in the marriage bed? It wasn't the first time it had happened.

He remembered one momentous occasion when the bride had run screaming into the street, followed by her distraught groom, both stark naked! There was an excuse for theatricals. Actors and actresses always seemed to be acting a part, on and off the stage. But it was not his business. They came and went, like ships in the night, and few remembered to tip the night porter.

Thomas was marching along the pavement with a purposeful stride. He knew exactly where he was going, and what he intended to do. To pick up a prostitute in Piccadilly would have been unthinkable an hour ago, but somebody had to relieve this painful frustration. What did it matter? A stranger to London, there would be no witnesses, he told himself, as he strode towards his quarry.

'Were you looking for me, dearie?'

He had hesitated for only a moment and the woman was there, hanging on his arm. The painted face had a garish unreality in the lamplight, and the cheap scent offended his natural fastidiousness. A mental picture of the girl he had left sobbing in the marriage bed flashed across his mind. What was he doing here? He must be mad. There was no agony, no erection, only a strong conviction that it was all a terrible mistake.

'I have changed my mind. I do apologize,' he told the woman, with gentle courtesy, pressing a coin into her hand, then he bowed and marched away.

'Christ! A bloody sovereign!' she muttered, biting it with her strong teeth. It wasn't a dud. It was REAL!

He was quickly back. Shiny-eyed, his face glowing, he marched across the foyer, lifted a hand in salute to the night porter, and raced upstairs, his heart pounding. Pushing open the door, he slipped inside. Rosalind had not moved. She was still sobbing. He flung his hat on the dressing table, sat on the edge of the bed and gathered her into his arms. With her tumbled hair and tear-wet face, she was just a little girl. He dried her tears, his voice husky with emotion. 'It's all right, sweetheart. Don't cry any more. I didn't understand.'

Gulping back a sob, she stammered, 'I – I thought you had left me.'

'Only to take a little walk.'

'You were so angry.'

'I was a brute. Can you forgive me?'

'It is you who should be forgiving me for being so stupid, so ignorant. It is very frightening to be so ignorant. I had not conceived such – such ugliness, and it is ugly, is it not, my darling?'

'Very ugly, my sweet.'

'Are all men made the same?'

'I am afraid so.'

'But what is the purpose?'

'Without the act of intercourse, the marriage is not yet consummated. In the eyes of the world we are not yet married.'

'But the Vicar married us?'

'He pronounced us man and wife, but that is just a

formality. The act of intercourse between a man and a woman, that is the reality. You remember the words of the marriage service?'

'Every single word.'

'Tell me.'

She repeated the solemn vows they had made and paused at the pronouncement '"Those whom God hath joined together let no man put asunder." Joined together – with THAT?' She shivered, involuntarily.

'Yes.'

'Through my private parts?'

'Yes.'

'It does seem so very unpleasant.'

'Not when you allow me to make love to you.'

'Without my nightgown?'

'Yes.'

'Then I suppose you must.'

'I will be very gentle. Because you are a virgin, it must hurt a little, but only for a moment.'

'And when you have finished, I shall really and truly belong to you till death do us part?'

'Till death do us part, beloved.' He smiled and kissed her, with such tenderness she was ashamed of her ignorance and fear. To have it explained was so very sensible, and Thomas was an absolute darling.

She wound her arms about his neck and whispered, 'I am ready now, but I shall close my eyes.'

So he took her, with the gentleness of a lover who had so nearly betrayed those marriage vows on their wedding night. And the momentary pain was forgotten in the ecstasy of complete surrender.

Thomas enjoyed his role as an adoring and

attentive husband. His duties still claimed the daylight hours, apart from that early morning hour, when they rode together and shared the pleasure of an exhilarating gallop beyond the confines of the garrison. They were as well matched in the saddle as on the dance floor. Both loved horses, and had ridden since childhood.

There were no concessions in these early weeks of their marriage for the young officer who must take his full share of the responsibility in preparing the ranks for their overseas service. But Army tradition and discipline was second nature to the Colonel's daughter, and she did not complain. There was no time to be lonely, and she was enjoying her role as mistress of the house they had been allocated. She was learning to cook, and Aunt Millie, who had found her an apt pupil, had declared, in her forthright way, that every woman, no matter what her station in life, should be capable of cooking and serving an appetizing meal – providing, of course, a servant was at hand to prepare the vegetables and wash up all the pots and pans.

Thomas became quite a bore in the Mess with his constant reference to his wife's culinary cleverness.

It was only when Aunt Millie was indisposed with a mild attack of influenza that Thomas was served with a burnt offering by a flushed and tearful little wife, but that was strictly a private matter, and her reputation did not suffer in consequence. A kiss and a cuddle and peace was restored.

'Cheer up, my sweet. You will be waited on hand

and foot in India, with all those native servants,' Thomas had reminded her.

But Rosalind was beginning to wonder whether she would care for such an idle existence. It was fun to have the dressmaker busy with yards of muslin and flowered prints for new gowns. It was fun to go shopping for suitable shoes and sandals, for straw hats and parasols, and silk petticoats. It was fun being married to Thomas!

'We must go home to say our farewells to the family,' Thomas decided, when the date of their departure had been publicly announced. He was dreading this inevitable parting, but having Rosalind might help. Grandmama never wept in public, neither did Mama, but the aunties and his sister Bella would be tearful. Women's tears were quite unbearably emotional.

'There is no need for us to stay overnight. We can manage the journey by train if we leave early. I will telegraph the time of our arrival, and Grandmama will meet us at the station.'

So it was arranged, and Amelia was there on the platform, wearing her Sunday best gown and hat, looking very dignified, smiling graciously. She kissed their cheeks. Her eyes were still as vividly blue as her grandson's, and she was still a very attractive woman.

Thomas handed her into the waiting cab, then handed in Rosalind, with the typical gallantry of an officer of Her Majesty's services. Amelia sat between them and held their hands on the short journey to The Haven. 'Not all the family could be here, my darlings. It was too far and too expensive for your

Auntie Grace and Uncle Henry to make the journey a second time, and they did attend the wedding. Prudence has recently given birth to a little daughter, and is consequently indisposed. You are Uncle Thomas now. Isn't that exciting? Bella has announced the date of her marriage to Roderic. Such a dear boy. They decided to wait till after you had sailed, the following week actually. Very sensible. It will give us another occasion to rejoice, will it not?' She smiled bravely, and squeezed their hands.

Rosalind found her quite enchanting and not a bit formidable. Thomas often spoke of his grandmother and their close relationship, but seldom mentioned his mother and sisters.

'I wanted you to myself for this brief period. Selfish of me, but the family will claim you as soon as we arrive,' Amelia explained. 'Here we are, and just what I expected. All out on the pavement to welcome you.'

Rosalind did not suffer from shyness, and thoroughly enjoyed the fuss and attention. It was fun to be told she belonged to the family now, and fun to have Uncle Charles bowing over her hand. Everyone agreed she was charming, and so pretty. That is to say, only Bertha found the Colonel's daughter a little precocious, but she was a difficult person to please.

'My darling boy!' enthused Kate, clasping her nephew to her ample bosom. The French perfume was a trifle overpowering, and her plump shoulders a trifle too revealing. In her fashionable gown and enormous hat, she stole the limelight, as always, at any family gathering. Thomas laughed, and kissed her most affectionately.

'How do you do, Sir,' Thomas greeted his Uncle Charles politely. There was no ill feeling. It was Charles who paid the cabby, and Charles who gave his arm to Rosalind and led the procession through the green gate, down the tiled path, and into the house. The hall smelled of polish, and a faint odour of gas from the basement. Nothing had changed.

Lunch was laid in the spacious dining-room, on a white damask cloth with gleaming silver, and Norah was carving roast lamb on the sideboard. She greeted them with a warm smile and a firm handshake, as befitted one who was neither family nor servant. Amelia took her place at the head of the table, with Thomas and Rosalind on either side.

During all this ceremony, Ellen had seemed to keep herself in the background. Her son had dutifully kissed her cheek and enquired after her health, and she had shaken hands with Rosalind. To be so vividly reminded of her husband, Jonathan, was almost more than she could bear, but she braced herself to endure the farewell gathering and the inevitable parting after an early tea. So she watched and listened, but took no part in the flow of animated conversation. Charles was at his best and wittiest, and Thomas entertained them with amusing anecdotes of a strictly proper nature.

Edward listened attentively, but his nervous stammer prevented any participation. With his gaunt features and black eyeshade, he still reminded Thomas of a rather melancholy pirate.

Rosalind and Bella giggled happily, and Kate's

shrill laughter embarrassed her husband and irritated her mother.

Amelia was playing hostess with her accustomed dignity, and only Charles, who was fond of his mother-in-law and admired her tremendously, was fully aware of the effort it cost her.

Leaving Norah and Bertha to clear the table and wash the dishes in the basement scullery, the rest of the family adjourned to the drawing-room, and seated themselves on the handsome brocade chairs and sofa. There were deep armchairs for the two uncles, and a number of occasional tables with photographs, in silver frames, and Victorian bric-à-brac much treasured by Amelia but disliked by Bertha, who had to keep it dusted.

Charles and Thomas continued to entertain them, and kept the sadness at bay. From time to time Jane or Bella or Rosalind would think of something amusing to relate and the rest would listen politely, and applaud their efforts.

When at last all were silent, and the atmosphere rather strained, Amelia played to them, and they settled down to listen with sighs of relief. Norah and Bertha had since joined the rest of the company. Norah's hands were red and shiny from the hot soda water as they lay on her lap. Ellen and Jane had both offered to help with the washing up, and received the usual refusal.

'We can manage,' Bertha insisted, and added, acidly, 'We are used to managing.'

Thomas was standing beside Amelia now, turning the pages of the music, and her aching heart refused to believe he was leaving her for five long years. Her fingers found their own way on the keyboard. A Strauss waltz and a Chopin Prelude, so familiar her thoughts could wander. If only she could put back the clock and relive those happy years before his seventh birthday when he went away to boarding school. In the Winter months the cab, which Amelia hired every day, would be a little stuffy, and Thomas would cuddle into the warmth of Grandmama's astrakhan coat. But they both loved the Summer, when the hood was down and Thomas stood up, smiling and waving like a little prince in his white sailor suit and sailor hat.

What was he thinking now, as he stood beside her? Amelia wondered. How it would have hurt her to know that he was longing to get it over, this family farewell party, that he was bored to distraction, and that he found the task of turning the pages so very tedious.

Poor Amelia! When she dropped her hands from the keyboard to consider what next to play, he whispered in her ear. She smiled and nodded.

'Rosalind, my sweet. Come here and sing for us,' he called imperatively.

She shook her head and answered, 'You must excuse me. I have a slight cold,' with misleading demureness. The tone of his voice had displeased her. It was not the first time she had to remind him she did not care to be bullied.

'Arabella, my dear, you will sing for us?' Amelia asked, kindly.

'If you wish, Grandmama.' Bella had no silly

drawing-room affectations. She enjoyed singing, and sang like a choirboy, her voice a pure treble. That she chose to sing 'All things bright and beautiful' was no surprise. It was her favourite hymn.

'Bravo!' cried Charles, clapping his hands enthusiastically.

'Encore!' That was Roderic, who could never get enough of Bella's singing. Now she sang 'Onward Christian soldiers' and Jane leaned forward to explain to Rosalind, 'That is the marching song of our Salvation Army band.'

'Indeed?' Rosalind was feeling rather piqued that Thomas's sister, who was not even pretty, and was wearing a gown of outmoded style, should possess an untrained voice that would put her own voice to shame.

'Thank you, my dear,' said Amelia, graciously. 'Now, Charles, let us have one of your charming ballads, if you please.'

'At your service, Ma'am,' said he, with mock solemnity, bowing from the waist. He sang with feeling. She was fond of Charles and thought him much too good for her naughty Kate.

'There is a lady, sweet and kind,' sang Charles, in his deep baritone. Kate was jealous, but could she honestly claim to be 'sweet and kind'? Then he sang 'Where are you going to, my pretty maid?' for Rosalind, and it pleased her enormously to be singled out, though it was hardly flattering to be likened to a milkmaid!

Thomas sighed with relief when Amelia decided it was time for tea, and they all moved back into the dining-room.

'Nothing has changed since that memorable tea party to celebrate my third birthday,' Thomas explained to Rosalind. 'Three kinds of jam, gentleman's relish, hot buttered scones, brown and white bread and butter, Madeira cake and fruit cake. I remember it exactly.'

'He was such a darling little boy,' said Kate, gushingly, patting his cheek.

'Showing off again,' muttered her prim sister, Bertha, as she seated herself beside Norah, who received no applause for the home-made jam, light scones, and delicious cakes.

'I remember the splendid birthday cake, with three pink candles,' Charles was saying.

'And I blew them out with a single puff!' Thomas laughed at the memory.

'He wore a paper crown and looked angelic, but there was nothing of the angel in three-year-old Thomas that day,' Jane recalled.

'Come now, Auntie Jane, I thought you were fond of me?' her nephew teased.

'I was, and am, my dear,' she insisted, her grey eyes tender with affection. Her sister's children had always been very close to her.

'How is my new little great-niece? Is she pretty?' she asked Ellen.

'She is very tiny, and will need a lot of care. I am staying with them, temporarily, until the baby is weaned. Basil was worried about Prue, and they seemed to need me. No, she is not a pretty baby, but so adorable.'

'Have they chosen a name for her?'

'Victoria Louise. Basil has already shortened it to Vicky. Shall you be coming to the christening, Thomas?' Ellen asked her son, but she knew already what the answer would be.

'I am sorry, Mama. I couldn't possibly manage it. Please convey my sincere regrets to Basil and Prue.'

'I will,' Ellen sighed. It was a thorn in the flesh that brother and sister had never been close, yet Thomas was not entirely to blame. Prue had such a jealous nature. She was actually jealous of the baby now because Basil made such a fuss of her. It was natural for a father to adore his daughter, but the breach between husband and wife was widening, and Ellen found herself the go-between. It was an uncomfortable situation, and her own peace-loving nature longed for the quiet of her small apartment on the top floor of The Haven. But they needed her, and she would stay until Prue was fully recovered.

Amelia had heard enough, and she changed the subject quickly. Such a fuss and bother over one child, and she had borne six! Ellen was too easily persuaded that she was indispensable. It was not a sensible arrangement with a daughter so emotionally disturbed that she always seemed to be on the verge of a nervous breakdown. Amelia was impatient with such a lack of self-control. Her own six daughters had been brought up strictly, and only Kate had challenged her authority; the result was absolutely disastrous. A cuckoo in the nest, that was her daughter Kate!

She turned to Rosalind and asked, 'Have you been

shopping, my dear, for suitable clothes for the tropics?'

'Yes, indeed. It has been such tremendous fun, and the dressmaker has been making my day gowns. The styles are simple, but quite adequate. I have chosen cotton and flowered prints for the day gowns. My evening gowns are rather more elaborate. I understand there will be lots of parties and an occasional ball. I can hardly wait. I am so excited.'

'My daughter, Ellen, employed a native dressmaker who was attached to the garrison. Isn't that so, my dear?' Amelia now addressed her eldest daughter, and Ellen agreed.

'Such a clever little man. One had only to show him an illustration in a magazine, and he would copy it. The tradition is handed down from father to son, and his two grandsons worked as apprentices, sitting on the floor. The linen costume that he made for me could have been bought at Harrods. There was such a fascinating display of materials from which to choose in the native bazaar. We were received like royalty, with polite salaams, and always served with tea and biscuits.'

'Did your husband accompany you?' Rosalind asked, eager for more information on such a fascinating subject.

Ellen smiled whimsically. 'He always declared I had been cheated, and he could have purchased the materials for half the price. It was considered the normal practice to bargain, but I hadn't the heart for it, and neither had my friend who always accompanied me. It seemed so mean when the materials were so reasonably priced compared to our prices, and they all had to make a living.'

'Isn't that just like Mama. Always defending the underdog,' teased Thomas, affectionately. 'My esteemed Papa should have accompanied you, darling, for safety's sake if not for the bargaining. I shall not allow my wife to go shopping in a native bazaar without a proper escort.'

'We came to no harm, dear, and we were treated with the utmost courtesy.'

'That was a long time ago, Mama. Times have changed since your day, and a native bazaar will probably be out of bounds for the wives of officers.'

'That would be a pity. Rosalind would enjoy it.'

'It all sounds so terribly romantic, life on the Northwest Frontier,' Rosalind enthused. 'I know I am going to love it. Papa has told me about the hill stations, where the women and children spend the hottest season of the year in delightful surroundings, and the men spend their furlough there, that is to say, the officers. The ranks remain on the plain in the charge of the sergeants. And when the men arrive at the hill stations it's all tremendous fun, with picnics and parties, tennis and polo, dancing the night away, and riding, of course. I know it's all going to be terribly thrilling, and I shall want to spend the rest of my life on the Northwest Frontier.'

Not if Thomas neglects you when you are pregnant, and the heat and the smells and the dust make you long for England, and you are so homesick you cry yourself to sleep every night, Ellen was thinking, her dark eyes sad with memories. How she wished she could spare this lovely child the suffering that seemed inevitable. Thomas could be charming and affectionate. But he would not be faithful. Too many women and too much whisky. They were so young and vulnerable, younger even than Jonathan and herself had been. She wondered if Rosalind pleased and satisfied her husband in the marriage bed. She had always been frightened of sex, and a bit of a prude. She had done her duty as a wife, and borne three children in less than four years. Only her own conscience reminded her she had loved her children too well.

'How are we getting back?' The question shattered the brave attempts to be cheerful, and everyone stared at Thomas as though he had committed a grave misdemeanour. He had the grace to blush, and Amelia answered the question with a calmness she was far from feeling.

'I have ordered the station cab to take you to the station in good time to catch your train.'

'Thank you, Grandmama. You think of everything.' He kissed her cheek.

'May we share the cab, Thomas? I have to get back to Town to keep an appointment by seven o'clock,' Charles explained.

'Of course,' Thomas agreed.

'Would there be room for Edward and myself? We also have to get back to relieve Aggie. She gets so agitated when she is left in charge,' said Jane.

'The more the merrier. We will squeeze you in. I will nurse Rosalind on my knees. She is light as a feather.'

'And I will nurse Bella. She is even lighter than a feather!' Roderic declared, flippantly, to make them laugh, for the women were near to tears now the last hour was slipping away.

'You won't mind, my darlings, if I do not come to the station to see you off? I would prefer to stand at the gate.' Amelia's voice was choked with emotion, and her blue eyes misted with the tears she would not allow herself to shed in public. 'I should have ordered a second cab, then all of you could have gone to the station in comfort. How about you, Ellen, and Bertha?'

They both shook their heads. To wave their farewells from the green gate would be less distressing than watching the train disappear round the bend.

'We will see them off. Their train leaves some twenty minutes before the London train,' said Charles, who always took the precaution to check in the railway guide.

'We six will travel back to London together and keep each other company,' said Kate, who was feeling sentimental over losing her darling boy.

'We have second-class tickets,' Jane reminded her. 'And you always travel first.'

'I will pay the difference.' Charles smiled at Jane and she thanked him and thought what a nice person he was.

So Amelia poured the last cup of tea and Edward ate the last crumbs of his second slice of fruit cake. He made no secret of the fact that he thoroughly enjoyed afternoon tea at The Haven.

The last few moments held an indescribable

sadness for Amelia and for Ellen, and when the cab had driven away and they stood there, clutching their handkerchiefs they had waved so bravely, they had no words to comfort each other. Norah was weeping unashamedly, and Bertha dabbed her wet eyes as they followed Amelia into the silent house.

Slowly, with dragging steps, Ellen climbed the stairs to weep in the privacy of her bedroom, while Amelia returned to the drawing-room and closed the door.

'It's like a death in the house,' sobbed Norah, as she cleared the tea-table with the help of Bertha.

'I will brew us a fresh cup of tea, love, before we start on the washing up,' promised her practical companion.

'*Five years*. It's an eternity,' sniffed Norah, miserably.

'My dearest, we have each other. Nothing in the world can separate us now. We will live, and die, together.'

Chapter Six

It had taken all day to embark, and the horses, with their attendant grooms, were the last to come aboard.

Thomas stood at the rail with Rosalind, jostled by fellow officers and their wives, all intent on watching the safe passage of their own particular mount up the gangway and into the well deck, where the stables had been prepared with even greater care and more comfort than the cabins for their owners.

Carriages had transported the officers' wives and families to the docks. Rosalind had been most indignant because she had not been allowed to bring her own favourite, and had been promised a suitable mount at the end of the journey.

'It's not fair!' she had complained, petulantly, but the Colonel was adamant. Other officers' wives who were keen riders and very attached to their mounts would expect the same treatment, and rightly so. He had always tried to be fair and kind in settling the many problems of a domestic nature as well as military.

Rosalind had now forgotten her disappointment in the excitement of embarkation and giggled happily at the antics of the handsome stallion who had to be persuaded by a patient groom to set foot on the gangway.

'It's not funny. He could injure himself. Then where should I be? I should never find another like him,' Thomas reminded her.

'I sometimes think you are fonder of that horse than of your wife!' she retorted, pouting her pretty mouth.

'Could be, my sweet,' he teased. But there was a grain of truth in her observation, and the bond between a man and his horse was very strong. But the regiment was his first love; it was in his blood, and no other career would have been possible.

During these early months of marriage, it had soon become apparent to Rosalind that she was not, and never would be, the most important factor in her husband's world. He adored her as a charming plaything and satisfactory bed-mate, but it was a superficial attraction that had no lasting value. In her innocence she had thought to possess him completely because he had taught her to enjoy the marriage bed, but Thomas had been encouraged since his earliest recollections to see himself as a favourite of the gods. He took what he wanted and gave little in return.

As Ellen had long since discovered, her handsome son was capable of inflicting grievous hurt by his careless disregard of other people's feelings. He could not bear to be disliked or ignored. Subaltern Jones was ignoring him these days. The bitterness of defeat had eaten into the soul of that morbid Welshman. Not for David a romantic courtship on the long sea voyage. If he couldn't have Rosalind, he would remain a bachelor, he had decided.

Now he stood a little apart from the rest, watching her with Thomas, his lean, sensitive face and melancholy dark eyes in complete contrast to that striking fair Adonis who had so completely captivated his love. Seeing them together tormented his senses, yet he could not take his eyes away. His hated rival was so confoundedly sure of himself, and had every right to be since he had won the hand of the Colonel's daughter with the apparent ease of a born conqueror. And he had changed her in a few short months from a coy, flirtatious little minx to a doting wife. They said there were stormy scenes between husband and wife – servants' talk – and David supposed her wilfulness was something that had to be tamed. His own romantic heart loved her to distraction. Cartwright was unworthy of such a jewel, incapable of worshipping her as his lovely Rosalind should be worshipped.

When he sang, he sang for her alone. His voice was the instrument that held all his emotions, all his deepest yearning. There had been a time, not so long ago, when he felt her responding to the invitation in his singing Welsh voice. They had danced together, and she was light as thistledown in his arms. But always he had to share her favours with half-a-dozen others.

It was a gala occasion, this embarkation. Their own regimental band was playing on the top deck, and the dockside was crowded with relatives and friends. He had taken leave of his own family in the Welsh village, and had begged them not to come to

Southampton. To go through it all again would be quite unbearable.

The haunting strains of 'Greensleeves' floated across Southampton Water, and women were dabbing their wet eyes. David felt the hot tears welling in his own eyes, and choked back a sob. Then it was over, and every man on board the troopship and on the dockside sprang to attention at the opening bars of the National Anthem. They were soldiers of the Queen, duty bound to defend the frontiers of her far-flung Empire. In this respect, Thomas and David were brothers.

Aunt Millie was sharing a cabin with the elderly governess attached to the family of Major Price-Browne; she had taught an earlier generation, and was loved and respected. The two women had much in common, had travelled widely, and possessed strong stomachs that had not disgraced them at the first rolling motion of the vessel on the high seas. But they would soon be required to minister to those who were not so fortunate. The governess would find all three of her pupils prostrate on their bunks when they should have been taking the air on deck. Her spartan nature deplored such weakness, and the three little girls would be reminded of their duty: as the daughters of a senior officer, they should be setting an example. They were much too sorry for themselves to pay attention, however, and would wallow in their misery for three days and nights, by which time the poor woman was wishing she had accepted the offer of retirement on a small pension.

In the meantime, Aunt Millie was playing nurse to

Rosalind, for the stewardess could not be expected to cope, single-handed, with so many seasick women and children. Thomas had tapped on their door that first morning at sea, and reported that his wife had succumbed to the malaise, and was threatening to die.

'Nonsense, my dear boy! Everyone fancies they are too ill to live. It does not signify. Leave her to me.'

'Bless you, Ma'am,' said he, gratefully, glad to escape to the quarterdeck, and his official duties as a junior officer on his first voyage. A sick wife in the confined space of a small cabin was no place for a man, and the early hours had been disturbed by her vomiting and moaning. It had happened so suddenly he had no time to move away. They had been making love in the lower bunk. Wrapped in each other's arms, he was feeling drowsily replete and satisfied. The stench was nauseating. He wrinkled his nose in disgust, muttered a curse, and slid to the floor. When he had sponged himself, he handed the wet towel to his discomforted spouse with a shudder of distaste, for he could not bear to touch her. Too weak to stand, she sat on the edge of the bunk, weeping helplessly, and he regarded her with the baleful glare of a disgruntled husband.

'You should not have eaten that chocolate pudding,' he grumbled.

She shook her head, dazed by the sickness and hurt by his complaining attitude. 'I want Papa,' she sobbed. But when she was married, Papa had given her away to her husband. Shivering and wretched, she groped for the dry towel Thomas was holding and lay back exhausted. Only once before in her short life had she felt so terribly ill, but she had recovered. This time she would die, and Thomas would never forgive himself. That look of disgust and the impatient tone of his voice, was that the attitude of a loving husband who only a few short weeks ago had vowed to 'cherish her in sickness and in health'? She could hear him moving about the cabin, and when the door opened and closed without so much as a word of comfort or sympathy, she knew those marriage vows had only one meaning for Thomas – to possess her body. It was a rude awakening and her heart ached with loneliness and misery.

When Aunt Millie walked in, unannounced, she found her niece sitting on the edge of the bunk, stark naked, clutching her stomach.

'Cover yourself, child!' said she, in horrified disapproval, and draped a blanket over her shivering little body. The stench of vomit clung to the tumbled bunk in the stuffy cabin, and the whimpering girl, with her pallid face and bedraggled hair had no resemblance to that blooming young woman of yesterday.

'Where is your nightgown, dear?' she asked.

Rosalind could only shake her head. Such a silly question. She had not worn a nightgown since their wedding night, and Thomas had not worn a nightshirt. He had no use for modesty.

Aunt Millie made no comment, and foraged in a drawer for a clean nightgown, removed the blanket, and draped it over the tousled head. She felt much less embarrassed by the situation. In seventeen years it was doubtful whether she had ever seen her niece unclothed. A step-mother has little authority in the nursery or the schoolroom, and her brother had been so foolishly indulgent.

'I want Papa,' said Rosalind, sulkily.

'When I have cleaned you up,' replied that good woman, filling a bowl with hot water. Gently she sponged face and hands, and brushed the tangled hair. The scent of lavender soap dispelled the sourness, and when she had sat Rosalind in a chair, she stripped off the sheets, and rang for the stewardess.

She arrived in due course with an air of brisk efficiency, and an armful of clean linen and towels. 'I been rushed off me feet with all me passengers ringing their bells,' she announced, glancing dispassionately at the limp figure on the chair. 'You wants to use that bowl, Ma'am, when you feel it coming up. There ain't no sense in waiting to spew it all over the place. There's worse to come. This ain't nothink. It can be real rough in the Bay.'

'A Job's comforter,' Aunt Millie reflected quietly when the woman had departed in a flurry of starched petticoats.

'Poor little pet. Did nobody warn you this could happen?' the Colonel asked, some time later, breezing into the stuffy cabin after his morning constitutional of twenty times round the upper deck, in the company of one of his senior officers. Smelling fresh and clean, and obviously disconcerted by the foul atmosphere, he was disinclined to linger, and averted his eyes from the bowl. What was the stewardess doing to neglect her duties in such a disgusting manner? The generous tip he had in mind for services rendered would be modified unless she bestirred herself more diligently. It did not occur to the Colonel that a small advance tip would be much appreciated by the poor woman, who was a widow with a family of children in the care of relatives who had to be paid. The wages were poor in anticipation of the tips but the majority of the passengers were reluctant to part with their money at the end of the voyage, when they had forgotten the unpleasant duties performed on that rough passage in heavy swell.

'I wish I was dead.' Rosalind's voice was weak and choked with misery.

The Colonel patted her hand. 'Be a brave girl. It will soon be over.'

'It won't. The stewardess said it gets worse in the Bay.'

'Stupid woman!'

'Thomas was disgusted. He does not love me any more.'

'I will have a word with him.'

'No, there is no need. I am too ill to bother.' She sighed, and closed her eyes.

'Your Aunt Millie will look after you. She is a kind soul. Try not to worry, dear heart. It will pass, and you will soon forget it once we are sailing on calm waters.'

'Must you be quite so bracing, Papa?'

'I am only trying to cheer you up.'

'I don't want to be cheered up. I want to be left alone.'

'Very well.' He kissed her damp brow and searched his mind for some further comment on the distressing situation, but could think of nothing but the trite suggestion, 'Try to sleep.'

He left her with a feeling of inadequacy, but it was no place for a man. The fried eggs and bacon he had enjoyed for breakfast suddenly erupted in his stomach, and he hurried up the companion-way and hung over the rail, very conscious of being observed by a dozen or more sufferers on the lower deck. The Colonel wiped his mouth, braced his shoulders, and went in search of a stiff whisky.

The horses were not liking it either. They were being coaxed out of their warm and comfortable stables to take a little exercise on the swaying deck. Three times daily, in strict rotation, they were led on a tight rein, prancing and dancing with nervous energy. Thomas slapped Jason's shining flanks with a hard hand, and promised a good gallop as soon as they disembarked on Indian soil. Jason flung up his handsome head and neighed impatiently.

Thomas laughed. 'My beauty. I couldn't agree more. It's a hell of a long time!' said he.

The doctor's face swam into focus on the third day. When a passenger became too ill for her limited ministrations, the stewardess handed over her responsibility. Rosalind had no recollection of seeing him in Aldershot, and no recollection of anything but the awful retching, the throbbing head, and the sour taste of vomit. Thomas was an insubstantial figure, floating in a grey mist, to ask the same stupid question, 'How are you feeling, my sweet?'

'Ghastly' was the only word that described her condition, and she could not be bothered to talk to him, so he went away, feeling guilty, but glad to escape.

'Thomas can sleep in my cabin, and I shall sleep here. The governess is sleeping with the children.' That was Aunt Millie at the end of the first day, or was it the second?

Rosalind had lost count. The days and the nights merged into one everlasting hour of unutterable misery. Aunt Millie was the only substantial object in the near vicinity, and her capable hands sponged her sticky face, changed her nightgown, and coaxed a sip of water down her parched throat. She had stopped asking for Papa. He smelled of fresh air and whisky, both of which she found incompatible with her suffering state.

Now the doctor was here, and Aunt Millie was discussing her symptoms, as though she had no substance, no eyes to see, no ears to hear, no voice to speak for herself. It was true, in a sense, and she lay there, alienated from her normal self, while the doctor took her temperature and felt her pulse.

'You were wise to send for me, Ma'am,' he told Aunt Millie approvingly.

'She has a slight rash on her chest, doctor. Is that all part and parcel of the sickness?' she asked.

'Not to my knowledge,' said he, unbuttoning the nightgown and peering more closely. 'That is a measles rash, Ma'am,' he declared, with calm deliberation.

'*Measles?*' she gasped, in some agitation.

'I have just given orders for the youngest Beresford child to be removed to sick bay, but I did not expect to find an adult case. Did Rosalind not have measles as a child?'

'She had nothing more serious than a feverish cold, I seem to remember.'

'A pity. It's as well to get them over, these childish maladies, in childhood. No wonder she is running such a high temperature. Has she been in contact with the Beresford children?'

'She was amusing them in the nursery soon after we embarked. Rosalind is fond of children, and they like her because she is normally full of fun.'

'Quite so, and I am annoyed that one foolish mother should be so inconsiderate. That youngest child must have had the rash when they came aboard. Now it will spread, and I shall have an epidemic on my hands.'

'I suppose she thought they would be left behind if she reported it?'

'They certainly would,' he growled. 'I must keep a strict eye on the rest of the children and have them removed to sickbay as soon as the rash appears.'

'I don't want to go to sickbay,' said Rosalind, tearfully.

The doctor hesitated. 'She could stay here, Ma'am, if you are willing to nurse her? But it would greatly restrict your own movements.'

'That would not worry me, Doctor. I could take a

walk on deck in the early morning, and again in the evening when the other passengers were dining.'

'That would be splendid, and I would arrange for your meals to be delivered to your own cabin. But you must not tire yourself, Ma'am.'

'I am perfectly healthy. It is only the arthritis that troubles me, but that is a common complaint, I have noticed. One has to put up with it since there is no cure. A small dose of laudanum eases the pain when it gets too severe.'

'Quite so.'

They both were remembering the fright Rosalind had given them when she helped herself from the bottle.

'Then that is settled, Ma'am. I dare say the several governesses attached to the regiment would prefer to nurse their own charges. I shall be in attendance twice daily and, any time you feel anxious, do not hesitate to send for me. When she has finished vomiting, try her with oranges. There is nothing more refreshing or beneficial in the early stages of measles in my opinion. She will not be ready for solid food for another week or so. It's a question of gradually getting back to normal. First a little broth, or beef tea, and calves' foot jelly. All very light and nourishing.'

Rosalind pulled a face, and he smiled and patted her hand. 'I know the very mention of food is repellent at the moment, my dear, but you will be surprised how quickly this will pass. With such a slight rash, it looks like being a very mild attack of measles. The Beresford child is smothered, poor mite. No two children are alike. They will be well cared for in sickbay. I am able to call upon Sergeant Martin's wife, who was a nurse at the Hospital for Women in London before her marriage. A kind and capable woman. It's unfortunate for it means that nobody will be allowed ashore at the ports of call *en route*. The health authorities are very strict, and anything of an infectious nature has to be reported. We may get held up at Karachi till the end of the incubation period. That is to say, the men will disembark, together with the families of the ranks.'

'What a disturbance, and what a lot of extra work for you, Doctor.'

'Quite so, and all because of one inconsiderate and rather selfish woman.' He sighed, and went on his way, a man no longer young, who would serve the regiment to the end of his days.

'I wonder whether Thomas had measles as a child,' mused Aunt Millie, as she closed the door.

But Rosalind was not listening. She had reached for the bowl.

'The children are going down like ninepins, Ma'am!' the steward reported, three days later, when he served their breakfast in the cabin the two women had shared for that first day at the start of the voyage. Miss Harrison, the elderly governess, known affectionately as 'Harry', was beginning to feel the strain of her responsibility, for the middle child, Emma, aged eight, was seriously ill. Her only rest was the brief interlude for meals and frequent cups of tea in the cabin that Thomas used for sleeping in. The two women took turns for a brisk walk on the deck, one being always in attendance on Rosalind and the three little sisters.

The mother of the children did no more than enquire how her poor little darlings were feeling, but it was 'Harry' they wanted, and 'Harry's' love and devotion that saved little Emma from an early death.

During this period of enforced isolation, the two women became firm friends. The days passed pleasantly enough when the doctor allowed the sick children to be carried outdoors to a sheltered corner of the deck. Wrapped in rugs, and thoroughly spoiled with all the attention they were receiving, their demands to be amused were cheerfully met by various members of the crew. 'Chippie', the ship's carpenter, was called upon to fashion a number of cradles for the dolls. Dusty Miller, a jovial quarter-master, played countless games of Snap and Happy Families in his off-duty time, and even Rosalind, who was inclined to despise such childish fun and games, could be seen tapping her feet to the rhythm of Charlie Potter's mouth-organ.

It was strange to wave to Thomas from behind a barricade of deck chairs. Yet she had no strength and no desire for closer contact, even if it had been allowed. It was Thomas who was feeling the segregation more keenly, and missing the sensual pleasure of the marriage bed. Short-tempered with his men, and rude to his batman, only Jason recognized the note of frustration in that familiar voice, because it was mutual.

With the sun hot on their sweating bodies, even

the tropical uniform was too cumbersome. The men were drilled with disciplined regularity in readiness for their appointed task as guardians of the Frontier. They were a mixed bunch of men who had enlisted to claim the Queen's shilling, and to escape from a world of poverty and vice. Their wives and children, housed in the hold, were allowed up on the lower deck for brief periods when the ship was no longer tossing and pitching. The stench was appalling. Three pregnant women died in child-birth, two babies were smothered in communal bunks, shared by their brothers and sisters. One small boy fell to his death from the top of a ladder, and the anguished weeping and wailing, too distant to disturb the more privileged passengers, set the sensitive nerves of the well-bred horses on edge. The grooms complained and were cursed by their officers.

While the troopship sailed peacefully across the calm waters of the Indian Ocean, and the officers' lady wives languished in deck chairs with parasols to protect their complexions, and a steward to serve iced drinks, women and children were panting for breath in the crowded, stinking hold. Such a hell could not have been envisaged but had to be endured, for it was the only accommodation available in that day and age for the families of men serving in the ranks when the regiment was drafted overseas. The barracks they had left behind were dirty and verminous, and bare of anything but the basic necessities, but at least they could breathe fresh air, and the children were free to run about in their own restricted area of the garrison. They escaped the measles epidemic because they were too far removed from contamination; few, if any, would have survived this additional hazard.

The gap between the privileged and the underprivileged was too wide to negotiate, and nobody, least of all the poor wretches in the hold, expected anything but segregation. Yet the majority survived. Self-preservation was a stong instinct in the underprivileged, born to fight for every crust of bread and every bowl of thin broth. No mention was made of their plight on the upper deck. The subject would be too indelicate. The officers delegated their sergeants, and the sergeants delegated their corporals to supervise the distribution of rations and water. Such was protocol, and such was the custom, to shift the responsibility.

Thomas felt only a vague pity for the women and children in the hold, but he made no attempt to see for himself the appalling conditions reported by the corporal to his sergeant. He could shut his eyes and turn a deaf ear to anything of a distressing nature. His duty to his men did not include their dependants.

Leaning on the rail, watching the flying fish cavorting on transparent wings, Thomas was brooding on the unfairness of Fate that had robbed him of the companionship of his adorable wife on this interminable voyage. She seemed quite oblivious to his sufferings, and had not replied to the loving little note that Aunt Millie had delivered. 'I long for the night when I can hold you in my arms, my sweet,' he had written. It was true. The tempation to share his lonely bunk with the fascinating Mrs Foster-Clarke was very strong. That she was willing, and that her husband had ceased to care whose bed she shared, was common knowledge in the Mess. But when you had married the Colonel's daughter, some discretion had to be employed!

An awning had been erected in that sheltered corner of the deck where the sick children were slowly recovering. Strong sunlight had to be avoided or the sight could suffer permanent damage, the doctor had emphasized. Rosalind was living in an unreal world, drifting through endless days and nights of a half-remembered past, and taking no hold on the future. She had no strength, no appetite, and no interest in the lively prattle of the children. The only adult to suffer the indignity of such a childish complaint, she sat a little apart from the children, in a gown of sprigged muslin and a drooping straw hat, looking so frail and wan that Subaltern Jones, who never missed an opportunity to play 'Peeping Tom', felt his throat tighten with pain. Like a wilted flower she lay there, with closed eyes, her hands folded in her lap, yet she seemed to his worshipful eyes more lovely than ever, and more unobtainable. His romantic Celtic senses were saddened by her helplessness. She was constantly in his thoughts, and in his dreams he held her in his arms and kissed her naked breasts.

At that moment as though prompted by the sentiments of a love-lorn Welshman, the regimental band came to life, and the vibrant notes of 'Land of my Fathers' caught at his throat. His dark eyes were moist as he lifted his voice in praise of his beloved country. Rosalind opened her eyes and smiled. Dear David.

Down in the hold, a bereaved mother caught an echo of her homeland, and wept, like Rachel, for her lost children.

Chapter Seven

They were all there to greet them – the native servants the authorities provided for the officers, drilled and disciplined to the required standards of the British Army.

A tall, grey-haired man in a white linen suit stepped forward with the gravity and dignity of an English butler, and salaamed politely. 'I am Bearer, Sahib, in your house. It is my pleasure to greet you. Many years I serve officer sahibs. Now I return to this house where I was servant to your father and your mother. It is the Will of Allah,' he pronounced in his careful English.

Thomas smiled disarmingly. Such a handsome young Sahib, and so like his father. It seemed to the Bearer that the clock had been put back twenty-five years.

'What do I call you, my good fellow?'

The voice was the same, and the arrogant manner was expected of an English Sahib.

'They call me Boy. Always I am called Boy.'

Boy? With that grey head. He must be all of fifty years. But with such gravity and dignity, one did not question such a statement.

'You remember my father?'

'Very well, Sahib.'

'In this same bungalow?'

'Yes, Sahib.'

Thomas turned to the girl hanging on his arm. 'Isn't that interesting, sweetheart?'

'Yes,' she agreed, listlessly.

Such a pretty little Memsahib. The perfect English rose. Such a pity she would have to fade, Boy was thinking. The climate was not kind to these young memsahibs. He remembered the young Sahib's mother, a dark-eyed lady, very calm and quiet, with nice manners to the servants. That was a rare thing. It was the memsahibs who made trouble because they would not be bothered to speak the language of the servants, and he, the Bearer, must always take the blame.

'Darling, I must lie down. I am quite exhausted.'

Boy recognized that petulant demand. It was the voice of a memsahib who would behave like a spoilt child. His own voice was gentle. 'On the back verandah, Memsahib, there are chairs to sit, and chairs to lie, with many cushions. I will show you.'

'Who are all these people?' she answered him haughtily.

'They are your servants, Memsahib. There is my daughter, to maid you. She speaks good English, no trouble. There is Cook, dhobi, sweeper, garden boy. No speak English. No trouble. You give me order, Memsahib. I give order to servant.'

Rosalind cast a cursory glance over her native staff. She supposed they would have to do since she had not been consulted. They all were dressed alike in

284

striped cotton trousers and white tunics. Only the old man and the girl wore sandals. The others had bare feet. Not very hygienic. The horrid, smelly natives, and the horrid, smelly camels who had collected them from the hotel at Lahore, had been quite revolting. It was all so strange and confusing, and the novels she had read on board ship had not prepared her for the heat, the dust, the pungent smells and barefoot servants. She sighed, and dropped her aching head on Thomas's shoulder.

The old man, called Boy, waved a hand in dismissal, and the others simply vanished into thin air. They followed him through the house. The windows were shuttered, and fans stirred the warm air.

'There, my sweet, now you can relax,' said Thomas, soothingly, as she sank back among the cushions and closed her eyes.

What an interminable journey! They seemed to have been travelling for months, and she had hardly seen Thomas for the regiment had had a long trek overland while the wives and children had travelled by train to Lahore, where they had been accommodated in an hotel awaiting the arrival of their menfolk. The rest of the journey, in a caravan of camels, swaying and jolting in bamboo baskets, had made her sick. She shuddered at the memory.

Thomas had lost his batman on that trek across country. He had died of a fever, poor fellow, and been buried the same day. Thomas was so disgustingly healthy. He seemed immune to measles and fevers. Now he was explaining to Boy about the batman.

'It makes no importance, Sahib. I valet you,' said he, proudly.

'Splendid! Then no need to bother with a replacement?'

'No need, Sahib. Now I fetch cold drinks. Will Memsahib have fruit juice? Very cold. Very nice.'

Rosalind nodded.

'Whisky for you, Sahib?'

'Yes.'

The young Sahib's father had been a heavy drinker, and Boy had watched and waited so anxiously for his return from the Mess. If he was drunk, Boy would pull off his boots and settle him comfortably on the drawing-room sofa. It was not good for Memsahib, in a state of pregnancy, to see her Sahib in such a bad state. When the morning came, there would be strong black coffee and a cold bath, and a reunion with Memsahib who never complained. A very brave lady. Two babas had been born, both girls, and Sahib had been bitterly disappointed. It was the Will of Allah, Boy had explained gently – and been cursed for his impertinence. Now here was the son, at last. What would the future hold for these young ones? Boy was wondering as he served the drinks. It was a new beginning. Sad memories of the past must not be allowed to intrude on the present. His daughter, Marja, was hovering in the kitchen, and he bade her attend immediately to the Memsahib.

'Remove her shoes and stockings. Bathe her feet.' He spoke sharply, and she obeyed. At the age of fifteen she was no longer a child, but a beautiful young woman, for whom he must find a suitable husband. The girl's eyes were downcast, respectfully, as she knelt to serve her new Memsahib. The long lashes that swept her cheeks hid the sullen expression. She knew she was being watched by the beautiful young Sahib. Her father was also watching. Always, until today, she had been kept in the background, observing, very carefully, all that was demanded, never actually making direct contact with these superior beings her father honoured. He had taught her to speak English, to be honest, respectful and obedient, and she had been whipped for speaking the truth when the last Sahib they had served, a loud-voiced, red-faced senior officer, had put his hand down her tunic and pinched her nipples so hard she had cried out with the pain. Her father had said she was to blame for flaunting the fact that she was no longer a child with a flat chest, but a woman with firm, pear-shaped breasts. Her father had taught her to speak quietly and to tread softly, but he had not been able to teach her humility because it was not in her nature to be humble. She knew she was beautiful. The only difference between herself and this new young Memsahib was the colour of her skin, her eyes and her hair. Allah could be blamed for that!

A wave of envy swept over her as she peeled off the silk stockings and touched the soft, fair skin. The pride in her own dark-eyed beauty and shapely limbs was suddenly eclipsed by this bewitching loveliness. She knew a moment of panic, of rebellion. Then she lifted her head and caught the meaningful glance in those mocking blue eyes. He understood!

Swift as an arrow from its bow, she was plunged into the fire of love, so consuming in its heat and passion, she stumbled as she rose from her knees to fetch a bowl of water.

'Steady!' The Sahib grasped her arm. She could feel the grip of his fingers through the sleeve of her tunic.

'Thank you, Sahib,' she whispered, and slipped away.

When she returned with the bowl of water, her father was signalling to the garden boy to play the hose on the lawn, and the boy obeyed. He was but a child of twelve years of age, and he spent all day watering the lawn and tending the flowers a homesick memsahib had planted to remind her of England. The green lawn was his pride and joy, as her own firm, pear-shaped breasts were her pride and joy. Everyone must have something to lift the spirit from the drudgery of service, for she found no pleasure in serving these white-skinned people who came from the land of the great Queen Victoria; it was a duty and an obligation. Yet she was her father's daughter, and a daughter has no status. To obey, or to be whipped. He had not spared the whipping because of their relationship. It was the only way to teach obedience. In the servants' quarters, beyond the garden with its shady trees, her father was much respected, and his word was law.

The spray of cold water from the hose was cooling the hot air, and the young Memsahib was sipping the iced fruit drink and looking better pleased.

'What is your name, girl?' she asked, as her feet were bathed.

'My name is Marja, Memsahib,' she answered, respectfully.

'Who taught you to speak English?'

'My father taught me, Memsahib.'

'And doubtless *my* father will have taught *your* father?' the Sahib suggested.

'That is so, Sahib,' the girl agreed.

Thomas was enjoying his new role. He would hardly miss his batman. This old man they called Boy would make an excellent valet, and if the girl pleased Rosalind, then he would have few worries. The doctor had warned him that the measles had left a certain weakness in his wife's constitution, and she might have to spend more time in the higher altitudes of the Murray Hills. In the meantime, he would advise plenty of rest and little exertion. No riding, dancing, or late night parties.

'Not much fun, eh, my sweet? But I will make it up to you when you are stronger,' Thomas had promised.

They had made love in the bedroom of the hotel in Lahore, after their enforced separation, but something had been lacking in Rosalind's response. She was tired, and a few cuddles and kisses would have pleased her more. There was a limit to a man's endurance, he had to remind her, and he had been deprived of sex all these weeks.

'I need something more than cuddles and kisses, sweetheart. Just relax,' he told her.

Then, as always, he knew exactly where to find the most vulnerable spots.

'Where have you been?'

Thomas was beginning to find the question irritating. The Mess was a lively place, and the company congenial. Rosalind was always tired and rather fretful these days. She had to be amused and entertained, and it was not always possible to arrange for one of the young wives to visit her. They had their own lives to lead, and were finding their new environment quite fascinating. The twins, who had been courted by two young subalterns on the voyage, would shortly be married by the chaplain. They could talk of nothing else but the delights of courtship, almost forgotten by a wife who had since suffered that wretched attack of measles.

Veronica Mowbray could talk of nothing else but the beautiful Arab mare her father had bought for her eighteenth birthday, and Penelope Fortescue, with her lisping voice, was hardly tolerable for more than an hour.

Rosalind was bored to distraction. All the things she liked best – riding, dancing and late night parties – being denied, the days were long and tedious, and often lonely. As Thomas had predicted, it was no fun, and having fun had hitherto been her main reason for living. All about her, in this swarming garrison town, life went on with unchanging rhythm and regularity. The sun rose to the strident call of Reveille and set to the softer notes of the bugle. It was much like Aldershot as far as duty and discipline were concerned. Sweating men had always to be reminded they were bound by iron rules to follow the drum to far distant outposts of the British Empire. They were here for the sole purpose of guarding the Frontier. With a few carefully picked men, Thomas would soon be detailed for this dangerous assignment. He would welcome the challenge with his usual disregard for danger. Aunt Millie would be in residence in his absence.

As for Jason, that indefatigable beast, he had quickly adapted to the climate and the environment. One place was as good as another for an early morning gallop, and a man on his back who belonged there. The handsome stallion and the handsome subaltern were inseparable. Thomas was happy and excited at the prospect of confronting a band of tribesmen in the hills. With his father's blood in his veins, and his father's honour to defend, the sooner the better. Rosalind had to be reminded that she was an officer's wife, and also had a part to play.

So he answered her question with another. 'How would you like a puppy to keep you company?'

'No, thank you. I am not very partial to dogs. Come and sit down and talk to me.'

He sighed and sat down. His breath smelled of whisky when he came from the Mess, and she turned her face away when he bent to kiss her. 'You smell horrid,' she complained, petulantly.

'It's the custom, my sweet. Everyone drinks whisky in this benighted climate. When in Rome, you do as the Romans,' he told her.

'There are other drinks beside whisky.'

'Soft drinks are not for men.'

She regarded him dispassionately. His face was

flushed. He was shiny-eyed and almost, though not quite, intoxicated. 'If you dare to come home drunk, I shall report you to Papa!' she threatened.

'You will never see me drunk. *Never!*' he shouted.

Boy was hovering with the usual tot of whisky and a syphon of soda water on a silver salver.

'Take it away! We will have coffee, iced coffee,' said Rosalind.

Boy hesitated, glancing from one to the other.

'Leave it. I will help myself when I am ready. Bring coffee for Memsahib,' Thomas contradicted authoritatively.

'Very good, Sahib.'

The atmosphere was charged with the angry resentment they made no attempt to conceal. Did they suppose a native servant had no feelings, no sense of danger in this strained relationship between husband and wife? Boy was deeply concerned and saddened by these obvious signs that his young Sahib was tempted to adopt the habits of the senior officers. There was a weakness in his character that he had inherited from the father who was here before him. The Memsahib was making a grave mistake. A man must be master in his own house.

As he set down the tray on the bamboo table, the Memsahib reached for the whisky and flung it into the garden.

'That was naughty.' The Sahib's voice was dangerously calm. 'Bring me another, Boy,' said he.

And Boy repeated, 'Very good, Sahib.'

'You are looking very handsome tonight, *mon brave*.'

Isabella Foster-Clarke's gloved hand rested on the sleeve of the immaculate white jacket, and her brown eyes were soft as velvet. Those same eyes could be black with anger, or cold with indifference. It was her changing moods that attracted her many admirers, for they never knew what to expect from her.

Tonight she was playing the role of the charming hostess, and her perfume reminded Thomas of Kate. They were waltzing to the strains of 'The Blue Danube'. It was not often that his thoughts wandered in the company of Isabella. He was much too occupied in pleasing her. As the wife of a senior officer, she held an advantage over the wives of the junior officers. She was able to pick and choose for these informal dinner parties. She invariably set the tongues of the matrons wagging by including two of the young subalterns. Thomas was a special favourite, and his wife was still under the care of the doctor.

Thomas was usually to be found among the bachelors, and in that role enjoyed the best of both worlds, or so it was assumed. He was amusing, he danced divinely, and he knew how to excite a woman. Isabella was thirty-five, and so practised in the art of seduction, she knew instinctively that Thomas was only waiting to be asked to share her bed. It was her pleasure to withhold that privilege as long as possible, however. Her own husband was having an affair with a plump matron, old enough to be his mother.

'A nice fat bum to pinch, my dear!' he had told her. Reggie could be so coarse!

It had been a pleasant evening, with the usual musical interlude between dinner and dancing. She had accompanied David Jones on the pianoforte. David was an asset to any party in a totally different way. His shy smile held a hint of sadness, and he seldom paid a compliment, but his singing Welsh voice was his passport to popularity. They said he was in love with Rosalind Cartwright, and that he and Thomas had actually fought over her on one occasion. They said David was only waiting for Thomas to be sent away on a frontier patrol to pay a call on Rosalind. They said . . . they said. Isabella enjoyed all the gossip and delighted in her own notorious reputation. It was much exaggerated, of course, but she encouraged that exaggeration. Her manner, her complete lack of decorum and her revealing gowns all advertised her sex appeal that Thomas, and others, found irresistible. Variety was indeed the spice of life to a woman of Isabella Foster-Clarke's mentality, and she had to keep boredom at bay.

In that respect, there was nothing to choose between the younger and the older woman, for both had an obsessive fear of being left alone. Isabella was tall for a woman and proud of her slender figure. When she danced, she could meet the eyes of her tall partners, including Thomas, and she seldom allowed herself to be partnered by a shorter man, unless it was the Colonel.

The rustle of silk petticoats accompanied the music, and the servants hovered at a discreet distance. Born and bred to serve the white Sahibs, the regiments that occupied the garrison town for the allotted span of five years were much alike. The officers and their families took possession of the spacious bungalows, and the native servants, with the self-importance expected of these superior beings.

Only the Ayah slept in the house, on a mat outside the nursery door, like a faithful dog. It was expected that the native servants would quickly adapt to the ways of a new family, and they were not consulted. The memsahibs seldom bothered to learn more than a few words of the language spoken by their servants. The Bearer and the Ayah would act as interpreters. This, too, was expected, and taken for granted. Native servants had status only among themselves. They were part and parcel of the establishment. Ayah would grow fond of her babas, but they quickly grew into dictatorial little demons, with spiteful tongues and slapping hands. Then the white sahibs were gone, and it started all over again.

It may have been a mistake for Boy to teach his daughter to speak English, and to cultivate the habits of the white Sahib and his Memsahib, for now she saw herself as superior to her own people, yet still no nearer to being accepted by her employers as an intelligent individual. Marja's mind may have been superior to Rosalind's, but her native blood was indisputable. If she had been able to claim one white parent, she could have called herself an Anglo-Indian. But her skin, her eyes, and her hair were native.

*　　*　　*

'How long will you be away?'

Another question that Thomas resented. Torn between the urge to prove his courage and resourcefulness on the Frontier, and his infatuation with the fascinating wife of a fellow officer, his nerves were taut and his temper short.

'It depends on the resistance we encounter. They are devils for surprise tactics, these hillmen. We never know what to expect from them. But my men are well trained and equipped with the new rifles that were issued before we left England. The old ones we used at Sandhurst are obsolete.'

'I did not ask for a lecture. I asked how long you would be away,' Rosalind reminded him in the fretful voice that had lately become habitual.

'Not long. Three to four weeks.'

'I could ask Papa to send one of the other officers?'

'No!' He leaned forward, his eyes blazing. 'Do you want me to look like a fool? When duty calls, I have to go. You, of all people, should know. What has happened to you, Rosalind? There was a time when the regiment meant as much to you as it does to me. There now, don't cry. I apologize for speaking so roughly.' He took her limp hand, and raised it to his lips. Her wet eyes reproached him. He could not bear to see her cry.

'Stay with me, *please*, darling,' she pleaded.

'Come, my sweet, sit on my knee. Tell me what is troubling you. Is it only that I am going away? Or something more?' He dried her tears. She had to be comforted and cosseted like a child, and she lay in his arms with her head on his shoulder. The warmth of her body under the silk tea-gown was a tantalizing reminder that they had not made love since that night in Lahore. He felt deprived. He *was* deprived. A man needs something more than cuddles and kisses, and Isabella was a bitch, teasing him with her seductive glances.

'Sweetheart, I want you,' he whispered, fondly.

'Now?'

'Now.'

'I don't know. The doctor said . . .'

'The doctor said to be careful, and we have been careful. I would be so gentle, you would hardly know I had taken you.'

'Oh, *Thomas*. You silly man.'

'I can prove it. Will you? Please say you will.'

She nodded tremulously. Perhaps if she allowed him to make love to her, he would not want to go away?

He carried her into the bedroom, Isabella forgotten. The door closed. The shutters were closed. The girl's eyes widened with surprise and resentment. She had been brushed aside as though she had no substance. She had lost her identity. They called her 'Girl'. They had forgotten she had a name. She was a slave to the demands of this Memsahib who behaved like a spoilt child. Even the garden boy could hide himself under a bush and close his eyes in the heat of the day while she was expected to keep awake, to be on call yet never intruding – a pair of hands to fetch and carry, a quiet presence, a servant with no status.

A servant has ears to hear, she reminded herself, and the foolish little Memsahib would lose her beautiful husband to that other woman of such worldly wisdom. Since they had come to live here, this was the first time they had shut themselves away in the bedroom to make love. Every night they had slept apart. The Doctor Sahib had ordained it. When her Memsahib slept soundly, her maid-servant could slip away to the servants' quarters in the compound. Doctor Sahib gave medicine to induce sleep and calm the nerves. She slept like a child till cockcrow, when she awakened ready for early morning tea, as was the custom. The girl's father would wait patiently for his young Sahib, to help him undress and put him to bed in the dressing-room. He, too, was a slave, but there was a difference. He had served the white Sahibs for so many years, he found pleasure and pride in the service and did not see himself as a slave.

The girl was too young for such devotion to duty, and too feminine to care whether the rest of the sahibs were sleeping or waking, in danger or safety, or making love to their memsahibs. Her world was small, and only one Sahib mattered. Her young virgin body burned with the desire to lie with her beautiful Sahib. When her father had put him to bed, he would be alone till Reveille, sleeping off the effects of the whisky, while she lay awake, tormented by the urge to go to him. She knew exactly what he would do when he found her in his bed. There was no mystery in a man's need of a woman, and she was a woman now. In the darkness of the night he would take her and be satisfied. It was as natural as breathing. She would not speak a word or her voice would betray her. She could not see beyond that moment, because her vision was blurred by the image of the Memsahib, with her soft, white skin, her golden hair, her blue eyes. Love and hate lived side by side in this household. Fear and respect for her father was a separate thing. A daughter was born to serve. This was the Will of Allah.

'What are you doing here?' Her father's voice broke the train of thought, and she answered dutifully.

'I am waiting to be summoned by the Memsahib, as you have instructed, my father.'

'There is no need for you to wait. The Memsahib will not require you again till cock-crow. Go to your bed.'

'Yes, Father.'

He watched her walk away, much troubled by her wet eyes. He knew her tears were no longer the tears of a child, to be wiped away on her sleeve, but the tears of a native servant who found herself in love with her white Sahib.

They would all be taking their instructions from the Colonel's Memsahib while the Sahib was away. She had taken over the household the previous day – a very capable Memsahib who had taught herself to speak and understand their language sufficiently. Boy was impressed by her clever achievement, and bowed to her authority. Her countenance was stern, and she walked with a limp because she suffered from a sickness of the bones called arthritis. It was the English climate. There was much rain and fog and grey skies. But now all the memsahibs were complaining about the heat and the dust and the smells. Girl had listened to the gossip of other native servants, and not one of the memsahibs had a good word to say of the climate they had exchanged for the rain and the fog and the grey skies. One of the ayahs had personally experienced these discomforts in the land of the Great Queen Victoria, for she had travelled to England with one family and travelled back with another to save expense. Poor Ayah. She had not been consulted, and had nearly died of the English climate in a few short months.

'What are you doing there, girl?' The Colonel's Memsahib had eyes in the back of her head!

Girl explained politely that she was returning the tray to the kitchen.

'Is this the way to the kitchen?'

'No, Memsahib.'

There was no time for scolding. The young Memsahib was calling imperiously. 'Aunt Millie! Come and talk to me!'

'Coming, dear.' The tone of voice had changed, and there was a smile on her tight lips as she limped away.

Marja sighed. Her heart was heavy. Her day had started an hour ago, when her beautiful Sahib had ridden away on his beautiful horse. Her father had wished him a successful expedition and a safe journey while she hid herself in the shrubbery to shed her silent tears in secret. He was gone, and there was no joy in this household without her Sahib. How many days must pass before his return? The clip-clop of hooves, the beloved voice – the voice of an officer and a gentleman. She would not wish to go on living if he did not return. He was her lord and master, and she was his willing slave. These thoughts occupied her mind and her heart constantly.

They were leaving at dawn. They would carry only the barest necessities in their saddle bags. Thomas would ride Jason, and the men would ride the tough little mules, who were familiar with the hilly terrain. Nothing had been neglected, and they all knew exactly what the expedition entailed and the dangers they must face. The men that Thomas had picked were as tough and fearless as the mules they rode. They would follow where he led, and Thomas was a born leader.

Too exhausted to sleep, he lay awake, his mind tuned to the operation for which they had been planning and training since their arrival in the country. In theory, nothing could go wrong. In practice, it was extremely hazardous.

Lying there, taut with eager anticipation, Thomas had never felt more fit or more ready for action. He smiled at his masterful approach to the tantalizing Isabella. He had waited till the servants had retired to their own quarters, then surprised her in the bath! What a lark! He hadn't enjoyed himself so much since that afternoon with Kate when her husband had returned home unexpectedly. Nothing of the kind last night, for he had taken the precaution to ascertain the husband's exact whereabouts. A man does not make the same mistake twice. It had been a lively and lustful encounter that he had every intention of repeating at a later date. In the meantime, he would forget the pleasures of the flesh in the harsh realities of the Frontier. This was the life for which he was born and bred. He wondered if his father had made love to his mistress the night before he went into action. It would not have been to his own sweet mother, because she would have been heavy with child at that time. His sister, Prue, must have been conceived on their honeymoon. It was difficult, almost impossible, to visualize his mother in the act of intercourse. It was much easier to imagine his father making love.

They had said goodbye and he had dried Rosalind's tears some hours ago. He would not disturb her again. 'Parting is such sweet sorrow.' Was that Shakespeare? Three to four weeks was a rough estimate. It could be much longer. He sighed with contentment. Boy had become an indispensable part of his routine, but he would have to manage without him for a few weeks.

Boy's grey head was nodding on his chest. He dare not fall asleep, for his Sahib was depending on him. His Sahib was a happy man now, but his servant was sad. It was happening all over again, and he was powerless to prevent it. Waiting in the shadows, he had seen his young Sahib leaving the bungalow of that other woman in the early hours. So the wagging tongues had spoken the truth.

'Has your master gone?' Rosalind demanded fretfully, as the girl placed the tray on her knees.

'Yes, Memsahib,' she answered.

'Was your father in attendance to serve his coffee?'

'Yes, Memsahib.'

Rosalind sighed impatiently. She was always fretful in the early morning. Her head ached, and she woke with a nasty taste in her mouth. The sleeping draught the doctor had prescribed was necessary. Without it, she would lie awake for hours.

'What is actually wrong with you, Wosalind dear?' Penelope had asked in her lisping, babyish voice.

'Nervous exhaustion,' she told her.

'Poor darling. Is it very painful?'

Such a stupid question, typical of such a stupid girl.

'Your master will be away for three to four weeks. It's too frightful to contemplate,' she told the girl.

'Yes, Memsahib,' she answered, dutifully.

'Yes, Memsahib! No, Memsahib!' she mimicked. 'If that is what your father calls speaking good English, I could do as well with a parrot!'

'I am sorry, Memsahib.'

'Oh, for heaven's sake, don't just stand there. Pour the tea.'

Girl poured the tea from the tiny teapot. It was China tea, served with a slice of lemon. The early morning tea service had been brought from England, together with all the rest of the china, glass, cutlery, linen and personal belongings. Eight trunks altogether, carried by the over-burdened camels. Three of the trunks had been filled with the Memsahib's clothes. Girl had unpacked the trunks, wondering at the luxury and extravagance of so many garments for one little Memsahib. Such pretty petticoats and drawers and nightgowns, all of the finest crêpe de Chine. This would be for the Sahib's pleasure. It was one of her duties to wash and iron these dainty garments, for they could not be entrusted to the dhobi. Two dozen pairs of silk stockings, and a dozen pairs of white gloves had been brought from England. Nothing could compare with the quality of English clothes, the young Memsahib had pointed out as her maid-servant had knelt on the floor, surrounded by finery that only the Memsahib could wear with such distinction. Quality was a word that described everything in those eight trunks.

When the Memsahib had finished sipping the tea and nibbling the biscuits, Girl took the tray away. Her father had served the Colonel's Memsahib with Indian tea, very strong, and biscuits of a different variety. This ritual of early morning tea to suit the tastes of the memsahibs was almost as important as the afternoon tea, following the siesta, when dainty sandwiches and cakes were served. Tea for the memsahibs, whisky and soda for the men. Strange customs, but Girl was trained not to question, only to serve.

'How are you feeling, dear?' Aunt Millie kissed her flushed cheek affectionately, and settled herself for a chat with her niece on the edge of the bed. The early morning was the worst time with this wretched arthritis, and her joints were so stiff and painful that she could have wept if she had allowed herself the luxury of tears. Self-pity was a deplorable indulgence to her spartan outlook on life, and she deplored Rosalind's lack of self-discipline.

'That girl drives me to distraction,' her niece complained, lying back on her pillows.

'Is she disobedient?'

'Good heavens, no.'

'Lazy?'

'No.'

'What has she done, dear? Tell me. I am here to keep the servants in order. Thomas has given me a free hand while he is away. He said you were not to be worried.'

'She is dutiful enough. Her father keeps a constant watch on her. She is like a puppet. He pulls the strings and she performs to his bidding.'

'I expect you are comparing her with Lizzie, and that is a mistake.'

'Lizzie was so lively and amusing. This girl is so deadly dull. I am sure she hasn't a thought in her head.'

'Native servants are not expected to think, dear. They have no intelligence, no understanding of life as we know it. Their mentality is that of a four-year-old white child. I know what I am talking about. Remember, I have lived in Singapore, and we had Malay servants there. One needs the patience of Job, and you have all my sympathy.'

Rosalind yawned. 'I am so bored, Aunt. So terribly, terribly bored, now Thomas has left me. And it's quite devastating.'

'He will soon be back, dear. Then it will be time for a holiday at the hill station. You will enjoy that. The air is so invigorating. You will feel like a new person.'

'Shall I?'

'Of course you will, dear.'

'Sometimes I wonder whether I shall ever be strong and well again.'

'Now that is being morbid, Rosalind, dear. Doctor assures me you are making excellent progress.'

'He does?'

'Yes.'

'Then why does he not allow me to ride and dance?'

'He will, when he thinks your heart can stand the strain of so much exercise.'

'Is my heart weak? Why haven't I been told that I had a weak heart? Now I shall be frightened to move. Oh, it's all so ghastly. I can't bear it!' The blue eyes swam with tears.

Aunt Millie sighed and patted the limp hand consolingly. 'Do not distress yourself, child. Your poor old Aunt Millie has suffered a weak heart for years, and your dear Papa has never suspected it. It's a question of mind over matter. One just keeps battling on.'

Rosalind looked doubtful, but she dried her tears and asked, plaintively, 'Then I am not going to die?'

Aunt Millie clicked her tongue impatiently. 'You will probably live to be ninety, with snow-white hair and a family of great-grandchildren.'

Rosalind still looked doubtful. 'One must first become a mother, and Thomas does not care for children. He thinks they are a nuisance.'

'He will think differently with his own children.'

'How shall I know when I am going to have a baby? Tell me about it. I am so terribly ignorant.'

'You will know when the time is ripe, dear. Now I must see Boy about the market.' She limped away. Such embarrassing questions could not be answered by a confirmed spinster!

Several days had passed without incident or any interruption to the careful routine that had been established since their arrival. With Aunt Millie holding the reins in her capable hands and with Boy's willing co-operation the household ran smoothly. He continued to do the marketing and managed to save a few annas for himself. He was saving towards a dowry for his daughter's marriage, so he did not see it as a form of stealing.

Although he had not yet decided on a suitable husband, he had received several offers. Marja was a beautiful girl, obedient to her father's wishes. What more could a husband expect? Even a modest dowry would make the choice more selective, and money was a useful commodity. It could purchase a small parcel of land and dwelling place in a village settlement. They could raise a family, cultivate the land, buy several clutches of eggs and broody hens. There was always a market for eggs and boiling fowls. Boy had given the matter much serious thought. A garrison town was not the best place for his daughter. He had made a mistake in teaching her to speak English, and to copy the habits of the memsahibs. Now she wept her silent tears. She was sullen and miserable because their Sahib was away. She was too young to hide her feelings, and too old to whip.

Marja would not care for the simple life in the

village, or for the husband he would choose because he would be native, and she would compare him unfavourably with the beautiful white Sahib. Be that as it may, she would obey his wishes when the time was ripe. An older man would be more suitable for a young, foolish girl, and the marriage bed the best place to teach humility if a father had not succeeded in doing so.

His thoughts were interrupted one evening when a visitor called. He salaamed politely, asked his name, took the large, heavy parcel from the visitor, watched him tether his horse to the railings, and led the way to the back verandah where the two Memsahibs were reclining after their evening meal.

'Lieutenant Jones to see you, Memsahib,' he announced, importantly.

His young Memsahib blushed prettily and exclaimed, 'David! What a lovely surprise,' and offered her hand, as was the custom. 'You have met my aunt, have you not?'

'I have indeed had that pleasure, Ma'am,' he replied, bowing over the hand of the old Memsahib.

'Have you brought me a present, David?' Rosalind asked, coyly, her eyes on the large parcel Boy was holding.

'I have taken the liberty, Ma'am. I saw it in the market, and wondered whether you would find it amusing.'

'It is most gratifying to be reminded of your sympathy in my unfortunate condition. I can hardly wait to inspect the contents. Put it here, on this table, Boy, then fetch a drink for the Sahib.'

'Very good, Memsahib.' He did as he was bid, and slipped away to fetch the whisky and soda. His young Memsahib seemed delighted to see Lieutenant Jones, and it was not only the gift he brought. Her cheeks were flushed, and her eyes were sparkling in a way that only happened when the visitor was a Sahib. Boy was very observant on these matters. This particular Sahib was strikingly handsome, and obviously a very popular visitor. With the Colonel's Memsahib as a chaperone, however, all would be well. He took up the silver salver and hurried back to the verandah. Wrappings were strewn on the floor.

'Isn't it exciting!' Rosalind lifted the lid of the box, peered inside, and gave a little squeal of pleasure. 'A croquet set! How clever of you, David. Isn't it clever of him, Aunt?'

'Very clever and very generous. It must have cost a pretty penny.'

'A trifling thing, Ma'am, of no value,' said he, modestly.

'But you could not have thought of anything more suitable in my present state of indisposition, could he, Aunt?'

'No, indeed. A little quiet exercise in the cool of the evening is just what you need, and Doctor will approve; of that I am convinced.'

'Then shall we play a game now? Can it be made ready for play without too much trouble?'

'No trouble at all, Ma'am. A pleasure.' And Lieutenant Jones took the croquet set, leapt down the steps, and proceeded to arrange the hoops on the green turf. His dark eyes glowed with the success of his carefully digested plan. He would never forgive that bastard, Cartwright, for stealing a march on him. With Cartwright away, the opportunity to be near Rosalind, to touch her, to steal a kiss, was too tempting to resist. He had not expected to see the Colonel's sister, however, and it had jolted his complacency, but only for a moment. She wore spectacles, he noticed, and had peered at him with the close scrutiny of a short-sighted person. With a little strategy, and Rosalind's co-operation, he still could steal a kiss and fondle those adorable breasts. She seemed to have lost the sparkle and vitality that he remembered, and there was a delicate air about her. Even so, she was so very desirable.

'You will join us in a game, Ma'am?' he asked Miss Maitland, when the hoops had been placed in the correct positions.

She shook her head. 'I am too old to play games, young man. I will sit here and watch,' said she. In truth, her hands were so stiff and painful, she had laid aside the tapestry on which she had been working. She planned to make covers for the drawing-room chairs and sofa. It pleased her to see her niece taking an interest in the game, for she had already realized it would need all her patience and tolerance to keep her amused in the absence of Thomas. So she sighed with relief, and closed her eyes as David gave a helping hand to Rosalind on the steps.

Rosalind was also feeling a sense of relief as he took her hand, for Aunt Millie had got stuck on her favourite hobby-horse – their young days. She had heard it all before, and there was nothing new in the tale of a little brother, and a worshipping older sister. It seemed that Papa had been the most clever child who ever lived, and had passed every examination with flying colours. He had no vices and his virtues were of the highest. Rosalind found this model of perfection a little tedious. Papa was a darling, and she adored him, but her ego preferred a more personal topic.

'It was sweet of you to come to my rescue, David. Aunt Millie can be rather tedious, though I should be grateful that I am spared the responsibility of taking charge of the household while Thomas is away,' she confided, when they were out of earshot.

'How you must miss the riding and the dancing. You have all my sympathy, Ma'am.' His singing Welsh voice was warm with his sympathy, and his strong fingers curled round her limp hand. His dark eyes held a disturbing reminder of their last meeting, and his passionate declaration of love.

'I have missed you, David. I have been so terribly bored,' she sighed.

'I have missed you, too, Ma'am, but the situation was a little indelicate.'

'I am fully aware of it, but now you can stop calling me Ma'am. My aunt has taken off her spectacles, always an indication that she is having a little nap, although she will stoutly deny it. Old age is so very tedious, is it not?'

'I hadn't really thought of Miss Maitland as an old lady. Apart from that slight limp, she seems quite energetic.'

'Oh, but she must be all of sixty years, for my Papa is fifty, and she is that much older.'

'Indeed?' David was anxious to drop the subject and steered her away from the verandah. When he had explained the simple rules, he handed Rosalind a mallet and she hit the ball with such force, it raced across the lawn into the shrubbery.

'Bravo!' he cried, perceiving she was not as weak as she pretended. She giggled, and started in pursuit, lifting her skirts to show a pretty ankle. He followed her nonchalantly, swinging his mallet. She was hiding, but he caught a glimpse of her blue gown and dropped his mallet. Then she was in his arms, and he was kissing her hungrily. Her arms crept round his neck. On tiptoe, her uplifted breasts were taut and strained. He could feel her fluttering heart, and her breath tasted of the pineapple juice for which she had such a liking. Her lips parted, and his thrusting tongue teased her own tongue till both their bodies were trembling. It was dangerous, and it was tantalizing. It was so far and no farther, for he dare not unfasten a single button or slip his hand in that enticing cleft between her breasts. He could feel the shape of her thighs and her flat stomach under the soft folds of the clinging tea-gown. She wore no corsets, only a silk petticoat and drawers for coolness and comfort. To hold her thus, tormenting his senses with a clamorous desire, was both pleasure and punishment. But she was first to break away when she felt the hard penis against her thighs, and she was frightened.

'No, David. *No!*' she whispered, and dropped her arms.

He stared at her. His dark eyes sultry, his face haggard. 'You torture me, my dearest,' he breathed, shuddering in an agony of frustrated desire.

'We must not do this again, David. It is too dangerous. Servants could be watching. I do not trust that girl. She is so sly.'

He was amazed at her recovery, and the cool assumption that such passion could be dismissed as easily as a stolen kiss.

'I love you with all my heart and soul, not only with my body. Don't you understand? Does it mean nothing to you?' he asked.

She stroked his face and smiled. 'Of course it does. Silly darling. I am so very fond of you. Next to Thomas, you are the nicest man in the whole world.'

'Next to Thomas,' he echoed bitterly, and picked up the mallets.

'Are you cross with me, David?' she asked, like a little girl, anxious not to give offence. A married woman, no longer a virgin, with a husband as virile and sensual as Cartwright – had she still no conception of a man's fundamental needs, his agonizing desires? He kissed the tip of her pert little nose and took her hand. 'No, I am not cross with you. Come and play. Miss Maitland will have finished her short nap.'

Aunt Millie opened her eyes as the two figures emerged from the shrubbery. To chaperone her naughty niece was a hopeless responsibility, she decided, and closed her eyes again with a sigh of resignation.

The croquet proved a most popular pastime. The

twins brought their husbands to play against David and Rosalind. Boy served drinks on the verandah. The shrubbery was out of bounds, and boredom was kept at bay.

'Everything has been arranged. You will be leaving for the Murray Hills on Sunday next with the other officers' wives and children,' the Colonel told his daughter.

'But Thomas has not returned, and I am dying of anxiety,' she protested.

'He is expected back any day, and you will be advised as soon as he arrives, my pet. Thomas is not the only officer engaged on patrol duty, and you are not the only anxious wife. Without this constant vigil on the Frontier, we should never be safe from a surprise attack, or an ugly uprising of thousands of tribesmen, similar to the one in which Thomas's father met his death. There have been quite a number of attempts in the past twenty years, repulsed before they reached the garrison. They have not been without loss of life, and the consequent distress of wives and children who have to be sent home.'

'Would you send me home if Thomas was killed?'

'Yes, with your Aunt Millie.'

'Where should we live?'

'With Thomas's family at The Haven. It has been discussed and your mother-in-law has been approached. Thomas was fully aware of the dangers he would face, and was sensible enough to make provision for you in the event of his death.'

'That was uncommonly handsome, Papa!' Rosalind

snapped, infuriated by such a cool assumption. 'I do not care for my in-laws. I find them singularly dull and parochial, apart from Charles and Kate. I should find it so very boring. What should I do with myself in such a place?'

'There is no need to get yourself in a state. We hope and trust that Thomas is safe and well, but there will be other forays on the Frontier, and one should always be prepared for bad news. I am not being pessimistic, my daughter. It is all part and parcel of Army life and you are no stranger to it. Wherever we serve, the danger is there, and must be faced bravely by our women.'

'I am not at all brave, Papa. If Thomas was killed, I would not wish to go on living. I love him so very much. They say that absence makes the heart grow fonder. It is true. He is constatly in my thoughts.'

'Then we must hope and pray for his safe return. Try to be cheerful, my pet. It worries your aunt when you get so depressed and have no appetite.'

Rosalind sighed. 'I am so tired of being treated as an invalid. Will you speak to Doctor, Papa. Surely I could start riding again in the cooler climate of the Murray Hills? *Please*, Papa.'

'Very well. If you promise not to overtire yourself.'

'I promise. Thank you, dearest Papa.' She would have promised anything for a gallop on her new mare, Mayfly, still being exercised by the groom.

So the croquet set was packed away in the box, and Rosalind was surprised to find herself joining in the feverish preparations for the long holiday at the hill station. The children were excited because they had been promised morning lessons only and all kinds of treats. It was a major operation to transport all the officers' wives and children, their governesses and ayahs, and the stacks of baggage. The servants would be left behind, all but Girl, who was expected to attend her Memsahib. Servants were employed all the year round in the bungalows at the hill station, where Civil Servants and their families also spent their holidays.

Only Isabella Foster-Clarke had the audacity to remain behind. Some hours after the cavalcade had departed, her irate husband discovered her calmly drinking a whisky and soda on the verandah!

'What the hell are you doing here, Isabella?' he shouted.

'I like it here,' she answered. 'I should be bored to distraction with all those women and brats.'

'One of these days you will find yourself on board a ship bound for England,' he threatened. But his threat carried little weight. She was a law unto herself, and she was waiting for Thomas.

He arrived back three days later, dirty and dishevelled, and weak from loss of blood. He had lost two of his men, and his right arm was hanging limp and useless. His bearded face was grey and haggard, and his eyes dull with pain and fatigue.

When he had reported to the Colonel, dismissed his weary men to the barracks, and seen Jason comfortably settled in his stable, he dragged himself up the verandah step and fell into the waiting arms of Boy.

'Doctor . . . get Doctor,' his beloved Sahib muttered, and collapsed in a dead faint.

It was better so, Boy was thinking, as he gently removed the blood-stained jacket and shirt, and staunched the gaping shoulder wound with a clean towel. He was still kneeling there an hour or so later, when the doctor hurried in.

'Good fellow. You did well to keep the pressure on that wound,' said he, brusquely. 'Now fetch a bowl of warm water and more clean linen. Then you can help me.'

'Very good, Doctor Sahib.'

It was agony to watch the doctor probing deep into the wound for the bullet, and Boy wept his silent tears as he held the bowl of bloodied water.

'A nasty wound, but it will heal. He is young and healthy. Lucky to get off so lightly. These devils shoot to kill,' the doctor was saying, as he stitched the gaping hole.

Boy shuddered. He could feel the needle in his own flesh. Such capable hands, the Doctor Sahib, he was thinking as the shoulder was bandaged and firmly strapped. Together they undressed his young Sahib and, when he was stretched on the bed, the doctor hurried back to the sick-bay and a dying corporal.

'Get him washed and shaved, and when he wakes, keep him quiet,' he instructed, as he mounted his horse.

'Very good, Doctor Sahib.' Boy salaamed politely, and went back to his patient. It was a labour of love, and Boy sponged the lean young body with the gentleness of a mother with a sick child.

When he had shaved the bearded face, it was once again recognizable – a boyish face, reminding him so vividly of the other.

He was kneeling there, thanking Allah for his safe return, when the Memsahib walked in, unannounced. He scrambled to his feet, put a warning finger to his lips. 'Doctor Sahib he say my Sahib must be quiet,' he told Isabella Foster-Clarke, his dark eyes hostile.

She pushed him aside, pulled a chair to the bedside and sat down. 'Bring me a drink,' she snapped.

'Fruit drink, Memsahib?'

'Whisky and soda, you fool.'

'Very good, Memsahib.'

'Then you can clear off and get on with your work. I shall stay here till the Sahib wakes.'

Boy made no answer. His hands were clenched, and his whole body trembled with a bitter hatred of this woman. For the second time in his life he was watching the downfall of his beloved young Sahib. It was happening all over again, and there was only one way to prevent a second tragedy. He must tell his Sahib the truth about his father's death as soon as he was strong enough to bear the shock. They had often spoken of Jonathan Sahib, who was a hero to his son.

'Tell me more about my father, Boy,' he would say, thirsty for every detail.

When he came back with the drink, the woman was holding his Sahib's hand, and her eyes were tender with love. He set the silver salver on the bamboo table and went away. All his movements were quiet and constrained, but his thoughts were hostile. The other servants crept about on their bare feet, wondering about this Memsahib who drank whisky like a man, and who stayed behind when the other memsahibs went to the hills. But only Boy knew the truth, and Boy did not gossip with the lower servants.

Hovering in the doorway some time later, he could see his Sahib was awake. The Memsahib was smoothing his hair, and talking in a low voice. '*Mon brave.*' What did it mean? It could only be an endearment, for a smile trembled on the grey lips. Boy crept away, for he could not bear to watch.

Doctor called every day to dress the wound, the Colonel also called every day, and his brother officers. Boy was kept busy serving drinks at all hours of the day and night, for his Sahib enjoyed the lively company. But the woman seemed to know when he would be alone, and slipped in like a shadow, usually at siesta time.

The days slid away, the wound was healing nicely, and Thomas wore the arm in a sling.

'You will take a month's leave at the hill station to recuperate, then you can all travel back together,' the Colonel decided. 'Rosalind is fretting, and in her last letter she threatened to come home to help nurse you, though I was careful to explain your injury was not serious, and gave her all your fond messages. She needs to stay at least a month in that cool climate, and we may have to send her to the hills from time to time, during the next five years or so. It worries me, as I am sure it worries you, dear boy, to see her looking so pale and languid.'

Thomas agreed he had been feeling worried about her health for some time, but to tell the truth, his guilty conscience was reminding him of his neglect. It had not escaped the Colonel's observation that the wife of one of his senior officers had stayed behind and was spending too much time with his son-in-law. He seldom interfered in the private lives of the men under his command, but it was a different matter with the husband of his adored daughter.

So he and the doctor had consulted, and both had agreed that Thomas was well enough to travel with a groom in attendance. Boy was pleased when he was told of the arrangement, and quickly gathered together the necessary articles to be carried in the saddle bags.

'I could have travelled with you, darling, and taken good care of you.' Isabella was piqued. Only a few stolen kisses and now he was snatched away. Her husband regarded her obvious dismay with some amusement as she watched young Cartwright helped into the saddle, for he still wore his arm in a sling.

'Serves you right!' he jeered.

'Give me a drink and shut up!' she retorted.

'Plenty more fish in the sea, my love. Don't tell me you are going to mope?'

She laughed, mirthlessly. 'How right you are. Damn you!'

But Thomas was her favourite. They were two of a kind. They took what they wanted. It was not love, and it would not last, but such a compelling sexuality had to be satisfied.

So Thomas rode away, glad to escape from an attachment that was beginning to get tedious. Women were all alike. They wanted to possess a man, body and soul. He was a law unto himself, free to come and go if only they had the sense to realize it!

Jason whinnied and tossed his handsome head. It was good to be back in the saddle. It was a man's world when all was said and done.

Chapter Eight

The girl's heart leapt with gladness when she saw the two horsemen in the distance. She had not been told of her Sahib's injury, but she had overheard the two memsahibs talking anxiously together, and there was little that escaped her acute hearing. For one thing, they hardly noticed whether she was present or not, and she was sly and secretive in her movements.

The days had passed slowly, for she did not associate with the other servants who were strangers, pretending to be as important as her father in the servants' hierarchy, when actually she was nothing more than a slave to the whims of the young Memsahib. Her only pleasure in this small world of the hill station was to lock herself in the bedroom when the two memsahibs had departed on some social event and she was free to please herself for a few hours. There she would strip off her clothes, and dress herself in the dainty crêpe de Chine drawers and petticoats, and the pretty gowns. She would smooth the soft materials over her hips, and lift the skirts in the haughty manner of a memsahib, and curtsey to her reflection in the long mirror. The rustle of silks and satins was music to her ears, and her luminous dark eyes glowed with the passionate conviction of her own beauty. The cotton tunic and trousers lay discarded on the floor as she flounced about the room with swaying hips, and preened herself at the mirror. If only her Sahib could see her now!

Against a background of luxury and refinement, the colour of her skin, her dark eyes and hair had a fascinating appeal and a kind of beauty which was more disturbing to the senses than the fairness of the Memsahib. It was altogether remarkable the difference that it made. Clothed in the garments of her Memsahib, she was no longer a slave or a servant. She was her equal. Back in her tunic and trousers some time later, she felt only a passionate resentment against the young Memsahib. It was not fair! The Will of Allah was a mockery.

But now her Sahib was on the way she was happy again and forgot her resentment. She could hear the excited chatter of her young Memsahib, for she, too, had seen the two horsemen in the distance. Standing in the shadows, tense with eager anticipation, there was pleasure and pain in watching and listening to the reunion.

A few yards from the balcony, the Sahib swept off his hat, bowed to his Memsahib, and announced, importantly, 'Greetings, good wife! Your lord and liege has returned safely from the field of combat. Come, kiss me, my sweet.'

'Silly darling,' giggled Rosalind, happily, and lifted her face for his kiss.

Jason stood absolutely still, sweating and exhausted. It had been a long and tedious journey at a slow pace.

'Girl! Are you there, Girl?' The Colonel's Memsahib was a thorn in the flesh, but she had to be obeyed.

'I am here, Memsahib,' the girl answered, dutifully.

With his arm about Rosalind's waist, Thomas stood for a moment looking back at the wooded slopes of the steep hillside. The cool air on his sweating brow was better than any tonic the doctor could prescribe. He wished he had brought Boy to minister to his needs, but he supposed one of the servants here would be capable of assistance with bathing and dressing until he was fully mobile.

'You are looking very well, my sweet. It suits you here. A pity you cannot live here all the time, but then we should be separated for most of the year, and that would be unbearable, would it not?'

'Even these few weeks have been unbearable, and I have been so very anxious since Papa wrote to tell me of your injury. My poor darling. But now you are here, you must relax. I shall wait on you hand and foot. I shall be your slave and yours to command.'

He laughed indulgently. 'It seems I am going to be thoroughly spoilt, but you must not tire yourself.'

'I am not at all tired. I have been riding with the twins, and playing games with the children. We have lovely picnics and tea parties, and I sleep without the draught.'

'That is spendid news, sweetheart, for now I can make love to you.'

'Now?'

'When I have bathed.'

'But your arm?'

'You will be surprised at my cleverness with my one good arm. Besides, you can help. We shall manage.'

'Are you sure? I can wait.'

'Well, I can't. Even to hold you like this is torturing me. I need you. It is so long since I held you in my arms.'

'What will Aunt Millie think if we go to bed at this hour?'

'Does it matter?'

'But we have had no supper.'

'I am not hungry for food, only for you, my love. Say you will, *please*.'

Rosalind sighed. Since her illness, something had been lost and the passionate love-making of those early months of marriage could not be endured. She loved Thomas dearly, and wished to please him. A wife should always try to please her husband in bed. It was her duty. Would Thomas be satisfied or would he demand more than she could give?

'Is there a servant here who could valet me?' he was asking.

'There is Abbas. He is old, but willing and obedient.'

'Then summon him if you please. Tell him to bring a change of linen, but first a drink.'

'The drink is waiting, Sahib,' a gentle voice interrupted from the balcony.

'Whisky and soda?'

'Whisky and soda, Sahib.'

'Now you can run my bath.'

'Very good, Sahib.' Abbas salaamed respectfully.

'So there you are, Thomas.' Aunt Millie had the good sense to keep out of the way. An emotional reunion between the young couple was to be expected, but she was not in the mood to witness it.

'How do you do, Ma'am.' Thomas smiled and bowed.

'I do very well, thank you, Thomas. My main concern at the present time is *your* health. The Colonel instructed me in his last letter to inform the doctor as soon as you arrived. I have sent a servant with a message. I understand you have been transferred as a patient from the garrison doctor to the one in residence here. So get your bath, like a good fellow. He will wish to examine you.'

'Confound it!' Thomas muttered irritably.

'I beg your pardon?'

'Nothing, Ma'am.' He kissed Rosalind's cheek and whispered, 'Tonight.'

'Tonight,' she echoed, with a sense of relief. It was awful to feel so reluctant and not at all what a wife should be feeling. 'Those whom God hath joined together', with that horrid THING. She wished he had thought of a less vulgar way! As for helping Thomas with the love-making, with one hand incapacitated, would it mean actually *touching* it? Time and again he had tried to coax her. How could he be so very indelicate? Yet he seemed to have a fondness for the ugly article, and boasted of its size. Men were odd creatures. She would never understand the way their minds worked. Even when you supposed they were enjoying a meal or a quiet game of croquet, they were contemplating the pleasure of the marriage bed. Thomas had told her that all men were alike, and all made in the same image, and she had no wish to prove it. One man was enough.

If only she could put back the clock to that very pleasant year after she left the schoolroom. Flirting so gaily and innocently with the young subalterns. The stolen kisses, the charming compliments. It was such fun. Marriage to Thomas had put an end to all the fun and frivolity. To be a wife was a very serious matter, and the marriage bed, according to Thomas, the most important factor in their life together. She did not understand her own feelings of reluctance for it since her illness. Was it entirely her fault? Was Thomas partly to blame? Could there be any foundation in the rumour that Thomas was besotted with that elegant Mrs Foster-Clarke?

'Is anything wrong, child?' Aunt Millie was asking, anxiously.

'No, nothing,' she lied. But the pleasure and excitement of the reunion had already been spoilt by the question that sprang to mind: why had Isabella Foster-Clarke stayed behind?

It was like a second honeymoon that first week at the hill station. No wife could have wished for a more attentive or loving husband. They were left alone to enjoy the pleasure of riding, picnic lunches and quiet games of croquet after supper. The days slipped away, and the nights were made for love, according to Thomas, whose insatiable appetite was partly due to the strong desire to make amends for past infidelities. Yet all thoughts of Isabella could not be entirely dispelled in the arms of his adoring little wife. She had no teasing tactics. No sophisticated blandishments. No surprises. He knew exactly what to expect from Rosalind, and when he had taken her, she fell asleep like a tired child, while he lay awake, only partially satisfied, his young, healthy body remembering the passionate Isabella. Comparisons were unkind and disloyal. Yet the image of his mistress intruded, as he lay awake. Sex was as natural as breathing, so why should he deny himself? He loved Rosalind dearly, and could not conceive of life without her. He lay there, tense and troubled by a situation that was becoming too difficult to handle and wished there was just one person in whom he could confide, but he had no close friends among his fellow officers. In his prep school days there had been Roderic; then Gerald had stepped into his shoes at public school. At Sandhurst he had enjoyed the friendship of George and Lance. That had been a jolly exciting period, in a world of men with hardly a thought for the opposite sex.

Yet always, with Roderic, Gerald, George and Lance, he was the acknowledged leader. Grandmama had encouraged his forceful personality from his earliest recollection. She would understand. She would sympathize with his need to keep both a wife and a mistress, if he so desired. Grandmama would never be shocked. The only time she had been critical of his conduct was when he had confessed to bedding a housemaid at Gerald's ancestral home. She had deplored his admission, at the tender age of fifteen, to being the father of the child. Dear Grandmama! Wasn't it a gentleman's privilege to take a mistress? Sooner or later, he supposed, Rosalind would discover he was being unfaithful, but he would hotly deny it, and he could be a most convincing liar! Being the son-in-law of his commanding officer was a bit tricky, however, and he must be careful. The risk was exciting, and he could not resist a challenge. He had challenged the right to court and wed the Colonel's daughter in the face of much opposition. He had won his spurs, so to speak, in his first encounter on the Frontier. His luck had held. The wound had healed. Now he was ready for the next challenge. A month's leave was long enough, and he would be glad to be back in action. It was a good life, providing you did not allow yourself to become too domesticated!

Aunt Millie would be glad to get back to her own household. She still enjoyed the company of the governess, since they had become close friends during the long sea voyage, and the measles epidemic. To have a confidante who listened sympathetically but did not gossip was good for both women.

Mrs Foster-Clarke had arrived with her husband and his fellow officers, all due for their annual leave at the hill station. The Colonel, in khaki shorts and shirt, looked rather like an elderly boy scout.

'You look so quaint, Papa, with your bare knees,' Rosalind teased, affectionately.

When the men joined their wives and children, the hill station became alive, with exciting contests and competitions, with tennis tournaments, cricket and polo matches, and gymkhanas. Casual sports wear was replaced by silk shirts and white flannels in the evening, when the women wore their prettiest gowns for dancing and informal dinner parties.

Thomas was bored as a spectator, but his arm was still too stiff for the strenuous sports he normally enjoyed. Riding was the only recreation the doctor permitted, and this, too, would have been frowned upon had the doctor witnessed those reckless early morning gallops. This was the only opportunity to meet Isabella alone. Rosalind had got into the habit of breakfasting in bed since her illness.

Thomas was not the only husband enjoying a secret rendezvous in the wooded hills, and a light-hearted romp on the good earth.

Back at the garrison and back on duty, officers and ranks once again awakened to Reveille at cockcrow, and the flag was lowered to the haunting notes of the bugle at sundown.

Girl was pleased to be back. The hot, dusty plain was her natural habitat, but her young Memsahib would soon begin to wilt. The servants had been kept busy. Every inch of the spacious bungalow had been cleaned, carpets beaten, curtains washed. Fresh paint gleamed on walls and shutters, and scarlet geraniums bloomed in the white urns on the front verandah. Boy had them all lined up, once again, in their clean cotton tunics and trousers, salaaming respectfully to the Sahib and his Memsahib. On the back verandah, the bamboo chairs and tables had been freshly painted, and cushions recovered.

'All is new, Sahib.' Boy gestured proudly.

'It looks very handsome,' said Thomas. 'Is it not handsome, my sweet?'

Rosalind agreed half-heartedly. She was sorry to leave the hill station where her health had improved. The holiday was over, and Thomas was back on duty. She would miss his company. 'Where have you been?' The question would soon begin to irritate him if he stayed too late in the Mess. Aunt Millie was back with the Colonel, and the other young wives all seemed to be expecting babies, and could talk of nothing else.

'I serve drinks now, Sahib?' Boy suggested, anxious to please.

'Thank you, Boy.'

Sahib was in a good mood. It was not often that a native servant was thanked, and they did not expect it. Thomas smiled at the girl, hovering in the background, and she dropped her lashes over her sultry black eyes.

'You can get unpacked,' Rosalind told the girl.

And she answered, dutifully, 'Yes, Memsahib,' and slipped away.

'I have to remind her of every single thing. She is so stupid,' Rosalind complained.

'She is very young. I expect she will improve,' Thomas suggested.

'Why must you always defend her? She hasn't a thought in her head. I wish we had brought Lizzie. She knew what had to be done without being told.'

'Lizzie was a woman of mature years. This girl is a child.'

'Then I wish she would grow up.'

Thomas sighed. She had put into words his own thought of a married woman who still continued to behave like a spoilt child. 'Cheer up, sweetheart. We must think of something to amuse you while I am on duty,' he promised, and kissed her petulant mouth.

'Why does the Memsahib weep?' Boy demanded of his daughter one evening.

'Memsahib unhappy.'

'Why is Memsahib unhappy?'

'Her Sahib come not home.'

He sighed, his loyal heart heavy with the burden he carried. The time had come to tell the truth, and he alone could tell. He loved the young Sahib, and such a disclosure would destroy the cordial relationship between master and servant of which he was so proud. But he had been troubled for many weeks, and could no longer postpone the disclosure. The servants were discreet, and his daughter obeyed her father, but even some hint of the Sahib's whereabouts must soon reach the ears of the young Memsahib. She could be weeping now because she was beginning to wonder if her Sahib was deceiving her. Boy knew where he spent most of his evenings since their return from the hill station, and it was not in the Officers' Mess. That other Memsahib had the same fatal fascination as the one who had seduced the father all those years ago; she had the wiles of a harlot and a body that few men could resist. Boy hated this woman, as he had hated the other. It would end the same way, unless he intervened.

He did not need any further proof, for he had seen

with his own eyes the horse tethered to a tree in the garden of Foster-Clarke Sahib on more than one occasion. So he waited with the patience born of long years of servitude, saddened by the words on his tongue that must be spoken, now, *tonight*.

Flushed and bright-eyed, Thomas leapt up the steps of the back verandah, still confident that his luck was holding, and he could enjoy the best of both worlds. But Rosalind was not in the mood to be petted. She pushed him away when he bent over her, and complained petulantly, 'Don't touch me, Thomas. You smell horrid. I am going to bed, and you need not bother to join me.'

'Please yourself.' He let her go. If she locked the bedroom door he would sleep in the dressing-room, not for the first time.

'I serve drink, Sahib?' Boy's gentle voice interrupted his thoughts.

'Yes,' he barked, irritably, and sank into the chair that Rosalind had vacated.

When he had placed the silver salver within easy reach, Boy stood there, his hands clasped tightly on his white jacket.

'Well?' Thomas demanded.

'I speak with you, Sahib?'

'What is it?'

'I have to ask if you see burial place of father Sahib?'

Thomas frowned. He had intended to enquire where his father had been buried, but it had slipped his memory. 'Why do you ask? It does not concern you.'

'Pardon me, Sahib. I am much concerned.'

'Well? Get on with it, man!'

'Your father not buried with regiment, Sahib. He lies in corner of cemetery with that other Memsahib.'

'What are you saying? Speak up, man!'

'Your father, Sahib, not killed by sniper's bullet. He shoot himself with pistol when he strangle that other Memsahib.'

'Liar! Liar!' Thomas shouted, leaping to his feet, his blue eyes blazing.

Boy stepped back, expecting a blow. 'I not lie to you, Sahib, I speak truth,' he said, the tears wetting his hollowed cheeks.

Tossing down the neat whisky, Thomas pushed Boy aside, ran down the steps and leapt into the saddle. He galloped furiously to a cultivated area, some distance from the garrison where sheltering trees and flowering shrubs surrounded neat rows of wooden crosses. Bathed in moonlight, the place had an eerie solitude, and Thomas shivered as he slid out of the saddle and led Jason along one of the paths that separated the regiments. In 100 years many had died in this far-flung outpost of the British Empire. Officers and ranks lay side by side in death. The graves were carefully tended, and English roses had been planted in the borders. This particular duty must have been handed down from one regiment to the next.

It did not take long to discover the two isolated graves in a corner of the cemetery, and he read the names on the small wooden crosses with an overwhelming sense of shock and shame. Here, in this grave, apart from the regiment he had served for those few short years, lay the mortal remains of the father he had idolized, the father in whose steps he had trodden with such proud confidence, the handsome officer in the silver frame on the mantelpiece in the nursery. He remembered his mother lifting him up to kiss the portrait even before he could talk. His mother? That gentle mother, with the sad, dark eyes, who seldom smiled. Had she carried the burden of his father's disgrace all these years? Did Grandmama know the truth? Had they both conspired to keep that image a hero in the eyes of his son? What purpose had it served?

'Betrayed! Betrayed!' he muttered, choked with bitter disappointment. It was a cruel blow to his pride.

He turned away, his head bowed in shame, weeping for the hero he had lost.

The village, with its native market on the outskirts of the garrison, was a favourite haunt of the ranks, who could trade tobacco for the local liquor, a very potent brew guaranteed to deaden the mind when the body was exhausted with drills and discipline. The market would remain open till midnight, to serve the men from the garrison when they came off duty. Now, at this late hour, they were gathered in groups, behind closed doors, trying to pretend the stuffy atmosphere reminded them of their favourite pub back in their home town.

The street was deserted when Thomas arrived, leading his horse, in a dazed state of shock. The old native who served him with the liquor and took the few annas he charged, salaamed respectfully. It was seldom that he served an officer sahib, for they drank their own whisky in the Mess and in their homes.

In the shadows, a short distance away, the girl was watching him closely. She had heard the disturbance on the balcony, and had waited for him, not really understanding what all the fuss was about. Her Sahib had called her father a liar, and gone rushing off to see something for himself. It was all very puzzling. Why should he want to visit the burial place in the middle of the night? Who was buried there? When he returned home, he had just passed by the gate. She followed. Why had he come to the village to buy liquor when whisky was there to be served in his home? And what was she doing here? When her father discovered she was missing, he would know she had followed the Sahib because her eyes had betrayed her adoration, and she was too young to hide her feelings. She worshipped the very ground he walked on, yet he hardly noticed her existence. To serve him, she would humble herself, as a slave humbles herself before her master. His every wish would be gratified. So she watched and waited.

He was sitting on the ground, leaning against his horse, drinking from the bottle. The horse stood quietly with drooping head. When at last her Sahib struggled to his feet, he threw the bottle away with a muttered curse. The girl crept forward and made no sound as she approached. The horse whinnied as his master scrambled clumsily into the saddle, and when he turned his mount away from the village and the garrison, the girl presented herself at the horse's head, and pleaded, 'Take me with you, Sahib.'

Thomas laughed, mirthlessly. In the light of the moon her eyes were black as onyx in her childish face. 'Why not?' he asked, and scooped her up. In the curve of his arm she had no weight and no substance, and he was hardly aware of her. 'Betrayed!' he muttered. 'Bloody ridiculous!' He swayed in the saddle and his speech was blurred, but she had no fear, only a blind trust and obedience.

Her young heart sang with happiness as they ambled along at a steady pace, the clip-clop of the horse's hooves the only sound. She could smell the liquor on his breath, for he was breathing heavily and muttering curses. They seemed to be the only living creatures around as the weary horse plodded on, mile after mile, because he had not been ordered to halt.

When the order came at last, on the perimeter of a plantation, it was the horse that took priority in the man's fuddled brain. Dropping the girl to the ground, Thomas slid out of the saddle, slapped the steaming flanks and promised water and oats. He seemed to be familiar with the terrain, and the girl followed them through acres of bananas to a watercourse where the horse drank thirstily. Under the spreading branches of a banyan tree, Thomas threw himself down and commanded huskily, 'Get hay an' oats, an' liquor.'

'Where, Sahib?'

He pointed vaguely in a northern direction. 'Village.' She answered obediently, 'Yes, Sahib,' and stood waiting.

'Go,' he said, and closed his eyes.

'Money, Sahib,' she reminded him, and he fumbled for his wallet, drew out a note, and pushed it into her hand. Then he closed his eyes again with a weary sigh, and slept.

The girl stared down at him. He looked very young and beautiful, lying there, in the shadows, with a shaft of moonlight touching his golden hair with silver, and his cheeks with a deathly pallor. Fear clutched her heart. If he should die, she would not wish to live. But he was not going to die. He would drink more of the liquor, and she would lie beside him in her nakedness while he slept.

The village lay in a hollow of the hills, and the eerie silence was broken by the frantic barking of a dog as she approached. She was very frightened, and would have turned away but for the Sahib's command to fetch hay and oats and liquor. She dare not go back empty-handed. A rough-looking man appeared in the doorway of the nearest hut, holding the dog on a rope. The dog growled, but she stood her ground and stated her business.

'I have money,' she said, and held out the note.

The man tied the dog to a post, strode towards her, snatched the note from her hand, and spat on the ground. The spittle was the colour of blood. He was chewing betel nut. Now she thought he was going to take the money and give nothing in return, and she stamped her foot and threatened angrily, 'My Sahib very important. Many soldiers. You give me what I ask.'

'Come,' he said and she followed him.

It was not the first time he had sold hay and oats and liquor to the white sahibs and made a good profit, but the girl was suspicious, and kept close to his heels. He stank of goats, and spat the blood-red betel nut as she followed him round the village. He knew where to find everything, and no other person was disturbed. The bale of hay and the bag of oats was too heavy to carry, so she dragged them in a sack and carried the precious liquor clutched to her chest.

She left the man staring after her with a puzzled frown. They had exchanged only a few words, but he had the money and she had the goods. The dog growled as she went past, and she stuck out her tongue in a childish gesture, and went on her way, stumbling over the rough ground with her heavy load, back to her beloved Sahib.

She received no thanks, but then she expected none. A lord does not thank a slave for service to him. He watched her feed the horse, then he drank more of the liquor and slept again. She slipped off her tunic and trousers and went to bathe in the watercourse. Now she was hungry, and picked a banana. It was green and hard, and it gave her a belly ache, but all the bananas were green, and would soon be gathered ready for shipping.

Nobody came to the plantation, and when she had dried herself with the tunic, she lay down beside her Sahib and flung her arm across his chest. He had removed his jacket while she went to the village. It was hanging on a branch of the tree. The silk shirt was damp with sweat. He slept on, breathing heavily, and her small, naked body pleaded in vain to be noticed.

'See, Sahib, I am woman,' she entreated, taking his limp hand to feel her little pear-shaped breasts. Still no response. Daringly, she pressed her mouth to his mouth. Still no response. She had seen men in a drunken stupor after drinking this potent liquor, but never expected to see her beautiful Sahib so drunk. Like a fallen idol he lay there, totally unaware of her, and she sobbed herself to sleep, her wet face buried in the soft folds of the silk shirt.

When she awoke, some hours later, it was daylight, and she dressed herself in her tunic and trousers, feeling despised and neglected. Her heart ached and more tears flooded her eyes. What had she expected? Her father, in his wisdom, could have told her the Sahib would not take her, no matter how many moons they lay together. She was native. Not in a thousand years could she change the colour of her skin.

Still weeping, she took the handkerchief from his pocket and dipped it in the water-course, and bathed his sweating face. Again and again she ran to and fro to the water-course, and knelt beside him, bathing his face. There was nothing else she could do for him.

The day slipped away into the second night, and then another day. In his waking moments, he drank more of the liquor, muttering curses, his bloodshot eyes staring into space, seeing nothing, feeling nothing till the vomit caught in his throat and he fought for his breath. Then the girl was beside him, lifting his head while he spewed the vomit over the silk shirt. The stench was horrible. He was shuddering with revulsion, weak and exhausted.

When she had stripped off the shirt to wash it in the water-course, once again she ran to and fro to wet the handkerchief, sponging his face and chest. Then she took off her tunic and dried him, crooning over him like a mother with a sick child.

'Water horse,' he croaked.

'Yes, Sahib,' she answered, obediently. Terrified of the huge stallion, she was torn between fear and the natural urge to obey. The Sahib was watching her with his bloodshot eyes. His face was grey. The vomit still stank, so did the urine.

'Water horse.' His voice held a threatening note.

She untied the reins and led the horse to the water-course. It lapped the water thirstily, and she led it back and tied it to the branch. It whinnied fretfully and hung its head. It seemed to be mourning for the fallen idol.

Another day slipped away. The girl bathed in the water-course and dried her tunic in the sun. Her stomach was empty, but there was nothing to eat, only the green bananas. She sat beside the Sahib while he slept, but she no longer wanted to touch him. Her feelings had changed. It was her father she wanted, and her father she feared. What form would her punishment take? Would he marry her to that old farmer with the pigs, the goats and the hens, and the dirty house that would be her home? All her short life had been lived at the garrison. She had never known hunger until yesterday, or was it the day before yesterday? She would fall on her knees and beg her father's forgiveness. She would bow her head in the dust and humble herself. To be sent away, to be the wife of that old man and to bear his children, was that the Will of Allah? Her father would say that it was, and she must obey. She wept till she could weep no more. The impulse that had driven her to follow the Sahib was dead. To be a woman, to have breasts and the longing to be with the Sahib, what did it mean? She, too, had been betrayed. But who and what had betrayed the Sahib? That was a question still to be answered on their return. The mystery lay in the burial ground, and her father held the key.

'What are you doing now, Girl?'

She had fallen asleep, worn out with hunger and misery, and she slept like a tired little animal, curled in a ball on the hard ground. The Sahib was standing over her, a gigantic figure in the shadows, with his bare chest and his head silvered in a streak of moonlight.

She struggled to her feet and salaamed respectfully. 'I been here all time, Sahib.'

'Since when?'

'Since three moons, Sahib.'

'Three *moons*? You mean three *nights*?'

'Yes, Sahib.'

'Good God!' He brushed a hand through his tangled hair and stared with horrified amazement at his bare chest and the uniform jacket hanging on a branch. 'Where is my shirt?' he barked, irritably.

'Here, Sahib. I have it wash and dry.'

'Why did my shirt need washing?'

342

'Very sick, Sahib. You not remember?'

He shuddered. His eyes were still bloodshot, his face was grey, but his voice held the old ring of authority. 'We must go back. I must have been mad. Absent without leave. You know what that means?'

'No, Sahib.'

'A court martial.'

She had never heard of a court martial, but she supposed it to be some kind of punishment.

'I could be dismissed from the service. A bigger disgrace than my accursed father. I couldn't bear it.'

'No, Sahib.'

The horse whinnied, and the man spoke quietly, fondling the proud, handsome head. 'Yes, my beauty. We must go back. There must be a way to get out of this ghastly mess, and we shall find it. I feel bloody awful, and I stink to high heaven.'

'There is a water-course, Sahib.' She pointed.

'You have watered Jason and he has been fed?'

'Yes, Sahib.'

He did not ask whether she had had food. Compared to the horse, she was less than the dust. He untied the reins and they went together to the water-course, where the Sahib stripped off his trousers and plunged into the water. The moonlight played on his strong, young body when he stood on the brink and pulled on his trousers. He waited for the horse to finish drinking, then they came back to stand beside her. She would have taken off her tunic again, but he snatched the shirt and pulled it over his wet, glistening body. Then he put on his jacket, smoothed his hair, and squared his shoulders.

'Come,' he said, and she obeyed.

Leaving the plantation, the Sahib sprang into the saddle. He seemed to have recovered from that drunken stupor and the hangover was short-lived. The shock of discovering they had spent three nights under the banyan tree, together with the plunge into the water-course had cleared his mind and cleaned his body. He looked down at her with a puzzled frown, still not remembering how she came to be there. Then he scooped her up to sit before him.

'Home, Jason! Home, my beauty!' he shouted.

And the echo came back from the hills, across the barren plain.

Back in the bungalow, Rosalind was inconsolable, and Aunt Millie was once again installed to supervise the servants. 'Where is the girl?' Rosalind had demanded, irritably, that first morning when an old woman served her early tea.

'My niece is sick with fever, Memsahib,' she answered. 'I Ayah. I serve Gilbert Memsahib, three babas, five year. Before that, I serve Jackson Memsahib, two babas, before that . . .'

'All right. All right. I did not ask for your life history,' snapped Rosalind. 'You may stay till the girl has recovered.'

'Thank you, Memsahib.' Ayah salaamed respectfully and crept away on silent feet.

As the second and third day slipped by and there was no news of Thomas, the annoyance that Rosalind had felt initially for her husband's desertion changed to anxiety, then to definite certainty that he was dead. Nobody had seen him since he left the Mess, early on the Wednesday evening. That is to say, nobody but Rosalind, who had retired to bed in a bad humour, leaving him to drink his nightcap, and Boy, who had served the drink.

The Colonel was increasingly puzzled by his son-in-law's disappearance, and, although he questioned his daughter in the gentlest manner possible, she was much too distressed to remember exactly what had happened that night.

'I heard them shouting,' she sobbed hysterically.

'Heard who shouting, my pet?' the colonel prompted.

'Thomas and that servant he thinks so highly of.'

'Boy?'

'Yes.'

'But native servants do not shout, dear.'

'Did I say he was shouting? It was Thomas who was doing the shouting. I covered my ears. His language was so very objectionable.'

'Does he normally swear at the servants?'

'Only when he is drunk.'

'And he was drunk that night?'

'His breath was horrid. I would not allow him to kiss me. I pushed him away. You cannot conceive, Papa, what it is like to have a husband who comes home drunk.'

'No, I cannot, but I am most displeased, and I shall speak to him very severely on his return.'

'But he may *not* return, Papa, and I shall have driven him away!' she wailed, miserably. 'I get so vexed I do not know what I am saying. He is so very provoking. I do declare I am at my wits' end to understand his intentions. Sometimes I wonder whether he has stopped loving me.'

The Colonel patted her hand and assured her that was not the case. Then he questioned the servant, but Boy was much too loyal to admit there had been a disturbance or that his beloved Sahib had been drunk. He shook his grey head.

'Never have I seen Sahib drunk, Colonel Sahib.'

'But the Memsahib tells me he was shouting and swearing.'

'It was nothing, Colonel Sahib,' said Boy, with his gentle voice and smiled, disarmingly.

'I can't get anything out of the fellow,' the Colonel admitted. 'He closes up like a clam. Perhaps Millie can persuade him to talk. She is good with the servants. I never interfere.'

But Millie met with the same polite but stubborn denial that anything unusual had occurred that Wednesday night. Nor would Boy allow her to visit his daughter in the servants' quarters. 'Not safe for you, Memsahib. Daughter very sick. Better soon,' said he. And since he had brought Ayah to deputize for the girl, Rosalind was not inconvenienced.

'It's my opinion that conceited ass is staging this disappearance to attract attention, then when everyone is convinced he has suffered the fate of so many others, he will just arrive on a sweating horse, as large as life, and twice as natural,' Subaltern Jones declared, spitefully, in the Officers' Mess.

'But would he risk a court martial just to satisfy a whim? I think not,' a fellow officer contradicted. 'He is much too keen on his army career, and seems ripe for promotion following that successful foray on the Frontier,' he added.

'Was it entirely successful? one wonders. He was somewhat reticent about the actual combat if you remember, and it's unlike Cartwright to play down his own part in any successful operation,' another interrupted.

'Then he could be finishing the job single-handed. In which case we shall see him back, covered in glory!' Subaltern Hawkins suggested, laconically, as the steward served more drinks.

'Whatever the reason, it's dashed bad form. That lovely girl must be breaking her heart. He doesn't deserve her,' sighed a young admirer, enviously.

Subaltern Jones made no further comment, but his thoughts had wings. If Cartwright failed to return . . . and it would not be the first time a British officer had been captured and tortured to death by those devils on the frontier. His body would be dumped a short distance from the garrison, and there would be an impressive military funeral in which the entire regiment would parade, with the flag at half mast, and the bugles sounding the Last Post. Rosalind would be devastated, naturally, but after a decent interval, he would court her for the second time. And next time he would not have to watch his hated rival in the role of the favoured suitor. That blond Adonis was probably having his genitals removed at this very moment – and serve him right, the bastard! Nothing was too bad for a fellow who was being unfaithful to his lovely Rosalind only a few months after their marriage. It was a dastardly trick, for the dear girl was still obviously so in love, and not yet aware of his infatuation for the elegant Isabella – or was she?

The girl was weeping quietly now. They were going back. Her Sahib had his arm about her, and she was leaning against his chest, but she knew he was hardly aware of her, and she had no part in his thoughts or his plans. She had offered herself and she had been rejected. Her father's anger was troubling her now, and the punishment awaiting her. To be banished to the country . . . to be given in marriage to that ugly old farmer who stank of goats . . . to bear his sons . . . She had no choice. A daughter must obey.

The thud of hooves on the hard ground was the only sound as the horse galloped towards the garrison. The man and the horse were as one in their eagerness and desire to be back in their own world. The Sahib loved his horse. It was a special kind of love. The Memsahib was jealous. She could not bear to share him with a horse.

The shot rang out, and the startled beast reared in terror.

'Steady, my beauty, steady.' The man's voice was soothing, his hand was firm on the bridle as they drew to a halt. The girl's small body had slumped, lifeless. There was no sound now but the snorting breath of the terrified horse, and the snap of a twig as a dark shadow moved out from the trees that sheltered the servants' quarters.

'I take her, Sahib.'

Was he dreaming? That was no sniper's bullet.

'Boy! What are you doing here?' Thomas demanded.

'I take her, Sahib,' the quiet voice insisted, holding up his skinny arms. They received the small burden with nothing more than a sigh of resignation. It was the Will of Allah. Then he was gone, back to the shadows.

Thomas shuddered, and wiped the warm blood from his clenched hand. Then he slid out of the saddle and led Jason slowly and thoughtfully across the moonlit garden.

From a lounge chair on the back balcony, Rosalind lifted a tear-wet face, gasped, 'Thomas!' and struggled to her feet. 'I thought? . . . They said . . .' she faltered.

His blue eyes were tender with love. 'Have I not told you, my sweet, never to listen to gossip?' said he, with gentle mastery, as his arms enfolded her.

THE END

THE FAIRFIELDS CHRONICLES
by Sarah Shears

Set in the heart of the Kent countryside and spanning the period from the turn of the century to the end of the Second World War, Sarah Shears introduces us to the inhabitants of Fairfields Village. As we follow the changing fortunes of the villagers we see how their lives and loves become irrevocably entwined over the years and watch the changing patterns of English country life through the eyes of one of our best-loved novelists.

THE VILLAGE
FAMILY FORTUNES
THE YOUNG GENERATION
and now, the long-awaited conclusion:
RETURN TO RUSSETS

Published by Bantam Books

THE SISTERS
by Sarah Shears

For the first time in paperback

When Amelia Brent's husband dies, a chapter closes in her life and she is forced to acknowledge the far-reaching consequences of widowhood. Required to live in greatly reduced circumstances, Amelia dismisses her household staff and begins to map out the future for her children.

For her two eldest daughters the future holds dramatic change and separation. Ellen, the eldest daughter, dreams of love and romance as the wife of a soldier stationed in India, but all too soon her dreams are shattered by a brutal and traumatic event. For her sister Grace, sent against her wishes to work in London, her future appears to be one of endurance, as she faces the bitter truth that the man she loves belongs to another.

The Sisters is a moving, romantic and richly evocative portrait by the author of *The Fairfields Chronicles*.

A Bantam Paperback

0 553 40582 9

A SELECTION OF FINE NOVELS
AVAILABLE FROM BANTAM BOOKS

☐ 17632 3	**DARK ANGEL**	*Sally Beauman*	£4.99
☐ 17352 9	**DESTINY**	*Sally Beauman*	£5.99
☐ 40429 6	**AT HOME**	*Charlotte Bingham*	£3.99
☐ 40427 X	**BELGRAVIA**	*Charlotte Bingham*	£3.99
☐ 40163 7	**THE BUSINESS**	*Charlotte Bingham*	£4.99
☐ 40428 8	**COUNTRY LIFE**	*Charlotte Bingham*	£3.99
☐ 40296 X	**IN SUNSHINE OR IN SHADOW**	*Charlotte Bingham*	£4.99
☐ 17635 8	**TO HEAR A NIGHTINGALE**	*Charlotte Bingham*	£4.99
☐ 40171 8	**STARDUST**	*Charlotte Bingham*	£4.99
☐ 40072 X	**MAGGIE JORDAN**	*Emma Blair*	£4.99
☐ 40298 6	**SCARLET RIBBONS**	*Emma Blair*	£4.99
☐ 40372 9	**THE WATER MEADOWS**	*Emma Blair*	£4.99
☐ 40321 4	**AN INCONVENIENT WOMAN**	*Dominic Dunne*	£4.99
☐ 17676 5	**PEOPLE LIKE US**	*Dominic Dunne*	£3.99
☐ 17189 5	**THE TWO MRS GRENVILLES**	*Dominic Dunne*	£3.50
☐ 40364 8	**A SPARROW DOESN'T FALL**	*June Francis*	£3.99
☐ 40504 7	**FLOWERS ON THE MERSEY**	*June Francis*	£3.99
☐ 17207 7	**FACES**	*Johanna Kingsley*	£4.99
☐ 17539 4	**TREASURES**	*Johanna Kingsley*	£4.99
☐ 17504 1	**DAZZLE**	*Judith Krantz*	£4.99
☐ 17242 5	**I'LL TAKE MANHATTAN**	*Judith Krantz*	£4.99
☐ 17174 7	**MISTRAL'S DAUGHTER**	*Judith Krantz*	£2.95
☐ 17389 8	**PRINCESS DAISY**	*Judith Krantz*	£4.99
☐ 17503 3	**TILL WE MEET AGAIN**	*Judith Krantz*	£4.99
☐ 40206 4	**FAST FRIENDS**	*Jill Mansell*	£3.99
☐ 40361 3	**KISS**	*Jill Mansell*	£4.99
☐ 40360 5	**SOLO**	*Jill Mansell*	£3.99
☐ 17630 7	**DOCTORS**	*Erich Segal*	£5.99
☐ 40262 5	**FAMILY FORTUNES**	*Sarah Shears*	£3.99
☐ 40261 7	**THE VILLAGE**	*Sarah Shears*	£3.99
☐ 40263 3	**THE YOUNG GENERATION**	*Sarah Shears*	£3.99
☐ 40264 1	**RETURN TO RUSSETS**	*Sarah Shears*	£3.99
☐ 40582 9	**THE SISTERS**	*Sarah Shears*	£4.99